WRAITH: THE OBLIVION

THE EBON MASK

DARK KINGDOMS TRILOGY

VOLUME ONE

By Richard Lee Byers

WORLD OF DARKNESS
www.worldofdarkness.com

Inside, the shack was smoky and stuffy. The torches mounted on the walls burned with hot Skinlands flame.

Probably a Spook or a Proctor had kindled them. Behind the bar stood a Sandman in a garish patchwork cloak, his eyes narrowed with concentration, maintaining the existence of the earthenware jug the wraiths before him were passing from hand to hand. Judging from their loud, slurred speech and the way they stumbled and swayed, the illusory corn liquor was quite potent. Another four ghosts, all masked, huddled whispering in a shadowy corner. One hulking man with a black handlebar mustache perched on a stool beside a large, ragged-edged Nihil in the middle of the floor, dangling a rope into the seething depths. But most of the crowd had formed a circle around an old Quick tramp in rags. The mortal reeked of sweat and urine. Tears and snot streaked his grimy, wizened face. His breath rasped in his throat, his heart pounded, and his aura flamed orange with fear. Every time he tried to edge out of the ring, the wraiths in his way would reach out and stroke his face, while others crooned, "Meat, meat, meat." Then the victim recoiled, even though it was apparent that he couldn't truly see, hear, or feel his tormentors.

As Montrose took a seat, he felt some of the other patrons looking at him, sizing him up. Though not unduly alarmed, he deemed it prudent to leave the AK-47 with its ebon soulfire crystals prominently displayed on the rickety table before him. He nodded at the old man in the circle. "Charming entertainment," he said dryly.

"Yeah," Valentine replied, "and they're breaking the Dictum Mortem, too. You should arrest them, milord Anacreon."

"That would be counterproductive," Montrose said. "I'm afraid the old fellow is on his own."

For Adrain

1

James Graham, onetime Earl and Marquis of Montrose, now Anacreon of Stygia, stood in the bow of the *Belleisle*, the galleon rising and falling beneath him, his auburn lovelocks and heavy black robe stirring in the wind. His blue eyes peered intently into the seething darkness ahead, seeking a current of water or wind that might bear his vessel along faster than the sleek cruisers pursuing her, or a warp in space through which she might escape.

All he saw was the black swell and faint veils of blue and purple light, not unlike the earthly aurora borealis, flickering across the starless sky. He hadn't expected any better. Though privy to many of the arcane secrets of the proscribed Harbingers' guild, he was a landlubber. Captain Pizarro possessed the same skills and had been sailing the Sea of Shadows for more than a century. Still, Montrose hadn't been able to resist the temptation to look for some means of escape the mariner had missed. It was better than loitering uselessly on the quarter-deck.

He turned, peered backward, and tensed. For the last three hours, the six enemy ships had seemed to creep closer with excruciating slowness. Now, suddenly, they appeared nearly close enough to seize their prey.

Wondering for the hundredth time just who the raiders were, Soul-Pirates, Renegades, Heretics, Spectres, or, just conceivably, the covert agents of one of his master's fellow Deathlords, Montrose hurried aft. Some of his Legionnaires, newly clad like himself in uniforms embroidered with the sigil of the Order of the Unlidded Eye, clustered anxiously around him. They were veteran soldiers, but, like their commander, most had never fought at sea.

"Are we going to be all right, milord?" asked one, a bald man with the massive chest and shoulders of a Spook.

How the devil should I know? Montrose thought. He forced a reassuring smile. "Of course we are. We're Black Hawks, aren't we? We should be grateful to the captain for finding us a little sport to break up the tedium of the voyage." He clapped the fool on the shoulder, then strode on.

Captain Pizarro was a squat fellow with a drooping, grizzled mustache. At some point in his postmortem existence, a flesh sculptor had surrounded his jet-black eyes with a mosaic of iridescent multicolored scales. Glowering, he was watching some of the sailors hang scrambling nets, while others spread sand on the deck. His mouth tightened at Montrose's approach. Probably he wished the landsman would refrain from bothering him at this critical time, though he might forbear to say so outright. The other wraith was his superior officer.

"They're going to catch us, milord," Pizarro said. "We have to fight."

"I understand," Montrose replied. "What are our chances?"

The captain shrugged. "We'll come about in a moment. Then, when they're in range, we'll start shooting broadsides into their bows. If we can cripple them before they maneuver into position to return fire, we'll win. If we can't, well, they have genuine warships and we only have transports, without all that many cannons or marines. But we'll do the best we can."

Montrose nodded. "Well, you and your officers are the ones who know what you're about. My men and I are at your command."

"Thank you for that," said Pizarro. "Truth to tell, it's more sense and less pride than I expected from a grandee newly descended from the Onyx Tower. Since your lads don't know their way around a ship, I doubt that I'll have any complicated orders for them. Tell them to shoot when they have something to shoot at, kiss the deck if somebody tells them to duck, and keep out of the way of the crew." He looked up at the topmen laboring aloft. Two of them, blessed with a Harbinger's power of levitation, floated from spar to spar and sheet to sheet like bees flitting from one flower to the next. "Give the signal!"

A thin, crop-haired woman kneeling on the fore-top cupped her hands around her mouth and emitted a long, ululating cry. After a moment the Chanteurs on the other two vessels in the convoy wailed back. The deck heeled beneath Montrose's feet as the helmsman brought the ship around. The timbers creaked and groaned.

Montrose returned to his men on the main deck, where two sailors, their faces tattooed with faux deathmarks, were dispensing arms from a bin. There were some firearms, but more cutlasses, pikes, bows, and crossbows, weapons which, by Skinlands standards, were as archaic as the *Belleisle* itself. But in the world of the dead, where raw materials were always scarce, and guns and machines had to be powered by a ghost's own essence or the mystical substance known as soulfire, archaic implements were more the rule than the exception.

Montrose already had a darksteel rapier sheathed at his side and a .45 automatic, a Stygian artificer's copy of a Sig Sauer Model 220, hidden under his sable Inquisitor's robe, but he took a bow and a bundle of arrows. Almost four centuries ago, at St. Andrews University, he'd won the silver arrow two years running, but he hadn't practiced his archery in almost thirty years. He hoped he could still hit a mark.

After he strung the bow, there was nothing to do but wait, wait and say what he could to hearten his soldiers. Inwardly he seethed. He didn't fear the Final Death any more than he'd feared his first, but he resented being summarily expelled from the luxuries of his master's court to face it. He'd already risked his neck sufficiently to satisfy any fair-minded overlord. And it galled him to have to fight a battle he couldn't direct, one, moreover, in which the daredevil, hit-and-run tactics which had served him so well on land had no application.

The enemy cruisers, long square-riggers flying phosphorescent scarlet pennants, heaved steadily closer. Suddenly the cannons below deck roared, shaking the planks beneath Montrose's boots, startling him. He'd expected Pizarro to shout an order to commence firing, but evidently the captain had left it to the gunner to choose his moment.

Cannonballs splashed into the dark water, and grapeshot

kicked up spray as it ricocheted along the surface. But some of the salvo reached its target, cutting rigging on the nearest cruiser to pieces and punching holes in its sails.

A number of Legionnaires cheered. Montrose studied the cruiser, trying to assess the extent of the damage, willing the vessel to be disabled. The raider, like its fellows, hurtled on.

The cannons thundered, still with insufficient effect. As always at such moments, Montrose couldn't help feeling that something was missing. Firearms powered by soulfire didn't fill the air with smoke and sulfurous reek like earthly guns. The cruiser turned, bringing its own ranks of cannons to bear. A sailor shouted, "Drop!"

Montrose hurled himself down, then noticed that one of his centurions, a gangly fellow whose baby-faced, adolescent features belied his centuries of existence in the Underworld, had made no move to do likewise. Perhaps fear of this unfamiliar form of combat had dazed him. Perhaps his Shadow, the perverse will to cruelty and self-destruction that dwelled inside every wraith, had momentarily seized control of his muscles. Or maybe the crash of the guns had deafened his hypersensitive ears, and he hadn't heard the sailor's warning.

Montrose knew it was too dangerous to jump back up, but some impulse, perhaps arising from his own suicidal thirst for Oblivion, made him do it anyway. As he grabbed the centurion, he saw the cruiser's cannons flash.

Frantically he flung the lad and himself to the deck. *Belleisle's* scantlings crunched and cracked as the salvo hit her. Severed lines whipped through the air. Portions of the rail dissolved into a barrage of splinters. People screamed, and sailors fell from the yards. A section of broken spar plummeted, missing Montrose by inches, crushing the skull of his companion.

Ghostly flesh rippled and bubbled sluggishly around the length of wood. Montrose rolled the spar off the centurion's head so the bloodless wound could repair itself without impediment. Since the lad hadn't been hurt by darksteel, the talons of a Spectre, or some arcane instrumentality, he should eventually recover, but not in time to influence the outcome of the battle.

Cannons thundered, steadily blowing *Belleisle* to bits, or so it seemed to Montrose. New casualties thrashed and shrieked. He lay flat for as long as he could, but eventually he simply had to get a better idea of how the fight was proceeding. Rising to his knees, he peeked over what remained of the rail.

The attacking cruiser had come within bowshot. Wraiths armed with arbalests, muskets, and a smattering of modern guns rose from behind its rails. Sharpshooters dangled in the tops.

"Stand up!" Montrose shouted. "Attack!"

Legionnaires and sailors scrambled up, and the two forces began to shoot. Quarrels and arrows thrummed through the air, guns barked, and a few automatic weapons chattered. Meanwhile the cannons blazed on.

Some of the combatants eschewed mundane weaponry in favor of magical means of attack. The crop-haired Chanteur on the foretop wailed and a musketeer on the cruiser went mad. Shrieking and clawing at his own eyes, he dropped his gun, lost his grip on the rigging, and fell to the deck thirty feet below. A willowy blond woman on the enemy vessel moved her hands in a complicated pattern. A Black Hawk's knees buckled. As his head thumped down on the deck, he began to snore.

Montrose loosed shaft after shaft, concentrating on the foes who seemed to be attacking most effectively, and was grimly pleased that most of his arrows found their mark. One missile, one *of* the few tipped with gleaming black darksteel, plunged into a burly rifleman's chest. Waves of shadow pulsed through the raider's body, and then he simply faded away, his carbine dropping straight through the dissolving substance of his fingers.

Montrose pivoted, seeking another target, and then, though it had been several seconds since the enemy ship had fired a broadside, the *Belleisle* lurched. Soldiers and sailors staggered, some yelping, some falling. Something stabbed Montrose in the back.

He clutched at the hurt and found a splinter sticking out of his shoulder. Yanking it free, he stumbled around to behold a second cruiser. The vessel had maneuvered to leeward of the

Belleisle and had begun bombarding it from that side.

His comrades were dropping like flies. It was obvious that the *Belleisle* couldn't long endure such a crossfire. Montrose peered about, hoping to see one of the other Stygian transports coming to the rescue, but they were as hard-pressed as his own vessel.

Perhaps, he thought desperately, *we could storm one of the cruisers. The enemy wouldn't be expecting that.* But no, it wouldn't work. Only a handful of his troops shared his ability to fly, not nearly enough for the sort of headlong, frenzied charge he had in mind.

Hurdling the bodies of the maimed and unconscious, he dashed onto the quarterdeck. Though Pizarro had an arrow protruding from his shoulder, he was still at his post, which was more than could be said for the majority of his subordinates. Some sprawled motionless or writhing on the deck, while others were simply gone. Montrose assumed that the Void had swallowed them.

"What can we try that we haven't tried already?" he demanded. .

"Nothing," Pizarro rasped, his voice harsh with pain.

"We're encircled. Half the crew are dead or disabled, and most of the guns have been dismounted. I recommend we strike."

No! Montrose thought reflexively, but he couldn't see any alternative. Further resistance would only result in additional casualties. "Very well," he said. "Do it." Pizarro gave the order, and a midshipman began to haul down the colors, a magenta flag bearing a grinning golden mask, the ensign of the Smiling Lord, and a slightly smaller black one emblazoned with the red and silver Unlidded Eye. The surviving crew and Legionnaires lowered their weapons.

The cannons on the cruiser to leeward roared. With a crack, the *Belleisle's* mizzen fell across the poop. Darksteel grapeshot tore a sailor apart, his form vanishing like a cloud of vapor dispersed by a gust of wind. Some of the Black Hawks cried out in shock.

Montrose shared their dismay. Souls were the one great

resource of the Underworld, prized by nearly everyone. Thus, it had never occurred to him that their attackers would decline their surrender and the attendant opportunity to take as many of them alive as possible. But perhaps it should have. The realm *of* the dead was full of depraved and demented spirits who delighted in carnage for its own sake, or who loathed the Hierarchy of Stygia with an unquenchable hatred.

He pivoted toward his men. "Keep fighting!" he shouted.

Each of the cruisers fired a final devastating broadside. Then the big guns fell silent, and the ships began to maneuver closer to the crippled *Belleisle*. Perhaps their cannons were finally running out of soulfire. In any case, it was obvious the raiders meant to board.

Montrose sent his remaining arrows winging at the cruiser to windward, then discarded the bow, drew his pistol, crouched behind the splintered rail, and began to fire. The luminous black crystals set just above the grip glittered with each shot.

He dispatched several raiders, but it wasn't enough. At this point, no one could do enough. With the grim inevitability of death itself, the cruiser locked yardarms with the *Belleisle*. The two hulls scraped and grated together. The attacking wraiths began to swarm onto the galleon. Montrose bolstered his empty automatic, whipped out his rapier, and ran to meet them.

A Masquer ripped at him with huge, misshapen hands like the forelimbs of a mantis. Sidestepping the attack, Montrose thrust his blade into his assailant's neck. As the raider began to topple and fade, Montrose yanked the sword free, whirled just in time to parry a cutlass slash at his head, and stabbed the enemy swordsman in the chest.

He raged down the length of the ship, dealing death, knowing once again that his efforts were futile. His remaining allies were falling by the moment. No matter how hard he fought, he couldn't turn the tide.

The raiders from the leeward cruiser came aboard, accelerating the slaughter. Shortly thereafter, Montrose found himself alone by the bowsprit with a hundred hostile faces, some human, some deformed by a Masquer's art or the malice of the Void, glaring up at him.

Only one chance left, a chance that only a Harbinger could take. Montrose couldn't fly away. His foes would shoot him out of the air. But it was just possible that he could swim. He attacked the front rank of his opponents savagely, recklessly, driving them back for moment, then threw his rapier in their faces, whirled, and dived off the bow.

He entered the cold black water cleanly. Pikes and javelins plunged down around him. Frantically, hampered by his heavy sable robe, he swam deeper, until the last of the light was gone.

2

Package stores, pawnshops, and tenements lined the street, and graffiti—gang names, racial insults, and obscenities—covered the grimy brick walls. Cars crept along the broken pavement as the drivers checked out the drug dealers and prostitutes loitering in the shadowy doorways. Gangsta rap pounded from an upper-story window. The air stank of exhaust and rotting garbage and left an acrid taste in Frank Bellamy's throat.

The lanky, crewcut FBI agent shook his head, wondering why he so often found himself huddling with weirdoes and lowlifes in hellholes like this. Whereas whenever James Bond had a clandestine meeting, it was with a beautiful woman in an exotic resort. It was just a darn shame that the job of a real-life Fed couldn't be more like working on Her Majesty's fictional Secret Service.

Still, Bellamy had no real complaints. His work was fascinating, and it gave him a sense of purpose. He couldn't imagine doing anything else. And he was making his mark. Though he'd barely turned thirty, he'd already racked up an impressive score of arrests and convictions with the Violent Criminals Apprehension Program. And this new case was a career-maker. The agent who caught the Atheist was headed straight for the top.

That was why Bellamy had caught the red eye up from Baton Rouge and was driving around East St. Louis in the middle of the night. He didn't intend to pass up any leads, even one he was ninety-nine percent certain wouldn't pan out.

At last, he spotted the meeting place, a shabby concrete-block motel tucked away between a tire store and a topless joint. The dump probably made most of its money renting by the hour. The buzzing blue neon sign over the office window read, VAC NCY. Bullet holes pocked the door beside it.

Bellamy turned his rented Camry into the parking lot. Hoping that no one would attempt to steal or strip it, he climbed out, locked it, and started looking for number twenty-five. It turned out to be the room farthest from the street. No light shone through the curtained window.

Bellamy rapped on the door. At first no one answered, though the investigator thought he heard stealthy movement inside. He knocked again. "Open up, Mr. Waxman. It's Agent Bellamy."

"Step back," quavered a tenor voice. "I can't see you through the peephole."

Bellamy did as he'd been told. After a moment he heard a chain rattle and a latch click. The door cracked open, and a bloodshot eye peered out. The FBI agent displayed his badge and ID. Waxman had already seen them at their first encounter, but you never knew what might be necessary to reassure a jittery informant. The door opened wider. "Get inside!" Waxman said.

Once again, Bellamy obeyed. Waxman was an obese kewpie doll of a man with a rosebud mouth and wispy blond hair, clad in a rumpled three-piece suit with the tie askew. His bed hadn't been slept in. The wan light leaking through the curtains gleamed on bottles of apricot brandy, peppermint schnapps, and mint chocolate liqueur, and as the FBI man squeezed past the other man's heaving, wheezing bulk, he caught an odor compounded of sweat, alcohol, and cloying sweetness.

The cramped little room itself smelled faintly of mildew. Even in the gloom, Bellamy could make out the water stain on the ceiling. The accommodations, he reflected, were a considerable comedown for a guy who'd spent the last few years living in mansions and five-star hotels, which was probably why Waxman had chosen them. He hoped no one would look for him in such squalid surroundings.

His hands trembling, Waxman shut and locked the door as soon as Bellamy was inside. "Are you sure you weren't followed?" the fat man asked.

"Yes," Bellamy said.

Waxman grimaced. "No, you're not. I mean, you think you are, but you can't be."

"Nobody knew I was coming to see you," Bellamy said reasonably. Actually, his statement wasn't quite true. Naturally he'd told Linus Hanson, his supervisor, that Waxman had phoned him. But it was close enough to the truth to make no difference. "So, it's logical to assume that no one would try to tail me. Right?"

Waxman's face twisted as if he was struggling not to cry. "I don't know! They have ways of discovering things, ways we can't understand." He grabbed the bottle of mint chocolate liqueur, raised it to his lips, and glugged down a long drink.

"Mr. Waxman," Bellamy said, "I understand that your employer's murder came as a terrible shock, but I honestly don't think that you need to feel so afraid. So far, the Atheist has always hit a site once and then moved on, usually to a different state. And he generally kills high-profile types like priests, nuns, and ministers, not people who work behind the scenes like you. But if you *do* have some legitimate reason to think you're in danger, if you held something back when we spoke before, then you owe it to yourself to tell me now. Once I understand the problem, I can protect you."

"But how? Eric was the only one who could. I was the watchful eye and he was the strong right arm, that's what we used to say. Maybe now the only way to be safe is to lie low. Maybe if I don't tell on them, they won't come after me."

"You mean, let the Atheist get away with cutting Reverend Weiss's heart out? From the way you talk, I thought you liked him."

Waxman's piggy eyes glared. "Of course I did! Eric Weiss was my friend! The only one who was never afraid of me, who never looked down on me for being different."

"Then help me catch his killer."

Waxman hesitated, and then finally said, " All right. I do have to do something, or I'll hate myself for the rest of my life. And maybe you *can* stop the killing. Sometimes they jump to this side of the Shroud. They have to, to hurt us, but maybe at that point you could hurt them back. And I've heard that the government has secret information. Secret weapons. Maybe your superiors will know about that end of it."

Inwardly, Bellamy sighed. Obviously, Waxman wasn't just drunk. He was crazy. Not that that came as any big surprise. The guy had been in and out of psych wards as a kid, and the FBI man had spotted him for a flake at their first meeting. If Bellamy hadn't already established beyond a shadow of a doubt that Waxman had been visiting his mother in Seattle at the time of Weiss' murder, he would have wondered if the fat man might not be the serial killer himself.

But despite Waxman's manifest lunacy, Bellamy still intended to listen to his story. What the hell, he'd traveled hundreds of miles to hear it. And it was just conceivable that he might discover some legitimate information mixed in with the raving. "Shall we sit down?"

Waxman nodded. "Yes. That's a good idea." He carefully inserted his wide butt between the arms of a dilapidated chair, one within easy reach *of* the bottles on the table.

Bellamy perched opposite him on the sagging bed. The springs squeaked. "I want you to know I admire you for having the courage to come forward, Mr. Waxman. You won't be sorry. Now tell me what you know and how you know it."

"If it's going to be any use," Waxman replied, "you have to put aside your prejudices. I'm not stupid. I know you know about Reverend Weiss's drinking and womanizing, and the investigations for tax evasion and mail fraud. I know what you must believe. Eric was no better, no different than any other t-televangelist, milking his viewers for millions of dollars in 'love offerings.'"

"Based on what I've learned about him so far, I don't particularly admire him," Bellamy replied, "but I promise you, my personal opinion doesn't matter. He was the victim of a heinous crime, and I'm absolutely committed to catching his killer."

Waxman's mouth twisted. In the dimness, his round, shiny face resembled an angry, misshapen moon. "That's not the point. I—" Suddenly he stiffened, then peered wildly about. "Did you hear that? Did you *feel* it?"

"No," Bellamy said.

After a moment Waxman's shoulders slumped. "Neither do I, now." He peered at the bottle in his hand. "I shouldn't do this. It takes away the only edge I have. But I keep feeling like I'm strangling, and my heart keeps pounding and pounding in my chest. I need something to calm me down." He took another swig.

"You were telling me about Mr. Weiss," Bellamy said.

Waxman nodded. "Yes. He had his weaknesses. Who doesn't? But they were trivial compared to the good he did. He truly did have the power of God inside him. He healed people, and when it was necessary, he cast out devils."

And *always with a camera rolling*, Bellamy thought. Two days ago, trying to get a sense of the victim, he'd watched one of the "exorcisms" on tape. What with the floating objects and the shadowy figures fading in and out of view, Weiss had put on a pretty good magic act, though nothing for David Copperfield or Penn and Teller to lose any sleep over.

"And I helped him," Waxman continued. "He could hurt the demons, hurt them so badly they ran back to Hell, but most of the time, he couldn't see what they were up to. I could, because I'm a sensitive. A clairvoyant. We told the outside world I was just his secretary because we didn't want anyone getting the wrong impression. Some people might have thought that he was consorting with a witch." He peered at Bellamy as if expecting a reply.

"That's very interesting," the agent said.

"Don't patronize me!" Waxman snapped. "You don't believe. You're not even *trying* to keep an open mind."

Bellamy sighed. "I'm sorry if my skepticism bothers you, Mr. Waxman. I don't mean any disrespect for you or your beliefs. But I'm a detective, and a detective is a kind of scientist. We operate on the basis of facts, not faith or colorful speculations. As far as I know, there isn't any hard evidence supporting the existence of demons or psychic phenomena. And I can't help wondering. If you do have ESP, why did you need to peek through the peephole to see who was on the other side of the door?"

"Because the power doesn't work all the time," Waxman

replied. "It gives me flashes of insight. Symbols. Fragments. And it gets hazier when I'm like this." He took another long drink, his Adam's apple bobbing up and down.

Bellamy wondered how anyone could guzzle so much sweet, syrupy liqueur. He was getting queasy just watching. "Maybe so. In any case, my personal beliefs about spooks and visions don't matter either. What's important is that I'm listening. If you can give me one new fact, one lead, I'll follow it up no matter where it takes me."

"All right," sighed Waxman. "I've already put my head in the noose, just by asking you here. I suppose I might as well finish what I started. But you'd *better* follow up. You remember that I was the one who found Eric's body."

"Of course," Bellamy said.

"I told you exactly how it happened," Waxman said. "I didn't lie. But what I didn't say was that when I smelled the blood, I started having visions. I saw the black whirlpool."

"You just lost me," Bellamy said. "What does that mean?"

"You have to understand," Waxman said, "Eric and I fought the devils, but we didn't know much more about them than what we *needed* to know. Even when the spirits try to tell you things, it puts your soul in peril to listen to their lies. But over the year, I couldn't help picking up a little. And I found out that even the most dangerous demons fear the terrible dark emptiness at the very bottom of Hell, a black pool that sucks down anything that comes too close. I think it might be Satan himself."

"And that's what you saw."

"Yes," Waxman said. "The whirlpool destroys anything that falls into it. Nothing can ever climb back out. But in the vision, something did, a host of shadows with the faces of animals and corpses, who walked unseen among their fellow spirits. And a voice warned me that the fiends had risen from the depths to kill and damn a million souls. Your 'Atheist' murders are only the beginning."

"Interesting," Bellamy said. "If these creatures are haunting the earth, do you know where they are right now?" It still seemed remotely possible that Waxman knew something about a real human killer, someone he'd identified with his imaginary bogeymen.

The fat man shook his head.

"Are you aware of any threats against Mr. Weiss's life, or any strange occurrences in the days leading up to the murder?" Bellamy persisted. "Anything you neglected to tell me before?"

"No," Waxman said.

So much for this, then, Bellamy thought, the first twinge of a headache throbbing in his temples. This'll teach me to be so gung ho. I could have arranged for a local cop to waste his time on this fruitcake. I could be home in bed. "Well, then, I guess we're finished. Thank you for the information. You know how to contact us if you think of anything else."

"That's it?" Waxman demanded. "What are you going to do with what I told you?"

"Report it to my superior," Bellamy said, rising from the bed, "as you suggested. He'll decide how best to follow up."

Grunting, Waxman struggled out of his chair. Bellamy wondered if the fat man meant to physically restrain him from leaving. "I told you, don't bullshit me! Whether you believe me or not, you promised to protect me!"

Bellamy sighed. "And I would if I thought you needed it. But try to look at the situation logically. What have you actually told me? Just that a mysterious gang of spirits is committing the Atheist murders. Even if that's true, it's pretty vague, and even if the devils somehow learned that you passed along the information, I doubt they'd feel that you'd done them any real harm. If you can't get over feeling frightened, maybe you should see a doctor. He could prescribe you something for your nerves."

"I don't need medication!" Waxman snarled. "I need—" He jerked around toward the door, the liqueur bottle tumbling from his hand to thud on the linoleum. He let out a shriek and backpedaled frantically, blundering into Bellamy and nearly knocking him down.

The FBI agent flailed his arms and recovered his balance. Reflexively reaching for the Browning Hi-Power in his shoulder holster, he pivoted toward the door, only to see that it was still shut, the chain still engaged. Nothing had come through it. Evidently Waxman was hallucinating.

Bellamy scowled, annoyed at the jolt of anxiety that had sent the adrenaline buzz tingling through his hands. He shouldn't have let Waxman spook him, not when he already knew the guy was nuts.

At least Waxman was no longer blocking the way out. But Bellamy couldn't just leave the "sensitive" alone in this miserable place, not now that he'd lost it completely. He'd have to get him to a hospital. The agent moved to where the other man was cowering against the back wall, reflecting that he was lucky his informant, if that was still the proper term, hadn't decided to lock himself in the bathroom. "It's okay," he murmured.

"No!" Waxman gibbered. "No, it isn't! It came through the *wall!* It knows I *told!*"

"You have to trust me," Bellamy said. "There's nothing there."

"There is!" Waxman insisted. He clutched Bellamy's forearm, his plump fingers gripping painfully tight.

At the contact Bellamy's head swam, and his vision blurred. When the dark room swam back into focus, it looked subtly different. Puzzled, he squinted, and spotted an additional shadow looming between the window and the door. A gray-black form roughly the height and shape of a man, with pale streaks like glaring eyes and pointed fangs gleaming dully in its long, narrow head. Bellamy gasped and jerked backward. The apparition vanished.

"You see it too!" Waxman said.

No, I didn't, Bellamy insisted to himself. *I just caught a touch of your craziness for a second.* Gently but firmly, he extricated his arm from Waxman's grasp. "Maybe I did see it," he said. "And I don't want to stay locked in here with it, do you?"

Waxman shook his head.

"Then let's leave. I'll take you somewhere safe."

"But we'd have to walk right past it!"

"We're only a few feet away from it as it is," Bellamy said. "And so far, it hasn't tried to hurt us. Maybe it can't yet. Maybe it's gathering its strength. We should get away from it before it does. Come on, I'll take care of you." He took hold of Waxman's arm and tried to lead him forward.

The psychic yelped and resisted, pressing himself against the wall. *Then to heck with this,* Bellamy thought. *There's no way I'm going to manhandle a guy this big out of here against his will, not by myself. I'm calling the local cops for backup.* But then Waxman sobbed, squinched his eyes shut, and lurched forward.

Bellamy guided the other man across the room. He tried not to move hesitantly. Assuring himself repeatedly that there was nothing blocking his path, he fought the urge to pull his gun. Struggled not to imagine the phantom intruder clawing at his eyes, or flinging its long gray arms around him and burying its teeth in his throat.

When, after what seemed an eternity, his fingers closed on the cool brass security chain, the tension quivered out of his muscles. Now smiling ruefully, he thought, *I need to get more sleep. Or drink less coffee.* His psych instructors at Quantico had taught him that hysteria could be contagious, but until tonight, he'd never imagined that he might be susceptible.

He and Waxman stepped into the night. The nude pink neon woman on the roof of the topless bar winked at them over and over again, as if she had a tic. A convertible with a crushed fender and no muffler snarled down the street. The pollutants in the air stung Bellamy's eyes. Still, after the claustrophobic confines and imaginary terrors of the dark little room, the scene seemed almost pleasant.

"Is it following us?" Waxman whispered.

Now that his own irrational dread had subsided, Bellamy felt a surge of pity for his charge. It must be awful to feel that scared all the time. "No, it stayed inside. Everything's fine. My car's right over here." He reached into his pocket for the keys.

A low growl rumbled through the night, and then a black form rose from behind the Camry. The process seemed to take forever, as if the shape was huger, taller, than it had any right to be.

Bellamy recoiled, unconsciously letting go of Waxman, fumbling for his automatic. He knew he was staring straight at the shape's—the *creature's*—face, and yet somehow, he couldn't see it. Because it was too horrible to see.

Now Waxman was goggling at it too. He made a faint whining sound, then clutched at his chest and collapsed.

The creature bounded lightly over the car. It glided forward, arms outstretched.

Bellamy fired a single shot, then bolted. With each stride, he felt the world slipping away, his thoughts dissolving into chaos like a radio signal breaking up into static. Soon the crackle and hiss of the white noise swallowed everything.

When he became aware again, he was crouched trembling and weeping in the corner of a convenience store, between a freezer and the wall. The barrel of his pistol gleamed in the harsh fluorescent light. When a cop spoke to him, in the same kind of soft, soothing voice he'd used with Waxman, he shrieked and nearly shot him.

3

Blind, cold, and weary, Montrose wondered grimly just how long he'd been in the water. It felt like days. He wondered if he'd ever experience light and air again.

Fearful that someone would shoot him, he'd discarded his cumbersome robe, pistol, and boots, then swum what he judged to be a good distance away from the *Belleisle* before striking for the surface, only to discover that the boundary between ocean and air didn't exist anymore. He'd kicked and stroked upward for what surely must have been hours, and the water had never grown a whit less black.

Such a prodigy was possible because the Sea of Shadows wasn't simply an ocean. Rather, it was a manifestation of the Tempest, the eternal storm that surrounded and underlay the rest of creation, an unstable, hyperdimensional labyrinth where natural law didn't exist, and any condition at all could come to be. Evidently Montrose had blundered into an area where space curved back on itself, creating the illusion of a universe completely full of water.

He ought to be able to navigate his way through. That was the fundamental purpose of the Harbinger's art. But the Arcanos wasn't infallible, and so far he hadn't had any luck.

At least the *Restless* didn't need air, food, or, in the general run of things, sleep. But he suspected that if he was trapped in this hellish place for too long, he'd run into a Spectre, or one of the other terrors infesting the Tempest. Unarmed, sightless, and floundering in the water, he'd be easy prey. And if the monsters didn't get him, despair or madness surely would, whereupon he'd plummet into the Void.

Once again, he labored to project his awareness as stooped, crotchety Adrain, his Harbinger teacher, had taught him, looking for currents and eddies, gaps and folds in the fabric of existence. And at last, he sensed *something*, too distant for him to determine precisely what, below him and off to the right.

Excited but wary as well—Spectres frequently lurked in the vicinity of Byways and gates, hoping to snare unwary travelers—Montrose swam toward it. A gray smudge of phosphorescence bloomed in the murk ahead, so faint that at first he wondered if his light-starved eyes were playing tricks on him. But then the glow grew larger and brighter, making him squint, changing from a dingy blur to a sharply defined white oval floating untethered and unsupported in the depths.

There didn't seem to be any creatures lurking around it. Eventually Montrose breaststroked near enough to determine that it was about four feet high and a yard across. Almost certainly a portal of some kind. This close, he could make out the patterns *of* fractured space coiling around it, like loops of iron filings defining a magnetic field. He tried to sense what lay on the other side, but to no avail. He wasn't surprised. It was relatively easy for a Harbinger to peek into the Tempest from outside, but usually impossible to spy from one section of the infinite storm to the next.

He'd have to pass through the portal without a clue as to what was waiting on the other side. But he didn't intend to go through utterly unprotected. Defying his own fatigue, he strained to invoke yet another Harbinger power. For a moment nothing happened, and then blobs of shadow oozed from his skin. The droplets expanded and flowed together, enveloping him in darkness. When the process was complete, he could still see his gray hands and forearms paddling in front of him, but while the effect lasted, no one else should be able to see him at all.

He swam into the oval. He didn't feel anything remarkable when his hands plunged through it, just more cold water on the other side. But when his face touched it, a barrage of sensations— searing heat, violent nausea, a throb of excruciating pleasure— assailed him, sudden and disorienting as the explosion of a bomb.

He thumped down on a tile floor. Transported from water to air, he instinctively gasped a superfluous breath, then lifted his head and looked around.

He'd emerged into what appeared to be an artist's studio, full of canvases in various stages of completion, the air tinged with the sharp smells of paint and turpentine. A row of French doors stood open, admitting a gentle breeze, the twittering of birds, and yellow sunlight. There was no sign of the gate through which he'd entered.

It all looked like a scene from the world of the living, but his Harbinger senses indicated otherwise. He was still inside the Tempest and he'd better start looking for a path that would carry him on to the true Earth. He stood up, water pattering from his sopping garments to the floor.

As he slunk toward one of the French doors, a painting caught his eye. He pivoted and gaped at it, startled because it depicted a moment from his own life. Perhaps ten years old, he was jumping a favorite bay gelding over a tumble-down fence. Kincardine, his family's principal castle, rose in the background.

Disconcerted, he prowled from one easel to the next and found himself the subject of every picture. In one, he was writing a poem at his desk at St. Andrews, in a second, marrying his young bride Magdalen, in a third, leading the wild charge at Tippermuir, and in yet another, weeping over the lifeless body of his son John, slain by the rigors of a ghastly winter march. Taken together the oils told the entire tale of his thirty-seven years of life.

And that, he reflected, wasn't good. It quite possibly meant that, his cloak of shadow notwithstanding, one of the denizens of the Tempest had taken an interest in him.

All the more reason to get out of this enclosed space and begin searching for a Byway. But as he turned back toward the French doors, another door in the far wall clicked and swung open. Princess Louise of Bohemia bustled into the room.

She was exactly as Montrose remembered her, willowy, graceful, and bright-eyed, with smutches of paint on her hands and the tip of her nose, and her honey-blond tresses intent on escaping her elaborate coiffure. Clad in a faded, unfashionable gown, perhaps a hand-me-down from some more affluent friend, she moved toward one of the paintings with the brisk air of someone about to set to work.

The sight of her flooded Montrose's heart with rage and, even knowing what he now knew, a bitter yearning. Fighting for self-control, he told himself, *It isn't really her.*

And yet it was just conceivable that it was. Since his own demise, he'd encountered a couple of his earthly acquaintances among the Restless, though never before someone for whom he harbored such powerful feelings.

Suddenly he was running toward her, as helpless to stop himself as a quarrel shot from a crossbow. His veil of darkness dissolving, he grabbed her by the arm and spun her around.

Startled, she squealed and recoiled, nearly upsetting her easel. A brush fell from her hand to clink on the floor. When she looked up into his face, her expression of alarm melted into a smile. "Darling!" she gasped. "You frightened me half to death." She tried to embrace him.

Gripping her forearms, he held her slender body away from his own. "Are you truly she?" he demanded.

She cocked her head. "If you're teasing, I must be slow this morning, because I don't understand the joke."

"Are you Louise," he asked, "or just something that plucked her image out of my memory? Either way, you must be a Spectre. Otherwise, you wouldn't be here."

"Where, in The Hague? It can be tedious sometimes, but I wouldn't be so unkind as to suggest that it's only fit for the dead." She smiled another smile, then knit her brows when he didn't respond in kind. "You aren't joking with me, are you? Something's wrong."

If she *was* real—and despite himself, with every passing moment he found it more difficult to recall that she probably wasn't—was it possible that she didn't know she was dead? He'd encountered wraiths suffering from a similar state of confusion, but always in the Shadowlands, the portion of the Underworld contiguous with the world of the living, not deep in the Tempest.

"Don't you understand?" he said. "We're spirits now. It's been three hundred and fifty years since Holland."

"Don't be silly," she said. "Touch my skin. Go on, don't be shy." Hesitantly he stroked her cheek. "Don't I feel alive?"

To his amazement, she did. Her soft flesh was warmer than the cool substance of the Restless, and when, trying not to derive any pleasure from the contact, he shifted his fingers to her throat, he felt a pulse. And then, impossibly, a similar throbbing in his own breast.

Perhaps *he* was the one who was addled. Perhaps they were *both* alive, and his long sojourn in the Underworld had merely been a kind of fever dream brought on by grief and care.

But no, surely that couldn't be. In the real 1649, Louise had painted his portrait. But she wouldn't have tried to capture his whole life on canvas, and she certainly wouldn't have used her art to prophesy his defeat and execution. Or if she had, she would have hidden the paintings away to gloat over in secret, not left them sitting out where he might see them. Roughly he turned her toward one of the nearest oils, in which a bound and bare-headed Montrose rode the hangman's cart into Edinburgh.

"If I've gone mad," he growled, "then explain this."

"I'm sorry if it disturbs you," she said. "It's just a bit of foolishness. I hoped I could paint away my fears. That it would help me be brave when you set sail for Scotland."

"Liar," Montrose said. "This scene already happened. You *made* it happen. You urged me to take that villain Van Lengen with me. I trusted him to scout, and he betrayed us to Strachan. Afterward he told me that you *bode* him betray me. Why? I adored you. I meant to ask for your hand once we installed young Charles on his throne. How could you turn on me?"

Louise sighed. "At this late date, I'm not sure I even remember, and what does it matter anyway? This, my dearest James, is a magical place and time. Let's not waste it talking of hurtful things. Let's savor the warmth and the tingle of life in our veins. Let's make love the way we used to." She attempted to enfold him in her arms.

Resisting a terrible urge to respond in kind, Montrose thrust her back. "The truth matters to *me*. Tell me or I swear I'll send you to the Final Death."

Louise grimaced. "Very well. If you must have it so. I

betrayed you for money. Your enemy Argyll paid handsomely to ensure that your expedition would come to a swift and inglorious conclusion."

Montrose stared at her.

"Is it so hard to understand?" she asked, her generous mouth sneering. "My family and I were impoverished exiles, living on charity. Did you think that didn't gall me?" She laughed. "You were always such a romantic fool that you probably did. You thought I was too ethereal for such base concerns."

"Perhaps so," said Montrose heavily. Paradoxically, now that she'd admitted her guilt, his anger had suddenly lost its edge, leaving him dazed and sick. "Van Lengen *said* you'd sold me for pay, but for some reason I always suspected there was a deeper explanation. I imagined that I'd dealt you some bitter hurt without even realizing, that somehow, it was my own fault—"

In the blink of an eye, Louise turned into a hunchbacked parody of her former self, with blazing, slit-pupiled green eyes, a slavering muzzle lined with jagged fangs, and tangles of writhing, hissing serpents sprouting from its shoulder blades. Even as the creature changed, it lunged, one of its huge, black-clawed hands streaking at Montrose's belly.

Miserable and befuddled as the Stygian was, the transformation caught him entirely by surprise. But his swordsman's reflexes wrenched him out of harm's way. The creature's claws shredded his shirt and merely grazed the skin beneath.

At once the Spectre pivoted to strike again. Drawing on what remained of his depleted strength, Montrose flew backward, knocking down easels as he went, until, his knees flexing, he touched down lightly on the other side of the room.

He'd never liked running from a fight, but it would be foolhardy to continue this without a blade, a bow, or a gun. He pivoted, seeking the nearest exit, and they all crashed shut at once. He launched himself at the nearest French door, ramming it with his shoulder, and rebounded. The panes of glass felt strong as iron.

The Spectre charged. Glancing up, Montrose saw that

the ceiling was too low to permit him to soar above the other wraith's long-armed reach. Pointless, then, to squander precious energy staying continually airborne. He snatched up an easel, dumping its picture—a depiction of a solemn Montrose signing the National Covenant—on the floor. When the creature pounded into range, he clubbed at it.

Its hands shot forward, grabbed the easel, tore it out of Montrose's grasp, and tossed it away. Without breaking stride, the Spectre hurtled on.

Montrose sidestepped, narrowly avoiding its talons, and slammed a punch into its side. The Spectre grunted and dropped to one knee, but as it did, two of the snakes growing from its right shoulder twisted and struck, biting the Stygian on the cheek and neck.

Even as he recoiled, Montrose felt an icy burning like the kiss of Underworld fire suffuse his substance, leaving weakness and a sensation of fluttery lightness in its wake. Like darksteel or a Spectre's ebon fangs and claws, the poison carried the taint of the Void. Another dose and he might dissolve into nothingness.

The Spectre lurched up, turned, and limped toward him, its uneven gait perceptible even inside the folds of its voluminous skirt. It had landed hard on its knee. Hoping to catch the monster by surprise, Montrose gave ground, trying to look as if he were even weaker than he felt, then sprang into the air and kicked.

The bold *savate* attack caught the Spectre squarely between the eyes. Montrose tried to tumble over its head and fly out of reach before it could retaliate. But his powers of flight abruptly failed and he plummeted on top of it. The two combatants collapsed in a heap together.

Montrose thrashed madly, trying to get clear, certain that he wasn't going to make it. In a second the Spectre would shred him with its talons, and the snakes would sink their fangs into his flesh. Finally, he realized that every part of the creature, including its serpentine appendages, was unconscious.

Trembling with weakness, fear, and loathing, he dragged himself to his feet and repeatedly stamp-kicked the monster, snapping its neck and smashing its skull flat, grimly aware that even those injuries wouldn't necessarily kill it. He'd need darksteel for that.

Darksteel, he realized suddenly, or the natural armament of a Spectre. Grinning, he knelt beside the creature and reached for its wrists, intent on slicing it to pieces with its own claws.

Ripping sounds split the air, as if a giant were tearing pieces of paper. Startled, Montrose peered wildly about.

Though everything still *looked* the same, his Harbinger senses revealed that the unstable substance of the Tempest was churning. This strange little world was about to come to an end, as if it had required the conscious will of its resident Spectre to maintain its existence.

Jagged black cracks snaked through the floor, the walls, the ceiling, and the air itself. Montrose extended his awareness, groping for a portal or a Byway, but found nothing. And then, with a crash and a roar, reality shattered, and water exploded through the breaches. An instant later, the light and the air were gone. He was floating in the ocean depths once more.

Grimly sure that the effort was futile, he reached out again, seeking another exit from this trap. And this time he sensed air and even a Byway above his head. Evidently, he hadn't returned to the same part of the sea. He floundered painfully upward.

The black water grew gradually lighter, until even dull mortal eyes would have noticed the change. Then Montrose's head broke the surface. Paddling feebly, he swiped his long hair out of his eyes, blinked, and looked around.

The rippling curtains of phosphorescence in the starless sky were predominantly silver and violet now. The rippling expanse of the Sea of Shadows extended as far as the eye could see in all directions, with no land anywhere.

Montrose was floating square in the middle of a Byway, a sea-lane leading out of the Tempest. But it didn't matter. He lacked the strength to swim or fly far enough to get to safety. Despite all his striving, he was going to perish.

The sheer unfairness of it infuriated him. A howling tide of darkness rose inside him as, at this moment of anguish, his Shadow fought to seize control.

He wasn't sure he could muster the will to resist. What did

it matter if his personal demon finally gained the upper hand? If it didn't destroy him, something else would.

And then a point of light appeared on the water.

Without meaning to, Montrose dived underwater. Frantically he fought to reassert control of his rebellious body. For several seconds, nothing happened. He couldn't even feel his limbs. But at last, he broke the Shadow's grip. Cackling, the demon scuttled back to its hiding place in the depths of his psyche.

Montrose struggled to the surface. The light was nowhere to be seen. Perhaps the Byway had already carried it to another layer of reality.

No! It had to be here. It was just that his vision had gone blurry. "Help!" he cried. "Help me!" The call sounded faint and thin, more of a wheeze than a shout.

But off to his left, a soprano voice answered, "Hang on!" Turning his head, he spied the light again. Gradually it glided closer, until he could see that it shone from a lantern hanging on the ornately carved prow of a small lateener. A tall woman perched by the tiller, her face shadowed by a black cowl. She studied the man in the water for a moment, then extended an oar. Montrose clutched at it, and with no apparent effort she hauled him aboard.

4

Montrose flopped down in the bottom of the boat. He doubted he had the strength to sit upright. It was a struggle just to roll over and look up at his rescuer. "Thank you," he gasped.

She reached into the folds of her layered cloak, brought out a tarnished silver flask, and handed it to him. "Drink," she said.

With considerable effort, Montrose managed to unscrew the cap and raise the bottle to his lips. The liquid inside it seared his throat much as liquor would burn a mortal.

At once he felt a glow of renewed strength and warmth, somewhat alleviating the chill he'd taken in the water. And simultaneously he experienced a flare of bitter resentment directed toward his savior. It was intolerable that she should see him, an aristocrat of the Hierarchy, reduced to a helpless, shivering supplicant! And surely that was a contemptuous sneer, half hidden by the shadow of her hood!

He was able to quell the surge of anger because he understood what medicine she'd given him. Though they had no need for conventional food and drink, wraiths derived sustenance from pure emotion, and centuries ago, some forgotten genius of an artificer had fashioned flasks which could capture the essence of hatred.

Montrose would have liked to guzzle the bottle dry and recover his vitality completely, but that, he judged, would be an abuse of his rescuer's kindness. Reluctantly, he replaced the cap and handed the elixir back. "Thank you," he repeated, his voice now only a little hoarse.

"Don't be too lavish with your gratitude," she replied,

replacing the potion inside her cloak. Somewhere off the starboard bow, something splashed, a sound like an earthly fish jumping. She peered into the darkness for a moment, making sure her craft was in no danger. "Ferrymen don't indulge in charity. We always claim a fee for our services."

"I'll pay it gladly," Montrose said. He laboriously sat up and set his back against the side of the boat. "I thought I was done for. I'm James Graham, in life Marquess of Montrose, now an Anacreon in the service of the Smiling Lord."

"And I'm Katrina," the Ferryman said. "I know you, Lord Montrose. How did you come to find yourself in such a predicament?"

My idiot master and his idiot minister sent me on a fool's errand, Montrose thought, his resentment fanned hotter by the influence of the potion. "Raiders attacked my convoy. After they overwhelmed us, I dived into the ocean to escape."

"And what was the object of your voyage?" Katrina asked.

Montrose hesitated. Two thousand years ago the wayfarers called Ferrymen had served Charon, the now-vanished founder of Stygia, as pathfinders, psychopomps, and warriors. But they'd renounced their allegiance when he proclaimed himself emperor. Since then, they'd wandered the Underworld pursuing their own mysterious ends, never foes to the Hierarchy, but no longer allies, either. And thus, no one to whom Montrose would ordinarily confide the Smiling Lord's affairs.

"I warned you that you owe me for my help," Katrina said. "I choose to claim my due in the form of information. I pledge to hold whatever you say in confidence."

Montrose decided that in that case, it wouldn't do any grievous harm to tell her. When he reached America, his business would become public knowledge anyway. "The Smiling Lord dispatched me to lead a campaign against certain Heretics fomenting strife along the Mississippi River."

"An Inquisition," Katrina said. "That explains your current affiliation. I'd heard you belonged to the Fifth Legion."

Montrose forbore to ask how she knew he'd been transferred from the Black Hawks to the Grim Riders when he was no longer wearing the Unlidded Eye. Rumor had it that Ferrymen were masters of all the old-time guildsmen's secret arts and other, stranger sorceries as well.

Katrina trimmed the sail. "And why this particular venture?" she asked. "Why now?"

Montrose shrugged. "You'd have to inquire of my master." *And that son of a whore Demetrius.*

"Since he isn't aboard," Katrina replied dryly, "you reduce me to conjecture. Perhaps the Smiling Lord aspires to Charon's throne. People whisper that all the Deathlords do. Perhaps your master hopes a string of successful raids against Stygia's enemies will further his ambitions."

"That's an interesting hypothesis," Montrose said. Actually, as far as he'd been able to judge, it was the exact truth.

The Ferryman smiled thinly at his show of discretion. "And who better to lead the crusade than the legendary Cavalier hero, the Earl of Montrose? All the sorrows of your life could be laid at the door of religion, couldn't they? I imagine you despise Heretics."

Montrose wondered just how much Katrina could tell about him, simply by looking at his face. Perhaps a wraith's entire history and personality were recorded in the invisible deathmarks graven on his countenance, if another ghost were Oracle enough to decipher them. At any rate, he didn't want to discuss his private emotions with the Ferryman. He was seldom comfortable discussing them with anyone. Perhaps he could redirect the conversation to more general topics.

"I think I'd dislike Heretics," he said, "even if I hadn't died trying to put young Charles back on his throne. Because they're a menace. Even the few who aren't actively plotting insurrection sow the seeds of discontent with their blather about paradisiacal realms beyond the Underworld and higher powers than the Deathlords. And they're contemptible fools besides. While people are breathing, we invest extraordinary hope and faith in some particular religion. Frequently we even wage war on our neighbors if they want to use a different prayer book. And afterward, when we die, we discover to our horror that the afterlife is nothing like what our priests and bishops taught us to expect. Our deities are nowhere to be found. At that point, rational men renounce the whole idea of gods and messiahs. But Heretics simply invent new religions, and commence the wretched farce all over again."

"Spoken with considerable fire," Katrina said'. "A person would almost think you *wanted* to lead the expedition. And yet you didn't, did you? Had you grown too fond of your concubines, and the dreams your Sandmen wove for your amusement? Or were you afraid that some rival courtier would steal your master's favor while you were gone?"

Montrose swallowed another surge of anger. "I don't know why you're baiting me, Ferryman, but I'm too grateful for your aid to take offense. Jeer away, and I'll bear it with as good a grace as I can muster."

"I'm trying to rouse you," Katrina said. "You're treading a dangerous path."

Montrose snorted. "Really! Do you say so? And my journey thus far has been so serene and uneventful!"

"I'm not talking about the common perils, phantasms, and portents of the Tempest. Something else, something strange and powerful, is lying in wait for you. A threat you must confront, and not merely for your own sake."

Montrose's eyes narrowed. "And what precisely is that?" Katrina sighed. "I don't know. I can't see it." Montrose couldn't help smiling. "This is just like half the romances in the Grand Archives. The Ferryman always warns the protagonist, and the warning is always too cryptic to be of any use. It's just as annoying as I always imagined it would be."

"Now," Katrina said, "you're mocking me."

"I don't mean to. But how did you expect me to react to such a vague report? Curl up in the bottom of the boat and blubber in terror? I already know I'm headed into danger. I'm sure the Heretics pose a considerable threat. But I'll handle them."

"Perhaps," said Katrina, "and perhaps not. Your Shadow is stronger than I'd hoped, and stronger than you imagine. But it's as pointless to second guess fate as it would be to counsel you any further." A brisker note entered her voice. "What will you give for passage to the Shadowlands?"

Montrose frowned. "If you recall, I already paid you. With information."

"That was for removing you from the water," Katrina replied, "and giving you the draught of Liquid Hate."

"You're too greedy by half," Montrose growled. His fists clenched, and he pried them open again. He didn't truly want to assault Katrina, and not just because he wouldn't have stood a chance. Grasping or not, she was his benefactor. It was the elixir seething through his system, and the seductive, malicious whisper of his Shadow, which insisted otherwise.

"If you don't want to pay," Katrina said reasonably, "you can simply disembark."

Montrose looked around. As he'd expected, there was still no land in view. And though he was in better shape than when she'd taken him aboard, he still doubted that he was strong enough to escape the Tempest under his own power.

"What do you want?" he sighed. "If I write you a note, the Smiling Lord will open his coffers for you, but you'll have to call at the Isle of Sorrows to collect your booty. All I have in my immediate possession are these sodden rags on my back."

"I rarely put in at the Weeping Bay," Katrina said, "and I don't believe your garments would flatter me. What I require is a service."

"What is it?" Montrose asked warily.

"Nothing that will harm you or compromise your loyalty to your master." She held out her hand. Suddenly a dagger with a curved darksteel blade, a silver hilt, and a carved owl's head pommel lay across her palm. Montrose jumped. "When you see this knife, forbear." The weapon blinked out of existence again. "Agreed?"

Bewildered, Montrose shook his head. "I don't even understand what you mean."

"You will when the time comes," Katrina said. "Do we have a bargain?"

Montrose shrugged. "You have me at a considerable disadvantage. So, if it won't conflict with my duty to my master, I suppose so."

"Then hang on," the Ferryman said. She trimmed the sail, then pushed the tiller to starboard.

As the lateener came about, Montrose sensed a zone of

fractured space yawning just a few yards in front of the bow. Even in his enervated condition, he didn't see how he'd missed it until now, unless Katrina had just created it by force of will.

As the boat glided through the gate, St. Elmo's fire crackled up and down the mast, filling the air with the smell of ozone. A tingling crawled over Montrose's skin, and his tangled hair did its best to stand on end.

The electrical phenomena ceased as soon as the lateener cleared the portal. Suddenly, towering walls blocked out most of the sky. Peering about, Montrose saw that Katrina had transported him from the open sea to a river hissing through a narrow canyon.

More rapidly than Montrose would have imagined possible, Katrina lowered the sail, dismounted the mast, and then leaned on the tiller. The lateener turned toward the canyon wall, space splintered, and an opening appeared in the rock. Beyond it, water roared and plunged into darkness, down an incline so steep it was nearly a waterfall.

The lateener shot over the edge and plummeted, in virtual freefall until it splashed down at the bottom of the torrent. By all rights the impact should have swamped it, or dashed it against one of the jagged rocks looming in a semicircle before it. But somehow Katrina kept it afloat and steered it through a gap.

The boat hurtled on, down a cramped subterranean channel, with boulders rarely more than a yard away. Montrose supposed he ought to be afraid. If the craft crashed into a rock or overturned, the accident might not destroy him, even in his weakened condition. But it might well cripple him, and the rapids could easily sweep him deeper into the caverns, separating him from his guide and leaving him in desperate straits again.

And yet he wasn't frightened. The precipitous, bucking flight of the fragile craft, the bellow of the rapids and the icy kiss of the spray, filled him with a joy he'd nearly forgotten, the same exhilaration that had once possessed him when he took a horse over a series of challenging jumps, or led his men to triumph at Alford and Kilsyth. Forgetting his frailty, laughing, he gripped the rail and raised himself up, the better to savor the ride.

Gradually the passage widened. The current grew gentler, its echoing roar fading to a murmur. The lateener glided into a circular grotto with a domed ceiling. Luminous crimson crystals studded the walls, providing a dim red illumination.

Montrose grinned at Katrina. "That was amazing. My teacher Adrain was a great Harbinger, but I don't know if even he could have taken a boat down that channel."

The Ferryman smiled slightly, then picked up an oar and rowed the sailboat to a dock hewn from the surrounding limestone. A flight of crude steps climbed from the platform to a cavity in the rock. "This is your stop," she said. "You'll find the Shadowlands at the top of the stairs."

Montrose wondered fleetingly how she was going to exit the grotto. Perhaps she meant to open another portal, though at this point, he would scarcely have put it past her to sail back up the rapids. "Thank you again," he said.

"Remember your promise," she answered. "And remember yourself. Remember why the Skinlanders still hold you in their hearts."

He didn't know how to respond to that, so he simply inclined his head. Then he clambered out of the boat and headed up the steps.

As he stepped through the gap, the world shifted, and he found himself standing in St. Giles' Cathedral in Edinburgh. A lovely place even though, for him, the moonlit stained-glass windows were sooty and broken, the stonework chipped and cracked, and the pews riddled with rot. A hint of decay underlay the scents of candles and frankincense, and the whispered prayers of the old woman across the chamber seemed to buzz and reverberate unpleasantly.

Montrose grimaced. He'd never quite grown accustomed to the way the Shroud, the barrier separating the living and the dead, warped a wraith's perception, encrusting his Shadowlands surroundings with a patina of ugliness and decrepitude. Another good reason to stay in Stygia!

But as always, for some reason, the white marble statue directly across from him was immune to the effect. Or at least he found it so. Another wraith, for whom it had no special significance, might have perceived it differently. Heedless of the elderly worshipper, knowing she couldn't see him, he approached the monument.

It was a carving of himself, clad in armor and lying in state. The steel sword beneath the stone hand was one he'd actually carried into battle. Above the image glowed the arms of his staunchest comrades—Gordon, Aboyne,

Hay, Macdonald, Airlie, and his own cousins—rendered in stained glass. At the center of them all gleamed his own red roses and golden seashells, with the Montrose device—*Ne oublie*, Do not forget—underneath.

As usual, the statue filled him with a profound ambivalence. By reminding him of his victories, it made him proud. But it also struck him as a mocking tribute to a fool and a life misspent.

Because in the end, everything he'd achieved on the battlefield had been undone by schemers and traducers whispering behind closed doors. As he'd blundered through life, drunk on a bookish idealism, one trusted associate after another had betrayed him for expediency's sake. In the end, even the young king for whom he'd risked everything had sold him out. Charles had repudiated him when him he'd already set sail for Scotland, a political ploy which kept the people from rallying around him and all but guaranteed his expedition's ruin. Van Lengen's treachery had merely administered the coup de grace.

Fortunately, in his postmortem existence, Montrose had learned to put his own interests first, to scheme as craftily and act as ruthlessly as any foe. And thus, he was faring far better as a Hierarch than he had as a champion of either the Kirk or the Scottish crown.

Every feeling the statue inspired, the nostalgia and bitterness alike, invigorated him, made him more *real*, fortifying him against the corrosive power of the Void. Wraiths generally found it easier to gain and exert strength in locations which reminded them powerfully of their mortal existences. That, perhaps, was why Katrina had delivered him here instead of taking him to the Mississippi.

The drawback was that such sites exerted a fascination

which made it difficult to tear oneself away. Some wraiths found it impossible, and spent eternity lurking near their graves or wandering the corridors of their earthly abodes. Finally, two minutes after he'd resolved to take his leave, Montrose squinched his eyes shut and wrenched himself around, turning his back on the memorial.

He strode to the nearest exit, pressed his hand against the seemingly worm-eaten panel, and shoved. The door wouldn't budge.

He scowled at his own deficient memory. He'd momentarily forgotten that here in the Shadowlands, wraiths and their surroundings existed on different levels of reality. It required extraordinary measures to move any object that properly belonged to the realm of the living.

Montrose hesitated, then stepped *at* the door. He couldn't resist bracing for an impact, but of course, there wasn't one. He slipped through the panel as if it were made of air.

Outside, the night was cool. A half-moon peered through shreds of cloud, and the easterly breeze carried the murmur and scent of the firth. Montrose strode down the cobbled street, wondering where the Quick kept the "airport," and how it would feel to fly inside a machine.

5

As the chubby blond secretary ushered him into the nondescript conference room, Bellamy studied the three men who were already sitting around the Formica-topped table. Linus Hanson, his boss, a bald gnome with round, gold-rimmed glasses, his features arranged in their customary expression of grave consideration. Carlton Nolliver, one of VICAP's resident shrinks, sleepy-eyed and puffy faced, fidgeting nervously with a Tic Tac dispenser. Rumor had it that he was constantly spritzing or sucking some kind of breath freshener to kill the telltale smell of alcohol. And Bill Dunn, the emissary from the Special Affairs Division. His shaggy black mane, russet suede jacket, and chinos made a marked contrast to the conservative suits and haircuts—pretty much the uniform for the average FBI officer—of his companions. He'd also opted to defy the ban on smoking in Federal offices, a transgression Hanson would never have tolerated from one of his subordinates. An acrid blue haze hung in the air around him.

As far as Bellamy could see, none of the trio had brought a rope, but he still felt like the guest of honor at a lynching.

"Good morning," Hanson said. "Would you like some coffee?"

"No, thanks," Bellamy replied. He'd drunk too much already, parked in the waiting room. Another cup and he'd be bouncing off the walls.

"That will be all then, Betty," Hanson said. The chunky secretary departed, pulling the door shut behind her. "Have a seat, Frank."

"How bad is it?" Bellamy asked.

"Let's not lose sight of the fact," said Nolliver, "that it isn't *all* bad." He tapped the stack of manila files on the desk before him. "Your tests came back negative. You didn't have any drugs or alcohol in your system, and your EEG and CAT scan are normal."

Bellamy grimaced. "Is that good? If it had turned out that somebody slipped me mescaline, we'd know why I wigged out and we could get on with our lives."

"It's damn good from where I sit," Hanson said. "It means that I don't have to fire you, and you don't have a brain tumor or some other terrible disease."

"But something drove me crazy," Bellamy said heavily. "I almost shot a policeman who only wanted to calm me down."

"But you didn't," said Dunn, a puff of smoke billowing from his mouth. "You didn't hurt anybody. So don't beat yourself up over that."

"I wish we did know what happened to you," Hanson said. "The facts simply don't add up to anything much. A known mental patient—"

"Former mental patient," Bellamy murmured, not certain why he'd bothered to correct him.

Hanson frowned. "Since you were convinced he needed to go back to the sanitarium, I'm not sure what difference that makes, but have it your way. A *former* mental patient gets drunk and babbles a preposterous story. For a second you imagine you see a shadowy figure in a dark room, but when you blink, it disappears. After you take Waxman outside, you think you see another goblin rear up from behind your car. Waxman drops dead of a heart attack—according to the autopsy, he was past due—and you go into a..." He glanced at Nolliver.

"Fugue state," the psychiatrist supplied.

"Thank you," Hanson said. He looked back at Bellamy. "You see? There's nothing to go on. If you could remember anything else...?"

"I'm sorry," said Bellamy, feeling like a pitiful excuse for a trained observer, "I can't." He turned to Nolliver. "You could try hypnotizing me again."

The ruddy-faced psychiatrist shook his head. "Judging from

our first two attempts, it wouldn't do any good. The memory is gone beyond recall. Besides, it's my professional opinion that at least on a superficial level, you assessed your situation correctly when you worried that Waxman's delusions were contaminating your own thinking. That phenomenon's called a *folie a deux*. It's more common than you might imagine."

"In other words," Bellamy said, "I didn't need LSD or a brain tumor to go crazy. I just had naturally had it in me." He looked at Dunn. "Or do you think there could be another explanation?"

In the past, Bellamy, like most of his peers, had derided the whole idea of the Special Affairs Department. It had seemed ludicrous that a law enforcement agency with real, flesh-and-blood felons to catch should devote any of its resources to investigating reports of Bigfoot and little green men from outer space. Now he was glad that Hanson had requested SAD to participate in the current inquiry. *Something* weird had happened in East St. Louis, and it was just possible that Dunn could throw some light on it.

But the agent in the leather jacket shook his head. "I'm sorry, Frank. I wish I could help you out. But nothing in your story rings any bells. Of course, it's like Division Chief Hanson said. What you told us is incredibly vague. It's hard to extract any details to correlate with the information in our database. Not"— he grinned wryly—"that that would be likely to do any good anyway. I'll be straight with you. SAD has been poking around alleged haunted houses and crop circles since 1952, but it's not like we've actually learned anything. It's still an open question whether the paranormal even exists.

"I can tell you this. We keeps tab on Satanists and other potentially dangerous occultist cranks." He smiled again. "We feel honor-bound to do a little honest police work once in a while. As far as we've been able to determine, none of the cults and covens in our files has anything to do with the Atheist murders. And a couple years back, we checked out Eric Weiss. We concluded he was a charlatan. There was no indication of genuine wild talents. And Waxman didn't even participate in the trickery. He was just a flake who answered the phone and licked envelopes."

"Look," Bellamy said. "I don't believe in the 'paranormal' either. But in the course of investigating cult leaders and phony mystics, didn't you people ever discover a technique for making a man see things that aren't really there, or giving him a panic attack?"

Dunn dropped the remains of his cigarette in a Styrofoam cup, extracted a leather tobacco pouch and a package of rolling papers from a pocket inside his jacket, and dexterously began to fashion another. "Sure. Any magician will tell you there're a million ways to make people see what you want them to see and feel what you want them to feel. But every trick requires either a prepared stage, the manipulator establishing communication with the manipulatee, or both. So, I don't see how anybody could have used them on you."

"Particularly since Waxman was in hiding," Hanson said. "Nobody besides you even knew where he was."

"We don't know that for sure," Bellamy said.

"I don't blame you for wanting to believe that some external agency was responsible for your experience," Nolliver said soothingly. "It's frightening to lose control. But look at it this way. You're a courageous individual. Since joining the Bureau, you've proved it time and again. No one could upset you to that degree by projecting a ghostly image on a wall, or popping up in a Halloween mask. Only a disturbance in your own psyche could do that."

Suddenly Bellamy felt tired. There was no point in arguing any further, particularly when he didn't have a coherent perspective of his own. "That's the verdict, then. You all think Waxman threw a scare into me, he dropped dead of natural causes, and I had a panic attack. Nothing that happened and nothing he told me had anything to do with the Atheist."

Dunn struck a match with his thumbnail. "I'm sorry, but yeah, that's about the size of it."

"But no one believes you're genuinely unstable," Nolliver said. "What you experienced was an isolated episode, and there's no reason to assume it will ever happen again. Not as long as we take the proper precautions now."

Crap, thought Bellamy. *Here it comes.*

"I've gone over your time sheets," Hanson said. "You work some very long hours."

"Everybody around here does," Bellamy said.

"Well, starting now, I want *you to* cut back to forty hours a week, and to meet with Dr. Nolliver as often as he thinks appropriate."

"To discuss whatever you'd care to talk about," the psychiatrist said.

"And finally," Hanson continued inexorably, "I'm taking you off the Atheist investigation. It's a gruesome case and it's possible you may have gotten too emotionally involved. Turn your notes over to Walter Byrd."

Under the table, Bellamy clenched his fists in frustration. He understood that Hanson was trying to give him every possible break. The older man would have been well within his rights to place him on formal probation, or suspend him pending further medical evaluation. All the same, his decision had dealt his subordinate's career a devastating blow. Once the word got out, no one in the Bureau would really trust him.

But he knew he couldn't talk Hanson out of it. If he tried, he'd just wind up looking like even more of a loose cannon. "I understand," he said, trying to keep his voice steady. "Is that everything?"

"I believe so," Hanson said.

6

As Nolliver hurried past the double doors to the morgue, he caught the stench of rotten meat underlying the sharp antiseptic smell that pervaded the building as a whole. Once again, he wondered if there was any chance that it was real.

When confronted, the medical examiners insisted that no one else ever complained of noxious odors leaking into the corridor. They swore Nolliver was only imagining the stink, and after some reflection, he'd decided they were probably right. But he still smelled it every time he passed.

He wished he could move his office to another area, away from the corpses, the labs, and the infirmary, but it would be a bad idea to request such a relocation. Some people already thought he was falling apart. He didn't want to give them any further cause for gossip.

The vile smell of death lingered in his nostrils and coated his tongue. He needed a drink to wash it away. His hands beginning to tremble, he fumbled his key ring out of his lab coat pocket and unlocked his office door.

Tendrils of pungent blue smoke caressed his face. "Good morning again," said Dunn.

Startled, the psychiatrist flinched. Just a twitch, really, but he could tell from the way Dunn's smile widened that the SAD agent had noticed. Nolliver scrambled into the room and locked the door behind him. "How did you get in here?" he asked.

Sprawled on the leather couch, his scuffed brown cowboy boots propped up on one *of* the arm rests, Dunn shrugged. "I'm a detective. I'm supposed to be able to get inside places."

"Well, you shouldn't have broken into this one," said

Nolliver petulantly. He sat down behind his desk, unlocked the bottom drawer, and took out a pint of Johnnie Walker Black, noting automatically how much was left. About a fourth of the bottle, enough to see him through until he went out to lunch, at which point he could smuggle in a new one. "We shouldn't talk here."

"I don't see why not," said Dunn. "We're colleagues, aren't we? We've worked cases together. Nobody's going to think anything about it."

"You can't be sure of that." Nolliver raised the pint to his lips, tilted his head back, and took a long drink, shivering with relief as the Scotch burned its way down. "For all we know, someone could have bugged this office."

"Wrong," said Dunn. "I do know. I checked. Are you going to give me any of that booze?"

Nolliver glowered at him. "Is that why you're here? To cadge a drink?"

Dunn shook his shaggy head. "Actually, I just wanted to touch base and celebrate a job well done, but your pissy attitude is making it hard to bask in the glow."

"I can't help it," Nolliver said. "I hate this." He realized that Dunn was looking pointedly at the bottle in his hand. And he supposed it would be foolish to antagonize him. Reluctantly he stood up, circled the desk, and handed the liquor over, wincing at how much his fellow conspirator guzzled down.

Dunn sighed in satisfaction. "There's nothing like the good stuff, is there?" He held on to the Scotch for another moment, as if teasing Nolliver, and then gave it back. "I'll be damned if I know why you hate our little cleanup operation. You *do* remember how you got involved?"

Nolliver winced. "Of course."

"Extorting sex from teenagers in exchange for a favorable psychiatric evaluation—"

Only four times! Nolliver silently protested. And the first time, it was the boy's idea!

"—abusing your trust as a doctor and an officer of the court. Convincing judges to put dangerous youthful offenders back on the street. The last one even killed some people, didn't he? Just imagine what would happen if the truth came out."

"I said, I understand my situation," Nolliver said. "There's no need to threaten me."

Dunn raised his bushy eyebrows. "Who's threatening? I'm just making a point. When SAD uncovered your sordid past, our first thought was, now we can just blackmail the poor perverted bastard into doing whatever we want. But fortunately for you, we're nicer than that. You aren't just getting blackmailed, you're getting paid."

"For concealing the truth."

"What can I tell you? People at the top level have decided that it isn't good for anybody who lacks the proper clearance, even your average, garden-variety FBI stiff, to get all hot and bothered about the paranormal. Unfortunately, every year or two, some Fed stumbles over something spooky, and guys like you and me have to spring into action to put out the fire. Sometimes it feels a little slimy, but it's our patriotic duty."

I wish I could be sure of that, Nolliver thought. It would be comforting to assume that even when deceiving people like Bellamy and Hanson, he was still serving his country. But he often had his doubts, not that it mattered. Whatever the truth, he had no option but to cooperate.

"We've wrecked that young man's career," he said somberly. He took another drink. When he lowered the bottle, he was dismayed to discover that, somehow, there was only a swig or two remaining.

"Bull," said Dunn. He blew a smoke ring. "We knocked him a rung or two down the ladder. If he's got the right stuff, he'll climb back up eventually. It's his own fault anyway. When he saw which way the wind was blowing, he should have changed his story. Claimed he got hit on the head and screw the medical report if it said otherwise. Hanson wanted to let him off the hook. He would have accepted any halfway plausible explanation."

"Bellamy was too dedicated an agent to lie," Nolliver said. At that moment, he felt the agent's plight nearly as keenly as his own. "He was one of the best young investigators in VICAP. If we hadn't discredited him, if I'd actually tried to help him recover his repressed memories instead of burying them deeper, he might have caught the Atheist. The next time that monster kills someone, I'm going to feel like it's my fault again." His eyes throbbed as tears welled up inside them.

Dunn grimaced. "Will you get over yourself? Do you think I'd ask you to hide the truth if it meant letting a serial killer go free? I'm a cop, too, you know. I told you, SAD knows exactly what happened that night, and it had nothing to do with the Atheist. Bellamy and Waxman were just in the wrong place at the wrong time."

"How can you know that for certain?" the psychiatrist demanded.

Dunn exhaled a plume of blue smoke. "It's like our friends in the Company say, Doc. I could tell you, but then I'd have to kill you."

7

A long, cream-colored sedan turned onto the wet, gleaming street, cutting off the speeding taxi. The cab driver, a stocky Middle Eastern immigrant with slicked-back pomaded hair, squawked, stamped on the brake, and wrenched the steering wheel. The taxi spun out of control, narrowly missing the white car but whirling to the left side of the highway. Luckily there was no traffic coming the other way.

Montrose was sitting in the back seat beside the paying passenger, a thin, scholarly-looking young mortal currently frozen with terror. As the taxi came to a halt, the Stygian wryly reflected that travel was becoming interesting again. After a series of uneventful flights, he'd stowed away on the cab with as little difficulty as he'd boarded the airplanes. But it had soon become apparent that his chauffeur could feel his presence, though probably without comprehending precisely what he was sensing. He'd started sweating, flooding the car with the stench of his perspiration, and his aura had glowed orange with anxiety. He'd kept twisting his head to peer into the back of the vehicle, and his driving had become increasingly erratic.

Montrose supposed he'd better take his leave before the Quick man wrecked the cab. Now that he'd recovered his vitality, it shouldn't be any hardship to finish his journey afoot. Indeed, he'd be virtually tireless unless something injured him, or he expended too much energy practicing the arcane arts. He slipped through the side of the cab, then watched it lurch into motion and speed away. His body tingled as the raindrops plummeted through him.

He walked on through the benighted streets, peering about,

not much liking what he saw. Even allowing for the distortions of the Shroud, the city seemed a vile, decaying place, its gutters choked with reeking garbage, its streetlights broken, many of its shop windows covered with plywood and the rest armored by rusty steel grates. Periodically guns cracked in the distance, or sirens wailed. Nihils—cracks and holes in the surface of Shadowlands reality, breaches opening on the Tempest—seethed and glittered everywhere, a few conceivably large enough for a Spectre to wriggle through.

Edinburgh had been bad enough, and this Natchez looked even worse. Montrose wondered if the Shadowlands had been quite this unpleasant on his last visit forty years ago. He thought not. Perhaps, as some wraiths believed, the destruction of Charon had shifted the balance of power between Being and Oblivion. Perhaps the universe was crumbling away, dropping bit by bit into the Void.

He scowled and tried to shove the notion out of his head. It was Heretical, and the gloomiest, most defeatist kind *of* heresy at that.

Ugly or not, the stigmata of urban decay had their uses. Shadowlands wraiths tended to establish their communities in the most desolate portions of mortal cities. There, they didn't have to coexist with the Quick when they weren't in the mood. Moreover, such places frequently radiated a palpable atmosphere of misery on which the dead could feed, it being one of the ironies of their existence that joy and love didn't invest a place with the same emotional residue as fear, grief, and despair. Thus, the increasingly empty streets and the multiplying stands of condemned buildings were like signposts, pointing the way to Natchez's Necropolis.

A strain of sprightly but oddly dissonant violin music skittered through the air. Hands clapped, raggedly keeping time. Quickening his pace, Montrose rounded a corner. Before him, a narrow cobblestone street ran up a hill. A number of wraiths, many masked, their clothing a hodgepodge of styles from the last three hundred years, stood clustered here and there.

Some had gathered around the fiddler. Another group

was inspecting the meager selection of goods—many no doubt forged in Stygia, the remainder cherished possessions some dying soul had managed to carry into death—laid out in an open-air market. Still other loiterers gawked as a petite blond flesh sculptor stroked a customer's features into a new configuration. Suddenly his whole head bubbled and flowed at once, the tide covering or simply annihilating his eyes, ears, nose, and mouth. The customer, a burly black man, made a muffled squealing sound, jumped up from his seat, and began to flail around. Now looking panicky, the Masquer tried to push him back down and was knocked sprawling for her pains. The spectators laughed and jeered.

At the top of the street rose a jumble of massive brick buildings which might have been an abandoned factory, a collection of warehouses, or some combination of the two. Sentries armed with crossbows prowled the rooftops. Torches ringed the entire complex as if to define a perimeter. Clearly the site was a Hierarchy Citadel, and Montrose's ultimate destination.

Smiling, he started up the street. Half a block from the top, he spotted a slender young woman, dressed like a flapper except for the gold and ivory crucifix hanging around her neck. Perched on a tenement stoop, she was haranguing several other wraiths, ranting in a shrill, excited voice about Christ, faith, and "Transcendence, our doorway out of this purgatory and into bliss."

The Stygian's smile twisted into a scowl. He took a stride toward her, intending to drag her off the stoop and take her into custody, before his better judgment reasserted itself. At the moment he was scarcely equipped to arrest anyone, particularly when it might entail facing down a mob. Hoping that the preacher would set up shop here again, he marched on toward the top of the hill.

Since his death, Montrose had seen any number of gruesome and, by Quick standards, unnatural spectacles. He liked to believe that he'd grown blase about such things. Even so, he didn't care for the sight of Stygian torches. The brand in front of him now was typical. A Masquer had paralyzed some poor slave, stretched his body nine feet long, melted his legs into a single rigid shaft, and fused his arms to his sides. A corona of amber barrow-flame whispered around his head, slowly, slowly burning his substance away. His mouth gaped in a silent, endless scream. Montrose shivered as he passed. He told himself it was only due to the chill radiating from the fire.

He walked on toward the two sentries flanking the nearest door into the Citadel. One could argue that it was idiotic for Shadowlands wraiths to pay any attention to doors. As Montrose had rediscovered in St. Giles', they didn't need them, nor, in the general run of things, did they even open them. They just glided through them as they would any other barrier. But security considerations mandated that everyone enter and exit a Hierarchy stronghold through one of a few checkpoints. Any ghost who opted to do otherwise was automatically considered a thief, an assassin, or a spy.

The guard on the left leaned on a long spear and wore a Bowie knife on his belt. He'd stitched a patch with the black raptor emblem of the Fifth Legion to the breast of his khaki fatigues. A Masquer had pulled his lips into an exaggerated jack-o'-lantern grin, a common symbol of fealty to the Smiling Lord. His companion was dressed in buckskin and carried an AK-47. The question-mark brand on his cheek signaled his allegiance to the Beggar Lord. Both soldiers had a green sash emblazoned with a black hourglass, evidently the regalia of the fortress at their backs, draped over their right shoulders.

"Good evening," Montrose said.

"I don't know you," growled the sentry with the brand. "Have you got a pass?"

Montrose hadn't expected them to recognize him or show him any deference, not while he looked like a mendicant, but he was surprised by the overt hostility in the other wraith's tone. Either the fellow was having difficulty controlling his Shadow, he was subtly unhinged, or he was simply in an uncommonly foul mood. "No," the Stygian said, "but I do have legitimate business inside. I'm an Anacreon, newly arrived from the Isle of Sorrows, and I have business with your commanders."

The man with the brand sneered. "Sure you are, and I'm the

Lady of Fate! Get out of here before we send you back to Stygia in chains."

The spearman cleared his throat. "You know, he seems harmless enough, just a little crazy. We could ask the Centurion of the Watch. Maybe he'd okay it for him to come inside."

The wraith with the brand rounded on his companion. His arms jerked as if he wanted to swing his gun up and slam the butt into the other spirit's teeth. "No!" he shouted. "Rules are rules! If he can't prove he belongs, he can't enter!"

"Okay, okay," said the spearman, shifting back a step. He looked at Montrose, the wariness in his eyes an odd contrast to the artificial hilarity of his rictus. "I'm sorry, pal. Maybe you should come back some other time."

"Oh, I will," Montrose said, half irritated, and half amused. "To assign some special work details to you and most especially your friend." It was too bad, he reflected, that an army of the Restless didn't need anyone to clean latrines.

The Stygian turned and sauntered back the way he'd come, through the ring of sentient torches and on down the hill. But as soon as he judged he was out of eyeshot of the Legionnaires on the roof, he slipped into the narrow walkway between two tenements and veiled himself in darkness.

A wraith learned to take it for granted that mortals couldn't see him, but despite the centuries Montrose had spent honing his Harbinger abilities, he sometimes found it nerve-wracking to operate on the assumption that his fellow spirits were similarly blind. As he crossed the open space around the Citadel, he kept expecting one of the Legionnaires to shout a challenge or open fire. The tension prickled along his nerves and made his mouth feel dry.

But no one noticed him, and finally he reached the base of the wall. As he stepped through it, his substance resonated to the buzz of emotion lingering in the brick. Children had suffered in this place, slaving at workbenches from before dawn until after dark, breathing hot, thick air, squinting against the gloom, muscles cramping and fingers bleeding. The Stygian shuddered, invigorated and repelled at the same time.

Shaking off the sensation, he inspected the interior of the

building. He was standing in a cavernous, musty-smelling chamber illuminated by the dim gray light leaking through filthy skylights. Nearby, a wraith, a budding Chanteur, was practicing her Arcanos by crooning to spiders. When she hit the right note, the small predators ran madly around their webs or tumbled out of them altogether.

Montrose prowled on through the complex, avoiding proximity to other ghosts when possible. Cloak of shadows or not, he saw no point in tempting fate. Where not given over to open work areas, the derelict buildings proved to be a maze of cramped rooms, snaking hallways, and blind alleys. Often compelled to backtrack, he might have saved time by slipping through walls, but he feared losing his bearings.

Finally, warmth began to prickle across his skin, warning him that his mask of darkness would soon evaporate. He supposed he had little choice but to expend the energy necessary to weave another. Then he heard a commotion up ahead.

He crept forward, reached the end of the hallway, and peered out into another open area, this one illuminated by greenish barrow-flame. A diversity of banners, emblazoned with hawks, question marks, crowns of thorns, grinning faces, begging bowls, and hourglasses, hung from the rafters. Various luxuries, including a large television, one side of the mahogany cabinet a web of jagged Nihil fissures, stood here and there about the floor.

In the middle of the chamber a number of Legionnaires in the ubiquitous green sashes—officers, judging by the quality of their clothing and gear—were jammed in a circle together, crowing, cursing, and shouting encouragement. Peering, Montrose glimpsed a pair of barghests fighting in the center of the ring. The frenzied thralls were lean as greyhounds, their sculpted heads more canine than manlike, their bodies altered to enable them to stand erect or lope on all fours with equal facility. The gray iron muzzles which denied them human intelligence also prevented them from biting one another, but didn't hinder the use of their long gray claws.

A man in a gleaming steel domino, a short magenta cape, and the cuirass and helmet of a conquistador stood calmly watching the battle. Heedlessly as the other spectators jostled one another, they took care not to crowd him or obscure his view. A smirking dwarf in green and violet motley crouched at his side, a leather bag in his stubby hand. It probably contained the coins his master had wagered on the bout.

Montrose walked up behind the masked man, dissolved his veil of darkness, and tapped him on his armored shoulder. The masked man jumped and spun around.

"Hello, Manuel," the Stygian said. "It's good to see you again."

8

Manuel Gayoso de Lemos's suite occupied much of the top floor of the derelict building, where, for some reason, the echo of ancient suffering was strongest. Montrose supposed that by Shadowlands standards, his fellow Anacreon's rooms were more than comfortable. The Spaniard had even arranged for someone to sweep, dust, and scour the place clean, a task which, considering that the accumulated grime had existed on the other side of the Shroud, must have been a major undertaking. Still, to a Hierarch accustomed to the luxuries of the Onyx Tower, the place was essentially a hovel. Montrose did his best to conceal his disdain.

Gayoso ushered him into a dark office, then snapped his fingers. Three white tapers in a brass candelabrum burst into cold blue flame, the reflections gleaming on Gayoso's breastplate and domino. After offering Montrose a chair, he sat down behind his desk, hesitated, and finally, as courtesy required, removed his mask, revealing pouchy eyes and a fleshy beak of a nose.

Montrose had known any number of wraiths who hated revealing their faces. Struggling to survive amid the rivalries of the Hierarchy, they didn't want anyone gleaning their private thoughts from a momentary flicker of expression. Montrose sympathized with their anxiety, but he didn't share it. He flattered himself that he was generally capable *of* concealing his true feelings without recourse to a tangible veil.

"Well," said Gayoso, "it's been a long time since we'd had a visitor from the Isle of Sorrows. To what do we owe the honor?"

"The Smiling Lord has ordered a war against the Heretics

operating along the lower Mississippi. He appointed me to the Order of the Unlidded Eye and ordered me to direct the campaign." Montrose gave Gayoso what he hoped was an ingratiating smile. "Needless to say, I'll be relying heavily on your advice and support."

Gayoso grimaced. "I can't believe that our master would send you alone. Does he expect me to give up *my* troops and *my* resources—"

"He expects you to provide any assistance required, but I did set sail from Stygia with my own troops. Unfortunately, raiders attacked and overwhelmed us en route. As far as I know, only I escaped. So as it stands now, yes, I'm afraid I will have to draw on local reserves for my entire army. Surely it won't be all that much of a burden."

"Spoken like a true Stygian," Gayoso said.

Montrose lifted an eyebrow. "I fancied we were *both* Stygians, my lord Anacreon."

"I'm a Hierarch," Gayoso said. "There's a distinction. Hierarchs do the dirty work and Stygians reap the rewards. *We* struggle to keep order and enforce the Code of Charon. *You* extort levies of thralls from us to feed the Soul Forges, and keep all the newly made goods for yourselves."

"A harsh man might feel that remark bordered on treason," Montrose said. "But I don't. I understand your frustration. These are hard times. Stygia isn't receiving nearly as many souls as it used to, which means we can't ship nearly as many articles back. That's why all Legionnaires should work together to restore the empire to its former ascendancy."

"And you're going to accomplish that by destroying a few Heretics."

"It's a start," Montrose replied. "I'm amazed you haven't already set about purging them yourself. I saw one preaching in the shadow of this very Citadel. How can you command the respect of the populace if you tolerate open sedition?"

Gayoso sighed. "You don't understand the situation here. Yes, of course the Heretics are a problem, but they aren't our biggest problem. Since the emperor perished, we've had a steady string of Spectres and Maelstroms laying waste to the province.

We can't afford to provoke a major confrontation with Heretics or Renegades. Particularly not right now."

"What do you mean?" Montrose asked.

Gayoso shook his head. "I wish I knew. But I governed the living folk of this settlement three hundred years ago when I was breathing, and I've dwelled here ever since. I'm attuned to this place, and I feel something new arising. Something foul."

Recalling Katrina's murky warning, Montrose felt a chill ooze up his spine. He did his best to quash the feeling. Even if Gayoso wasn't lying to excuse his reluctance to cooperate, there was always danger lurking in the Underworld. A Legionnaire who permitted that realization to cow him would never accomplish anything.

"Perhaps," Montrose said, "the Heretics are responsible for the new threat. If so, a preemptive strike could nip it in the bud."

"I don't believe that," Gayoso said. "And even if I did, there's another consideration. I don't rule here alone."

"I'm well aware of that," Montrose said, striving not to lose his patience. During Charon's reign, a council of seven Anacreons, each representing one of the Deathlords, had governed every Citadel in the Shadowlands. In recent years, however, with manpower shortages endemic, no Legion maintained a presence in every single Necropolis. According to Montrose's information, Natchez currently belonged to the minions of the Smiling Lord, the Beggar Lord, and the Emerald Lord, a datum confirmed by the particular banners and other insignia he'd seen since his arrival. "I expect your peers to assist me also."

Gayoso snorted. "You can expect it all you like. It won't happen."

"Are you telling me that *they're* traitors, then? Every Legionnaire owes obedience to the will of every Deathlord."

"What we owe and what we pay can be two different things. With Charon gone, some people in the Shadowlands believe that propping up the Hierarchy is a lost cause. They want to establish their own kingdoms to rule as they please."

Montrose smiled. "I trust you're not speaking for yourself."

"Of course not," Gayoso said. Montrose couldn't tell if he was lying or not. "But that's what Mrs. Duquesne and Shellabarger want to do. If I turn my troops over to you, they'll seize the opportunity to depose me."

Aha, Montrose thought, *the truth at last.* Gayoso had finally revealed the primary if not the only reason he didn't want to help.

"And by ousting me," the Spaniard continued, "they'll remove Natchez from the Smiling Lord's sphere of influence. Surely, he doesn't want that."

"If he didn't have faith in you," Montrose said, "you wouldn't be in charge here. I daresay he assumes you're resourceful enough to retain your position even if placed at a momentary disadvantage. By the Scythe, man, I don't mean to take every Black Hawk you've got! I'll leave you an adequate bodyguard."

"I don't understand why our master ordered this done here," Gayoso said sullenly. "Here, out of every place on Earth."

"For one thing, he has the impression that the Heretics have grown particularly impudent in this area."

Gayoso's dark eyes narrowed. "Why the devil does he think that?"

Montrose shrugged. "He's a Deathlord. One of the most powerful beings in the universe. I don't know how he comes by all the secrets he uncovers. I suspect he may also have chosen to attack the Heretics hereabouts because he assumed he had a loyal commander in place to help me carry out his will." He stared into the other wraith's eyes. "And you are going to help me, Manuel. Just between the two of us, I don't have any great enthusiasm for this venture, either. I went through hell just getting here. I'd far rather have been at home, savoring a Sandman chef's fantasy of roast pheasant and champagne. But we have our instructions, and that's the end of it."

Gayoso's lips twitched into a smirk so fleeting that Montrose nearly missed it. "You may have your orders. I don't know that I do."

"What are you talking about?" Montrose said. "I just now delivered them."

"By word of mouth," Gayoso said. "Surely such an important directive would arrive in writing with the Smiling Lord's seal attached. And if you've joined the Grim Riders, where's your black robe? Your lantern with the Lux Veritas shining inside it?"

"I lost everything but these clothes on my back when I fled my ship," Montrose said. "What of it? *You know me.* We met when you came to Stygia for Charon's funeral obsequies."

"Precisely," Gayoso said. "And you were a member of the Fifth Legion, not the Order of the Unlidded Eye. A fellow Anacreon, not anyone who outranked me. In these chaotic times, with duplicity everywhere, I couldn't possibly place my command at your disposal. Not without clear instructions from higher up. I'll tell you what I'll do. I'll send a messenger to Stygia, asking for confirmation of what you've told me, just as soon as I deem it feasible. In the meantime, I invite you to enjoy the Citadel's hospitality. Fair enough?"

"Evidently it will have to be," Montrose said.

9

The small emergency room was full to overflowing. From what she'd overheard, the blond wraith gathered that a pickup with no brake lights had stopped suddenly in the rain, initiating a seven-vehicle pile-up. Hearing the wail of the ambulances, a number of the Restless had hurried to the county hospital to watch the proceedings. Some were soaking up the agony and terror in the air, palpable to a ghost as the reek of blood, bodily waste, and disinfectant. They looked as if they were becoming more *real* in some indefinable way. A second contingent wagered on who would die, how soon, and whether the unfortunate in question would join the Restless. A few Reapers hovered possessively over the injured, intent on capturing any souls who did materialize in the Underworld. Those with the ability to reach into the Skinlands subtly hampered the efforts of the mortal doctors and nurses.

The blond wanderer, a slender young woman dressed in faded jeans, a baggy flannel shirt, and a silver pendant cast in the shape of an owl, climbed up onto the wheeled gurney in the corner. Beneath her insubstantial feet, the cart was no more likely to shift than a slab of granite. Next she sang, first a plaintive lament for delights and loved ones sealed away forever behind the Shroud, then a lewd, raucous satire on the Deathlords, and finally a hymn of Transcendence, of reconciliation and release. She was no Chanteur, but she had a pleasant soprano voice and did a reasonable job of accompanying herself on the mandolin. By the end of the third song, she'd lured several of her fellow spirits away from the ongoing drama of the carnage.

She took another look around the room, checking for

Legionnaires, and then launched into her speech. The Sisterhood of Athena was an odd, hybrid sort of organization, Heretics or Rebels depending on how one looked at it, and her oration reflected the dichotomy. It was partly an exhortation to seek Transcendence and partly a call for revolution. But a fiery abhorrence of slavery infused every syllable. Catching the thrust of her remarks, the Reapers glared.

She kept the sermon short, partly out of concern that Legionnaires might wander in, but primarily to avoid boring her audience. As she neared the end, she searched their faces, looking for an indication that her words were hitting home. She didn't find it, though one or two of the wraiths looked genuinely thoughtful.

At least, the Sister reflected, no one had heckled her. And after she finished, some of them asked questions.

"You didn't tell us what path really leads to Transcendence," a stooped old man in a bow tie, suspenders, and zippered leather bondage mask said querulously. "Should we believe in the Third Coming, the Needle Dancers, the Invisible Tabernacle, or what?"

"The Increate is infinite and therefore infinitely diverse," the Sister replied. "That being the case, many creeds embody aspects of the truth. Follow the path that suits you best. Just make sure it isn't a corrupt faith, one that feeds your Shadow and grovels to the Void."

A slender woman in a red halter and a mask of peacock feathers raised a hand with a bright blue eye in the center of the palm. Wondering if the sculpted organ could actually see, the Sister gave her a nod.

"A friend of mine got depressed," the masked woman said. "Over the course of a few months, he just lost the will to go on. I was there when Oblivion took him."

"I'm sorry," the missionary said.

The masked woman scowled as if the Sister had jeered at her grief. "That isn't the point! I knew somebody else, a Holy Roller like you. She spent most of her time meditating, looking for Transcendence, and finally she disappeared. I was there that time, too, and you know what? It looked exactly the same!"

"Many people do believe that Transcendence is just another name for annihilation," the blond ghost conceded. "That's what the Deathlords and the Legions *want* you to believe, and I can't prove they're wrong. But I *feel* it, and I think that if you look into your hearts, you'll feel it too. There has to be something beyond this desolate, lonely place. Somewhere better. Something to hope for."

The masked woman sneered.

Scowling, a doctor stepped back from a motionless, gory body. The Reaper poised at the head of the bed, a rangy man wearing a latex Newt Gingrich mask and a chainmail vest, quivered with expectation, eager to snap the shackles in his hands on an Enfant's wrists. But no new wraith appeared in the Shadowlands. Finally the Reaper abandoned the corpse and looked around. No doubt discerning that other scavengers had already laid claim to the rest of the dying, he wrapped the manacles around his waist and swaggered toward the Sister.

"I take thralls," he said curtly. "I catch them, I chain them, and I sell them."

"I can see that," the Sister replied.

"If you want to chase after Transcendence," the Reaper said, "go ahead. It's your funeral. But why do you want to screw up the world for the rest of us?"

"Whatever their differences, nearly every faith agrees that you Transcend by becoming a good person. How could I aspire to virtue yet ignore the suffering and injustice all around me? How could I ever deserve ultimate freedom if I didn't care that others were trapped in the vilest sort of slavery?"

"That sounds real noble. But what's that mandolin made of? Or for that matter, the shirt on your back?"

The Sister frowned. "Quite possibly, they came from a Soul Forge. But—"

"You bet your ass they did! This is the Underworld. There's nothing *but* souls to make stuff out of. It's a tough break for the losers who go to the smelters, but if we let them go free, the rest of us would have nothing!"

Some other wraiths muttered in agreement.

"I realize it wouldn't be easy to shut down the Soul Forges," the Sister said. "I don't claim to know how we could get by without them. But I'm confident we'd find a way. After all, they're an invention. They didn't *always* exist. Freeing the thralls would change our world in a fundamental way. Perhaps we'd find it had changed us as well. Perhaps we could all Transcend."

The Reaper made a spitting noise, turned, and disappeared through the wall.

After his exit, the discussion lost momentum, and the Sister's audience began to drift away. To her surprise, the old man in the S&.M hood tossed a worn copper obolus on the gurney. She couldn't tell if she'd actually moved him or if he was merely rewarding her for a few minutes of diversion.

Either way, she thought, she'd be happy to take the offering. She'd learned the value of money from childhood on, and her long mortal career as a nun and abbess had disabused her of any notion that clerics didn't need cash as much as anyone else. She hopped to the floor and picked up the coin, wincing at the ache that twinged through her fingertips. Oboli were frequently unpleasant to handle. Some wraiths believed it was because the coins still had a vestige of human consciousness suffering inside them. Unfortunately, few other Soul Forged goods emitted similar vibrations, and thus it was all too easy to overlook their gruesome origin.

As she slipped the obolus in her pocket, she took a final look around the ER, wishing the accident victims life, or, failing that, a happier destination than the Shadowlands. Then she slipped outdoors.

The pounding rain had ebbed to a drizzle, though lightning still flashed to the west, out over the wide expanse of the Mississippi. The cool air smelled clean. For once, the Shroud notwithstanding, she didn't catch even the subtlest whiff of decay, although, to her eyes, the pines at the edge of the parking lot looked twisted and blighted, with dry brown needles, and oozing chancres mottling the bark.

Skirting the large Nihil hissing and shimmering in the middle of the asphalt, her mandolin slung across her back, she headed down a narrow side street. Soon she reached one of Greenville's Haunts, an area of dilapidated, abandoned clapboard houses three blocks square.

Legend had it that in the 1840s, one of the residents of the district had brutally beaten a slave, and the unfortunate woman had cursed him with her dying breath. Shortly thereafter, a terrible disease resembling a fast-acting leprosy had swept through the neighborhood. Horrified by its virulence, the city officials had taken extreme measures to contain it. Armed sentries had patrolled the perimeter of the area, shooting anyone who tried to leave. The municipal leaders had even considered burning the district down, but feared that the fire, too, might spread to the city as a whole.

The Quick had tried to demolish the old houses on any number of occasions since, but so far the local wraiths had always managed to sabotage their efforts. The miasma of grief and despair still festering in the shuttered bedrooms and moldering parlors was far too bracing to surrender without a fight.

As the Sister strolled, she looked for someone who could direct her to a market, or a venue where Sandmen and genuine Chanteurs performed. At the moment, no one was in view. Perhaps the downpour had driven everyone indoors. Rain couldn't hurt a wraith or even get him wet, but some spirits disliked the tingle of the droplets falling through their bodies. No doubt what many actually disliked was any experience that served to remind them they were dead.

So many ghosts pined endlessly for the lives they'd left behind! The Sister occasionally fell prey to the same longing herself, but when she did, she fought hard to quash it. At best, it was a demoralizing distraction from the quest for Transcendence. At worst, it could lead a wraith into unspeakable crimes.

Prompted by such reflections, she began silently reciting the Pledge of Athena. *I am dead, and death is a journey. Spirit clothed in light, risen and sundered from my chrysalis of mortal clay—*

Somewhere behind her, something made a soft, brushing sound. She turned smoothly, her weight centered, the way her sifu had taught her, only to discover there was still no one in sight.

It was quite possible that she'd imagined the noise. Or that it had nothing to do with her. Still, the Underworld was a dangerous place, especially for missionaries and other subversives, and it paid to be careful. She spent another moment peering about, straining her hypersensitive vision to the utmost.

She didn't see anything threatening. Somewhere to the north, a Quick baby started crying, a sweet, vital sound, and, like the scent of the rain-washed air, blessedly undistorted by the Shroud. A few feet away from the infant, a man emitted a groggy groan and clambered out of his waterbed. The mattress sloshed.

Now smiling at her own edginess, the Sister turned and walked on. Just as she completed the second stanza of the Pledge, she heard the noise—a stealthy footfall?—again. This time it sounded a little closer.

She whirled. Stare as she might, there was still nothing to see. Just the moonlight gilding the glistening streets, and the feverish glitter of the Nihils defacing the decaying houses.

Unfortunately, just because she couldn't see anyone, that didn't mean there was no one there. Certain wraiths, Harbingers, for example, could become invisible. She strained her ears, listening. Lacking a heartbeat or the need to breathe, the Restless could be extraordinarily quiet when they wanted to be, but they were also preternaturally perceptive. Sometimes it balanced out.

But not this time. Down along the river, frogs chirped, and the current murmured. Engines moaned, and car tires hissed over wet roads. But she still couldn't pinpoint anyone creeping along behind her.

Maybe no one was. Or perhaps he was simply good at it. In any case, now that she was concerned about the possibility, the chances of her enjoying the night life of Greenville, Mississippi had dropped to just about nil. She decided to head directly for her skiff and get away from land as soon as possible.

As she turned toward the river, a figure ducked behind an overgrown hedge on the other side of the street. Startled, she jumped, and soft laughter pulsed through the dark. There was something odd about the rhythm of it.

In any case, the mockery angered her. Though she generally

tried to avoid violence, she was no one's helpless victim, and she would have liked to ram the laughter back down the wretch's throat. But it wasn't a practical notion, not when there was also someone skulking along behind her.

She wondered who it was. Conceivably a band of Legionnaires, though the locals hadn't persecuted missionaries with any great zeal in the last couple years. Nor did Hierarchs generally play cat-and-mouse games. Halt-or-we'll-shoot was more their style. Most likely it was the Reaper who'd accosted her and one or more of his friends, come to enslave *her*. The notion made her muscles clench in fury.

But whoever it was, they wouldn't get her. The Sisterhood had trained her too well. She turned back toward the north and started to run, only to glimpse a flicker of motion in the darkness directly ahead.

Now truly alarmed, she lurched to a halt. Was she surrounded? If there were that many people after her, why couldn't she catch a good look at any one of them? And why didn't they just close in for the kill?

She couldn't imagine, but by hanging back, they'd given her a chance. Pivoting, she dashed across a weed-infested yard, up three steps, and through a warped door with a few flakes of yellow paint, the mark of the old-time quarantine, still clinging to the wood. In a musty foyer, she turned and ran south, plunging through the exterior wall of the house, across a strip of coarse grass, and through the side of the derelict home next door.

A wraith's power to flit through solid objects gave him an advantage when trying to evade pursuit, even when the pursuers were ghosts, too. The quarry could always dodge behind a wall, thus escaping the hunters' scrutiny, and then flee in a different direction. Intelligently employed, the tactic generally served to shake even alert and energetic adversaries off one's trail.

And so, for the next few minutes, she ran, constantly changing course but trying to work her way gradually downhill toward the river, hurtling through rotting walls and filthy, broken windows, across yards where rats rustled through the underbrush and streets with weeds poking between the cobblestones. Periodically she tried to spot the hunters, but without any further success. She supposed that was all right if they'd lost sight of her as well.

Unfortunately, her strategy had one drawback. It took energy to slip through solid objects. Finally, panting just as if she still needed air, she bounded up a flight of rickety stairs and into a small bedroom, where a tiny skeleton lay in a cradle, and the stale air screamed with ancient heartbreak. A ghost in a gingham dress stood staring down at the dead baby. She slowly raised her head to regard the Sister with vacant eyes.

"I'm sorry for intruding," the missionary said, peering out the windows. No one was in sight. "I just want to rest for a moment, and then I'll go." She could already feel the grief trapped in the room revitalizing her.

The other ghost returned her gaze to the bones. Her own predicament notwithstanding, the Sister couldn't help wondering if her companion had spent the last one hundred and fifty years doing nothing but staring down at the remains of her child. It was a ghastly thought. Perhaps she could come back later and talk to the poor woman, convince her to abandon her vigil and—

She felt something rushing at her back.

Her hands snapping up into a guard position, she sidestepped and pivoted to face the newcomer. In the gloom, all she could make out was a hulking figure with something strange about its head. Agile as a panther, he hacked at her with a jagged-edged two-hand sword.

Ducking, the Sister silently called her own weapon, and the leather-wrapped hilt of the darksteel knife with its owl's head pommel popped into existence inside her fingers. She feinted a kick at her attacker's crotch, then lunged in close, stabbing at his breast.

Her adversary twisted aside, evading the thrust. Unable to use the sword at such close quarters, he slammed his elbow against her temple, driving a spike of pain through her skull. Off balance, she stumbled toward the fungus-spotted, Nihil-riddled wall. From the corner of her eye, she glimpsed him charging after her, whirling the sword above his head for a lethal stroke.

She could see that she'd never recover her equilibrium in time to ward off the blow. Struggling to focus past the pain in her head, she willed herself completely insubstantial.

She caught a last glimpse of the wraith in the gingham dress, still staring down at the cradle as if she were all alone. Then she tumbled through the side of the house and out into the night.

When she hit the ground, she did her best to roll, her mandolin shattering beneath her. By good luck as much as facility, she managed to avoid serious injury. As she scrambled to her feet, she peered frantically about, expecting to see her attacker leaping down after her, or his accomplices charging toward her. But everything was still.

Her head and left hip aching, limping slightly, she turned and ran, trying to understand how the swordsman had tracked her, how he'd appeared so suddenly in the little nursery, and why his companions weren't already on top of her. Once he'd located her, he should have signaled them to move in. None of it made sense.

Her strategy of evasion hadn't kept her safe before, but, lacking any better plan, she held to it, working her way out of the Haunt and into a Quick public housing project, rows of identical gray concrete-block buildings with slogans like GENERATION LAST and BLOOD AND SILENCE spray-painted on the walls. Now every move through a solid barrier brought a throb of pain.

Ahead of her, six giggling teenagers, four boys and two girls, were squatting in a circle. Their auras flickered a murky violet with malice and excitement. As the Sister ran by, she saw that they were dissecting a writhing guinea pig. The animal's glistening gray viscera bulged through a long cut in its belly.

All but exhausted, the Sister peered back down the street. She didn't see any pursuers. Praying that at the moment, none of them could see her either, she tried to step into a small barbecue joint that had already closed for the night. For a second, she could feel the wall resisting her intrusion, clinging to her like flypaper, and she imagined herself getting helplessly stuck halfway through. But a final wrench of her shoulders and a last exertion of will carried her on into the interior. The shadowy diner smelled of hickory smoke and half-spoiled pork. The inky fissures in the back wall hissed.

The Sister scurried around the greasy counter and hunkered down beside it. *They can't check every room in every building*, she thought. *If they didn't see me duck in here, maybe they won't find me.* She resisted the urge to peek over the counter, for fear that one of the hunters would look through the window and see her. Instead, she listened with all her might, hoping her ears would warn her if any of her enemies drew near.

For a minute she couldn't hear anything but the Quick, their breath hissing, hearts thumping, and bowels gurgling, babbling, chewing, and grunting in the apartments all around her. Then she seemed to catch a different sound, but she couldn't make out what it was. Not a whisper and not the creak of shoe leather. Not the click of a gun being cocked, nor the metallic sigh of a blade leaving its—

Abruptly she realized that the hissing of Nihils behind her had grown infinitesimally louder. Just as her head snapped around, a long vertical crack gaped open. It still shouldn't have been wide enough to admit the swordsman, but somehow he flowed through it anyway, sweeping his jagged weapon down at the top of her head.

Kneeling, she couldn't fling herself out of the way in time. All she could do was try to deflect the blow. She whipped up her arm and the sword skated along it, gashing it, leaving a trail of momentary numbness that abruptly flared into pain.

The swordsman kicked her in the chin, flinging her back against the counter. From the sharp crack and the fresh jab of agony, she knew he'd broken her jaw. Suddenly her vision was blurry and dim. The jagged blade swung up for another blow.

Reflexively she scrambled backward, through the substance of the counter. Once again the coarse, gummy matter fought her, clutched at her, but somehow she dragged herself clear. Desperately she struggled to her feet, certain that her assailant must already be leaping over the pitifully inadequate barrier she'd placed between them.

But he wasn't. He was still standing by the wall, watching her frantic efforts to get into a fighting stance. He laughed his disturbing syncopated laugh, and as her vision swam back into focus, she finally saw what made the sound so peculiar. It was coming from both of his wedge-shaped, jet-black reptilian heads.

The head on the right licked its upper fangs with a gray, forked tongue. Then the apparition stepped backward, and the Nihil oozed shut in front of it.

The Sister trembled. Her arm and head throbbed. Absurd though it was, she could have sworn she felt a living heart pounding with terror in her breast.

Though wraiths didn't need to breathe, her sifu had taught her the proper way to do so to facilitate meditation. She forced herself to take long breaths and let them out slowly. After several exhalations, her pain and fear lost some of their edge.

Her impulse was to resume running, but she resisted the temptation. Headlong flight hadn't helped her so far. Her only chance was to think. To figure out what was happening to her.

Now that she'd gotten a good look at him, and seen the singular method he used to sneak up on her, she surmised that the swordsman was a Spectre. In the Shadowlands, where wraiths of all persuasions engaged Masquers to sculpt them into gaudy monstrosities, simple freakishness was no indication that a spirit had sold himself to the Void. But most of those who took on such forms opted for the exotic allure of an angel or a sphinx, useful modifications like retractable claws or spiked knuckles, or the macabre humor of a devil's horns or a grinning skull face. Few sane ghosts aspired to look as hideously inhuman as the two-headed bipedal crocodile.

Moreover, nearly all of them, even Harbingers, whose arcane skills had been invented to allow them to negotiate the Tempest, considered such travel a perilous enterprise. Whereas, she now suspected, the reptile man was traversing it with ease, while peeking out into the Shadowlands to keep track of her. Only one enemy had ever actually attacked her because there was only one. Exploiting the chaotic spatial distortions of the storm, he'd materialized behind her, ahead of her, and then off to the side, all in a matter of moments. Convinced she was sorely outnumbered, she'd run and so squandered her strength.

And any second now, he'd pop up behind her to finish her off! She fought to quell another surge of panic.

He'd stepped through a Nihil. Evidently, he could flow through any such opening, even the smallest, but maybe he couldn't emerge where there were none at all. If she could find such a place, he might abandon the chase, and at least he wouldn't be able to leap up out of nowhere.

Her skin crawling with tension, constantly turning this way and that, she edged toward the window and peered out at the street. Then she laughed, and her eyes throbbed as if they could shed tears.

Nihils, most no bigger than hairs or grains of sand but Nihils nonetheless, pocked and creviced every surface. The walls, pavement, ground, lampposts, fire hydrant, overturned newspaper box, and parked cars all glittered with a poisonous sheen. Dear God, had there always been so many?

She supposed there had. Loath to recognize the voracity with which Oblivion was eroding the world, she'd simply avoided looking at them. At any rate, it was apparent that she couldn't possibly find some untainted corner of creation in time for it to do her any good.

Such being the case, she might as well make her stand where she was. She told herself firmly that she had a chance. She now understood the Spectre's tricks. It hadn't even seen hers. As it happened, Freda Schmidt, the founder of the Sisterhood, was an accomplished Spook, and most of her followers learned at least the basics of the rowdy guild's Arcanos. The Sister herself had often used the magic to good effect, when pain and fatigue weren't hampering her efforts.

She moved to a clear section of floor, making sure there were no Nihils immediately under her feet or in the ceiling above her head. Then she reached out with her mind, trying to *feel* the tables and chairs around her, and the metal rack, laden with bags of potato chips, Moon Pies, and other snacks, standing by the back wall.

At first, she couldn't establish a connection. Then the seething sound of one of the Nihils at her back changed timbre. Desperately she reached again, and at last the power rose inside her. Suddenly it was as if she had twenty extra hands, their fingertips lightly resting on various objects scattered about the room.

She turned and saw the Spectre rushing her, his sword upraised. She scrambled backward, leading him on. When he was directly opposite the metal rack, she seized it with her invisible fists, and, grunting, jerked it into the air and lashed it at his heads.

He threw up his arms for protection. Strewing snacks across the dingy linoleum, the rack slammed into him, penetrating his form without resistance, and knocked him staggering sideways. The makeshift weapon slipped out of her psychic grip.

She didn't bother to fumble for it. Instead, she picked up a round table, sending a napkin dispenser, ashtray, and salt and pepper shakers clattering to the floor, and bashed the Spectre with it. The blow hammered him to his knees.

She managed to club him twice more, and then the table simply hurtled through his body without changing his position an iota. He'd shifted himself completely out of phase with the material world, although he and his weapon—a length of wood or bone, she now observed, the edges lined with sharp black stones—would still be dangerously real to her. Both mouths snarling, baring his now-broken fangs, he started to lurch upright.

She'd wanted to batter him unconscious from a distance before he managed to neutralize her Spook magic. Now she could only hope that the punishment he'd taken had slowed him down sufficiently to give her the edge in hand-to-hand combat, despite her injuries and exhaustion. Knife leveled, she lunged at him, striving to get inside his reach before he hoisted his sword into position for a swing.

She didn't make it. The weapon streaked at her neck. Instinctively she shoved at it with her mind.

It was a risky move. She had no right to expect that she could make psychic contact with an object that small, moving that fast. But with a crack, the sword rebounded, some of the black rocks shattering, as if it had collided with a shield.

Scrambling on, the Sister buried her dagger in the Spectre's breast. The two-headed wraith reeled backward, the sword tumbling from his hands. As his knees began to buckle, waves of dark light ran through his flesh, washing his substance away. When he vanished, the knife fell out of his chest.

The Sister sank to the floor, gasping, trembling with the fear she hadn't permitted herself to experience during the battle, her arm and jaw throbbing as her body labored to repair itself. She wondered exactly what she'd done to attract the Spectre's attention. Whatever it was, she hoped she wouldn't do it again.

10

The shooting range, a large, low-ceilinged room in the basement of the Federal Building, popped with gunfire and smelled of burnt cordite. Bellamy loitered by the exit, waiting for Walter Byrd to finish practicing. He'd known he could catch his fellow agent here. Byrd, a fortyish man whose doughy physique belied his mental and physical toughness, showed up at the range every Monday afternoon at five, no matter how busy he was. He'd been fanatical about honing his marksmanship ever since his first shoot-out three years ago. On that occasion, he'd fired three shots at close range, missing each time, and then the perpetrator had shot him in the neck. The surgeon had told him it was a miracle he'd survived.

Scowling ferociously, Byrd emptied his Browning, then pushed the button mounted on the rail. The paper target with its black human silhouette floated across the room to him like an obedient ghost. He inspected the holes he'd put in it, then, evidently satisfied, pulled off his goggles and ear protectors, reloaded his pistol, and returned it to its shoulder holster. He stooped to collect his brass, then headed for the door. When he saw Bellamy, his mouth tightened.

So much for my winning personality, Bellamy thought. "Hi, Walt."

"Hi," Byrd replied, trying to slip past.

Bellamy turned and fell into step beside him. As they pushed through the door and out into the corridor, he asked, "So what's happening with the Atheist?"

"Nothing much," said Byrd, rubbing the scar beneath his chin.

"Oh, come on. There've been three more murders. You must

have something new to chew on."

Byrd glanced up and down the hallway, obviously making sure no one else was in earshot. "You're going to get both our butts in a sling if you keep doing this. You know I'm not supposed to talk about the case to anybody outside the task force, especially you. Hanson's orders."

"Nolliver's, really."

"And he's your doctor. All the more reason to go along with the program."

Bellamy snorted. "Give me a break. Since when do you have any faith in shrinks? Come on, Walt, put yourself in my shoes. Imagine that you were looking for the Atheist and then got yanked off the case. Wouldn't it drive you crazy if you couldn't at least find out what was going on?"

Byrd sighed. "Probably. Here it is, then, short and sweet, and you didn't hear it from me. We've got three new victims and three new crime scenes, but it hasn't helped. We still don't have any real leads."

"Damn it, that shouldn't be. When a serial killer murders as frequently as the Atheist, it usually means he's coming unwrapped. He gets sloppy, takes more chances, and makes mistakes."

"You must put some stock in shrinks. Otherwise, you wouldn't be quoting me that psychological profile crap."

"I used to put a lot of stock in them," Bellamy said. "Then I started therapy with Dr. Breath Mint."

They rounded a corner. Byrd quickened his pace, possibly hurrying toward the vending machines that had just come into view. "Hasn't he sorted out your Oedipus complex yet?"

"He doesn't seem to be sorting out anything, just going through the motions. It's like he just wants to support the idea that I need counseling."

Byrd inspected the sandwich machine. Most of the compartments were empty. "Do you believe this? Nothing but egg salad again. Of course, if I had any brains, I'd be on my way home for supper. Look, what are you saying, that Nolliver wants people to believe you had a breakdown when you really didn't? Why the heck would he care?" He fished in his pocket and pulled out a handful of change.

Bellamy shrugged. "I know it sounds paranoid—"

"Bingo."

"—but on the other hand, I've thought a lot about it, and whatever happened to me that night, I sure don't feel mentally disturbed now."

Byrd grinned. "The real whackos never do." He fed coins into the slot, then pressed a button. The yellow and white sandwich in its glistening cellophane wrapper slid forward, dropped, and thumped down in the bottom of the machine.

"There's something else bugging me," Bellamy said. "Dunn, the rep from SAD, decided that what happened to me had nothing to do with the paranormal. He also pointed out that since my memory has a hole in it, my story is vague. But precisely because it is, how could he rule the paranormal out? Look at what I *did* give him. A psychic who talks about evil spirits and then drops dead. Shadowy figures that appear and vanish mysteriously. An experienced field agent who inexplicably loses his mind. My god, what kind of stuff does SAD investigate, if Dunn isn't willing to look into all that?"

Byrd extracted his sandwich from the bin in the bottom of the machine. "So Nolliver and Dunn are in it together, working for the Atheist, who just happens to be Count Dracula. Is that about the size of it? I wonder how much he's paying them. If it's good money, maybe we should join the conspiracy ourselves."

Bellamy fought to quash a surge of irritation. "You know damn well that isn't what I think. But *something* weird is going on. Waxman worked for Weiss, he was worried that if he talked to me, he'd die, too, and right on cue, he did."

"Of a heart attack, after he'd drunk enough booze to float a boat."

"It's still too much of a coincidence."

Byrd turned to look Bellamy in the eye. "Listen to me. I don't want to believe you've lost it. We've been through a lot together. I keep thinking I ought to be able to kid you out of this foolishness, but it doesn't look like I can, so I'm going to talk to you straight. Nobody's out to get you. There's no such thing as the paranormal. Forget about it and the Atheist too. Otherwise, you're going to trash your career. And you and I are not going to discuss this bullshit anymore. The next time we run into each other, we're going to talk about cars, or pussy, or football. The important things in life. *Capice?*"

Bellamy grimaced. "Okay. I know you're right."

"You bet I am. Now I should get back to work. Nothing goes better with stale egg salad than a nice juicy autopsy report. You get out of here. Go out and have a life. You can tell me what it's like."

Bellamy stood and watched Byrd walk away. *Have a life*, he thought. He *had one*, once, until his work had squeezed it out of existence. First, he'd gradually stopped spending time with any friends who weren't involved in law enforcement, and then Janice had divorced him, complaining that she never saw him anymore, and even when she did, his mind was still a million miles away.

He guessed the truly sad thing was that, deep down, he hadn't cared. His career had been too rewarding, and if he'd had to sacrifice friendships and even his marriage to keep it revving, that had been a price he was willing to pay. He'd never dreamed a day might come when *he* would feel forsaken, betrayed, and abandoned by his colleagues.

He didn't want to stick around the building, yet he couldn't quite bring himself to leave. Perhaps it was because he had nowhere else to go. He took a slow, groaning elevator upstairs, then trudged on, moving warily past Hanson's corner office. He slipped into his own workspace and quietly closed the door.

The air was stuffy. Evidently the air conditioning was getting ready to die again. Bellamy spent a moment gazing out the dirty window, hoping it would cheer him up a little. Generally speaking, the view was a depressing vista of huge, soot-stained towers, their bases scarred with graffiti and their upper stories crawling with indecipherable hieroglyphics and leering gargoyles. But at the end of North Boulevard he could just make out one end of the Old State Capitol, a quaint Gothic Revival castle with a gorgeous colored-glass skylight, and beyond that, a slice of the Mississippi, the water sparkling in the sunlight.

Sighing, he turned away and removed the top manila folder from the tall stack before him. Like the others in the heap, it was the file on an old, cold case that VICAP had never managed to close. Procedure mandated that someone periodically review such records, on the theory that he might suddenly deduce the solution like Sherlock Holmes. As far as Bellamy knew, no one had ever enjoyed this happy experience, nor did his superiors seriously expect that anybody ever would. That was why they allowed the reviews to pile up until someone needed some busywork, like an agent they no longer trusted to do anything important.

This particular record detailed VICAP's efforts to apprehend a serial killer of streetwalkers who'd terrorized Little Rock from 1986 to 1990. Bellamy made an honest effort to focus on the investigators' notes and the photos of the corpses and crime scenes. But he couldn't keep his mind off the Atheist, who was killing people now.

At last, he decided, to hell with it. Hanson had ordered him to cut back to a forty-hour work week. That meant he was on his own time anyway. He set the file aside, switched on his computer, and logged on to the Internet.

He hadn't told Nolliver that he'd started reading the wildcat bulletin boards devoted to Wicca, crystal power, flying saucers, and a host of other crackpot subjects. The psychiatrist wouldn't have approved. He would have warned Bellamy that he was regressing into delusional thinking again.

But I'm not, the agent thought. I don't believe in all this crap. But I've got to start looking for answers somewhere.

After a moment's thought, he decided to begin with Grailnet, a board which attracted a more eclectic and peculiar mix of eccentrics than most of the others. Sliding and clicking the computer's mouse, he selected the proper address from his directory. Grailnet's opening screen, a cloaked, hooded figure beckoning mysteriously, appeared on his monitor.

Bellamy joined the first real-time conversation area, or Circle of Discourse, as Grailnet's menu called it. The screen displayed a benighted clearing, where shadowy figures with luminous eyes squatted around a pale green campfire. Lines of

Gothic type, messages from other users, crawled in and out of existence beneath the illustration. "Alhazred" was raving about his pet theory that the fiction of H. P. Lovecraft was based on truth, while two other regulars ridiculed his every statement.

Bellamy thought that if the average user caught as much flak as Alhazred did, he'd flee the board forever. But the Lovecraft buff seemed to thrive on the abuse. Indeed, the FBI agent wondered if he *ever* went off-line.

In any case, Bellamy didn't want to talk to him. He'd already endured several of Alhazred's harangues about "slumbering Cthulhu," "the Lake of Hali," and all the rest of it, and if any of it had anything to do with what happened in East St. Louis, it would take a smarter man than he to make the connection. He moved on to the next Circle. The clearing became even darker, the figures subtly more misshapen. A couple seemed to have blood on their mouths and hands. Periodically a demonic face took shape in the midst of the flames. As near as Bellamy could make out, Grailnet's progression of increasingly sinister visuals was intended to suggest that as a user explored the system, he was descending deeper and deeper into hell.

Two people had arrived before him. Bellamy knew one of them, "Astarte," whose great ambition in life was to become the "handmaiden" of some supernatural entity. He gathered that a vampire would be ideal, but any sort of phantom or uncanny beast would do. The agent imagined her as an obese, slovenly woman with a dozen cats, a bookshelf crammed with Anne Rice books and Harlequin romances, and no off-line social life whatsoever. "Vulture," the user with whom she was presently conversing, was a stranger to him.

I know they're out there, Astarte said. They're all around us. I just have to figure out how to find them.

They don't want to be found, Vulture replied.

They don't want to be found by the wrong people, Astarte said. They don't want to hunted or exploited. They do want to be adored as the gods they are.

You don't know that, Vulture said. You don't know them. You think you do, from movies and stories and your own dreams, but they're more alien than you can possibly imagine.

How do you know that? Astarte fired back. Have you ever seen one?

For a while there was no response. Bellamy guessed that Vulture had abandoned the conversation. He reached for the mouse to move on himself. Then another message appeared.

I've glimpsed things at a distance, Vulture said. I can't be any more specific than that. Please, just believe that I know what I'm talking about. You wouldn't be the first human admirer to knock on a supernatural creature's door. Most of them wind up regretting it, even in relatively peaceful times, and the dark world hasn't been peaceful in a long while. And there are indications that it's going to get worse.

Bellamy no longer got excited merely because someone on-line claimed to have first-hand information about the paranormal. Heck, cyberspace was swarming with people who claimed to be paranormal entities themselves. But vague as it was, Vulture's comment seemed to echo Waxman's fearful babbling. The agent quickly typed, What *kind of indications?* His keyboard clicked.

Hello, Frank, Vulture said. I wondered if we were going to hear from you, or if you were just going to lurk in the background.

Hi, Bellamy typed. What kind of indications?

To his irritation, the next message to appear was from Astarte. *If you really have seen supernatural creatures, tell me what kind, and where.*

I'm sorry, Vulture said. There are certain facts I can only share with kindred spirits. People who already possess a certain amount of information. Otherwise, I'd wind up luring defenseless people into danger.

That's a crock, Astarte said.

Bellamy couldn't decide whether it was or not. Vulture was quite possibly striking a pose, pretending to knowledge he didn't possess. But his genuine reticence set him apart from other on-line charlatans the agent had encountered. They'd claimed they couldn't reveal their deepest, darkest occult secrets, but they'd given up any number of intriguing hints and lurid details. They'd understood they needed to say something specific in order to seem impressive.

If Vulture didn't care about looking impressive, maybe he was a different breed of cat. Even if he was a crank, perhaps he had inside information about some dangerous cult or coven. Bellamy wondered how he could get him to spill it.

Until now, the FBI man had avoided telling anyone on Grailnet who he was, or why he was interested in all their New Age mumbo jumbo. A lot of people were reluctant to talk to cops, and he didn't want somebody contacting the Bureau reporting that one of its agents was spending hours on the boards, chatting about cattle mutilations and the Bermuda Triangle. But instinct told him it was time to take a risk. Frowning, he typed, *I understand more than you realize, Vulture. Do you know who Milo Waxman was? I was with him when he died.*

I don't know, Astarte said. To Bellamy, the white characters on the black rectangle at the base of the screen seemed to convey a plaintive whine. *Who was he?*

Once again, it took Vulture a moment to respond. *I thought Waxman died of a heart attack.*

There's more to it than that, Bellamy typed.

WHO WAS WAXMAN? Astarte demanded.

Who are you, Frank? Vulture asked.

Now it was Bellamy's turn to hesitate. An *investigator,* he answered after a moment. *And you?*

A *student,* Vulture said. A *watchdog sometimes. If you don't already know precisely what you're dealing with, walk away from it. Take a long vacation in another country.*

That's not an option, Bellamy typed.

It's *RUDE to cut somebody out of a conversation,* Astarte sulked. *You can both go to hell.*

Tell me about Waxman, Vulture said.

What's in it for me? Bellamy replied. Will you share what you know?

After another pause, Vulture said, *Not on-line. And not over the phone or through the mail, either. We'd have to meet.*

Bellamy tried to swallow away a sudden dryness in his mouth. *Where?*

Can you get to New Orleans?

Yes, Bellamy typed, feeling even more excited. Heck, he could drive there in a couple of hours. Considering that Vulture could have been anywhere in the world, his proximity was a piece of luck. But more than that, it lent weight to the notion that the guy might actually know something about recent events in the Mississippi basin.

How will I recognize you? Vulture asked.

Bellamy described himself. *I'll wear an LSU cap,* he added.

Meet *me in Jackson Square at noon on Wednesday,* Vulture said. *Come alone or you won't see me.* His cartoon buzzard icon vanished from the corner of the screen, indicating he'd exited the Circle.

Bellamy did the same, wondering if he'd just taken the first step toward discovering what had happened to him, or established beyond any shadow of a doubt that he was every bit as crazy as everybody thought he was.

11

Scowling, Montrose prowled the corridors of the Citadel, his new cloak swishing about his ankles. The cape was as full and black as a Grim Rider's outer garment was supposed to be, but it didn't have the Unlidded Eye affixed to it. Gayoso had promised that he'd instruct a seamstress or metalworker to fashion a proper badge for his guest, but so far, none had been forthcoming.

Happening upon a pyramidal stack of old, rusty paint cans, Montrose gave in to the impulse to kick them. Since his insubstantial foot couldn't shift them an iota, the result, a muffled bong, was less than satisfying.

The Scot had studied the secrets of the Proctors as well as those of the Harbingers. If he wanted, he could project himself into the Skinlands and give the cans a proper kick. But it would hardly be a wise expenditure of his energies, particularly here, in what he was rapidly coming to regard as the lair of his enemies.

But to hell with it. It wouldn't take much strength. The Shroud was even thinner here than it was in most Haunts. And more to the point, in his present humor, he didn't care about being prudent. He focused his power, his body throbbed, and a wraith in the distance vanished from view. He booted the cans, and the stack flew apart with a satisfying clatter.

His frustration vented, he immediately began to feel sheepish for behaving so childishly. He relaxed his will, and the spiritual magnetism of death instantly drew him back to his proper sphere. As he reentered the Underworld, he heard a pair of hands applauding behind him. Tiny bells chimed in time with the clapping.

Montrose turned. Gayoso's jester, whose name, he'd learned, was Valentine, stood behind him. Tonight, his motley was red and green, with brass bells decorating the horns of his cap, the ragged cuffs of his gloves, and the upturned toes of his boots.

The Anacreon smiled ruefully. "You're right to mock me. That was an asinine display. When I was breathing, I rarely lost my self-control that way—"

"But now that you're a ghost, you can blame every tantrum on your mean old Shadow," the dwarf said, smirking. "Just like the rest of us. Why not? It's the perfect alibi. May a humble entertainer ask why you're so exasperated?"

Montrose hesitated. Considering that Valentine was one of Gayoso's underlings, he seemed a poor choice for a confidant. But the Stygian was still feeling reckless, or too full of annoyance to contain himself, because he finally said, "I've just come from an interview with Mrs. Duquesne."

The jester nodded. "That's enough to ruin anybody's evening."

"She refused to give me any Legionnaires to fulfill my mission. Nathan Shellabarger and your master had already rejected the same request."

"None of that bunch is going to put himself in a position where he's vulnerable to the other two. So it's three strikes and you're out."

Montrose cocked his head. "I beg your pardon?"

"It's a reference to baseball. You know, the American national pastime. Ah, don't worry about it. The point is, you're out of luck. Except that the scuttlebutt around the Citadel is that you had written orders and a passel of soldiers when you left the Isle of Sorrows."

The Scot nodded. "The 'scuttlebutt' is correct."

"So why don't you just go back and get some more?"

"For one thing," said Montrose, sitting down on the grimy floor, "I daresay your governors don't want me telling a Deathlord they defied his wishes. They wouldn't give me an escort, and it's dangerous to travel the Tempest alone. And even if I did make it home, what then? Do I go whining to the Smiling Lord with my tail between my legs? 'I'm sorry, milord, but I lost my Lantern of Truth, my ships, and my troops, and the impudent Hierarchs of Natchez refuse to heed my commands. Please, give me fresh credentials and another expedition so I can go out and try again.' I'd look pathetic. And you can rest assured that if my master ever begins to lose faith in me, I have an abundance of rivals ready to whisper slander in his ear and speed the process along." The swarthy, lantern-jawed face of Demetrius appeared before his inner eye.

Valentine chuckled. "Nice to know that the big shots in the Onyx Tower are just as kindly and honest as us little shots here on Earth. I guess you really are screwed."

Montrose scowled. "No, I'm not. There has to be a way. If I had just a few men—" He paused as an idea struck him.

"What is it?" Valentine asked.

Montrose jumped up. He almost dusted off the back of his cloak before he remembered that dirt on the other side of the Shroud couldn't stick to him. "How would you like to show me the sights?"

Valentine eyed him quizzically. "You mean nobody's showed you around?"

"Around the Citadel, yes. The entire Necropolis, no. I've seen how feebly your Anacreons hold the reins of power, and I'd guess there must be a quarter where the criminal element congregates. A section of Natchez which Hierarchs rarely enter except in force."

"And that's where you want to go tonight."

"Yes. Are you game?"

Valentine grinned. "You know, I guess I am. It could be interesting."

"Can you find me a weapon?"

The jester frowned. "Hard to say. There's a shortage. Any grunt or quartermaster who loses one can be enslaved, so everyone keeps track of his gear pretty well. But if we take a look around—"

"Never mind," Montrose said. Now that he'd decided to act, he felt too eager to waste time snooping about the Citadel. "I'll take care of it." He set out for the front of the complex, and Valentine trotted along beside him.

When they slipped through the fort's front door, Montrose was pleased to see the same two sentries he'd met on his arrival. Evidently in no sunnier humor than before, the Legionnaire with the question-mark brand gave him a sneer.

"Good evening," said Montrose, smiling. "I need your rifle."

The soldier snorted. "What are you, crazy?"

"Some people have said so," Montrose said. "Even you, if memory serves. But I also truly am an Anacreon, as I believe you've been advised."

"I don't care if you're Charon risen from the Labyrinth. You're not *my* Anacreon, and nobody told me to obey y—"

Montrose kicked the other wraith in the stomach, then grabbed him by the collar of his buckskin shirt and slammed his head against the wall behind him. The stunned sentry's knees began to buckle. The Stygian tore the AK-47 out of his hands and whirled to cover the spearman with the jack-o'-lantern grin, who was still trying to fumble his weapon into position for a thrust.

"Is there a problem?" Montrose asked.

The spearman swallowed. "No. No, sir."

"Good," the Stygian said. "Before my appointment to the Grim Riders, I was Fifth Legion myself. At heart, I still am. It would have saddened me if you'd turned out to be insubordinate, too. I'm also going to need your dagger."

The Black Hawk unclipped the Bowie knife from his belt and handed it over.

"Thank you," Montrose said. "Have a pleasant evening." He turned and sauntered toward the ring of human torches. Valentine followed.

"You know," said the dwarf as they started down the hill, "Winston—the jerk you just beat up—is going to run straight to Mrs. Duquesne."

"I don't care." Thinking that for the moment he might as well be as anonymous as possible, Montrose put on his glossy black ceramic mask. "The Smiling Lord put me in charge of these wretches. It's time I started acting like it. Besides, Mrs. Duquesne ought to thank me for disciplining the man. He needed it."

"Maybe," said Valentine, "but he wasn't the only one. We turn here." His bells jingling, he led his companion down an alley that reeked of rotting produce. A black cat, vastly more perceptive than the average Quick human, peered at them with gleaming golden eyes. Nihil cracks in the oil-stained asphalt hissed. "A lot of people have been in a nasty mood lately, inside the Citadel and in the rest of the Necropolis too. There've been a lot of fights, not the usual chickenshit but serious ones, the kind that don't end until somebody goes to the Void."

"That's interesting," Montrose said. For a moment he wondered if the phenomenon could have anything to do with the mysterious threat that Katrina had blathered on about, then pushed the witless notion out of his mind. "Do you have any idea why?"

"Nope," Valentine said, leading him around another corner. Montrose realized they were wending their way west, toward the river. The breeze carried the scent of the muddy water. "Maybe you can figure it out."

"It isn't my job to figure it out," Montrose said. Something whispered overhead. With reflexive caution, he looked up, to see a bat fluttering after insects.

"But I've read some British history," said Valentine, leering, "and I know who you are. A hero."

Montrose grimaced. "You should have read through to the last chapter, where Argyll and his cronies strung me up."

"Okay, so you were a *tragic* hero."

"Rubbish," the Stygian said. "But if I was, the moral of my saga would seem to be that heroism doesn't pay. Only an ass places an ideal ahead of his own interests, or trusts his fellow man an inch further than he has to."

"You're trusting me, a virtual stranger, to lead you through these dark streets to an unknown destination."

"That's true," Montrose said. "But since it was my idea to come, it's unlikely that you're guiding me into an ambush. I am curious, though, as to why you're helping me, when you know Gayoso wouldn't want you to."

"Reverence for the Deathlords?"

Montrose chuckled. "Somehow I find that hard to credit."

"Pretty smart on your part. Actually, I don't like Gayoso much. I don't like his idea of entertainment. A dwarf in cap and bells? I know he was born on another continent in another century, but give me a break! Hell, most of my jokes aren't even funny. He just keeps me around because he thinks it's stylish for a ruler to have a retainer like me. Mainly he uses me for a gofer."

"You aren't a thrall, are you?" asked Montrose. Valentine shook his head. "If you don't want to be a clown, and Gayoso won't accept you in any other capacity, why do you stay? You could strike out on your own. Hire a Masquer to give you normal height, if that would please you."

"I've seen how you turn up your nose at the Citadel when you think nobody's looking. It seems like a dump to you, doesn't it? But the quarters Gayoso gave me are a lot more comfortable than any Haunt I could find anywhere else."

"Don't be so sure. The Hierarchy has any number of strongholds, and they all need clever, hardworking functionaries to keep them running. Perhaps you could find a comfortable berth elsewhere."

Valentine glowered up at him. "I thought you said you don't care about other people's problems."

Montrose shrugged. "I do appreciate it when someone tries to help me, and I hoped I could repay you with some." Valentine took him all the way down to the docks. Now the water smelled foul, as if someone upriver had dumped something noxious in the current. Wavering yellow light and a jumble of voices spilled through the doorway of a tumble-down shack. Somebody with no pretensions to artistic talent had daubed a green skull and crossbones on the warped boards of the wall. The paint had run, as if to suggest that the bones were dripping putrescence.

"The Green Head," said Valentine. "I think I understand what you have in mind, and from one point of view, this is the place for it. But if you do go in, you'll be taking one hell of a risk."

"Why?" asked Montrose. A jovial shout and a smattering of applause sounded from inside the tavern. "Do you expect the place will turn out to be full of Heretics and Renegades?"

"No," Valentine replied. "They usually hang out in other dives. That's why I brought you to this one. Most of the guys in here don't give a rat's ass about politics or religion. But just because they don't sit around plotting the overthrow of the Deathlords, that doesn't mean they like Hierarchs. In their eyes, people like you are cops, pure and simple."

Montrose smiled. "I imagine I'll be all right. But you needn't come in if you'd rather not."

Valentine's mouth twisted. "Oh, don't worry about me. I've been inside before. They'd rather laugh at someone like me than destroy me."

"In that case, after you."

Inside, the shack was smoky and stuffy. The torches mounted on the walls burned with hot Skinlands flame.

Probably a Spook or a Proctor had kindled them. Behind the bar stood a Sandman in a garish patchwork cloak, his eyes narrowed with concentration, maintaining the existence of the earthenware jug the wraiths before him were passing from hand to hand. Judging from their loud, slurred speech and the way they stumbled and swayed, the illusory corn liquor was quite potent. Another four ghosts, all masked, huddled whispering in a shadowy corner. One hulking man with a black handlebar mustache perched on a stool beside a large, ragged-edged Nihil in the middle of the floor, dangling a rope into the seething depths. But most of the crowd had formed a circle around an old Quick tramp in rags. The mortal reeked of sweat and urine. Tears and snot streaked his grimy, wizened face. His breath rasped in his throat, his heart pounded, and his aura flamed orange with fear. Every time he tried to edge out of the ring, the wraiths in his way would reach out and stroke his face, while others crooned, "Meat, meat, meat." Then the victim recoiled, even though it was apparent that he couldn't truly see, hear, or feel his tormentors.

As Montrose took a seat, he felt some of the other patrons looking at him, sizing him up. Though not unduly alarmed, he deemed it prudent to leave the AK-47 with its ebon soulfire crystals prominently displayed on the rickety table before him. He nodded at the old man in the circle. "Charming entertainment," he said dryly.

"Yeah," Valentine replied, "and they're breaking the Dictum Mortem, too. You should arrest them, milord Anacreon."

"That would be counterproductive," Montrose said. "I'm afraid the old fellow is on his own."

Yet the unpleasant spectacle nagged at him. Though he no longer felt any real solicitude for others, cruelty for its own sake, directed at a helpless, innocent victim, still disgusted him on a visceral level.

Besides, he had important business to attend to. He didn't want to sit idly in this wretched stew until the entertainment concluded. For all he knew, his fellow wraiths might keep baiting the tramp all night.

Abruptly he stood up.

"What are you going to do?" Valentine asked.

"What I came to do," Montrose replied. "You might watch my back if you feel so inclined." He pointed the assault rifle straight up at water-stained ceiling, then, on impulse, aimed it just over the heads of the wraiths in the circle instead. He fired a burst. Some ghosts dived to the floor, some cried out in shock, and others lurched around, fumbling for their weapons. The Shadowlands bullets disintegrated against the wall without doing any damage.

Montrose knew that when one wanted to persuade people of anything, it helped to display a bold eye, a firm jaw, and a confident smile. He doffed his mask and tossed it aside to clatter on the floor. "Good evening, ladies and gentlemen. I apologize if I startled anyone, but I wanted your attention."

"You've got it now," said the Sandman behind the bar. The phantasmal jug now lay shattered on the floor in a pool of clear, pungent liquor. Abruptly the wreckage vanished, along with all symptoms of the topers' intoxication. "And it may turn out that you didn't know when you were well off."

"I trust not." To the Stygian's right, cloth rustled. Pivoting, he spied a lanky wraith in a red leather domino easing a throwing knife from its sheath. When Montrose pointed the AK-47 at him, he quickly took his hand away from the hilt. "Allow me to introduce myself. I'm James Graham, in life Earl and Marquess of Montrose, currently Anacreon of the Order of the Unlidded Eye."

The crowd babbled and growled. "You keep getting yourself in deeper," the Sandman said. "We get a few Hierarchs in here, slumming, like your midget friend. Some of them even make it out of Under-the-Hill in one piece. But they have the good sense not to brag about kissing the Deathlords' asses."

"I understand that you aren't unduly fond of the government," Montrose said. "But how do you feel about Heretics? The Smiling Lord sent me to Natchez to make war on them. I'd like you to join me."

Some of his audience laughed. Others babbled in bewilderment. One woman shouted, "I'd rather *die* than join a stinking Legion!"

"I'm not asking you to," Montrose said. "I want you to sign on as free mercenaries. You'll serve on your own terms and quit whenever you like."

"In return for what?" demanded a bald man in dark glasses. Bandoleers crisscrossed his otherwise naked chest, and judging by the bulge in his tight gray jeans, a Masquer had enlarged his genitals to Priapic proportions.

Montrose grinned. "I assumed that was obvious. Plunder, of course! After we subdue the Heretics, we'll take everything they have and sell them into slavery. Valentine told me that one or two of you are familiar with the basic modus operand!."

Several wraiths laughed. The bald man said, "Why do you need us? Why aren't you using Legionnaires?"

"That was my original intention," Montrose said, "but your illustrious local officials apparently can't spare me any troops. I've been advised that the desperadoes of Under-the-Hill are far more formidable than Hierarch soldiers anyway. I hope you deserve your reputation."

"You don't have a Lantern of Truth," said the Sandman. "How do we even know you really are a Grim Rider?"

"I suppose you'll have to take my word for it," Montrose replied. "And if that's a problem, consider this: As long as the venture turns a profit, what does it matter who I really am?"

A number of the onlookers were regarding him differently

now. Their scowls and sneers had given way to more speculative expressions. The Scot didn't entirely know just how he'd swayed them, but he'd assumed from the outset that he had a reasonable chance of doing so. He'd discovered he was a natural leader three hundred and fifty years ago, when he'd held his ragtag army of unruly Highlanders together through sheer charisma.

"I'll tell you what matters," rumbled a gravelly voice. Craning, Montrose saw that the speaker was the burly man, still dangling the coarse hemp rope into the Nihil. He stood up and began to haul it in, hand over hand, neither his voice nor his movements betraying appreciable strain. "What matters is that there are *river men* here. *Real* men. What makes you think we'd follow *any* stranger, let alone a limp-wristed Stygian noble, with dainty curls and a frilly velvet cape?"

The end of the line emerged from the Nihil, knotted to a heavy iron hook transfixing the torso of a semi-conscious, feebly writhing thrall. Montrose gathered that the wraith with the black mustache had been fishing for Spectres, a hazardous sport to say the least, though safer for the angler than the bait.

"You should join me because we'll win," said the Anacreon. "I know how to command an army."

The other wraith tossed the slave and hook to the floor. "Well, nobody 'commands' me. Nobody but a better man. And there aren't any better men than *Mike Fink!*" He paused dramatically, as if expecting Montrose to cower at his name.

"Never heard of him, I'm afraid," the Stygian said.

Fink quivered. His dark eyes glared, while his hulking body seemed to swell like a frog's. "Well, let me educate you," he said, his voice beginning softly but building in a relentless crescendo. "My mother was a Malfean and my father was the Tempest! I can outfight, out-brag, out-sail, and out-hoodoo any spirit on the river! I eat Nephandi for breakfast, wolfmen for lunch, and bloodsuckers for supper, all with Oblivion ice cream for dessert! I'm faster than lightning, meaner than a gator, and crazier than the Laughing Lady! I pop little pissants like you like pimples!"

To Montrose, Fink's outburst seemed more humorous than threatening, in spite of his clenched fists and outthrust jaw. But the Scot could tell that the audience had a different reaction. They were amused, but wary as well. They wouldn't have wanted the big man to think they were laughing at him. Buffoonery aside, they held considerable respect for him.

And because they did, they'd resumed glowering and sneering at the Stygian, reasoning that if the local strongman scorned him, he couldn't be worth heeding after all. Montrose realized that if he still wanted to recruit them, there was only one way to go about it.

"What a colorful oration," he drawled, becoming the languid, condescending aristocrat Fink had accused him of being. "But let's get down to cases. A moment ago, you said that you would follow a better man. Meaning a man who can humble you in battle, I assume."

Valentine tugged urgently on his cloak, presumably to warn him he was headed for disaster.

Fink grinned. "Oh, sure, Anacreon. We'd all follow a superman like that."

All? That was even better than Montrose had dared to hope for. He lifted an eyebrow. "You speak for the entire room, do you?"

Fink turned, regarding his fellow outlaws. "Anybody here think he's too good to fight in the same gang with me?" Apparently no one did. Smiling crookedly, the big man pivoted back toward Montrose. "But here's the thing, Lord Jimbo. If I'm going to bet, you have to put up something, too."

Valentine yanked on Montrose's cloak even more frantically than before. The Stygian tugged it out of the small man's grip. "What did you have in mind? I don't have any cash on my person. But this is a valuable rifle, and as you pointed out, my cape is rather nice as well."

Fink made a spitting sound. Lacking bodily fluids, it was as close as the Restless could come to actual expectoration. "That's not good enough. You want a limited amount of service from all of us? Well, that equals out to an unlimited amount of service from you. You lose and you become my slave."

Inwardly, Montrose winced, even though it was precisely the proposal he'd been expecting. "Done. How shall we duel? Guns?" Unless Fink had a modem weapon stashed away somewhere out of view, the Stygian's assault rifle would give him a sizable advantage.

Fink grinned. "I don't think so."

"Blades, then." The Scot was more adept with a rapier or saber than a knife, but he was still confident that his swordsmanship would stand him in good stead.

Fink's leer stretched even wider. "Uh uh. As the challenged party, I get to pick, and I say, no weapons at all. Just muscles, and whatever Arcanos either of us knows."

"Fine," Montrose said, setting the rifle back on the table. He pulled off his cape, dropped it over the back of a chair, and unclipped the scabbard from his belt. Fink stripped off his denim vest and then his homespun shirt. His physique looked even more powerful without it. Meanwhile the other wraiths moved back, clearing a space for the fight, and the old Quick tramp finally crept unnoticed out the door.

"Run for it," Valentine whispered.

"I think not," Montrose replied. "Although I must say, if this Fink character is so dangerous, you might have mentioned it when we first entered the building."

"I didn't know he was going to take a dislike to you. Nobody knows what he'll do until he does it. He's crazy."

"What Arcanos has he mastered?"

"I don't know. I don't come here all that often. I've only seen him fight once, and that time, he only needed his hands to tear the other man apart."

Montrose smiled. "You're doing wonders for my confidence. Look after my things. Otherwise, someone is likely to walk off with them."

The Stygian stepped out into the clear area. Crouching, his hands poised to grapple, Fink grinned. "Do you like fishing, Anacreon?" he asked. "I've decided to let you take Beauregard's place on the hook."

"Really," Montrose said. Fists raised, he circled, looking for an opening. "And here I thought you wanted me for your catamite. You seem like the type." He lifted his foot for a kick and the world turned red, as if he were viewing it through a pane of scarlet glass.

Startled, he hesitated. Fink bellowed and rushed him. Montrose dodged, and just barely managed to avoid the larger man's clutching hands. Fink blundered past, and the room returned to its former colors.

The Scot thought he understood how Fink had affected his vision. The outlaw was a Haunter, a wraith who knew how to disrupt someone else's mind or even reality itself with a blast of primal chaos. Montrose decided it was high time he used one of his own powers. Cool shadow flowed across his skin. By the time Fink lurched back around to face him, he was invisible.

Unfortunately, he'd reckoned without the spectators, who'd watched him conjure the veil. "He's right in front of you!" shouted the Sandman. "Kill him!"

Montrose started to sidestep. Once he changed position, his adversary's cronies would no longer be able to give him away. But before he could move, his thoughts shattered into confusion. Where was he? Who were these people, and what was going on?

A powerfully built man with a black mustache lunged at him, slammed into him, and knocked him to the floor, then dove on top of him. The attacker fumbled at him as if he were trying for a chokehold but was having difficulty locating his neck.

The shock of being assaulted jolted Montrose's thoughts back into partial focus. He remembered he was fighting someone named Fink, and that the larger man was having difficulty grappling with him because he'd cloaked himself in shadow. But the Harbinger trick could only buy him a few seconds.

Montrose was certain he couldn't out-wrestle Fink. He had to break away before the stronger man got an unbreakable grip on him. Trapped beneath Fink's weight, he punched and thrashed as best he could, but couldn't buck him off.

Another wave of confusion swept through the Stygian's mind. Struggling to resist it, he called on his Harbinger abilities again. For an instant, nothing happened, and then he floated into the air. He'd hoped Fink would tumble off him, but the Haunter kept his grip. The audience gasped and babbled.

Now in danger of falling, Fink stopped trying for a stranglehold. Instead, he wrapped his arms and legs around his opponent and started biting, plunging his teeth into Montrose's shoulder. The pain was excruciating.

Montrose rolled in midair, placing Fink beneath him, and then hurled them both at the floor. The impact hurt, particularly the way it jerked the teeth buried in his flesh. But presumably it had hurt the Haunter worse, considering that Montrose was in effect the hammer and Fink the nail.

He raised the big man up and smashed him down again. Fink's grip loosened. Simultaneously levitating and shoving the other wraith away with all his strength, Montrose broke free altogether. The Scot rocketed upward, just managing to stop before he collided with the ceiling. Meanwhile Fink struggled to his feet.

Aching and weary, Montrose desperately craved a moment's rest. But he knew he mustn't give Fink the opportunity to recover from the pounding he'd just received. Flying around the big man like an invisible hornet, he lashed out with one kick after another, snapping the Shadowlander's head back and forth. The crowd couldn't tell precisely what was happening, but it was obvious that Fink was taking a lot of punishment. Some of the spectators groaned and winced in sympathy. Others smirked.

Another kick dumped Fink onto his back. With his flattened nose, torn lips, shattered teeth, and the raw, shiny patches on his skin—lacking blood, the Restless neither bled nor bruised—he looked incapacitated. Montrose floated back a pace and cocked his leg to administer the coup de grace. Then Fink bellowed and brandished his fist.

Bolts of crackling radiance blazed across the room, turning some of the onlookers into vibrating, charring statues and flinging others off their feet. One jagged shaft of lightning blasted through Montrose's chest. He blacked out, and woke up sprawled on the floor. His ears rang, and the left side of his body was numb.

He looked around. A few tendrils of electricity still danced sizzling about the tavern, and Fink was still on his back. Apparently, Montrose had only been unconscious for a moment. He struggled to his feet and hobbled toward his opponent.

As Fink scrambled up, his body shrank, and his hair

changed from black to honey-blond. In the blink of an eye, he'd become Louise.

Was it really Montrose's lost, treacherous love staring at him with terror in her eyes? He didn't know, but it didn't matter. He hated her even more than he hated Fink, and her image merely served to energize him with a fresh burst of rage. He blocked the roundhouse punch she threw at him—an extraordinarily powerful blow, a part of him noticed, for a slender woman—and slammed his fist into the point of her jaw.

Louise reeled backward. By the time she hit the floor, she was Fink again. As Montrose studied the outlaw, making sure he truly was unconscious, the residual haze of bewilderment evaporated from his mind.

But his anger didn't. Fink had both sought to enslave him and caused him a considerable amount of pain, and he wanted to keep hurting the big man in return. He could stamp his body to jelly. Pick him apart with the darksteel Bowie knife. Ram the iron hook through *his* body and lower *him* into the Tempest—

No! Montrose thought. What was the matter with him? He wanted to *use* Fink, not alienate his admirers by torturing him. It was his Shadow, roused by the pain of his wounds and the fury of battle, that was filling his head with these vicious fantasies. Closing his eyes, he drew a long breath, trying to calm himself. After a moment, his lust for violence faded.

Montrose regarded the spectators, who were silently gaping at him. "So," he said. "Are you with me or not?"

"I am," said the wraith with the bandoleers. "I always said that if we all threw in together, we could own this burg."

"Me too," said someone else. The next moment they were all pushing forward to shake Montrose's hand.

When he got a chance, he turned to Valentine. "I won't be accompanying you back to the Citadel," he said. "Now that I have the resources I need, I have no intention of giving Gayoso the opportunity to stop me from putting them to use. Tell him he'll see me by and by."

12

Whenever he climbed the spiral staircase to the Pinnacle of Lamentations, Howard Potter felt grateful that the Restless were virtually immune to physical fatigue. Of course, he could have flown to the top of the tower and saved himself considerable time, but to do so would have violated tradition. And so he trod slowly, striving for stately dignity, his plate armor clinking, the butt of his ceremonial halberd thumping on the basalt steps, and the train of his mantle whispering along behind him.

Occasionally a narrow window afforded him a view of the landscape outside. Like every other eye in the infinite storm of the Tempest, Stygia was a realm of eternal night, dimly lit by barrow-flame torches, Charon's lantern shining atop its obelisk, and the random flickering in the mass of thunderheads that covered the Isle of Sorrows like a dome. The metropolis of the dead was a sort of pyramid, with the Onyx Tower—actually a crazy quilt of palaces, ramparts, reflecting pools, and faux gardens surrounding a huge central keep—at the top. Beneath the domain of the aristocrats, level after level of chambers and hallways descended to the forbidden labyrinth of caverns and crypts buried deep beneath the surface. Rumor whispered that the latter connected to the Labyrinth itself, though Potter had never believed it. The emperor had been far too sly to link his capital to the heart of Oblivion.

On one side of the city rippled the waters of the Weeping Bay, where much of the Stygian fleet, a hodgepodge of ships from many cultures and eras, floated at anchor. Had Potter been closer to the shore, he might have seen anguished faces forming and dissolving in the waves, or heard faint, whimpering cries arising from the depths, for by Charon's decree, the entire Sea of Souls was a liquid mass of imprisoned spirits designed to hold Oblivion at bay. Beyond it rose the seawall, another bulwark against Spectres, Maelstroms, and the terrible power they embodied, a mammoth construction of iron, steel, and less refined soul stuff. Here, too, an observer could discern the shapes of human faces and bodies protruding from the surface, although unlike the ones in the water, these were motionless and silent. One could at least try to believe that the imprisoned thralls weren't suffering.

Mighty bridges extended from the landward side of the Isle, linking it to the sprawl of tenements, warehouses, factories, rail yards, and fortifications on the mainland. In the last eighty years, fed by an exponentially increasing mortal birthrate and the harvest of two World Wars, the city had finally outgrown its original bounds, necessitating expansion into the Iron Hills.

At last Potter reached the flat, circular roof of the Pinnacle, to find that all of his fellow Deathlords had arrived before him. Masked and otherwise clad in full regalia, each stood on his appointed pedestal near their departed master's empty throne.

They looked so powerful and enigmatic, so *totemic*, that Potter had to repress a shiver of awe. He firmly reminded himself that he was the Smiling Lord. These others were his peers, not some sort of deities. "Forgive me if I'm late," he said, "but at least I arrived before the prisoner." To his surprise, he realized he didn't recall just whom they had assembled to judge. It must be either a traitor of the highest rank or a rebel of the greatest importance to merit the attention of all seven members of the council.

He headed for his own position. The Quiet Lord stepped in front of him, barring his path. Potter's colleague, traditionally the patron of wraiths who'd died of despair, wore a murky red robe dyed with the blood of suicides. He carried an empty sack—from which Potter had on occasion seen him extract a diversity of bizarre and lethal objects—and his silver mask had been cast in the form of a face without a mouth. Because Charon had taken a piece from each of his lieutenants' masks to forge his own, it had a triangular hole in the left cheek.

The Quiet Lord pressed his index finger to his invisible mouth. It looked as if he were commanding silence, but Potter knew better. The gesture helped the other Deathlord focus his power.

Potter hesitated. Was the Quiet Lord threatening him, here, in open council? Surely not, though it seemed nearly as unlikely that he could be making a joke. Puzzled but not too alarmed, he began to edge around him.

For once eschewing her affected tremulous shuffle, the Ashen Lady moved to bar his path, her gnarled cane raised like a sword. Shadows slithered up and down the prop like serpents. Her gray robes hung loosely on her stooped, shrunken frame, and wisps of fine white hair escaped from the edges of her mask, the wrinkled, sagging, carved-wood countenance of an ancient crone, with one corner broken off to reveal the smooth, firm jaw beneath. Her flesh emitted the stale smell of senility.

Potter stared at her, trying to read her intent from her pale gray eyes. He couldn't. Cloth flapped, and, startled, he pivoted in the direction of the sound. The other four Deathlords had descended from their low daises as well, and were moving to surround him.

"What's the meaning of this?" Potter demanded. He tried to use his haughtiest tone, but his voice quavered.

"You have transgressed," said the Emerald Lord, turning his crimson dice over and over in his white-gloved hand. Somewhere above the tower, purple lightning flared, glinting on his jade crown of thorns, his verdigris-encrusted brazen mask—an expressionless, androgynous face with its eyes closed—and the emerald-studded wheel-of-fortune amulet hanging on his breast. "You must be judged."

"What do you mean?" Potter said. "What are you accusing me of?"

The Ashen Lady tapped her mask with her withered, liver-spotted forefinger.

For a second, Potter had no idea what she was trying to convey. Then he realized he could feel a cool breeze caressing his face, and that there were no steel rings sharply defining the edges of his vision. Somehow, he'd come to council without his visor!

He pressed his hands to his features, concealing them. Peering out between his fingers, he said, "Forgive me! It was an accident!"

"Perish," said the Emerald Lord. "Go to the Final Death."

The six Deathlords brandished their symbols of office, blasting Potter with bolts of arcane power. His halberd and armor shattered. Convulsed with agony, his substance shriveling, he reeled off the edge of the tower and plummeted toward the spires and rooftops below.

And then he emitted a strangled cry and joked half out of his chair.

He was sitting alone in his scrying chamber with the clay figurine, a nude woman with fleshy thighs, stubby arms, and two smiling faces adorning her head, resting on the ornately carved teak stand before him. The statuette was an artifact, a magical object which, destroyed in the Skinlands, had begun a second existence in the Underworld. When Potter opened himself to its power, it granted him visions, often containing useful intelligence about the enemies of the state.

This time, however, it had made him an *actor* in the vision, subjecting him to an experience much like a mortal nightmare. Even now, grasping what had happened, he was still shaking. He grabbed his mask, the leering steel countenance of a savage warrior, pressed it to his face, and invoked its persona.

As always, Charon's magic took effect at once. A new parade of images flashed through Potter's head. He was Cain, striking down Abel. He was a Roman retiarius thrusting his trident into another gladiator's belly on the hot sands of the Flavian Amphitheater. An airman dropping firebombs on Dresden. A highwayman on a moonlit road, shooting a coachman who'd rashly made a grab for his own flintlock pistol. A teenage mother, her blood aflame with crack, pounding and pounding on her baby until the tiny creature finally stopped crying.

He was War and he was Murder, the rightful lord of every soul who perished at the hands of another. Ecstatic, his nose and mouth tingling with the coppery scent of gore, he rose, took up his halberd, and began to perform a *kata,* turning and striking with impeccable grace and lethal precision.

With the final thrust and bellowed *kiai,* his exhilaration waned a bit. He remembered Howard Potter, the human spirit sheathed inside the ferocious archangel he'd just become. And despite the ecstasy that always overwhelmed him when he reaffirmed his mastery of his powers, he still wasn't altogether happy.

Is this what it takes for me to feel secure? he wondered. *Have I become so neurotic that I can never unmask, even when I'm alone?*

No. Surely not. He'd simply become upset because the vision had been inherently disturbing. Instead of wasting time on morbid introspection, he should try to figure out what the mystical dream had signified.

Unfortunately, as he recognized immediately, that train of thought led to speculations that were equally disturbing.

He realized that he no longer wished to be alone. He wanted the company of one of the handful of trusted retainers he'd occasionally permitted to glimpse the human being hidden behind his godlike facade. Montrose—

He grimaced, remembering that the Cavalier wasn't available. He'd sent him off to slaughter Heretics. Demetrius, then. He took hold of the golden bellpull and rang for a thrall.

13

The cramped office reeked of cigarette smoke. An overflowing ashtray sat on the desk, and a yellowish film clung to the windows. As Nolliver took a seat, he wished again that he could have handled the current situation on the phone. He never enjoyed meeting Dunn face to face, and when he had potentially troublesome news to report, he liked it even less.

Unfortunately, he'd become leery of conferring with the SAD agent in any other fashion. Dunn *claimed* that no one had tapped their phones, but it was quite possible that he simply didn't know. Of course, it was also possible that someone had bugged the office, but somehow, that seemed less likely, and in any case, Nolliver knew the other man would dismiss any suggestion that they needed to talk outside the building.

"You look like crap," Dunn said. "Have a drink if you need one."

Startled, the psychiatrist blinked. "Excuse me?" "Have a drink," Dunn repeated. "I can see you aren't just stashing booze in your desk anymore. You have a flask in your coat."

"How do you know that?" Nolliver asked. *God, if Dunn had noticed, then who else—*

The shaggy-headed agent grinned. "Don't panic, Doc. I'm *amazingly* observant, even for a Fed. Nobody else would be able to tell. But I hope you aren't getting careless. You don't want to get caught, do you?"

"No, of course not," Nolliver said, feeling both defensive and vaguely ashamed. He removed the silver flask from his pocket, unscrewed the cap, and took a swallow. The whiskey kindled a warm glow in the pit of his stomach.

"Feel better?" asked Dunn. Nolliver nodded. "Then tell me what's up."

"Bellamy phoned this morning and asked Hanson for the rest of the week off. Hanson okayed it without consulting me. What concerns me is that Frank never told me he wanted to take a break. In fact, he seemed grimly determined to hang on here, do his job, and convince everybody that he's still competent. Of course, people do impulsively change their minds. For that matter, they catch the flu. This is probably nothing. But you said I should tell you if there was even the slightest indication that he might be inclined to make any kind of waves."

"As his kindly physician," Dunn asked, "did you call him to see if he's home in bed with the crud?"

"Yes," Nolliver said. "He didn't answer. But that doesn't necessarily mean anything, either."

Dunn stood up. "Let's pay a visit to his office."

"You mean, to search it?"

"No," said Dunn, "I thought we'd redecorate it. Of course, to search it."

"Do you think that's wise? What are the odds that he left something significant lying around in there? And what if someone notices us snooping?"

"Then we'll just have to kill them," answered Dunn. He looked into Nolliver's face, then grimaced, rolling his eyes. "It's a joke, Doc. My god, will you lighten up? You said yourself, probably nothing's wrong. But on the other hand, I at least have to go through the motions of keeping tabs on Bellamy. If anybody asks what we're doing, we'll make up a story, that's all. Now pop a Certs and let's get to it."

Nolliver could see there was no way to talk him out of it. By the time they reached the corridor outside Bellamy's office, his underarms were clammy with sweat. But no one paid them the least attention. Dunn turned the brass doorknob. It rotated slightly, then stopped.

"Locked," Nolliver whispered.

"No, it isn't," Dunn replied. He twisted it again, and this time the door swung open. Bewildered, Nolliver scrambled inside, and the SAD agent stepped in after him.

Dunn surveyed the room, a drab space decorated with a few mementos of Bellamy's career in law enforcement, but only one, a baseball covered with signatures, that reflected any extracurricular interests. "How come everybody has a bigger office than mine?" asked Dunn. "I know, our pal Bellamy has a great arrest and conviction record, but *Earl Maxwell* has a bigger office than mine, and he couldn't catch a cold."

Nolliver took a tentative step toward the beige metal file cabinet in the corner. "I could look in here."

"Just stand back," said Dunn. "Tossing a room is *my* area. If I find something you ought to look at, I'll let you know."

The SAD agent sat down behind the desk with its Rolodex, phone, PC, ceramic coffee mug, and imposing stack of manila folders. He picked up one of the files from the considerably smaller pile in the Out basket, held it near his face, and inhaled deeply. "Bellamy hated processing these," he said. "It bored and depressed him."

"How do you know that?" Nolliver asked.

"Call it instinct," said Dunn. Swiveling the chair, he picked up the phone, placed it to his ear, and set it back in the cradle. "He hasn't been burning up the wires with any exciting conversations lately, either. We should give him the number of a good 900 line." He turned again, to face the computer. Suddenly he frowned and bent forward over the gray plastic keyboard, his nostrils dilating, reminding Nolliver of a hound taking a scent.

"Is something the matter?" Nolliver asked.

"He *was* excited when he was working here," Dunn replied, straightening up. He switched on the computer, which came to life with a crackle and a tinny fanfare. "Let's see if we can find out why."

"You might need a password," the psychiatrist said.

"I told you, I'm good at getting into things."

Dunn spent the next few minutes reviewing the contents of Bellamy's hard drive. Finally, he turned in the swivel chair. "There's nothing here. Maybe he's got it on a printout or a floppy." He rummaged through the desk drawers, then rose and did the same thing with the file cabinet. "No luck."

"If he did have some kind of significant information, maybe he took it home with him."

"You could be right." said Dunn, sitting back down at the desk. "On the other hand, this thing has a modem. Bellamy didn't store any funky numbers in his directory, but it's still possible that he was getting into mischief online." The agent picked up the phone, punched 9 for an outside line, and dialed a long-distance number.

For a moment Nolliver could just hear the ringing on the other end of the line. Then Dunn said, "Pyramid." He paused. "No, it's Madonna, calling to ask if you like my new CD. Sure, it's me. Is Chester there? I need a house call." He recited a phone number with a Baton Rouge area code. It puzzled the psychiatrist for a moment until he realized it must be the computer's phone line. "Now would be better. There's an outside chance my problem is important. And I have company, so tell Chester to cool it with the fireworks. Right. Thanks, buddy." The agent hung up.

"Who were you talking to?" Nolliver asked.

"SAD," Dunn answered. "Who else? You and I need a hacker, and fortunately, the Department has one of the best."

Lines of text ran across Bellamy's monitor. Dunn typed a response. A few seconds later, multiple columns of words and numbers appeared.

"These are the sites Bellamy logged on to over the past week, and the dates and times," said Dunn, scanning them. "Shit."

Nolliver tensed. "What's the matter?"

"Most of these are bulletin boards for people who are into the paranormal." He gave Dunn a sour stare. "Am I confused here, Doc? Weren't you supposed to do everything in your shrinkly power to discourage Bellamy from taking any further interest in stuff like this?"

"I did my best! I swear it!"

Dunn sighed. "Yeah, I'm sure you did, and the odds are, he still doesn't pose any real problem, so calm down." He resumed typing. The keys clicked. "His last visit was to a board called Grailnet, late yesterday afternoon. I'm asking Chester to dig out what he did while he was there."

"He can do that?"

"Probably. When it comes to cyber-crap, he can do almost anything. But it may take him a couple minutes."

Dunn leaned back in his chair and stretched, then slumped down so comfortably that he looked as if he might doze off. Reluctant to make the SAD agent think him any weaker or more ineffectual than he did already, Nolliver fought the impulse to take yet another drink.

At last new lines of text paraded across the screen. After skimming them, Dunn said, "Jumping Jesus on a pogo stick."

"What's wrong?" Nolliver asked.

"Bellamy is going to New Orleans to compare notes with somebody else who's interested in Waxman's death."

"Who?"

"Somebody who called himself Vulture. That's all we know. You don't have to give your real name to anybody to use Grailnet, and lots of people don't. Your patient just went by Frank. Very creative, right?"

"Whoever Vulture is," said Nolliver, "we don't know that he actually has anything to tell Bellamy. It seems more likely that he's just a crackpot."

"I know that," said Dunn. He removed his tobacco and papers from the inner pocket of his jacket and began to roll a cigarette. "But unfortunately, we can't count on it, just like we obviously can't trust Bellamy to keep his nose out of SAD business. Damn. I really thought that, working together, you and I could get the poor bastard out of trouble. Now I have to get tough."

Nolliver swallowed. "What are you saying?"

"That Bellamy and his new friend will have to drop out of sight for a while." He struck a match with his thumbnail and lit his cigarette. "Don't you worry about it. Disappearances are my area, too."

"You're going to kill them, aren't you?"

Dunn's eyes widened with every appearance of shock. "No, of course not!"

"I don't believe you!" Nolliver said, appalled at his own sudden burst of audacity. "And I'm not going to be a party to it. Covering up the truth is one thing. Murder is different. You can't expect me to go along with it when I don't even really know what any of this is all about!"

"I know you have a problem with the idea of being implicated in anybody else's death," said Dunn, staring him in the eye. "I understand why it's hard to trust me. But even if you've decided you don't care about losing your job, your profession, or going to prison, I guarantee you, you still can't afford to give me any crap."

Nolliver felt his momentary defiance crumbling. "Why not?" he stammered.

Dunn smiled. "Because if you do, you might find yourself looking at the same sight that stopped Waxman's ticker."

14

Ensconced on a sunlit bench, a paper cup of *cafe au lait* warming his hand and a half-devoured oyster po-boy resting in his lap, Bellamy twisted this way and that, peering about. He supposed he looked like a rubbernecking tourist, drinking in the sights of Jackson Square. The bronze equestrian statue of Andrew Jackson. The Greek Revival portico of St. Louis Cathedral. The sidewalk artists' paintings and sketches, hanging on the wrought-iron fence. And the jugglers, magicians, white-faced mimes, and musicians who'd appeared to entertain the lunch crowd. A banjo player a few feet away was filling the air with a plangent bluegrass tune.

Actually, of course, Bellamy was trying to spot Vulture, most likely an exercise in futility, considering that he had no idea what the other man looked like. But he couldn't help making the attempt.

He was well aware that Vulture might not show. The guy might have been pulling his leg. Even if he did keep the rendezvous, there was every chance that he'd turn out to be a faker or a crank.

But so what? Bellamy thought, suddenly feeling, at least for a moment, relaxed and free from care. Even if Vulture himself proved to be a waste of time, a trip to New Orleans sure beat reviewing inactive files in Baton Rouge. When he was younger, he'd spent a lot of weekends and holidays in this wonderful place, but gradually he'd gotten so busy that such excursions no longer seemed practical.

He crunched down another succulent bite of his sandwich. La Madeleine's take-out was as good as he remembered. Then he felt eyes peering at him.

He turned his head, to see the same motley array of pedestrians who'd been drifting past all along. No one seemed to have been staring at him unless, perhaps, it had been a pale, long-legged girl dressed in ragged jeans and a leather jacket. She was eighteen or nineteen at the oldest, and might have looked pretty had it not been for her punkish, magenta-striped haircut, the steel rings in her right eyebrow, left nostril, and lower lip, her black lipstick, and her sullen sneer. If she *had* been looking him over, she seemed to have lost interest. She was turning away in the banjo player's direction.

Behind her, a plump, flushed little man in a sweat-stained powder-blue sports coat, a narrow-brimmed straw hat tilted far back on his head, and a wide, bright red tie came busting through the crowd. He grinned and mouthed the name, "Frank." Bellamy nodded. The chubby man hurried over and plopped down on the bench. Up close, he smelled rather pungently of Old Spice

"Obviously, I'm Vulture," he said, wiping his hand on his slacks and then extending it. "I'm delighted you could make it."

Bellamy shook hands with him. "Nice to meet you. Do I have to keep calling you Vulture in real life?"

Vulture smiled. "Ah, that is the question, isn't it? One we merely postponed confronting when we'd decided to meet face to face. Dare we trust one another? Does either of us have enough information to offer to make it worth the other one's while?"

"I guess one of us has to take the plunge first," Bellamy said, "and just hope the other will reciprocate." Inwardly he resolved that if he spilled his guts and then Vulture tried to walk away without doing the same, he'd lean on him hard. "My full name is Frank Bellamy. I'm an FBI agent."

Vulture cocked his head. "From Special Affairs?"

"No," Bellamy said, mildly impressed that his companion had even heard of SAD, "VICAP. Violent Criminals Apprehension Program. I work out of the district office in Baton Rouge, so as you might guess, until recently I was trying to catch the Atheist."

"You aren't now?"

"Not officially." Once again, Bellamy felt the weight of

an onlooker's scrutiny. He looked casually around, but still didn't catch anyone staring. The sensation was beginning to remind him unpleasantly of his experience with Waxman, but he supposed it was just his imagination. Even if something supernatural *had* occurred that night, it was preposterous to imagine it happening again in the middle of a crowd on a bright spring day. Besides, nobody had known that he was coming here, and never mind that that was what he'd said the last time.

As succinctly as possible, he told Vulture about his encounter with Waxman. Usually, doing so made him feel like an idiot, but this time, the other man's expression of grave interest somewhat alleviated his embarrassment.

When he finished, Vulture said, "And your friend from SAD didn't take anything in your story seriously?"

"No," Bellamy said.

Vulture shook his head. "Extraordinary. They must be even more ignorant than we supposed."

"'We'?"

Vulture smiled. "Ah, yes. It's my turn to confide in you, isn't it? Either that or terminate the conversation, which is what some of my colleagues would recommend." Bellamy tensed. "After all, your story isn't all that illuminating. But it *is* information, and I *am* an activist in my small way. I believe that when it's feasible, somebody should stop the atrocities, and perhaps if we combine my esoteric knowledge with your police powers, we can. My name is Roscoe Jefferson Keene—R. J. to my friends—and I belong to an organization called the Arcanum."

"What kind of organization is it?" Bellamy asked.

"A lodge," said Keene. "A one-hundred-year-old brotherhood of scholars united to study the occult. Sort of a civilian counterpart to your Agent Dunn's organization, except that where SAD presumably exists to defend America from paranormal menaces, the Arcanum supposedly exists to further the cause of pure research."

"You say, 'supposedly.'"

"Many members pursue other agendas. We 'Templars,' for example, aspire to protect mankind from supernatural predators." He smiled wryly. "It could be argued that the vast majority of paranormal creatures fall into that category, so we have our work cut out for us."

Yet again, Bellamy's skin crawled with the near certainty that he was being watched. The fine hairs on the back of his neck stood on end. Unable to ignore his intuition any longer, he asked, "Do you mind if we walk as we talk? It'll help settle my lunch."

"By all means," said Keene. Grunting, he stood up.

The two men began to stroll around the square. Bellamy kept stopping and changing direction, seemingly to gawk at the shop windows, or to take a better look at a painting or a performer. In reality, he was putting his hunch to the test. If someone was following them, that person would stop and start and pivot with them, unless he was adept at the craft of shadowing others.

"What do you know about Weiss and Waxman?" Bellamy asked.

"That for all their greed and chicanery, they actually did cast out devils on occasion."

Bellamy paused to watch a prestidigitator in a red silk top hat pluck a white paper rose from the air. "That's not what SAD thinks."

"SAD also thinks you're insane, do they not? Do you share their opinion on that point?"

"Only when I'm having a bad moment," Bellamy said, pretending to inspect a painting of a horse-drawn carriage on a benighted street. "Were Weiss and Waxman members of the Arcanum?"

Keene snorted. "Lord, no! Weiss had a rather narrow perspective, metaphysically speaking. He would have regarded us as practitioners of black magic, or pawns of Lucifer at the very least."

By now, Bellamy was all but certain that someone was tailing them. He *felt* a person behind him, that other's movements mirroring his own, as if in a dance. It would be awkward to accost the shadow in the middle of a crowd, but perhaps he could lead him into a more private place. Resisting the impulse to look back again and so risk spooking his quarry, he headed for the facade of St. Louis Cathedral, framed between the Cabildo and the Presbytere.

"But you know something about the murders," Bellamy said. He felt torn between the urge to plunge into the heart of the matter and the wary reflection that it might be better to stall until he'd dealt with the spy at his back, even though the shadow quite possibly already knew more than either he or Keene did anyway.

"Perhaps," Keene replied, sidestepping to avoid a giggling, staggering Japanese couple with cameras hanging around their necks and half-empty Hurricane glasses in their hands. "Right from the start, I've made it a point to read the newspaper accounts of the Atheist murders, because it was conceivable that a supernatural being might slaughter ministers and Sunday school teachers for ritual purposes. But until recently, I didn't pay all that much attention, because I was pursuing other studies, and it actually seemed more likely that the killer was just a cunning maniac with a grudge against the clergy."

"Let's step in here for a second," said Bellamy, leading Keene onto the covered ambulatory of the basilica. "It'll be cooler. I gather that something eventually convinced you that the murderer probably *is* connected to the paranormal."

"First off, Weiss's death," said Keene, removing his hat and pulling open the church door. Bellamy pulled off his LSU Bengals cap and stuffed it in his pocket. "If you *were* a supernatural creature committing the crimes, you'd want to eliminate one of the few religious figures who might actually pose a threat to you, would you not?"

It was cool inside the church. The air smelled of stone and incense, and after the brilliant sunlight outside, the interior of the building seemed shadowy and dim. Two old women sat motionless as waxworks in the pews. Bellamy moved past the font and a wrought-iron rack of votive candles toward a small chapel built into the right-hand wall. Once he and Keene were inside, they'd be out of sight of the worshippers in the nave.

After a moment, the door whispered open and shut behind them, and a shoe scuffed faintly on the gleaming marble floor. The shadow was still skulking along behind them.

"But you don't need an occult killer to explain Weiss's death," Bellamy said. "If the murderer craved notoriety, he could guarantee himself a lot of press by knocking off a televangelist. And even if he didn't, well, he's killing preachers, and Weiss was one. It could just be the luck of the draw."

"You're playing devil's advocate," said Keene, fanning his flushed, sweaty face with his hat. "Good for you. Hardheaded critical thinking is crucial to the success of any investigation. But the rebuttal to your argument is that the Atheist killed Waxman, another individual with psychic abilities, immediately afterward, even though Waxman was neither a member of the clergy nor a figure in the public eye. Indeed, by killing one of his previous victim's close associates, he broke his pattern."

"My colleagues in the Bureau would point out that Waxman wasn't murdered," Bellamy said. "He died of a heart attack."

"I think we can assume the Atheist would have killed him, if he hadn't saved him the trouble by dropping dead of terror. The puzzling thing is, why didn't he murder you as well?"

The two men stepped under a basket-handle arch into the chapel, a small space dominated by a marble life-size statue of the Virgin, standing, arms open, smiling sadly, in a niche in the back wall. As Bellamy had hoped, no one was praying here.

"I've wondered the same thing," the FBI agent said. "All I can figure is, he was afraid of my gun. But look, R. J., so far, all you've given me is conjecture. Intelligent conjecture, assuming a person accepts the existence of the paranormal, but only speculation even so. Haven't you got any facts?"

"A few," Keene said, "although I don't know if you'll regard them as such. My friends and I do our best to keep the various supernatural beings in New Orleans under surveillance."

"Do you know who they are?" asked Bellamy. He strained his ears, listening to the background noise in the church. He could *feel* the eavesdropper, lurking outside the chapel, but he couldn't pinpoint the shadow's location.

Keene sighed. "Not really, but we have intimations. We've devised techniques, mostly indirect measures, which allow us to monitor or at least infer their activities. We're fairly certain that the city has a large population of spirits."

"You mean ghosts?"

"That's what I believe, although others favor different hypotheses. I also think they have two rival kings or masters. There are indications that around the time of the first Atheist murder, open hostilities broke out between the factions."

Abruptly, though he hadn't consciously registered a telltale sound, Bellamy felt certain that he knew precisely where the eavesdropper was standing. Just to the left of the arch. "What makes you think there's a connection?" he asked. Then, holding up his hand to caution his companion, he tiptoed toward the opening.

Fortunately, Keene reacted to the signal appropriately. He didn't say or do anything that would have given Bellamy away. He simply pursued the thread of the conversation. "Just a hunch, I must admit, prompted by the knowledge that the Atheist has done some of his bloodiest work at this end of the Mississippi. Be that as it may, other odd things are happening hereabouts. There's a, well, call it a clan of peculiar people living over in Lafayette. The Arcanum doesn't know if they're diabolists, the descendants of people who interbred with something inhuman, or what, but we're virtually certain they're involved in the high rate of unexplained disappearances over there. Until recently, they rarely came into New Orleans, but now—"

Bellamy lunged around the pier of the arch, grabbed the eavesdropper by the arm, and whirled the shadow inside, all in a single instant, moving so rapidly that he didn't really register that his captive was the girl with the magenta hair and the piercings until he'd already completed the maneuver.

"My goodness," Keene exclaimed.

Bellamy pressed the girl back against the wall. "Who are you?"

For a moment, she looked flustered, and then her black-painted lips grimaced. "Nice," she said. "Go ahead, FBI man, rough me up. Rodney King me. I'll scream my head off. I'll put your ass in prison."

Bellamy realized that whoever she was, she wasn't the towering figure that had risen from behind his rental car in East St. Louis, nor did she appear to pose a threat. Technically speaking, he probably hadn't had the right to put his hands on her. Reflecting that he could always grab her again should she try to run, he released his grip on her fragrant black leather jacket. "I don't want to hurt you," he said "But I am here pursuing an official investigation—"

"Bullshit. I've been listening to you, remember? I know there's nothing official about this."

"Trust me," said Bellamy, giving her his best intimidating stare, "I can make it as official as it needs to be."

Keene stepped forward. "Miss, as you've evidently heard, we're trying to stop a series of murders. If you have information that could help us, simple human decency demands that you disclose it."

The girl sighed. "You're barking up the wrong tree. I didn't even have any idea who Waxman was until a few minutes ago. I asked two nights ago, but you jerks ignored me."

Bellamy gaped at her. Though he knew he shouldn't feel so astonished, considering that he hadn't anything to base it on, he couldn't help marveling that his mental picture had been so far off the mark. "Astarte?" he asked.

"Of course," she said. "Who else was in the Circle of Discourse when you arranged your little party? I hitchhiked all the way from Ohio to crash it."

Bellamy's shoulders slumped as the tension flowed out of his muscles. "You're lucky I didn't bounce you around a lot harder than I did. For all I knew, you were somebody who came here to kill us."

"But why are you here?" asked Keene.

"So, you could tell her where to go to meet Count Dracula," said Bellamy. He looked back at the girl. "Isn't that about the size of it?"

"Basically," she replied. "And so far, you're a big disappointment to me, Vulture. I hope you've got more to say."

"Me, too," said Bellamy. "But you're not going to be around to hear it. Take a hike."

"Screw you," she replied.

"Believe me," said Keene, "I understand your fascination with the paranormal. But we're not obligated to help you pursue it."

Astarte scowled at Bellamy. "What if I phone the FBI and tell them what you've been up to? They'll kick you out. They might even lock you in a rubber room."

Bellamy's instincts assured him that the chances of Astarte following through on her threat were minute. She wasn't the kind of kid who'd rat out anybody to heavy-duty authority figures like the Feds. "Do what you want. We're still not going to talk to you anymore."

Astarte's large blue eyes, rather pretty ones despite rings of eye shadow so heavy and black they made her resemble a raccoon, glared at him. "Then I'll go to Lafayette and ask questions there!"

"I wish you wouldn't," said Keene. "But tens of thousands of people live their whole lives there without ever running up against the paranormal. I doubt that you could ferret it out in the course of the next few days."

"You are two of the—" Astarte began. Then her eyes widened, her mouth fell open, and her body jerked in surprise. A faint rasping sound whispered through the chapel.

Keene and Bellamy spun around. At first the FBI agent didn't see anything strange. Then he realized that the statue of Mary was very slowly twisting its head, apparently in order to aim its blank white eyes directly at them. Crunching and popping, tiny cracks appeared in the marble.

Bellamy felt dizzy and sick to his stomach. A terrible fear gripped him. Not so much of the statue itself—though he was afraid of it—as of the possibility that his mind was about to shut down again. He struggled to get past the shock, to *hang on,* and after a moment, his head cleared somewhat. He reached for his Browning.

"Everyone take it easy," said Keene, a slight quaver in his voice. "Whatever it is, it may not mean us any harm."

Crackling, the statue's lips tore apart, creating a space where none had existed before. Bits of broken stone fell from the opening to rattle on its pedestal, as if it were vomiting. Evidently it was clearing an area inside itself, manufacturing a mouth and throat.

When the cascade of pebbles stopped, the statue's lips

worked stiffly. The motion reminded Bellamy of a stroke victim straining to speak. And a sort of grinding whisper did emerge from the figure's mouth, but too faintly for him to make out any words. Evidently realizing that the humans hadn't understood, the statue beckoned for them to come closer.

And Astarte did.

Keene shouted, "No!" He lunged after her, an action which carried him within the statue's reach as well.

Keene grabbed Astarte and started to pull her back. Suddenly moving as fast as a human being, fresh cracks zigzagging through its arms, the statue struck him a backhanded blow. The occultist reeled into the wall. The figure pivoted toward Astarte, raising one hand high as if for a karate chop.

Gripping his gun in both hands, feet spread wide in one of the marksman stances the Bureau had taught him, Bellamy began to shoot. The bullets hammered pockmarks in the statue's beatific face and the graceful folds of its mantle.

Astarte scrambled backward, but too late. The marble hand whipped down, striking her shoulder and dropping her to the floor. Then the figure's feet separated from their base, and a vertical fissure split the skirt of its robe. With a rumble, chunks of stone fell away from it, sculpting the lower half of its body into two crudely formed legs. It sprang off its pedestal and charged at Bellamy.

The FBI agent got off two more shots before the statue plowed into him. As he stumbled backward, his assailant hit him in the head, a jolt of raw sensation that he knew would turn to a blast of pain in a moment. But before it could, he blacked out.

The bark of a gun recalled him to his senses. Dazed, his head aching, sprawled on his side, he pried his eyes open. Every inch of its pale white form now webbed with cracks, the statue stood over Keene with Bellamy's smoking Browning in its hand. A splash of red bloomed on Keene's chest.

Still pointing the automatic, the stone figure turned toward Bellamy. The FBI man lurched up off the floor and threw himself at it.

It sidestepped, and he only struck it a glancing blow. It

stumbled backward, but stayed on its feet and kept its grip on the automatic. His own balance equally impaired, the agent fell back onto the floor, certain that he'd only succeeded in winning himself one more moment of life.

Then Astarte rushed at the statue, still tottering from Bellamy's assault, and shoved it with all her might. The image's feet flew out from under it. When it crashed to the floor, its overstressed stonework body shattered into a hundred pieces.

Panting and trembling, Bellamy struggled to his feet. "Are you all right?" he asked.

"I don't *think* it's broken," Astarte said, experimentally rolling her shoulder. "How's your head?"

Bellamy gingerly touched the sore spot on his scalp. His fingers came away tacky with blood. "It doesn't feel like a concussion. We were both lucky."

She abruptly pivoted toward the man on the floor, as if she'd just remembered him. Quite possibly she had. Violence could jumble anyone's thoughts. "We have to help Vulture!"

Bellamy looked at Keene. The hole in his chest was directly above the heart, and the fecal stench of death mingled with smells of gore, gun smoke, and marble dust hanging in the air. Nevertheless, kneeling beside the occultist, the agent held his hand in front of the other man's nose and mouth, hoping to discover a whisper of exhalation, and pressed his fingertips against the carotid artery, checking for a pulse. He didn't find either. "I'm afraid it's too late to help him," he said. "Let's find a phone. We have to call the police."

Something clinked and scraped across the floor.

Bellamy whirled. The pieces of the broken statue were beginning to roll and scoot together in an apparent effort to reconstitute the whole. Already bits of finger and hand had locked together to grip the pistol anew. The remade hand flopped and rocked, struggling to turn itself around to point the weapon at the humans.

Crying out in rage and disgust, Bellamy stamped on the hand as if it were a cockroach. The bits of stone flew apart again. He snatched up the gun and thrust it back in its holster. Then, driven by a common terror, he and Astarte bolted. The two old women, now huddled in the far corner of the nave, goggled at them as they scrambled for the exit.

15

Bellamy surveyed the green fields of Woldenberg Riverfront Park. Camellias, azaleas, and irises were blooming. Smiling, chattering tourists strolled in the sunlight, admiring the plant life, making for the entrance to the Aquarium of the Americas, or heading for the *Cajun Queen*. The white paddle wheeler sat moored at its dock, waiting to embark on its afternoon cruise, plumes of white vapor rising from its twin smokestacks.

It all looked so pleasant. So normal. So *real*. For a moment Bellamy couldn't help wondering if the horror he'd experienced in St. Louis Cathedral had been real.

Impatiently, he thrust the treacherous thought away. *Yeah,* he told himself, it *did happen. Keene was right. The paranormal exists, and it's out to get me. I have to accept that, no matter how much it scares me, or I won't have a snowball's chance.*

"Can we stop and rest?" Astarte asked, rubbing her shoulder. Desperate to put some distance between themselves and the church, they'd fled the French Quarter, not quite running—instinct had warned Bellamy not to make himself that conspicuous—but striding along rapidly enough to tire anyone who'd just been through the stress and exertion of a fight.

"Sure," Bellamy said. He knew he had to pull himself together and think.

"You could call the cops in there," Astarte said, pointing at the aquarium.

"I could," Bellamy said. A twinge of residual fright prompted him to look around and make sure nothing was creeping up on him, although, God knew, his experience with the statue suggested that he might not recognize a source of danger even if he saw it. "But it might not be a good idea."

"You still don't think your buddies in the FBI would believe you, do you?" said Astarte. For the first time, Bellamy glimpsed the steel stud embedded in the tip of her tongue. Despite his focus on genuine, indeed overwhelming problems, he winced. How many piercings did she have? How could people *do* that to themselves?

"What's the matter?" she demanded.

"Nothing."

"You made a face."

"Really, we're okay. To answer your question, yeah, I am worried that my colleagues wouldn't believe me. I doubt that the pieces of the statue are still moving around back there. Any ordinary homicide detective would zero in on one fact: Keene was shot with my gun. Heck, that's why the statue bothered to pick it up, instead of just beating our brains out with its hands. It wanted to make it look like I killed you and Keene and then turned the gun on myself."

"You've got me to back up your story," Astarte said.

Bellamy smiled ruefully. "I'm not saying this to put you down, but you're not the kind of person that cops consider a reliable witness."

To his surprise, rather than losing her temper, she grinned back at him. "Isn't that the truth. And when they found out I have a jones for ghoulies, ghosties, long-leggedy beasties, and things that go bump in the night, that wouldn't help, would it?"

"I'm afraid not," Bellamy said. They started to saunter on toward the water. A pigeon wheeled overhead as if checking to see if they were likely to drop any food, then soared away.

"If we're worried about being accused of the crime, should we be worried about being identified by the old ladies in the church?"

"I hope not. I doubt they noticed us at all when we came in, and with luck, they only caught a glimpse of us from across the nave when we ran out."

"Good," said Astarte, turning her head to watch an Irish setter chase a Frisbee. The dog's coat glowed red in the sun. "So, what are you going to do next?"

"Catch the Atheist," Bellamy said. When he said it out loud, it sounded so absurdly macho, heck, just so absurd, that he had to smile. "Why not? I've got plenty of time. I took the whole rest of the week off."

Astarte stared at him. He couldn't read her expression. "You mean it, don't you?" she said at last. "Even after what we just went through. Who do you think you are, John Constantine?"

Bellamy didn't know the reference, but he understood what she meant. "No, but I am a guy who catches murderers. I like it, and I'm pretty good at it. And I even feel that I have a *duty* to do it." He looked at his companion, expecting her to jeer at what he assumed she would consider a corny sentiment.

But she merely said, "Especially if you think nobody else is going to do it."

"Yeah. There may be someone else involved in the investigation who could relate to the idea that paranormal forces are involved, but if so, it's because he's on the Atheist's side."

"Do you think somebody is?"

"I wish I knew. I told Hanson where I was meeting Waxman. Anybody else in the office could conceivably have found out from him, and then tipped off the killer. Of course, I didn't tell anybody where I was meeting Keene, but if somebody was keeping tabs on me…" He shrugged. "The only thing I'm certain of is that I'm on my own."

"I'm not saying you *should*," Astarte said, "but you could pretend today never happened. Go home and do what the FBI tells you to. Eventually your boss would probably decide you're still trustworthy. Then you could chase a bunch of other murderers."

"If I were still alive," Bellamy said. "Remember, somebody or something just tried to kill me. For all we know, it'll keep trying until it succeeds, or I take it down. And even if my life weren't on the line, this would still be personal. The Atheist has killed two informants right under my nose. He's ruined my reputation with my colleagues. He's made me doubt my own nerve and even my own sanity. I won't lie to you, this supernatural stuff scares me, but I have to keep after him. Otherwise, I'll lose my self-respect."

He faltered, surprised at himself. He rarely disclosed so much of his feelings, even to trusted friends like Walter Byrd. He guessed the ordeal in the cathedral had loosened his tongue.

"Do you have any idea how to catch him?" Astarte asked.

"Keene suggested a couple of possibilities. I'll pick one and run with it."

"Well, I think we should go to Lafayette," Astarte said. The *Cajun Queen* blew a blast on its whistle.

Bellamy stared at his companion in amazement. "Don't be ridiculous. You're not going to be involved in this any further. You're a civilian."

"So, deputize me or something."

"Not even if I could. I'm stuck in this mess. You're not. The Atheist only knows you as Astarte. You can go back home and be safe."

"You don't know that."

The cut in his scalp, where the statue had hit him, began to throb. "It's a reasonable assumption."

"Maybe," she said, "but I'm still not leaving."

"Look," he said, "I realize that your great goal in life is to find a vampire and"—to his surprise, the first image that popped into his mind was too pornographic to express; he paused for a beat to think of another—"uh, get its autograph. But this isn't a game. It's deadly serious."

"Well, that would explain the corpse," she replied sarcastically. "I know it's serious. That's why you need my help."

"Oh, and you've been a huge help so far," Bellamy said. "Keene might have told me a lot more if our conversation hadn't been cut short. But he got killed trying to pull you out of danger."

Astarte stared at him for a moment, and then her face twisted. She jerked around, turning her back to him. He suspected that it was to keep him from seeing her cry.

Bellamy had merely told the truth as he saw it, but still, he suddenly felt a pang of guilt for making her miserable. He stepped closer to her, catching the sharp scent of her body—evidently, she hadn't bathed since leaving home—mingled with the scent of leather. Awkwardly, he tried to lay his hand on her shoulder, but she wrenched herself away from his touch.

"I'm sorry," he said. "That came out harsher than I meant it to. I'm as much to blame as you are. I'm supposed to be a professional, but I froze. If I'd started shooting a second sooner, Keene might still be alive. And ultimately, neither of us is responsible. The person or power that made the statue move is.

"All I was trying to say is, you haven't been trained—"

She rounded on him. "Don't you think I know Mr. Keene is dead because of me? I was trying not to think about it, but I did. That's part of the reason I want to help you, to make up for it. And I did as well against the statue as you did. I'm the one who finally knocked it down."

"And I'm grateful," Bellamy said. "But you have to admit, it was a lucky shot."

"Maybe so," she said, wiping her nose with the back of her hand. He noticed that she'd bitten her black-enameled nails to the quick. "But think about this. I've read a ton of books about the occult. Maybe I don't know as much as Vulture did, but he's gone. I'm the closest thing to an expert you've got left. *Please* let me stay."

"I can buy my own books—"

"If you won't let me stick with you, I swear, I'm going to poke around on my own. Vulture didn't think I could find anything, but I will!"

The hell of it was, she just might, and get herself killed in the process. Certain people had a genius for blundering into trouble, and Bellamy suspected she was one of them.

Maybe he should keep her with him for the time being. There was an outside chance she could be useful. And once he learned her real name and address, maybe he could arrange for her family to come and drag her back to Ohio.

"All right," he said, "provided you agree that I'm in charge."

She twisted her black lips back into their customary half sneer. "*Jawohl, mein Fuhrer,*" she said.

16

Montrose's tiny fleet, a motley collection of *pirogues*, broadhorns, keelboats, and skiffs, glided with the black current. The murmuring water smelled of silt and acidic industrial waste. Gradually the lights of Natchez faded away astern, leaving only the stars to alleviate the darkness.

Standing with Fink on the bow of the latter's keelboat, Montrose remembered what had happened the last time he took an army onto the water. He hoped his luck had changed.

In an effort to distract himself from his misgivings, he mused on the paradox his miniature armada represented. Generally speaking, Underworld objects weren't solid in relation to matter existing in the Skinlands. Yet the boats appeared to sit in the water. Their sails bellied with the breeze, and their rudders, poles, and sweeps served to maneuver them, even though they never raised a splash. It was one of the countless enigmas of Shadowlands physics. Montrose had watched newly deceased scientists and logicians go half mad trying to puzzle such mysteries out.

Fink pointed at the shore ahead. "There," he whispered. His crew began to steer the flatboat into the shallows.

Peering, Montrose could just make out the vague shapes of what might be a cluster of houses, and then a vague flicker of movement in their midst. "And you're absolutely certain that this is a Circle of Heretics," he said.

"I'm certain the bastards'll look good in chains," said Fink, and then he grinned. "Yeah, yeah, I'm sure. I told you, nobody knows more about what goes on along the banks of the Mississip' than I do."

Montrose nodded to the Chanteur, a small man protectively cradling a cello case. In the Shadowlands, where material goods of all sorts were scarce and theft consequently endemic, many wraiths carried their prized possessions everywhere, even into situations where they were likely to prove cumbersome. The Chanteur set his instrument carefully on the deck, clambered atop the low cabin in the center of the boat, cupped his hands around his mouth, and whistled a bird call. The sound seemed so faint as to be nearly inaudible, but Montrose was confident that everyone in the raiding party would hear it. And sure enough, in a moment the other boats began to turn in toward shore.

The guerrillas beached their vessels, and then Montrose led them southward. As the raiders glided through a stand of mossy, resiny-smelling pines, their commander felt a thrill of anticipation. He'd tried not to relish warfare when he was breathing. It had scarcely seemed Christian to do so. Yet he hadn't been able to deny that a part of him delighted in the challenge and the risk, and evidently, despite his expectations to the contrary, the years at his master's court hadn't rendered him too jaded and sophisticated to experience the same excitement now.

A cluster of two- and three-story houses emerged from the gloom ahead. Like many Haunts, the structures were ruinous, riddled with Nihils, and seemingly abandoned by the Quick. They filled the air with the smells of mildew and wood rot. Peering between the derelict buildings, Montrose could see they formed several concentric circles around an open space. When the breeze gusted, the long, coarse grass in the clearing stirred, revealing crumbling gray tombstones and precariously leaning granite crosses. Scattered among the monuments, vague silhouettes swayed back and forth as if the wind were tossing them. A wordless chant like a whimper of pain murmured through the air.

Montrose wondered fleetingly just what sort of Quick village had been morbid enough to focus its communal life on the town graveyard, and then shoved the reflection aside. His business was with the current inhabitants of the hamlet, who had apparently assembled at its center for some sort of Heretical rite, like lambs obligingly congregating for the slaughter.

The Scot peered at the shadowy doorways, windows, and porches of the nearer houses, checking for sentries. Seeing none, he pointed right with the AK-47 and left with his empty hand. His force split up, three wraiths remaining with him but most, Fink included, skulking away in the directions indicated. The guerrillas would converge on the cemetery from every side, surrounding it, making sure none of their prey escaped.

Montrose waited a minute, giving his men time to encircle the Haunt, and then crept into the outermost ring of houses. His companions slunk after him. Rage, agony, and terror, the echo of an ancient massacre, still sang through the soil beneath his boots. A sickening exhilaration juddered up his legs and spine.

Still no sign of any guards. He noticed a Tudor-style door hanging by a single corroded hinge. Long ago, someone had carved lines of text into the top panels. Despite the worm holes and the mushiness of decay, Montrose could still read them. I am a child of the Wasteland. Dust is my drink and stones are my bread.

The Stygian raised his hand. His three companions halted. He glided forward to peek around the corner of a collapsed porch. As he'd hoped, he now had a clear view of the graveyard.

Standing in a ring, a dozen wraiths swayed and crooned there, their faces slack with mindless ecstasy. In the middle of the circle, and the very center of the village, for that matter, was a bare patch of earth occupied by a single gargoyle-encrusted mausoleum. The tomb's doorway was a glittering Nihil, and what at first glance appeared to be an androgynous angel hovered ten feet above the roof, its iridescent wings beating in slow motion.

On further inspection, Montrose could see subtle signs of the creature's true nature, notably the hungry blackness, a match for the restless dark in the opening to the Tempest, seething in the center of its eyes. Whatever its worshippers imagined it to be, it was actually a Spectre, no doubt risen from the portal beneath its flawless alabaster feet.

Montrose's stomach clenched in loathing and disgust. It was just as he'd told Katrina. Wittingly or otherwise, Heretics were the lackeys of Oblivion. He opened his mouth to shout a demand for surrender, and then a ragged volley of shots rang out. A wraith behind him made a choking sound.

The Stygian spun around. One of his companions, a woman in a parti-colored red and white mask, collapsed to her knees, fumbling at the crossbow bolt protruding from her neck. Waves of darkness pulsed from the wound, and then she faded away. Behind her, at the edge of town, figures were advancing. Guns flashed and barked, bows twanged, and a Chanteur wailed.

Another missile—Montrose didn't see whether it was an arrow or a bullet—ripped through the back of his mantle, passing between his torso and his arm. He turned again. The Heretics in the graveyard had hunkered down behind tombstones, snatched up weapons which had apparently lain hidden in the tall grass, and begun shooting also. Still floating serenely above the mausoleum, the Spectral angel looked at him and smiled.

Evidently the community of Heretics had grown considerably larger than Fink had imagined, large enough to outnumber the little band of raiders by a considerable margin. And just as obviously, they'd somehow detected Montrose's approach and set a trap for him, an ambush he'd rendered even more effective by dispersing his force through the Haunt. Now he and his men were the ones who were truly surrounded, and caught in a crossfire to boot.

Unless he could rally his troops and rally them quickly, the expedition was doomed. Throwing off his cape, he turned to his companions. "We have to charge and take the graveyard."

"That's crazy!" replied a squat little Spook with a ruby embedded in the center of his brow. "The Spectre's there, and they've got us outnumbered besides!"

"If we don't pull our force back together," Montrose said, "we're all going to die. And the cemetery is the only place to rally. It's the only area that everyone on our side can see. Now come on!" He ran through the rubble of the collapsed porch, on across a strip of weeds, and through the side of a house which listed drunkenly to one side, not bothering to glance back to see if his companions were following him. Either they were or they weren't, and if not, he didn't have time to coax them. He resisted the urge to cloak himself in shadow. If the men *were* charging after him, they might well falter if he vanished.

Racing through the interiors of houses, he covered part of the distance to the clearing without coming under additional fire. But inevitably loomed the moment when he'd have to break from cover. Exerting his will, not allowing himself to break stride, he hurtled through another wall, a broken porch railing, and bounded down onto the grass. Still running, he began to shoot.

He cut down two of the Heretics before any of them spotted him. Then all the survivors pivoted in his direction.

He fired another burst, blasting an ancient-looking, gray-haired woman's head apart. Her body imploded like a broken balloon. He turned, seeking his next target, and then someone with Chanteur powers wailed.

The screech penetrated his head and reverberated on and on inside. Fighting the pain and the sheer distraction of it, his vision blurring, he tried to pivot toward the source of the noise, but his movements were halting and spastic.

A bullet slammed into his thigh, staggering him. Even with the Chanteur's scream scrambling his senses, he could tell that he hadn't sustained a serious wound. He didn't feel the numbing caress of Oblivion scraping away his substance from within. But no doubt the next bullet or arrowhead, or the missile after that, would be both better aimed and made of darksteel.

Guns barked and rattled behind him. The screech stopped abruptly, releasing him from his partial paralysis. He realized that his companions *had* followed him, and just now saved his life.

He shot a Heretic kneeling behind a broken tombstone. The man flew backward and lay thrashing in the grass. Montrose spun toward another target and saw that this one, a thin man with enlarged, pointed ears and protruding canines, was goggling at the space above his would-be attacker's head.

Montrose threw himself to the ground. Something swooshed through the air above him. He frantically rolled onto his back and glimpsed the Spectre flashing past. No longer content simply to hover above the graveyard, the creature had changed its form—its arms had elongated, and its fists had enlarged into knobs studded with black spikes—and joined the fray. It wheeled for another pass.

Scrambling to his feet, Montrose tried to fire at the Spectre. His gun only clicked. It was out of ammunition, and he didn't have time to reload. The bogus angel was already plunging down at him. He dropped the assault rifle and whipped out his new rapier.

He waited an instant, and then, when the Spectre was nearly on top of him, hurtled up to meet it, hoping that the creature hadn't realized he could fly. And perhaps it hadn't; in any case, the sudden, all-out attack seemed to catch it by surprise. Montrose's blade rammed into its breast. Cancerous black light began to lick away its flesh.

Wrenching his sword free, Montrose grinned savagely, and then a new pain stabbed him in the shoulder. Someone had shot him from the ground.

He could tell it wasn't a mortal wound, but it startled him and broke the focus necessary to use his Arcanos. He crashed to the ground. The arrow in his shoulder snapped beneath him.

Gasping reflexively, dazed, he struggled to gather his strength. It began to return, but it would take a few seconds. He managed to lift his head and looked around.

Fink stood over him, leering and pointing a Mag-10 Roadblocker shotgun at his nominal commander's chest. Certain that the burly Haunter meant to avenge his humiliation in the Green Head, Montrose gave him a level stare. He hadn't lost his composure on the scaffold in Edinburgh, and he wouldn't now, either.

But Fink merely mouthed the word, "Boom," and then roughly hauled Montrose to his feet. "How are you?" he asked.

"I'll make it," Montrose said, peering about. The only remaining Heretics in the graveyard were incapacitated. So was the Spook with the red jewel in his forehead, who lay motionless beside a headstone with several white, glistening slashes in his throat and chest. Montrose's other companion had vanished and had probably been destroyed. Judging by appearances, Fink and three other raiders had charged up to complete the task of taking the area.

The Stygian gingerly tested his legs. The wounded one throbbed, but it could support his weight. Extricating himself from Fink's grasp, he picked up his AK-47 and sword and swung the latter over his head. "Everybody, come to me!" he bellowed. "Use the houses for cover!" Any soldier worthy of the name should have sense enough to take advantage of any available cover without being told, but one never knew what even seasoned troops would forget in the heat of battle, particularly when they were losing.

Alone or in pairs, their faces white and their eyes rolling with incipient panic, the raiders limped into the cemetery. About a third of the initial force failed to appear.

Behind the survivors, guns banged and a Chanteur wailed as their pursuers harried them.

"What are we going to do?" cried the Sandman from the tavern, his rainbow-colored mantle now hanging in tatters. "We're outnumbered and surrounded!"

"We're going to charge," Montrose said. "Through the open this time, so we can keep together. The Heretics are spread out in a ring. We'll outnumber the ones comprising any given section of the circle. If we hit hard and fast, we can break out of this crossfire. Are you game?"

"It sounds like a plan to me," said Fink.

Some of the raiders cheered. Others grimly nodded their agreement.

"Then let's go," said Montrose, striding toward the edge of the cemetery. By the time he left its confines, he was running. His soldiers thundered after him.

In the darkness ahead, guns flashed, but this time, no one hit him. Montrose held his own fire, waiting till he got close enough to have a reasonable chance of hitting someone himself. After a few seconds, bullets and arrows began to whiz at the column's flanks. Witnessing the raiders' sudden maneuver, Heretics fighting elsewhere around the ring had scrambled into new positions in order to continue shooting. But they didn't produce enough fire to break the momentum of the charge. Too few of them had moved up quickly enough.

The faces of the Heretics in front of the guerrillas swam out of the murk. As they continued shooting and their opponents kept coming, their eyes began to widen in dismay. Eventually one threw down his longbow, wheeled, and fled toward the edge of the village. A moment later, a second rebel bolted.

Montrose judged that he was close enough to start firing. He squeezed the trigger and the AK-47 rattled and shook in his hands. A Heretic in bib overalls, armed with a slingshot, of all things, flew off his feet.

The Stygian's column smashed into the Heretics. He shot someone, then sensed an attacker lunging at him from the side. He pivoted, ramming the butt of his rifle into the other wraith's face. Bone, or what passed for it in a ghost's anatomy, crunched. The Heretic collapsed, a tomahawk slipping from his fingers.

Montrose looked around, but failed to find another opponent. The only figures standing in the immediate area were his own troops. Evidently recognizing that they'd succeeded in breaking free, one of them threw back his head and let out a war whoop.

The Scot supposed that since they were tired, in some cases wounded, and still outnumbered, the prudent thing would be to disengage and run for the boats. But if he led them away without a victory, without loot, they'd never follow him again. Heedless of the risk of attracting enemy fire, he levitated over the outlaws' heads so everyone could see him.

"We just took away the enemy's advantage," he said. "If you're as tough as you're supposed to be, we can beat them now. We can form into squads, sweep through this rat's nest, and drive the bastards before us. We can avenge our fallen comrades and capture a fortune in thralls!"

The freebooters shouted their assent, a sound like a pack of wild dogs snarling. They divided into groups of five or six, and then began to spread out.

At the head of one such party, Montrose led it from lane to lane, yard to yard, and house to house. The battle became a game of cat and mouse, blasting away at the shadowy figures that pounced out of nowhere, chasing the ones that fled, proceeding fast but warily in case the Heretics were leading them into a trap.

It was dangerous work. One of his men perished, decapitated

by a blow from an ax. Another was temporarily crippled when a blast from an assault rifle all but tore his leg off. But the Heretics fared worse than their enemies. Montrose didn't know if they'd been demoralized by the destruction of their Spectral patron or if, indeed, they simply couldn't match the prowess of his own band of ruffians. In any case, it soon became apparent that they didn't stand a chance.

With victory all but certain, the excitement Montrose had been experiencing, a kind of wild abandon seasoned with fear, gave way to a feverish ecstasy. Without his quite realizing it, the grim satisfaction of driving home a telling blow, of staying on one's feet while the other man went down, warped into a gloating enjoyment of the terror and agony in his victim's face.

Christ, he hated Heretics! Or at least he supposed he did. At certain moments, as he slipped deeper into his delirium, he imagined that he was striking down not a rabble of deluded Shadowlanders, but Argyll, Hamilton, the two Charleses, Van Lengen, and Louise. Finally, wreaking vengeance on all the traitors.

Until at last he and his companions prowled through two more houses without finding anyone else to maim. Despite the haze of cruelty clouding his mind, he realized he no longer heard shooting anywhere in the Haunt. Evidently the battle was over. Suddenly feeling dazed and empty, he simply stopped and stood in the center of a ruinous parlor, like a clockwork toy running down.

After a moment, a raider in a green hood said, "Anacreon?"

Montrose jerked as if someone had startled him awake. He felt his Shadow writhing inside him. He supposed that the events of the last few minutes had nourished it in some way, though he wasn't entirely sure how. He'd just been defending himself, hadn't he, doing what needed to be done.

In any case, he didn't have time to think about it now. He looked at the outlaw. "What is it?"

"I was thinking you could fly up over the town and get a bird's-eye view of what's going on."

"Good idea," Montrose said. He floated through the ceiling, a bedroom, and finally the attic, flitting through a mass of filthy cobwebs filled with the husks of flies, roaches, and termites in the process. His passage didn't disturb a single strand, but sensing him, the spiders skittered madly about.

He soared through a warped expanse of roof that had shed half its shingles, up another twenty feet, then stopped and looked around. Below him, his men herded staggering, whimpering prisoners toward the edge of the village. Though some of the surviving Heretics had no doubt fled into the countryside, the raiders had rounded up an excellent haul.

A number of outlaws were cuffing, shoving, kicking, or obscenely fondling their prisoners. The spectacle made Montrose feel obscurely ashamed. Throughout his Scottish campaigns, he'd forbidden his soldiers to engage in gratuitous cruelty, and made the edict stick. Shouldn't he do the same thing now?

He scowled, disgusted by his own momentary squeamishness. No, of course not. The Quick Montrose had been a fool to fret about securing gentle treatment for his own enemies. And the Heretics were pawns of the Void itself, condemned to slavery and an eternity of rough treatment by his own decree. Besides, an attempt to alleviate their distress might cost him the respect of his band of thugs.

He spotted Fink marching along between two houses with his arms full of rifles and shotguns, booty as valuable as the newly made thralls themselves. He flew down and landed in front of him.

Something had singed the left side of Fink's face, charring shiny white patches and grooves on his skin and burning away an eyebrow, much of his hair, and a section of his mustache. But if he was in pain, he didn't show it. His eyes were as full of devilish mirth as ever. "I thought the Marquess of Montrose was supposed to be some kind of hotshot Cavalier general," he said.

Montrose raised an eyebrow. It was the first time Fink had indicated that he'd ever heard of his new leader's mortal career. "We Won, didn't we?"

"Yeah, but not very elegantly," said Fink. "First, we sneak into town, then we run back to the edge of town, then we sweep into town again. Kind of a Chinese fire drill, in my opinion."

"Well, if my worthy lieutenant had provided adequate intelligence…"

Fink's burnt cheek rippled, repairing itself. He shrugged. "You wouldn't even have found the Heretics if it hadn't been for me. I said I knew more about the river than anybody else. I didn't say I knew *everything* about it. Nobody does."

Montrose could well believe that. The vast expanse of the Mississippi seemed more akin to the open sea than any of the rivers he'd known in Europe. In many respects, it was as awesome as the River of Death itself, the colossal waterway twisting through much of the Tempest.

"We both did an adequate job," the Stygian said. "But we did take heavy losses. I hope the rest of the men will continue to follow us."

Fink snorted. "Don't worry about that. They're too afraid of me to quit on you unless I do. Besides, you know how it is with sons of bitches like us. We think nobody could possibly kill *us*, *even* though a lot of us became wraiths because somebody *did*. If we didn't believe we're indestructible, we'd find less dangerous pastimes to get us through the centuries.

"Trust me. Manpower is no problem. When word gets out about the plunder we took tonight, you'll get all the volunteers you need. Every cutthroat and lowlife from Cairo to the Gulf of Mexico will beat a path to your door."

Montrose smiled crookedly. "Now there's something to look forward to," he said.

17

Potter prowled restlessly about the enormous, high-ceilinged chamber, where Hittite chariots and Sherman tanks cast blurred reflections in the gleaming gray marble floor. Stealth bombers and Fokkers, supported only by an artificer's magic, hung above his head, and glass cases full of polearms, machine guns, and grenades lined the walls. The air smelled sharply of oil, and the dripping tick of a water clock echoed through the gloom.

Sometimes it soothed the Deathlord to wander the museum, or one of the twenty like it scattered through his allotted portion of the Onyx Tower. The surroundings evoked the godlike spirit inside his mask. But tonight, they failed to silence the fretful human soul hiding at the core of the transcendent entity he'd become.

The door clicked. Potter turned, reflexively holding his halberd across his body as the images of the Smiling Lord in all the paintings and statuary did, standing straight and still. By the time the door swung open, he'd become a figure that might easily have been mistaken for some enigmatic idol.

Tall, thin, and saturnine, the folds of his toga draped as elegantly as ever, Demetrius stepped into the chamber. He'd tucked his carved sardonyx helmet of a mask under one arm, his naked face a token of submission and respect. Bowing deeply, he said, "My lord."

Potter relaxed a little. He didn't feel the need to maintain absolute formality with the advisor, though the question of just how much of the inner man he ought to reveal to anyone was often troublesome in its own right. "Good evening," he said.

"I hope I didn't summon you away from anything you were reluctant to set aside."

"Dispatches from our Citadels in South America," Demetrius replied, advancing. His sandals made a scuffing sound on the floor. "They'll keep. Is something troubling you?"

"Another vision," Potter admitted. "In this one, this section of the castle collapsed in around me and crushed me, while everyone else's quarters remained untouched."

"I rue the day I ever brought that miserable statuette to your attention," said Demetrius. "We don't even know who made it, or how it found its way into that storeroom. And I think there's a malignancy about it, some subtle taint of Oblivion, even if we can't detect it directly. Let's cast it into a Forge and be done with it."

"No," Potter said. "You don't kill the messenger for bringing bad news. You do your best to comprehend what he has to tell you."

"That assumes your dreams truly are portents of things to come."

"Since I haven't slumbered since you gave me the image," Potter said, "they can't be simple nightmares. I'd rather consider them warnings than signs of impending insanity." Feeling restless again, he turned and walked toward a trebuchet, using his halberd as a staff. The butt of the weapon clopped rhythmically on the stone.

Demetrius fell into step beside him. "I assume that was a joke."

"You shouldn't," Potter said. "It wasn't particularly easy to be a Deathlord even when Charon was in power, and it's far more difficult now. How would *you* like to have final responsibility for preserving the Hierarchy?"

"I'm sure I'd snap like a twig," Demetrius said. "But I'm not Charon's anointed lieutenant. As Hierarchs, we know there's no God, but by all accounts, our late master came close. He wouldn't have chosen you if you weren't equal to the challenge."

"No one understood Charon," Potter replied. "Not unless it was the Lady of Fate, and she's not talking. No one knew why he did the things he did. Perhaps he made me his deputy precisely because I was strong enough to assist him, but no stronger. Not nearly strong enough to cast him down and fill his place."

"Come now," Demetrius said, "naturally the Emperor's disappearance left turmoil in its wake. But Stygia has weathered times of trouble before. Your Council of Seven will hold the realm together."

As they veered around the catapult, Potter resisted a childish impulse to pull the triggering lever and send the stones in the basket crashing against the wall. "Perhaps," he said, "but will it still be a Council of Seven when things finally settle down? I'm certain that some of my peers are scheming to expand their power at the expense of others."

"Schemes that will likely come to nothing," said Demetrius. "But I'm confident that whatever happens, *you'll* still be securely ensconced in your place, if not more influential than before. The Master of War and Murder is too formidable a personage to assail. And your campaign against the Heretics can only serve to enhance your prestige."

"Naturally you think that," said Potter, drifting toward a mannequin in a doughboy's uniform equipped with a gas mask, carbine, and bayonet. "It was your idea."

"You miss Montrose, don't you? I don't blame you. He has a keen mind, when he can be induced to put it to use."

"Do you like him, then? I imagined otherwise."

"I appreciate his virtues. I can't afford to like him just at present. He seems to think that his own place at court won't be secure until he drives a wedge between you and any other courtier whom you've chosen to trust. Which is to say, he's fallen victim to a case of the same envy and ambition which you believe afflicts your fellow Deathlords."

"Perhaps I'm doing them an injustice," Potter said. "But it's hard to trust people when you don't even know their names and have never even seen their faces. I often wonder why the Emperor forbade us to reveal our human identities even to one another." He grimaced. "He probably figured that if we never became intimate, we'd never dare to conspire against him."

Demetrius uttered a noncommittal grunt.

"I often imagine that some of the others *have* broken the

prohibition," Potter continued moodily. "I can see them, faces bare, whispering in some secret crypt. Sometimes I picture all six of them there, plotting the destruction of the only person they've elected to leave on the outside."

Demetrius frowned. "Forgive me for saying so, my lord, but that does sound paranoid."

"Probably so," Potter sighed. "Why don't you prophesy for me? With luck, your findings will reassure me. And then you can quell my Shadow. Perhaps it's responsible for my more troublesome fancies."

As always, he felt somewhat sheepish making such a request. A quasi-divine entity like a Deathlord was supposed to be a supreme master of every conceivable Arcanos. He shouldn't require the talents of some other Oracle to interpret the weave of destiny for him, nor should he need the services of a Pardoner at all. But in Potter's experience, the old notion that a seer couldn't foretell his own future was absolutely valid. And while Charon had granted him reserves of willpower and spiritual strength that lesser wraiths could scarcely imagine, the ugly realities of governing the Hierarchy, the daily trafficking in war, execution, and slavery, nourished the dark parasite lurking inside him to an astonishing degree.

Demetrius's long, thin-lipped mouth tightened. "As I've warned you before, my lord, that isn't a good idea."

The advisor raised the same objections every time. An Oracle denied the opportunity to read the deathmarks graven in a supplicant's countenance stood a fair chance of misinterpreting that individual's karma, while a Pardoner ignorant of his client's history might conceivably strengthen his Shadow instead of weakening it.

Potter felt a sudden, reckless urge to go ahead and fling his visor away. Establish a genuine intimacy with someone. What kind of bizarre joke had Charon played on him anyway, granting him the power of a god but isolating him from every other person in the universe?

But he knew he wouldn't unmask, nor should he need to. Demetrius was one of the most gifted Oracles or Pardoners he'd ever encountered. That was one reason the Deathlord had welcomed him into his inner circle of lieutenants so rapidly, much to the chagrin of Montrose and certain others.

"Please," said Potter. "You've done an adequate job so far."

Demetrius grimaced. "So *far* is the proper way of putting it. Still, if my lord commands it..."

Potter inclined his head.

"Then I suppose we might as well sit over there." The two Hierarchs walked to an alcove occupied by a low, round table and three chairs. Demetrius extracted a pack of cards from the folds of his toga, sat down opposite his master, and handed the pasteboards to him. "You know what to do. Shuffle and then cut the deck twice with your left hand."

"The hand closer to the heart," said Potter wryly, removing his steel gauntlets. The cards whirred as he riffled them. "Even though the Restless don't *have* hearts. And most people would say that Deathlords are even more heartless than most."

"You aren't heartless," the Oracle said. "And in any case, the symbolism is still valid."

Potter set the deck down. Leaning forward, Demetrius turned the first card over and laid it face up on the table. The illustration depicted a high stone wall with a door set midway up. A figure standing on the ground, out of reach, gazed up at the portal in seeming frustration or perplexity.

"The Rampart," Demetrius said. "You feel cut off. Friendless and alone. Vulnerable."

Potter sighed. "I didn't need you to tell me that."

Demetrius turned a second card. The new one depicted a man crouched over an open coffin in a mausoleum. Knife in hand, he was violating the corpse of a lovely young woman, cutting off her fingers to steal her rings. The Oracle stiffened.

"What is it?" Potter asked.

"The Tomb Robber," Demetrius said. "Sometimes called the Archaeologist or the Resurrection Man."

"I know that," said Potter impatiently. "Tell me what it means."

"There are a number of possible interpretations...."

"Stop stalling and tell me what you see in it!"

Demetrius grimaced. "Betrayal, my lord. Someone, perhaps

several someones, will try to do you grievous harm."

Potter glared at him. "Why were you unwilling to warn me of that?"

"Because I'm not at all certain I'm right, and I wouldn't want to alarm you needlessly, or turn you against some innocent person."

"But this agrees with the visions from the statuette. It confirms what I feel every time I see the other Deathlords in council. How many validations do you need?"

Demetrius shook his head. "Perhaps I simply don't want to believe such a thing. The Hierarchy can survive a lot of political maneuvering, but if you Deathlords start trying to assassinate one another—"

"I need to know who my enemies are, and precisely what they're planning," Potter said. "Turn the final card."

Demetrius obeyed, revealing a picture of an ebony mask covered with runes. Darkness seemed to shimmer in the left eye hole, almost as if it were a Nihil. The pasteboard emerged from the deck upside down.

"The Visor reversed," the Oracle said. "All three cards are Greater Trumps. Your current situation is of the greatest possible consequence."

"In other words, I'm in the greatest possible danger."

Demetrius hesitated, then said, "That's certainly conceivable."

"What more does the Visor tell you?"

"Nothing," Demetrius said.

Potter glared at him. "How can that be? I've seen you spend half an hour interpreting a three-card spread like this."

"The Visor masks the countenance of fate. I can't see any more."

Potter felt a surge of fury, which energized the godlike persona resident in his mask. Springing up, he seized his halberd, whirled it over his head, and, despite the close quarters, effortlessly poised the gleaming black blade for a thrust at his minister's head.

"How dare you try my patience with lies and evasions?" the Deathlord thundered. "You *do see* something more. What is it?"

Demetrius quivered. "Forgive me, my lord. What I saw is simply what I warned you of already. It's your own mask, your own secrecy, which prevents me from helping you any further."

Potter's anger and feeling of near omnipotence ebbed, giving way to a bitter sense of frustration. Once again, he had to resist the temptation to bare his face and tell the Oracle his name. "We'll just have to keep trying," he said glumly, even though he suspected the effort would prove useless.

Abruptly he felt his Shadow stirring inside him. The sensation wasn't physical, but it still conveyed a sense of frenetic activity, as if the dark side of his nature was dancing with glee. He could almost hear it taunting him with a kind of singsong chant. *We're going to die , we're going to die, we're going to die.*

He tried to block the Shadow from his awareness, but it was impossible. The spiritual parasite had waxed too powerful, fattening on his distress. He sat back down. "Thank you for the divination," he said to Demetrius. "Now give me your Pardon. And I'd appreciate it if you'd hurry."

18

After he finished his third drink, Nolliver zapped the TV off, hauled himself up off the couch, and trudged toward his study. He left the liter of Johnnie Walker Black sitting on the coffee table. He always needed alcohol to fortify himself for the ordeal ahead, but he couldn't drink while it was actually occurring. It would have felt like a kind of sacrilege to do so.

Stacks of professional journals sat atop his carved maple desk, while a shelf crammed with psychiatric texts ran along a shelf on the wall above it. As he sat down, a little unsteadily, in his leather swivel chair, he thought, I *don't have to put myself through this.* But that wasn't true. There were evenings when he *did* have to look, and this was one of them.

He fumbled his key ring out of his pocket, unlocked the bottom left-hand drawer, pulled it open, and removed the fat yellow folder lying atop the .38 Special, a weapon he'd purchased one drunken weekend when his suicidal impulses were particularly compelling. Leaning back, he began to review the file.

Everything was there. The arrest and court documents, his interview notes, affidavits from social workers, teachers, and probation officers, and the Minnesota Multiphasic Personality Inventory profiles the psychologist had provided. His own recommendations that four vicious young criminals be released back into the community. And, of course, the newspaper accounts of the murders that Billy Cantrell had subsequently committed. Two men, a woman, and a little girl gunned down in the course of a carjacking.

Nolliver's eyes ached, brimming with tears. Even after all

these years, he wondered how it had all gone so wrong. The four offenders he'd lied for had only been *boys!* They'd deserved another chance, hadn't they, no matter how much trouble they'd caused in school, or how elevated their scores on the Psychopathy scale of the MMPI. What had been the alternative? Try them as adults and send them to prison? Surely that would have ended any hope of their ever adjusting to society. And in many ways, Billy had seemed the least malevolent in the lot. There'd been an underlying vulnerability—

Nolliver grimaced, disgusted with himself. How pathetic that he could romanticize the little monster even after everything that had happened. Billy had been a sadistic, amoral punk with subnormal intelligence. Unfortunately, he'd also possessed an angelic face and body beautiful enough to seduce a shy, lonely pedophile into imagining hidden virtues where none existed.

After the murders, Nolliver had waited, half in dread and half with a masochistic eagerness, for somebody to discover that he'd traded favorable evaluations for sex, or at least to question his competence. But no one ever had. The truth of the matter was that predicting criminal recidivism was such an inexact science that people rarely found it remarkable when a shrink or a caseworker made a bad call.

Though Nolliver hadn't endured prosecution or professional disgrace, he hadn't escaped punishment either. He'd simply punished himself, with impotence and alcohol. Desperate to ameliorate his guilt, he'd joined the Bureau and VICAP. He'd spend the remainder of his career helping to take murderers off the streets.

And for a while, it had helped. He hadn't felt cleansed. He'd known he never would. But sometimes he'd managed simply to do his work and live his life for hours at a time without his guilt and self-loathing coming to the forefront of his mind.

That had changed when Dunn came to him, revealed that, somehow, he knew the psychiatrist's sordid secret, and demanded cooperation in return for his silence. Nolliver had tried to tell himself that the arrangement was nothing he couldn't live with. He'd surmised—accurately, as it turned out—that the SAD agent would call on him only rarely. And then Nolliver would merely use his professional powers of persuasion to convince investigators that they hadn't really experienced any paranormal phenomena after all. How much harm could that do?

Yet as soon as he capitulated to Dunn's blackmail, he'd sensed his life spinning out of control again, hurtling toward a second disaster. And sure enough, in due time, the catastrophe arrived. Once again, he'd borne false witness, to discredit Bellamy, and now his every instinct warned him that as a result, another innocent person was going to die.

Unless Nolliver prevented it.

He could. Dunn had contacted him earlier today to say that his "people" had failed to apprehend Bellamy in Jackson Square, and that Nolliver should try to set up a rendezvous if the younger man contacted him. By escaping, Bellamy had given the psychiatrist another chance to reveal the truth to Hanson, who could then mobilize the resources necessary to locate his subordinate and keep him safe.

The catch, of course, was that Nolliver couldn't inform on Dunn without informing on himself as well. Then his life as he knew it would come to an end. Not that he enjoyed his existence, but still, to have his secret shame exposed to the world! To stand revealed as a liar, a pederast, and, in effect, an accomplice to murder! He didn't know if he could bear it.

He looked down at the papers rattling faintly in his tremulous hands. A black-and-white newspaper photo of a car with four shrouded bodies laid out on the ground beside it was on top of the sheaf.

How did you you feel knowing that Bellamy's dead, too? he asked himself. Will that be any better that losing this shabby little pretense of a life you have now, posing as a decent human being and drinking yourself to death?

Abruptly, he knew that it wouldn't. Eager to act quickly, before he lost his nerve, he made a grab for the phone on the desk.

Clumsy with intoxication, he only managed to knock the receiver *off* the cradle. The dial tone whined. And then the smell of tobacco that clings to a smoker's hair and clothing suffused the air.

Nolliver froze. It's *like the stench of the bodies from the morgue,* he told himself frantically. It's *all in my mind. Dunn couldn't just appear in my house out of nowhere.*

A large, rather hairy hand with slightly yellow fingertips reached from behind Nolliver and hung up the phone. "Hello, Doc," said Dunn. "I hope you don't mind me dropping by. You keep saying we had better talk away from the office."

Nolliver jerked his chair around. "How did you get in here?" he demanded, his voice breaking in the middle of the question.

Dunn smiled. "You've got pretty good home security, but nothing a real pro can't handle. Who were you about to call?"

"I was going to have some supper delivered."

Dunn gestured at the papers in Nolliver's hands. "Does reliving all this give you an appetite? Of course, I'm no psychiatrist, but that's hard to understand."

Nolliver realized that he didn't like looking up at the other man. It made him feel vulnerable and subservient. But at the same time, he was afraid to stand up. "I have to eat," he said. "No matter how much I regret the past, life has to go on."

"Not necessarily," said Dunn.

Nolliver trembled. "What do you mean?"

"That you might as well cut the crap. I know you were calling Hanson. I could smell it on you, even through the stink of the whiskey."

"That isn't true!" Nolliver said.

"It's a shame," Dunn continued, as if the psychiatrist hadn't even spoken. "Hanson couldn't help Bellamy anyway. No one could. In the unlikely event that my friends in New Orleans can't throw a net over him, I'll go down there and catch him myself. But that's tomorrow's little problem. Right now, we're focusing on you."

"I'm telling you, I'm loyal!" Nolliver said.

"I wish that were true," Dunn replied. "But you know, even if it was, you've been falling apart for months. Changing from an asset to a liability. A loose end I need to tie off."

Nolliver's bladder felt swollen. For a moment he thought he was going to wet his pants. He realized that despite his guilt, he wanted to live, if only to undo the harm he'd done to Bellamy.

And ironically, his .38 seemed to represent his only hope of surviving the next few minutes. He dangled his arm beside his chair and stealthily began to move his hand toward the drawer containing the gun.

Simultaneously, hoping that conversation would keep Dunn from noticing what he was doing, he said, "You haven't really been carrying out orders from SAD, have you? You're a rogue agent."

"Sure," said the man in the suede jacket. "Deep down, you've known that for a long time. Although the term 'infiltrator' might be more accurate, since I was never truly on the Bureau's side to begin with. My real job has always been to keep SAD or any other part of the government from finding out anything much about the paranormal."

Nolliver's groping fingers brushed the cold metal handle of the drawer. Now, he realized, he'd have to pull it open, grab the .38, lift it, and shoot, all before the lithe, powerful Dunn could jump him. And a minute ago, he hadn't even been able to pick up a phone!

Was there any chance at all that he could talk his way out of danger instead? "If you kill me, the Bureau will find out about you. I left sealed letters with a number of people, to be opened in the event of my death."

Dunn smiled like a parent dismissing a child's transparent lie. "No, you haven't."

Nolliver's fingers closed around the drawer handle. But he found he couldn't make himself open it, for fear of provoking Dunn into killing him *now*, as opposed to one or two precious minutes from now.

"I beg you," the psychiatrist said, "let me live. I swear I'll cooperate. Think about it, if you murder me, there's a good chance that the Bureau will figure out who did it. Your work inside SAD will be over. Even if you manage to avoid immediate capture, you'll be on the run for the rest of your life."

"That's an interesting perspective," said Dunn, "but I'm afraid I can't buy into it. It would require me to trust you, which I don't anymore. Besides, I'm not worried about exposure. I can make it look like poor, troubled Dr. Nolliver committed suicide.

Everybody in the Bureau will believe it, especially when the truth about Billy Cantrell comes out.

"In other words, you can't talk me out of this. If I were you, I'd go ahead and make a try for that gun in your desk. It's your only chance."

Nolliver gaped at Dunn, stunned to learn that the rogue had known about the revolver all along. Then he jerked around in his chair, tore open the drawer, and fumbled madly for the weapon.

To his surprise, he was actually quick enough to snatch it up. But the instant he did, a hand gripped the back of his neck and jerked him into the air. Thrashing, he blindly pointed the .38 over his shoulder. Before he could squeeze the trigger, Dunn tore the firearm out of his grasp, painfully wrenching his fingers in the process.

Dunn tossed the .38 back into the drawer. The gun landed with a thud. Taking the psychiatrist in both hands, the SAD agent turned him around with no more difficulty than Nolliver would have had shifting a squirming kitten.

The psychiatrist tried to kick Dunn in the groin. The agent twisted, and the blow merely glanced off his hip. He began to shake Nolliver, jolting him back and forth, not quite hard enough to injure him but forcefully enough to demonstrate his vastly superior strength. Much as he suddenly wanted to live, Nolliver realized it would be pointless to struggle any further. He went limp in the other man's grip.

Dunn stopped bouncing him around. "Aha, you've finally shown some fight," he said. "A man shouldn't die like a sheep."

"Who are you really?" Nolliver asked. "*What* are you?"

Dunn shook his head. "I said I'd show you if you crossed me, but it's better you never know. You finally found some courage, here at the end. I wouldn't want to take it away from you again. Now, where's your john? We'll do the dirty deed in the bathtub and give the cleanup crew a break."

19

Astarte looked at the line of French doors which made up the facade of the Old Absinthe House. A number of them stood open, leaking bright swirls of Dixieland jazz into Bourbon Street. "I think I've heard of this place," she said.

"Probably," Bellamy replied, "it's reasonably famous." A trio of sightseers, as drunk as nearly everyone else in the Vieux Carre seemed to be tonight, stumbled off the sidewalk to detour around him.

"Let's go in. I'm starved."

"I'll get you some take-out next time we pass a stand." He discovered during the course of their first afternoon together four days ago that she had no credit cards, no checkbook, and only a few dollars in cash.

She grimaced. "You're a real sport. I can probably pay for myself, at least if I order something cheap."

"The money isn't the point," Bellamy said, although heaven knew, he couldn't see any reason why he should be expected to pay for her food and motel room, even though that was the way it was working out. It wasn't as if she was his date. "I'd rather not take the time."

"What's an hour going to matter?"

"You never know. It could save someone's life. Maybe even ours."

"If a person carried that attitude to the extreme—and I bet you do—he could never have any fun. No wonder your wife dumped you."

Bellamy clenched his jaw, holding in an angry retort. He wished he hadn't told Astarte anything about his personal life, but it had been a ploy to induce her to open up about her own. And it seemed to have worked, at least to some degree. She'd told him her real name was Emily Dodds—but *nobody*, she'd added with a scowl of warning, called her that—she was eighteen, and she worked part-time in an alternative boutique. Her father was dead, and her mother received disability benefits for crippling migraines, chronic fatigue syndrome, and a bad back. Judging from her daughter's description, the woman would lack both the motivation and the moral authority to compel Astarte to go back to Ohio even if Bellamy could get in touch with her.

"You have no idea why my wife divorced me," he said, "and I have no intention of telling you. Now, maybe *you* aren't in any rush to get to the bottom of our situation. Maybe you've forgotten what happened to Keene. Maybe you feel safe. But—"

"All right!" Astarte said. "I get the point. Which way is it?"

"This one," Bellamy said. He led her northwest on Bienville Street. As they moved away from the press of giddy tourists and the raucous bars and souvenir shops on Bourbon Street into a more residential section of the Quarter, the night grew quieter, darker, and more desolate. The narrow streets were nearly empty, and most of the streetlights were broken. Wooden gates leaned drunkenly, and cryptic graffiti—GENERATION LAST, ADORE THE PALE QUEEN—blemished the walls. One of the ubiquitous balconies overhanging the sidewalk groaned ominously as Bellamy and Astarte stepped beneath it. A shadowy figure rooting through a reeking trash can scuttled away at their approach.

The gloom and general atmosphere of decay reminded Bellamy of the area in which he'd found Waxman. Grimacing, he tried to push the comparison out of his mind.

Finally, a point of blue light appeared in the darkness ahead. "Bingo," he said.

"Amazing," Astarte replied. "I thought you were lost."

"You shouldn't have," he said. "I know the Quarter about as well as a nonresident can, or at least I used to."

As they moved forward, quickening their pace, the smudge of blue radiance became a tinted bulb burning beside a dilapidated, iron-bound gate. Somewhere beyond it, someone was playing the piano, the music a schizophrenic medley of schmaltzy passages from fifty-year-old Broadway and Hollywood show tunes which shattered into crashing dissonance after the first few bars.

Bellamy knocked five times, just as a furtive clerk in a dusty little rare-book shop on Royal Street had told him to do. After a few seconds a brown eye appeared behind one of the cracks in the gate. "Step back," said a bass voice. "I can't see you."

Bellamy did as he'd been told. "She can come in," said the doorman brusquely. "I think you'd fit in better someplace else."

Bellamy held up his FBI credentials. The gate clicked and swung open, the hinges creaking. The agent noticed that the doorman, a handsome young black man with mocha-colored skin, a shaven head, a bodybuilder's physique, and a pink triangle tattooed on his left biceps, had to hoist the barrier up slightly so it wouldn't drag along the cobblestones.

"Did I see that right?" he asked, his tone considerably less truculent. "Was that an FBI badge?"

"Yes, but it's all right," Bellamy said. "No one's in any trouble. I just need to talk to Marilyn Sebastian. A friend of hers told me I might that I might find her here."

"Come in," said the doorman, stepping aside. "I just came on duty, but I'll find out if she's around."

The black man conducted them down a short, dark passage into a courtyard which had been converted into an open-air bar illuminated by strings of blue and yellow paper lanterns. At first glance it appeared that about half the customers were men and half, women. On closer inspection, however, it became apparent that most of the latter were transsexual or males in drag, though in some cases the illusion of femininity was nearly perfect, marred only by the breadth of their shoulders or the prominence of their Adam's apples. Same-sex couples embraced in shadowy corners, moaning and gasping, their clothing in disarray. The odor of marijuana hung in the air.

Just as Bellamy smelled it, the doorman winced as if he'd just noticed it too, and expected the Federal agent to make an impromptu drug bust on the spot. "Can I get you anything?" he asked. "On the house, of course."

"Nothing," Bellamy said.

Astarte shot him a glare, and he belatedly remembered he'd promised to feed her. "I could *really* use something to eat," she said to the doorman. "And a beer."

"We've got some good jambalaya," he said. "I'll get you some." He hurried over to the bar, and Bellamy and Astarte sat down at a small round table with a Cinzano umbrella rising from its center. When the FBI agent rested his forearm on it, it rocked precariously.

"Sorry," he said. "I forgot you were hungry."

"No harm done," she said, smirking a superior little smirk. "You're probably lucky you remember what we even came here for. I'll bet this place really weirds you out."

He smiled back at her. "Sorry to disappoint you, but no, not much."

The doorman brought two mugs of beer and two paper plates heaped high with a steaming mixture of rice, shrimp, and sausage. When he smelled the spicy aroma, Bellamy realized that he was hungry, too.

"Now I'll find Marilyn," the doorman said. He turned and vanished through a door in the far wall, into what had probably been an apartment house at one time.

Astarte eyed Bellamy skeptically. "I figured a straight arrow FBI agent would disapprove of stuff like this."

"Don't believe every stereotype you see on TV," Bellamy said, wondering fleetingly why he was explaining himself to her. "I got into police work to keep violent people from hurting innocent ones, not because I'm some kind of moral fascist. I admit, I don't go to places like this for fun, but I also don't care about what consenting adults do for sexual gratification, or if somebody smokes pot. I don't think their private lives are any of my business. Mind you, if I had to chase marijuana dealers for a while to have a career in law enforcement, well, I guess I'd do it. But I'm very glad to be part of VICAP instead." He picked up his plastic fork and scooped up some jambalaya. It tasted as good as it smelled.

"If you say so," she said, clearly not entirely convinced.

"It's true," he insisted. "I've lost count of how many times I've come to New Orleans for Mardi Gras. Do you know what it's like in the Quarter on Fat Tuesday? Thousands—well, lots—of drag queens wandering the streets in sequin gowns and feathery headdresses. People exposing themselves and groping each other everywhere you look. If I had a problem with things like that, I couldn't enjoy the party, but I do."

"I've always wanted to go to Mardi Gras," Astarte said wistfully. "Is it still as good as it used to be? Somebody told me it's getting too commercialized and touristy."

"I don't think that's true," said Bellamy, not remembering until he spoke that he'd missed the celebration for four years running, and thus was scarcely in any position to judge.

Astarte took a long drink of beer. "Okay," she said, giving Bellamy a challenging stare, "if you don't have a problem with gays, drag queens, or pot heads, why don't you like me?"

"I like you all right," he said. "But you aren't trained to handle dangerous situations. You shouldn't be here."

She shook her head. "I'm not talking about that stuff. There's something personal going on."

Well, if she really wanted to know… "Don't you think you're a little sarcastic and a little hostile?"

She peered at him as if she was honestly surprised. "I guess maybe," she said at last. "But it's just my style. It doesn't mean anything. I'm glad we stuck together. I mean, considering what happened to Mr. Keene."

"Your piercings bother me, too," he admitted. "Don't get me wrong, I know that what you choose to do with your body is none of my business, either. But it's just something that's always creeped me out. It's like self-mutilation."

She gave him a wicked smile. "Don't knock it until you've tried it. It's supposed to be great for sex. It increases sensitivity and creates new sensations for your and your partner both."

He imagined how it might feel to kiss her, the contrast between her warm, soft flesh and the hard steel in her lower lip and tongue. He tried to push the phantom sensation out of his mind.

The doorman emerged from the table and strode back over to their table. "Marilyn is here," he said. "If you'll come with me, she'll see you now."

Abandoning his half-eaten meal with a pang of regret, Bellamy wiped his mouth with a paper napkin and stood up. Astarte carried her plate and mug with her, a decision which annoyed him. An investigator shouldn't arrive to interview an informant with food and drink in hand, and neither should the detective's unofficial assistant. It was unprofessional.

The doorman led them through the door, up two shadowy flights of stairs, and along a narrow hallway lit by two dimly glowing cut-glass fixtures designed to resemble gaslights. Judging from the ornate molding and the peeling, faded flock wallpaper, the onetime apartment building had been pretty posh in its day, but the current owner had allowed it to fall into decline. There were rat holes in the baseboards, rat droppings on the threadbare runner, and a stale, musty smell hanging in the air.

Sighs and moans whispered through the gloom. Evidently people were making love in various spots throughout the building, though some of the soft cries seemed less expressive of rapture than despair.

Bellamy's guide opened a door and said, "This is them."

"Come in," said a breathy contralto voice. "That is to say, 'Enter freely and of your own will.'" The speaker giggled.

Bellamy stepped across the threshold. The room beyond displayed the same kind of rotting elegance as the other parts of the tenement he'd seen. A grimy, flaking painting of fleshy nymphs and cherubs occupied the center of the ceiling, and a veil of cobwebs shrouded the softly glowing blue and red Tiffany floor lamp. Someone had chalked a line of cryptic blue symbols or hieroglyphics around all four walls, just above the floor. Glancing backward, the agent saw that the characters ran across the inside of the door as well, completing the circle, creating an indecipherable text with no apparent beginning or end.

On the brass bed in the center of the room lounged another drag transsexual, an angular figure in a lacy black negligee and a long platinum wig. From the wrinkles at the corners of "her" eyes and mouth, lines which heavy makeup couldn't quite disguise, she was probably in her forties. Propped up on a mound of red satin pillows, she held the mouthpiece of a hookah in one of her large, powerful-looking, red-nailed hands. The scents of hashish and sex hovered around her, and she had needle marks on the insides of her forearms.

"Marilyn Sebastian?" asked Bellamy, displaying his credentials.

"Yes," she replied. "Go on, Tony, it's all right." She waved her fingers in a languid shooing gesture. The doorman frowned as if he didn't want to leave, but then retreated down the hall.

Marilyn nodded toward a vanity, its surface covered by a jumble of cosmetics, stained tissues, paddles, vibrators, and handcuffs, and the straight-backed chair in front of it. "One of you can sit down, anyway," she said. Astarte took the seat and balanced her plate in her lap. The voice of the piano sounded through the open window, still alternately crooning and snarling as if the instrument were afflicted with Tourette's syndrome.

Bellamy told her his name. "And this is Emily Dodds."

"Astarte," his companion corrected through a mouthful of jambalaya.

Bellamy tried not to grimace. "She's not in the FBI—"

"*Really*," said Marilyn, as if she could scarcely believe it.

Bellamy felt his face grow warm. "—but she is helping me with my current investigation."

"I'll bet she is," said Marilyn with a trace of a leer. "And what might that investigation be? What brings an upright young detective and his—" she hesitated, evidently searching for the proper turn of phrase,"—plucky girl Friday into this den of sin?"

Astarte shot him a glance which seemed to say, See? It *isn't just me that thinks you look like a homophobe.*

"I spoke to a book dealer named Oscar Grace today," Bellamy said. "He told me you're one of his best customers for rare volumes pertaining to the supernatural, and that he suspects you belong to a secret society called the Arcanum."

Marilyn arched a thin, painted eyebrow. "I'm very disappointed to learn he's so talkative."

"We threatened to sic the IRS on him," Astarte explained.

"He's keeping two sets of books."

"How did you know that?" Marilyn asked.

"Instinct," Bellamy said, and he really couldn't explain it much better than that. Once in a great while, he met someone and just *sensed* what crime the stranger had committed. Of course, it helped if the guy was as jumpy as Grace had been, and kept sneaking guilty glances at the ledger sitting beside the cash register. "Was Grace right? Do you belong to the Arcanum?"

Marilyn tittered. Bellamy wondered just how stoned she was. "My goodness, darling, if it's a secret society, I wouldn't be very likely to admit it if I was, would I?"

"If you are a member," Bellamy said, "you probably knew a man named R. J. Keene. Someone killed him earlier this week, evidently because he was trying to help me solve a series of murders. If you want to see the killer brought to justice, you should cooperate with me."

Astarte set her paper plate on the vanity, knelt beside the bed, and took one of Marilyn's hands in both of hers. "Please," she said. "I've been searching for something like the Arcanum my whole life. If it's real, you've got to let me in."

Marilyn looked her in the eye, then sighed and shook her head. "You poor kid," she said, her voice dropping half an octave, "what do you think the Arcanum is?"

"A doorway," Astarte said. "The path into something wonderful."

Bellamy wondered how she could possibly say it with such conviction, with such a gleam in here eyes, after what she'd experienced in the cathedral.

"That's what I used to think, but it isn't like that," Marilyn said. "Human beings shouldn't try to shine a light into the darkness. You never like what you see."

"Then you are in the lodge," said Bellamy, just to nail it down once and for all.

Marilyn smiled. "Do I look like your image of an intrepid ghost breaker?"

"I don't care about your personal life," Bellamy said.

"I don't blame you," Marilyn said. "Some evenings, I have trouble staying interested in it myself. Lying here with one cruel young man after another, knowing that, if I had to rely on my rather faded charms, every one of them would choose to spend the hour with someone else. But they think I can work magic to help them accomplish their hopes and dreams. Some of them even think my kiss can make them immune to HIV."

Astarte stared at her. "Can it?"

Marilyn laughed, a sound like glass breaking. "My goodness, child, where are you from? Of course not."

"Then how can you play such a terrible trick on them?" Astarte asked.

"Easily," Marilyn said. She paused to take a long drag on the mouthpiece of the hookah, held the smoke in her lungs for about ten seconds, and then coughed it out. "Once upon a time, my sordid little trysts would have repulsed me. I wanted one true love to last my whole life through. But that was before I looked into the heart of the night. Now I need something more intense than romance to help me forget what I saw. When I'm lucky, my adventures in this bed do the trick, and so I'll do anything necessary to keep the cruel young men coming back.

"Besides, I'm not really hurting anyone. The whole world already has AIDS, haven't you noticed? It's rotting away, right on schedule, just like St. John the Divine warned us it would."

"Maybe not," Astarte said. "All through history, people have thought the world was about to end. They believed the prophecies in Revelation referred to events happening in their time. But so far, they've always been wrong, and you could be wrong, too."

Marilyn cocked her head. "*Touche,* little Phoenician. Perhaps you're not a credulous New Age idiot. But if one puts any stock in the occult tradition at all—and I take it you do—then one does have to accept that something like St. John's gibberish will eventually come to pass. And I see a great many signs that chaos is about to clench its mighty fist and crush us in its grip."

"This is all very interesting," Bellamy said, "but we didn't come here to talk about the Apocalypse." He smiled wryly. "Our problem isn't quite *that* big."

"Let's hope not," Marilyn murmured.

"I'm investigating the Atheist murders," Bellamy continued

doggedly. "I believe the paranormal is involved, and apparently Keene did, too. But before he could tell me why, a statue came to life, attacked us, and killed him." Despite Marilyn's avowed belief in the supernatural, the agent still winced to hear himself utter such a seemingly preposterous statement. "I'm hoping another member of the Arcanum—you—can tell me what he wanted me to know."

"And perhaps a member could," said Marilyn. "But I'm not one, not anymore. I resigned two years ago. I beat a hasty retreat from paranormal investigation after one memorable night in an old house on Conti Street."

Astarte frowned. "But you still buy occult books."

Marilyn shrugged. "Old habits—old interests—die hard."

"And you must still remember the secrets you learned," said Bellamy.

"I never discovered any real secrets," Marilyn said. "I just learned to be afraid."

Bellamy scowled. "Keene made it pretty clear that every member of the Arcanum knows *something*. Look, I just want to pick your brain. I'm not asking you to go back into the field. Why are you so reluctant to help me?"

"Keene tried, and he's dead. The dark powers don't like being gossiped about, and they have ways of finding out who's been meddling in their business."

"If you don't want to be involved," said Astarte, "we understand." Bellamy could see from her eyes that for her part, the statement was a lie. She couldn't imagine how anyone could discover a path into the supernatural and then decline to follow wherever it led. "Give us the name of somebody who still is a member of the Arcanum, and we won't bother you anymore."

Marilyn grimaced. "Just because I left the lodge, that doesn't mean I don't care about my oath. I swore I wouldn't reveal the identities of my fellow members under any circumstances, on pain of bringing a terrible curse on my head." He smiled ironically, as if to deride the notion that the Arcanum could actually muster the magical power to lay a hex on anyone.

"That's it," Bellamy said. "I've been trying to be patient with you, but enough is enough. The Atheist kills victims two and sometimes three times a week. If you can't see that that's more important than any pledge, you've got a problem. Since I'm not your friend, your pastor, or your shrink, I don't intend to try to fine tune your sense of right and wrong. Instead, I'll warn you the Federal government can be just as obnoxious as any goblin you ever saw. We've got any number of perfectly legal ways to make your life miserable until you give us what we want. With your lifestyle, you're practically begging for it."

Marilyn glanced at Astarte. "I'm not just trying to keep my word. I'm also trying to protect this young lady from the consequences of her own folly."

The girl bristled.

"I can appreciate that," said Bellamy, "but it isn't the most important consideration, and it wouldn't work anyway. If we can't find any answers in New Orleans, she'll just go looking in Lafayette." Marilyn winced. Evidently she, like Keene, regarded the town as dangerous.

"If I steer you on to the true Arcanum," said Marilyn, "to people far more knowledgeable than I, will you really leave me in peace?"

"Yes," Bellamy said.

"Well, maybe I can help you without violating the letter of my oath." A moth flew in the window and flitted around Marilyn's face. She brushed it away. "Did you notice the"—she tittered—"pardon the cliche, the writing on the walls?"

"Is it written in the Witches' Alphabet?" Astarte asked. Bellamy gathered that she was referring to some sort of occultist's cipher.

"Very good," said Marilyn, like a teacher complimenting a clever student. "Yes, it is, more or less. I wrote it shortly after I realized I intended to spend most of my evenings in this room. It serves several purposes. Theoretically, it affords me a tiny measure of protection. I suspect that, like the sex and drugs, it provides a measure of therapy. And if you examine it closely and oh so cleverly, you may find the information you need, without my having to speak it aloud."

"I can't actually read the runes," Astarte admitted. "Not without a translation chart."

"And I didn't even know what they were," Bellamy said. "Let's not play games. Just say what you know."

"Please," said Marilyn. "Try for at least a few seconds.

Give me one opportunity to feel that I haven't *entirely* betrayed my brothers."

Bellamy sighed. "All right. Where does it start?"

"Everywhere," Marilyn replied enigmatically. "Begin wherever you like."

Bellamy moved to the center of the room, the spot from which he could most easily see the entire ring of symbols. Astarte came and stood beside him.

"This is kind of cool," she whispered. Annoyed by her frivolous attitude, he scowled.

He began staring at the runes, looking for the shapes of ordinary letters hidden in them, or in the spaces between them. He couldn't imagine what else there might be to discover. At first, he turned, shuffling slowly, to examine the characters on every wall.

And then, to his surprise, the characters on one section of crumbling plaster seemed to change. Although he still couldn't read them, the curved and angular shapes seemed charged with meaning, like a distant billboard that was just about to come into focus. Fascinated, he peered even more intently than before.

The sense of imminent comprehension increased. He turned once more, and his eyes locked on a string of six symbols. Suddenly certain that they spelled out a single word, which he was on the brink of comprehending, he fixed his attention on them.

He heard Astarte gasp, though the sound seemed muffled, as if it had come from a long way off. He guessed that the symbols had changed for her as well. He considered asking her what she saw, but the impulse faded quickly. Speaking would only distract him from his own gazing.

The six runes seemed to squirm like flies in a spider's web, their tails and serifs writhing like limbs. He blinked and the characters froze once more, but only for a moment. Then they crawled to the left, like stock quotations on an electronic sign, though somehow without ever really changing their location. For a second, he felt as if he were hanging above them, about to fall.

Bellamy's excitement gave way to nausea and a dazed sense of dread. Eventually it occurred to him that perhaps he ought to look away. He was still mulling the possibility over when the six runes began to give up their secrets.

To his surprise, it wasn't like reading. A word or phrase didn't pop into his mind. Instead, he hallucinated a scene so intensely it was as if he were really there. He stood on a desolate shore, a cold, howling wind knifing into his flesh, peering across a channel at an island city like a fantastic stone wedding cake, level after level of chambers, corridors, and balconies capped by an immense castle from which rose a black tower. After contemplating the forbidding vista for several seconds, he noticed that, imposing as the cyclopean city was, it was far from the largest thing in view. The flickering thunderheads massed above it weren't actually clouds at all, or at least, not *merely* clouds. They were the heads and shoulders of mammoth demons, one with two draconic faces on a single head, one with no flesh on his skull, and some with forms so alien that it was only through intuition that Bellamy realized he was looking at sentient entities at all. Each glared down at the world below with a tangible malevolence.

The sheer vastness of the creatures was intolerable. Nothing, not even God, should appear so huge. And though common sense told Bellamy that a single human being was beneath their notice, that their loathing and loathsome gaze was actually focused on the island city, he couldn't shake the feeling they were looking directly at him. He heard himself whimper.

It's *only an illusion!* he insisted to himself. *You aren't really in this place. Close your eyes or turn your head. Break eye contact with the symbols on the wall and the vision will go away!* But he couldn't. Something, either a power in the runes or his terror of the devilish things looming over him, froze him the way the stare of a serpent paralyzed its prey.

He hated himself for that. It was just like the night of Waxman's death. Once again, the supernatural was stripping him of his courage and sense of self. But even his outrage couldn't energize him sufficiently to break the bonds that held him.

Faintly, through the wail of the phantasmal wind, he heard the voice of the piano, the soothing strains of "Moon River" disintegrating into cacophony. Then bed springs squeaked. Marilyn must have gotten up.

He realized that she was the true threat, not the giants in the vision. Yet the latter were so awesome, so much more compelling even in their unreality, that he still couldn't tear his eyes away.

A floorboard squeaked as Marilyn approached, even though the surface beneath Bellamy's feet seemed uneven, studded with pebbles he could feel through the soles of his shoes. Remembering his Browning, he strained to draw it from its holster. His arm merely trembled, the same power that kept his gaze locked on the runes afflicting it as well.

Astarte sobbed. Bellamy realized that whatever Marilyn meant to do to them, she was doing it to his companion first.

The ghastly but hypnotic vision faded and blurred a bit, and as a result, the spectacle of the colossal demons became a little less overwhelming. From the corner of his eye, he glimpsed the murky figures of Astarte and Marilyn, overlaid on the desolate landscape of the hallucination like images in a double exposure.

Exerting every bit of willpower he possessed, Bellamy wrenched himself around to face them. The giants, the island, and the beach vanished like a bursting bubble.

At the same instant, Astarte fell, sprawling against his legs and knocking him backward. He was still trying to recover his balance when Marilyn grabbed him and rammed a hypodermic needle into his neck.

20

Standing beside the Green Head and the moon-dappled river, Montrose surveyed the spectacle before him—his troops, their ranks swollen by scores of new volunteers, the hastily fashioned banners emblazoned with emblems of the Smiling Lord and the Unlidded Eye, the slave coffles, and the wagons loaded with less animate loot, drawn by still other Heretic prisoners locked in the traces—and realized that he was of two minds about it.

Montrose the Anacreon rejoiced in his triumphs and the humiliation of his enemies. But another James Graham who occasionally stirred in his memory, a young man who'd written poetry and taken up arms only when his principles demanded it, regarded the spectacle as barbarous and shameful.

The Stygian grimaced. The new Montrose was a victor. The old one had perished on the gallows. It was obvious whose perspective had more merit. He tried to thrust his qualms out of his mind.

"Something wrong?" asked Fink.

"No," Montrose replied. "I was just thinking."

The black-haired wraith grinned. "Better you than me. Too much thinking's bad for your liver."

Montrose smiled back. "The Restless don't have livers, but still, I believe you have a point. Everything seems to be in order. Let's be on our way." He turned, put his foot in his stirrup, and swung himself onto his mount, a magnificent white stallion with shining crimson eyes.

The creature was a Phantasy, a spiritual being analogous to a Skinlands horse, although, according to the more highly respected Stygian metaphysicians, not actually the ghost of an Earthly animal. Such valuable rarities were occasionally found and captured in the Tempest. Montrose's ragtag army had seized this one in their last raid.

The horse—which he'd named Alexander, after the conqueror whose exploits had inspired him as a boy—was the one piece of loot he'd insisted on keeping for himself. A Grim Rider ought to have a steed, shouldn't he? Besides, he liked to ride.

He brandished his rapier. Chanteurs shouted commands or blew flourishes on their instruments, whips cracked, and harnesses creaked. Kicking Alexander into motion, Montrose began to lead the procession on a winding route through Under-the-Hill and other ruinous sections of the city.

The Chanteurs provided martial music, effortlessly drowning out other ruffians who, bereft of musical ability but caught up in the jubilant spirit of the moment, elected to sing along. Sandmen conjured fireworks and showers of fragrant rose petals.

Whenever the parade passed a Haunt, the inhabitants watched it, often peeking warily from their lairs until Montrose's men lured them outdoors by tossing handfuls of oboli onto the sidewalks, whereupon the guerrillas pressed plundered garments, jewelry, books, boom boxes, bound thralls, and even guns into their eager hands. Afterward, many wraiths elected to march along behind the army, either in the hope of collecting further bounty or simply for the fun of it.

Periodically it was necessary to traverse a section of Natchez still belonging primarily to the Quick. Despite the thickness of the Shroud, a number of mortals sensed that something uncanny was in their midst. Some peered nervously about, some quickened their pace, and a prostitute in a red leather miniskirt and a coppery wig fainted outright. Instantly a teenager in a baseball cap scrambled out of a recessed doorway, snatched up the unconscious woman's purse, ripped the gold chains off her neck, and sprinted away down an alley.

Eventually the procession entered the principal street leading to the Hierarchy Citadel. As the raiders climbed it, they continued dispensing gifts, and their demeanor still bespoke swaggering pride and exhilaration. But, glancing backward, Montrose noticed some of them checking their weapons. He'd warned them they might meet with a hostile reception at the top of the hill.

The sprawling Citadel complex came into view. Legionnaires were hastily scrambling through the walls and trying to arrange themselves in formation in front of the entrance. As Montrose rode through the ring of frigid human torches, his Sandmen produced the most dazzling display of fireworks yet. Simultaneously the Chanteurs' song culminated in an earth-shaking fanfare. The Stygian halted Alexander on the last note. His troops stumbled to a ragged stop behind him, slightly marring the pageantry of their entrance. But it didn't bother him. His Highlanders, of whom they increasingly reminded him, hadn't known or cared how to stand at attention or march in step either.

The echoes of the fanfare died away. A final blaze of gold and crimson light flickered out, and the shadows deepened again. Montrose regarded the soldiers massed in front of the door, and they peered nervously back at him.

Finally he said, "Good evening, fellow Hierarchs. I've come to confer with your commanders."

A small figure squirmed through the front rank of Legionnaires. His face shadowed by the dangling horns of his pink and orange jester's cap, Valentine gave Montrose an enigmatic smile. "My master instructed me to invite you inside for that very purpose."

Fink, who'd marched through the city by Montrose's stirrup, looked up at him. "I wouldn't go in alone," he murmured, so softly that no eavesdropper, not even a wraith, was likely to overhear. "Make them come out here, or at least insist on taking a few bodyguards with you."

"I'd prefer to," Montrose whispered back. "But we marched up here the way we did to conjure the image of a dauntless conqueror, a hero so formidable that only a madman would defy him. If I do anything to appear fearful, I risk cracking the facade." He looked at Valentine, raised his voice, and said, "That will be fine." He swung himself down off Alexander.

"You're the boss," Fink said dubiously. "How long should we wait for you before assuming the worst?"

"An hour should tell the tale one way or the other," Montrose said. He handed his lieutenant Alexander's reins. "Keep an eye on our flanks and rear. Don't let any Legionnaires sneak down the hill and surround us."

He walked forward into the empty space between the two groups of soldiers, his new spurs jingling and his long cloak swishing around his boots. It seemed to take a long time to cover the distance. Despite himself, he couldn't help imagining the assembled Hierarchs suddenly leveling their guns and opening fire. But they didn't, and finally Valentine walked out to meet him.

"This way, my lord," said the dwarf. He waved his hand, the bells attached to his glove jingling, and the Legionnaires shifted, opening a path to the entrance. Four soldiers with shotguns fell into step behind them.

As they slipped through the door into the derelict building, Montrose thrilled to the echo of ancient anguish still jangling through the air. "We've been hearing stories about you," Valentine said.

Montrose tried to shake off the disorienting, vaguely nauseating shock of empowerment. "I thought you would," he replied, "if only because so much of our plunder has already reached the marketplace. You should have stuck with me that first night. Joined the crusade. My men are getting rich."

"Rich or killed," Valentine said. "I told you, I've got a good thing going here."

Montrose shrugged. "Whatever you say."

Valentine led him past two sentries, up a rusty wrought-iron staircase which looked as if it might collapse under the heavy tread of the living, and down a hallway toward Mrs. Duquesne's office. Beside the door stood yet another guard holding a pale, gaunt barghest on a leash. The creature growled as the Stygian and the dwarf approached. Its nostrils flared inside its gray iron muzzle.

Ignoring the bloodhound, Valentine gripped the brass

doorknob and twisted it. The door swung open. As Montrose had discovered on his previous visit, the portal existed on the deathly side of the Shroud. No artificer himself, the Scot could only imagine what sort of Arcanos magic was required to hang a Shadowlands door in a Skinlands frame.

Inside the room, sheets of Stygian iron mesh overlay the floor and walls and even covered the ceiling, a guarantee that no ghostly assassin could flit in or out by the usual method. When Montrose and Valentine entered, the guard pulled the door shut. A key clicked in the lock.

The three governors of Natchez regarded their visitor. Beneath his steel domino, Gayoso's mouth was drawn so tight he was nearly snarling. Nathan Shellabarger, the Emerald Lord's nominal lieutenant, a small man whose features were completely concealed beneath a green hood, seemed nearly as tense. He had at least managed to sit down, but his right hand kept opening and closely, clutching and plucking at the gray fabric covering his thigh. Only Mrs. Duquesne, the Beggar Lord's vicar, a thin schoolmarm of a woman with round, steel-rimmed glasses and gray hair pulled back in a severe bun, seemed completely unruffled. Ensconced behind her massive ebony desk, its surface empty except for a large black hourglass, a glazed white mask of Tragedy, and a wooden bowl containing several coins, she studied Montrose with the slightest hint of an ironic smile.

"Hello, Anacreon," she said.

"Hello," Montrose replied. "It's nice that at least two of us are courteous, don't you think? Perhaps good manners haven't vanished from the world entirely."

"We've already shown you more courtesy than you deserve," Gayoso said. "We should have ordered our troops to whip you away from our door."

"You unmasked when I came to you as something little better than a mendicant," Montrose said. He shot Mrs. Duquesne a grin. "No offense to your master intended." He switched his gaze back to Gayoso. "It seems reckless if not perverse to refuse to do as much now that I'm addressing you from a position of strength."

"For heaven's sake, both of you, show your faces," Mrs. Duquesne said testily. "This is no time for posturing. We have business to discuss."

Gayoso hesitated, then grimaced and removed his domino. Shellabarger pulled off his hood, revealing bulging faceted eyes like huge emeralds embedded in an otherwise nondescript face. Crouching in the corner nearest the door, Valentine smirked to see the two Anacreons pressured into doing something against their will.

Montrose inclined his head to them. "And good evening to *you*, gentlemen. Once again, I've come to discuss the mission which our august master the Smiling Lord entrusted to me, or rather, to all of us."

"Come with a band of cutthroats at your back," Shellabarger growled.

Montrose raised an eyebrow. "Pardon me, my lord Anacreon, but 'cutthroats' is a harsh term for valiant members of the Order of the Unlidded Eye, even if they are irregulars."

"Are you mad?" Gayoso demanded. "Do you seriously claim that those rabble are Legionnaires? I recognize some of them. You've got the worst scum from Under-the-Hill out there, Mike Fink and twenty others nearly as bad. Condemned criminals!"

"Not anymore," said Montrose. "I pardoned them."

"You can't do that!" Gayoso said. "You can't just abrogate our edicts and policies—"

"You're mistaken," Montrose said. "With the authority of the Smiling Lord behind me, I can do anything necessary to fulfill my responsibilities. Now let's talk frankly. I asked you to help me crush the Heretics operating in your bailiwick. You knew it was a legitimate request, but for your own reasons, you seized on every pretext to deny me. Evidently you assumed I'd spend the next few centuries sitting idle hoping you'd relent, or slink back to Stygia with my tail between my legs, and that either way, that would be the end of the matter.

"But it wasn't. Denied the use of your troops, I found soldiers where I could and commenced the campaign without you. In just a few days, I've destroyed several Heretic Circles and enriched the economy of Natchez by filling the markets and barracoons with new merchandise. I've made you look timid and weak by reminding the loyal Hierarchs of the province how an Anacreon is supposed to behave. It's conceivable that I could convince them to rise against you and install me in your place, and even more likely that I could prevail upon the Deathlords to depose you, now that I'm in a position to get a message to them.

"But I don't want to. Despite our rocky start, I don't bear you any ill will, nor do I have any desire to be an Earthly governor. I just want to finish my appointed task and go home to the Isle of Sorrows. And you can still help me. As effective as my mercenaries are, they'd be far more effective fighting in tandem with regular Legionnaires. And knowledgeable as my man Fink has proven to be, I have no doubt that you three have access to intelligence beyond his ken.

"So, I'll ask you one last time. Will you put your resources at my disposal as our masters bade you, or rebuff me again and suffer the consequences?"

"By the Scythe," said Gayoso, "how dare you threaten us?"

"Is it a threat to delineate the reality of your situation?" Montrose asked. "Some might regard it as a kindness."

"Let's talk about the reality of *your* situation," Shellabarger said. Montrose noticed that the man's hand had slipped inside his hip pocket, probably to grasp a small pistol, or, conceivably, some more arcane weapon. "You rashly walked into this room alone. What makes you think we'll let you walk out again?"

Montrose sighed. "Now who's dealing in vulgar threats? I came here without bodyguards, but scarcely unarmed." He opened the front of his mantle, exposing his rapier and pistol. "And at the risk of sounding immodest, I imagine I'm a better fighter than any native of this Citadel, and that my Arcanos are at least as formidable as any of yours. I'm reasonably confident that I can cut my way out of your clutches if I need to."

Gayoso sneered. "And I'm just as confident you're wrong."

"All right, for purposes of argument, let's say I am," the Scot replied. "My army is at the gate. If I don't emerge from this parley within forty-five minutes, they'll assume the worst and react accordingly."

"A band of criminals," said Mrs. Duquesne crisply, "driven by avarice. I question whether such men are capable of loyalty, and therefore, that they'd risk their necks on your behalf. I imagine they'd be just as happy to continue their plundering without you. If you don't return to them, they'll merely slink away."

Montrose suspected that was a shrewd guess, but he wasn't about to say so. "You might be surprised. I'm making them rich. That can inspire a measure of affection even in the most depraved. Moreover, they hate you people for putting prices on their heads, and they know the Citadel holds an abundance of treasure. They just might storm the place."

"Let them try," said Shellabarger, his insectile eyes glinting. "They're just muggers and gangsters. No match for real soldiers. Our men could defeat them anywhere. Crushing them on our home ground will be child's play."

"Once again," Montrose said, "you might be surprised. My fellows are the *creme de la creme* of the muggers and gangsters, as my lord Gayoso pointed out himself. Besides, you could encounter difficulties even if you win. Let's suppose that in the battle, the force controlled by one governor sustains heavy casualties, while the troops of another escape relatively unscathed. Wouldn't that upset the balance of power among the three of you? Are any of you inclined to risk it?"

"You make a convincing case," said Mrs. Duquesne, fingering the base of the hourglass. "Not that I needed convincing. As a loyal vassal of the Deathlords, I always meant to place my soldiers at your disposal, just as soon as I could work out the administrative details."

Montrose bowed. "Thank you, my lady. I humbly apologize for misconstruing your intentions."

"We don't have to do this," Gayoso said to her. "Natchez is our territory. We don't have to cede control of it to anyo—"

Mrs. Duquesne picked up the hourglass, inverted it, and set it down with a thump. Sand, barely visible through the dusky glass, began to trickle from the top chamber into the lower. Though they tried not to show it, both Gayoso and Shellabarger quailed. Montrose surmised that the hourglass was some sort of magical weapon, and that the woman in the spectacles had just cocked it.

"I'm throwing in with our guest," said Mrs. Duquesne. "I advise the two of you to do the same. Otherwise, I suppose we'll have to consider our *détente* at an end."

Scowling, Shellabarger took his hand out of his pocket, stood up, and extended it to Montrose. "I'm with you, my lord Anacreon."

"And I," said Gayoso through clenched teeth.

21

As the Sister climbed the path to the ruinous church on the bluff, doing her best to tolerate the choking stench of the paper mill in the nearby town, she realized something was wrong. She didn't hear any voices, merely the cries of birds, the sighing of the wind, and the churning of the muddy river below her. *No!* she thought. Please *don't let it have happened again.*

She often sojourned with Heretic Circles as she traveled up and down the river. Since the Sisterhood of Athena didn't proselytize on behalf of one particular faith, many of her fellow religionists didn't regard her with the same loathing they felt for missionaries of rival sects. And over the course of the last few days, working her way south toward Natchez and the Louisiana border, she'd stopped at two Heretic Haunts, only to find them silent and empty.

When the Restless fought, they didn't leave behind the same kind of mess as the Quick. The slain dissolved, their bodies devoured by the Void. No stench of blood or gun smoke hung in the air, and ghostly missiles and explosives couldn't mark the walls of a Skinlands structure. And with raw material at a premium, scavengers usually gleaned every broken arrow and spent cartridge.

Thus, the Sister hadn't found any concrete evidence that the strongholds had fallen to violence, but she couldn't think of any other explanation. Perhaps there were more of the same type of Spectre that had nearly destroyed her in Greenville, attacking Heretics up and down the river.

She wondered if there might be some still lurking in the derelict church above her.

If so, they were likely to spot her as soon as she reached the top of the rise. Since the building sat alone on the bluff, well removed from the shanties of Grand Gulf, she couldn't see any way to sneak up on it, certainly not in broad daylight.

She hesitated, weighing caution against her desire to examine the site for some clue as to what was actually going on, and then a wail of anguish sounded overhead.

If some of the Heretics were still here and in trouble, it was her sworn duty to help them. Thrusting her trepidation aside, she broke into a run. Her owl pendant bounced against her breasts.

Fleetingly grateful that wraiths didn't get winded, she scrambled onto the top of the bluff, and then heard other noises. A rapid shuffling of feet. Pieces of wood swooshing through the air and clacking together. A whack and a gasp of pain when one of the sticks slammed against flesh. Evidently two people were fighting with clubs.

The Sister ran on past a pair of sharp-smelling pine trees. Sensing her presence, a circle of bobwhites exploded up from the tall yellow grass. As she plunged through the crumbling brick wall, between two arched windows now covered with plywood, she pulled off her sunglasses. The tinted lenses, invaluable for protecting sensitive wraith eyes against the sunlight, would only hinder her inside the building.

Indeed, the musty nave, illuminated only by the light sifting through a few tiny holes in the rotting walls and ceiling, was so gloomy that a mortal would have experienced difficulty navigating around it at all. Worshipers of Odin, Thor, and the rest of the ancient Viking gods, the resident Heretics capable of exerting power across the Shroud, had painstakingly erased every bit of Christian iconography, replacing crucifixes and saints with hammers, Valkyries, miniature longships, and representations of the world tree, Yggdrasil.

In front of the altar, carved with scenes that owed more to Jack Kirby than thousand-year-old Norse art, one lanky young man stood over another, hammering his victim with a baseball bat. The fellow on the floor had curled into a ball to shield his head and the more sensitive areas of his body. His own broken cudgel, another bat, lay a few feet away from him.

The Sister knew them both, and since each was a member of the Valhalla Circle, she couldn't imagine what had brought them to this pass. "Stop it!" she cried. "He's had enough!"

Philip, the wraith on his feet, kept on swinging as if he hadn't even heard. The body of Warren, the man on the floor, began to ripple and steam. Even though the bat wasn't made of darksteel, he'd taken so much punishment that he was about to vanish from the Shadowlands into the depths of the Tempest, a transit so perilous few survived it.

The Sister sprinted forward. Unwilling to take the time to circumvent the pews, she simply ran *through* them, simultaneously marshaling her Arcanos. As soon as she felt the power rise within her, she reached out with it, grunting with effort, snatched up the spear on the altar, and whirled it at Philip, seeking not to drive the darksteel point into him but to bash him with the shaft.

The length of wood cracked him across the back of his head, staggering him, sparing Warren another blow. Plunging through one of the benches in the first row, the Sister grabbed Philip by the arm.

The contact stung her hand so badly that she nearly yanked it away again. She could feel the rage and self-loathing boiling through Philip's substance like a swarm of angry hornets.

"Your Shadow has taken control of you!" she told him. "You have to push it back down!"

Snarling, the pupils of his gray eyes seething, he tried to break her grip. She strained to keep him helplessly off-balance. He didn't manage to tear himself free, but despite her *sifu's* assurances that the grapple she was employing would neutralize any opponent, no matter how big and strong, he managed to shift the bat into his free hand and lash it at her skull.

She jerked up her arm to block. Pain stabbed through her wrist. She thrust her face so close to Philip's that an onlooker might have imagined she meant to bite him. "Fight it!" she said. "Ask Tyr to help you!" If she recalled correctly, the one-handed god was his particular patron.

He pulled the bat back for another blow, and then the

shimmering darkness vanished from his eyes. His weapon tumbled from his hand and clattered on the floor. His knees buckled as if he meant to follow it down. Awkwardly, her battered arm throbbing, she caught hold of him anew, and he slumped against her.

She hoped he wasn't going to faint. Some wraiths did when such an episode ended. "You're all right now," she said. "It's gone."

To her relief, he drew himself up, supporting his own weight, and looked wildly about. "Warren! My god! Is Warren—"

She turned Philip around until he was looking at the motionless form on the floor. "There. See, he's out cold, but he's not fading. He'll be all right, too. What unleashed your Shadow? And where is everybody else?"

Philip began to sob.

"Please," said the Sister, "tell me. If I don't understand the problem, I can't help."

The Heretic shook his head. Strands of his long, mousy brown hair slipped down his high, bony forehead. "You couldn't anyway. No one could."

"You don't know that," the missionary said. She guided him to a pew and sat him down. "Just pull yourself together, start at the beginning, and tell me the story."

He shrugged miserably. "All right. Why not? Have you heard about the priests and the Pardoners disappearing?"

She cocked her head. "No, not unless you're talking about what the Quick are calling the Atheist murders. A string of serial killings."

He irritably waved his hand. "I don't know anything about that. I'm talking about something that concerns us wraiths. I heard a rumor that over the past few weeks, in various Necropoli along the river, a few Heretic teachers and Pardoners—"

"The two sorts of counselors to whom a wraith might turn for spiritual guidance," the Sister murmured thoughtfully.

"—have vanished. Personally, I didn't think much of it. The Restless disappear for all kinds of reasons all the time.

Slavers or Spectres catch you. Oblivion grabs you and you become a doomshade yourself or fall into the Void. Or maybe you just get sick of where you are and move on, either to somewhere else in the Shadowlands or into the Tempest to look for your version of Paradise. So, I wasn't particularly worried that anything would happen to our own priest and priestess, and certainly not to our entire Circle.

"But last night, Warren and I went down into Grand Gulf to watch a couple movies and then hang around the Necropolis. About two in the morning, we heard shooting and screams coming from the temple here. When we looked in this direction, we saw the muzzle flashes of the guns. We ran back as quickly as we could." He averted his face. "But we didn't charge right back into the thick of things. We stopped a ways back and tried to scope out what was going on."

The Sister didn't understand why he was ashamed. Resting her hand lightly on his forearm, she said, "I would have done the same thing."

"What we saw," Philip said, "was that the temple was under attack by a whole bunch of people. A lot of them looked more like bandits or river pirates than any Legionnaires I ever saw, but they had banners with emblems of the Smiling Lord, the Beggar Lord, the Emerald Lord, and the Unlidded Eye on them, so I guess they must have been Hierarchs. The leader, a guy with long, wavy red hair, had a black cape and a fancy sword, like some kind of Stygian honcho."

A swordsman with a mane of auburn hair. Old joys and sorrows stirred in the Sister's breast. But of course, Philip couldn't be referring to the same person she'd known. Surely such a splendid soul had never found himself mired in the purgatory of the Underworld in the first place. Annoyed at her own sentimentality, she tried to push aside her memories and focus on the present situation.

"Warren and I could see right away that our people were losing," Philip continued. "The Hierarchs had us outnumbered and they were better armed. And so—" He faltered, then took a deep breath. "And so, we just hid and watched while the Stygians took everyone else prisoner, chained them up, marched them down to the river, and carried them away on their boats. I saw what happened to Barbara. My girlfriend. They took her clothes off and put their hands all over her. There was so much fear in her eyes!"

"Do you think you actually could have helped her?" the Sister asked. "Or would you merely have gotten killed or captured yourself? I'm sure she wouldn't have wanted that."

"You don't understand," he said. "When I joined the Circle, I swore to Tyr that I'd never back down. That I'd make myself a warrior fit to stand against Oblivion at Ragnarok. I promised myself that from then on, I was going to be a different person. But when the crunch came, I chickened out again, just like I always did when I was alive!"

"Courage doesn't mean throwing your existence or your freedom away uselessly," the Sister replied. "Moreover, people *do* change. I believe that's why we become wraiths in the first place, to refine our natures until we're worthy to Transcend. Even if you froze yesterday, you can be brave tomorrow. Simply resolve to do better. When you do, perhaps you can even free Barbara and the others."

He blinked. "Do you really think so?"

"I don't know," she admitted. "The Underworld is a bleak, cruel place, and the Hierarchy is one of the cruelest things in it. Your friends could already be on their way to Stygia. But until we know that for a fact, we mustn't abandon hope. Please, finish your story."

"There isn't much left to tell," Philip said. "After the raiders sailed away down river, Warren and I just hung around here. I guess we were too dazed to do anything else. And gradually I started to blame him for my cowardice. I told myself that if he hadn't stopped, I wouldn't have either. I would have run right out and attacked the Hierarchs. And maybe I could have taken out the redheaded guy, and that would have turned the tide. In the end I hated Warren so much that I just had to tear into him."

"Did any of the Legionnaires have two reptilian heads?" the Sister asked.

Clearly puzzled, Philip frowned. "Not that I noticed. They all looked pretty human, give or take the usual sprinkling of horns, cloven hooves, and that stuff. Why do you ask?"

As briefly as possible, she told him about the assassin who

had stalked her through Greenville.

"Do you think there's a connection?" he asked.

She grimaced. "I wish I knew. We have too many unanswered questions. Has someone truly been systematically destroying missionaries like me, Heretic leaders, and Pardoners ? If so, one would logically suspect Spectres, since wraiths of every other stripe value Pardoners, given that we all need to quell our Shadows on occasion. But now that we know the Hierarchy is raiding Heretic communities, logic *also* suggests that it's responsible for the disappearance of the priests as well. Otherwise, the synchrony of the two campaigns is too much of a coincidence."

"But why would you even bother to assassinate individual Heretic masters if you intended to destroy entire Circles at once?" Philip asked.

"It doesn't make any sense, does it? Perhaps you were right, and there's nothing to the gossip you heard. Maybe it was just the luck of the draw that made the double-headed spirit decide to hunt me. In any case, we should be glad we aren't entirely in the dark. We do understand the nature of the greatest threat facing us. For some reason, the local Hierarchs have grown militant again. It's imperative that we Heretics strike back hard enough to convince them to leave us alone. Otherwise, they'll pick off our enclaves one by one."

"But what can we do?" Philip asked. "Does the Sisterhood of Athena have an army?"

"A small one," the blond woman said, "but it won't come east of the Rockies. It has too many commitments on the West Coast."

"Then we're beaten," Philip said. "There were too many Hierarchs, and they fought too well. No Heretic Circle in the area is a match for them."

"Possibly not individually. If they unite, it could be a different story."

"It won't happen," Philip said. "They all hate each other as much or more than they hate Stygia."

"But they all want to survive," the Sister said. "And some of them don't hate me." She smiled wryly. "That's the advantage of preaching wishy-washy, nondenominational fluff. No one worries that I might lure his parishioners away. I might be able to bring a selection of the local Renegades into the coalition, too. Some of them are shrewd enough to grasp that once the Hierarchy finishes crushing Heretics, it's likely to come after them."

"But do you really think we can defeat Legionnaires?" Philip asked.

She had no idea. Perhaps no one would listen to her, or everyone who did would perish uselessly on the battle' field. But with the ease of long practice, before death and after, she concealed her doubts behind a smile. "With the Aesir's help, why not?"

22

Bewildered, Bellamy paced the frigid walkways and galleries of the dark stone city, past grotesque statuary and small, iron-bound doors sunk in odd corners of immense carved tableaux, almost as if the architect had been trying to hide the entries amid the details of the sculptures. The FBI agent's wandering took him across a narrow iron bridge, where, looking over the side, he saw level after level of chambers and corridors, sporadically lit by some of the ghastly anthropomorphic torches, falling away into darkness beneath his feet. He blundered onto a terrace, where huge towers with crenellated ramparts loomed above him.

He scurried back inside as quickly as possible. For some reason he couldn't—or didn't want to—remember, the black, starless sky with its flickering thunderheads disturbed him even more than the suffering and death manifest in many of the carvings, the soft moans whispering from the gulfs below him, or even his inability to remember how he'd come to this place.

After what seemed like hours, he climbed a staircase and found himself on a balcony connected by an arch of gray metal to a similar platform jutting from the rococo facade of the adjacent tower. On the other side of the bridge stood a slender, feminine figure in a voluminous scarlet robe. A red wooden mask concealed her features, but not the magenta streaks in her spiky hair.

"Astarte?" he asked.

She stretched out her hands as if she could neither speak nor run to him, but was beseeching him to come to her.

Even though it meant stepping out under the open sky, he

was eager to. She was the first familiar thing he'd seen since his arrival, indeed, the first *person*. With a pang of trepidation, forbidding himself to look either up or down, he strode onto the unrailed bridge. The metal surface clinked beneath his tread.

The world blazed white, and a deafening crash split the air. Dazzled, he sensed rather than saw the length of bridge in front of him shattering like glass. He dropped onto his belly and wrapped his arms around the span of metal beneath him.

From the way it was shuddering, he doubted that he'd actually done himself any good. He wasn't sure if lightning had struck the bridge itself, but it felt as if the entire structure was about to tear away from its moorings and fall into the man-made canyon below.

But it didn't, and when the vibrations subsided, he cautiously raised his head. Now separated from him by the gap in the bridge, Astarte sank to her knees in a pantomime of despair.

He felt an urge to run and jump to her. But even had he been sure he could leap far enough, either of the remaining sections of bridge might collapse at any moment, particularly if subjected to stress. As he wormed his way backward, he said, "Don't worry! I'll still get to you. There has to be another way across."

As if to make a liar out of him, lightning flared and thunder boomed again, violently shaking his perch. This time, he saw a forked bolt of glare strike the cornice of the building on the other side of the drop. The wall disintegrated, the rumble echoing the growl of the thunder. An avalanche of stone fell down the side of the structure, and Astarte and her balcony fell with it.

"No!" Bellamy screamed, and then her tiny form vanished into the gulf.

He sobbed, though strangely, his eyes remained dry. Then he realized the rumbling sound was still grinding on and on. In fact, it was growing louder, with a steady, rhythmic beat which suggested laughter. His section of broken bridge began to shudder.

After a moment he realized that it wasn't just his perch. All of the towers around him were swaying, also. The lightning strikes seemed to have triggered an earthquake.

One by one, the mighty buildings collapsed, the rubble streaming into the darkness below. Bellamy expected the broken bridge to fall at any moment. But for some reason it and the edifice to which it was attached endured while other structures crumbled, as if God wanted him to witness the devastation.

Still trying to inch backward to a safer position, ludicrous as such a concept now seemed, he *did* watch. And at first he wasn't particularly afraid. The spectacle unfolding before him was so huge and strange that it inspired wonder instead of dread.

But as the city dissolved, he began to glimpse what lay below it. The shards of stone weren't just tumbling to the ground, or even into some gigantic crevice that had opened in the earth. They were falling into a well of darkness that glittered and spun like a whirlpool. As soon as Bellamy caught sight of it, he sensed that it was the pure essence of annihilation, the primal fountainhead of cruelty and madness.

The overwhelming probability that he was doomed to drop into the vortex filled him with terror. He tried to creep backward faster, while the bridge began to creak, squeal, and shake more violently. His groping foot brushed the edge of the balcony, and then something snapped. He and his perch lurched forward—

—and he thrashed, his arms immobilized, metal clattering. After a moment, panting, his heart hammering, he realized he'd just awakened from a nightmare.

He lay on a bed in a small room, his hands shackled, quite possibly with his own handcuffs, to a post in the carved oak headboard. A figure stood over him. He had to peer for a moment to be certain it was Marilyn. Her lean body clad in a nondescript suit and narrow knit tie, her face scrubbed clean of makeup and her wig discarded, she might almost have been mistaken for a man. Only her plucked eyebrows, crimson nail polish, and the modest bulge of her breast implants betrayed her transsexuality.

"Did you have a bad dream?" she asked mildly.

He certainly had. Something about the dark city the mystic symbols had shown him. And a black whirlpool. Waxman had claimed to have seen something similar in his visions! Maybe the dream had actually meant something.

Or maybe it hadn't. Bellamy was no psychic. He'd probably dreamed about the vortex because Waxman had told him about it. And in any case, he had more immediate problems. He tried to speak and discovered that his mouth was painfully dry.

Marilyn picked up a crystal tumbler of water from the nightstand and held it to his lips. The cold liquid soothed his throat wonderfully. He was tempted to guzzle it all, but he knew too much could make him sick.

His captor took the glass away.

"Where's Astarte?" Bellamy asked.

"She's safe," said Marilyn. "She's resting comfortably in another bedroom."

"Good," Bellamy said. "Who are you really?"

"The Chancellor of the New Orleans Chapter House of the Arcanum," Marilyn said with a hint of pride.

Bellamy shook his head, trying to understand, his mind still fuzzy from the drug she'd given him. "Then the place we found you in, the story you fed us..."

"Some of what I said was true. I do frequent that establishment, and I do partake of what you might consider rather sordid pleasures there. When a person carries as much responsibility as I do, it can be an exquisite relief to feel helpless and weak. But more importantly, the bondage and humiliation are a means to an end. To perform the Great Work, an alchemist has to explore every facet of his character, psyche and shadow, animus and anima, master and slave. That's why I haven't had my final surgery yet, even though my body is ready. I think it benefits me to be hermaphroditic."

"Are you telling me you let people tie you up and spank you so you can learn magic? If so, I think you can stop now. Your Witches' Alphabet hexed the heck out of me."

Marilyn shrugged. "I can create one or two minor effects, sometimes, with hours of preparation. So could you, if you undertook the proper course of study and meditation. But my tricks are nothing compared to genuine sorcery. I once spied on a true mage through a pair of binoculars. The miracles he created, one after another, as easily as you or I could snap our fingers!"

"Maybe you should have asked him to give you a lesson."

"A number of Arcanists have tried. Some have been turned away. Some have been cursed for their presumption. And a few have disappeared, perhaps because the mage accepted them, perhaps because he killed them. Suffice it to say, even if I were given a chance to make the same request, I don't like the odds. I'd rather try to discover the wizards' techniques of empowerment independently, through study and experimentation."

"I see your point," Bellamy said, flexing his shackled arms to ease a cramp. "What I don't get is why, if you are one of Keene's colleagues, you witched me, doped me, and handcuffed me. I showed you my credentials."

"Identification can be forged. And even if you were a genuine FBI agent, what does *that* mean? What master do the Federal police serve?"

Bellamy grimaced. "I think you've been watching too many Oliver Stone movies."

"You may be right," Marilyn said. "On the other hand, it may be that all of us, the ordinary people, the uninitiated, are simply cattle, and our laws, institutions, and the dogma we've been raised to believe are the fences our owners use to keep us in our place.

"Be that as it may, I had good reason to be wary of you in particular. It seemed unlikely that a legitimate investigator would conduct his business with someone like Astarte in tow."

"I admit, I'm poking around without Bureau authorization," Bellamy said. "That's because my boss doesn't believe in the paranormal. And I just sort of wound up saddled with Astarte."

"You also told me that R. J. was killed by a statue that came to life. I have heard of such occurrences, though I've never had the good fortune to witness one. But the news media said he was killed with a gun." Marilyn picked up Bellamy's Browning from a small parquet table. "If I gave this pistol to the police for a ballistics test, I wonder what the results would show."

"That it fired the shot that killed your friend," Bellamy said. He could feel a cold sweat breaking out under his arms. "Because the statue picked it up and used it. I didn't tell you everything. I didn't see any reason to. But I can if you want."

"You already have. Shortly after you arrived, we gave you a second shot, of truth serum, and interrogated you extensively." Marilyn smiled thinly. "We Arcanists are more than a society of bookworms and theoreticians. We train ourselves to handle desperate situations as competently as Federal agents do."

Bellamy felt mingled resentment and relief. "If you questioned me under truth serum, then you know I'm on the up and up. Stop playing mind games and take off the handcuffs."

"It isn't quite that simple," Marilyn said. "I now find myself in the awkward position of having assaulted and kidnapped you."

"I'm not going to arrest you," Bellamy said. "God knows, I should, but if Astarte really is okay, and you help me catch the Atheist, I'll let you off the hook."

"But you'll know about the Arcanum. You'll know I'm a member. And you're an FBI agent. Aren't you duty-bound to report your discoveries to your superiors?"

"I know how to protect an informant," Bellamy said, "even from my bosses when I have to. Don't you want to help me nail whoever—or whatever—killed Keene?"

"I liked R. J. but he was a liability. He held the shortsighted attitude that we ought to run around protecting people and righting wrongs as if we were the police ourselves, bringing the wrath of the supernaturals down on our heads before we were remotely prepared to cope with it. You see where it got him."

"In other words, he deserved to die. And so do the rest of the Atheist's victims."

Marilyn scowled as she set the Browning back on the table. "No, of course not. You're deliberately distorting my point of view. Which is that the Arcanum has to walk softly until it can acquire enough information to make a difference for the entire human race, not just a few isolated individuals."

"If the individuals don't matter, then the whole human race doesn't either. And maybe to you, it doesn't. Maybe all you really care about is scoring some magic for yourself."

Marilyn's eyes narrowed. "You can't provoke me with insults."

"What about with logic? If you don't help me, or even let me go, what's the alternative? Are you going to hold Astarte and me prisoner forever? Or murder us? Are you that unscrupulous, and that stupid?"

"I hope it won't come to that," the Arcanist said. "We know how to use drugs for brainwashing as well as interrogation. We can expunge your memory of the Arcanum so thoroughly that no trace of it will remain, and then release you unharmed."

A ghastly picture popped into Bellamy's mind. He imagined a cop loading him into the back of a squad car again, dazed, and disoriented, with a second hole in his memory. Such a fiasco would unquestionably cost him both his career and any hope of ever catching the Atheist. At that moment, even death seemed preferable.

He struggled to think of another argument, to find a way to convince Marilyn to help him, when a scream reverberated through the building. She frowned, wheeled, and ran out the door, leaving her captive alone.

23

A man shouted, "My God!" Then something crashed. Bellamy wondered what was happening.

Whatever it was, he knew he didn't want to stay handcuffed to the bed if the disturbance was going to spill into the room, or, come to think of it, even if it wasn't. He inspected the carved post the handcuffs were looped around, and then he smiled.

The Arcanist might *think* she knew as much about security and restraint as any Fed, but she was kidding herself. The headboard looked reasonably substantial, but a strong man might be able to break it.

Bellamy rolled off the mattress. The motion brought a surge of dizziness and nausea. Silently cursing Marilyn and her drugs, he knelt on the gleaming hardwood floor with his body pressed against the side of the bed, anchoring himself as best he could. Then he gripped the post and pulled.

The wood cut into his fingers. It flexed and squeaked, but didn't break. Elsewhere in the house, something thumped. It sounded like a body falling to the floor. A pistol with a silencer coughed twice.

Bellamy tried to make his muscles loose and relaxed and then, shouting, wrenched at the wood again, attempting to exert every iota of his strength in one explosive burst, the way his unarmed combat instructor had taught him.

The post snapped at the top. He hastily fumbled the handcuff chain free, scrambled up, and swayed to another surge of vertigo. Ignoring it as best he could, he snatched a handcuff key off the little table and unlocked his restraints. He grabbed his Browning, made sure it was still loaded, jacked a round into the chamber, pivoted toward the door, and hesitated.

What was waiting beyond the threshold? A ghastly marvel like the living statue or something even worse, something so awful the mere sight of it would drive him out of his mind?

Grimacing, he told himself it didn't matter. Whatever it was, he had to deal with it before it murdered another potential informant, or wandered into Astarte's room and found her lying helpless.

Moving warily through the door, he found himself at the end of a gloomy hall, beside an upper-story window. Beyond the glass were the night sky, towering oaks, cobblestone sidewalks, and elegant houses with colonnaded facades and cornstalk fences. It looked like the Chapter House was in the Garden District.

He noticed that the palm of his left hand was bleeding. He must have cut it on a splinter when the headboard broke. He wiped it on his pants leg, then stalked on down the corridor.

The hallway led him to a curving staircase. He surmised that the noises he'd heard had echoed up from the ground floor, but everything was quiet now.

Trying to be silent, he crept down the steps, past a series of small Impressionist landscapes that looked familiar, as if he might have seen them, or other works by the same hand, in the Art Appreciation course he'd taken in college. His mouth felt dry as desert sand again.

As he neared the foot of the stairs, he caught the smells of blood and gun smoke. At first glance, the ground floor of the house seemed to be furnished with the sort of antiques one would expect in an antebellum mansion, but also with shelf after shelf of books and an assortment of strange curios. The freakishly misshapen skull of either a man or some other primate. A desiccated coffin lying on trestles. An alabaster statue of a kneeling witch kissing a goat-headed Satan on the rump.

Alighting in the foyer, Bellamy saw an Asian woman sprawled motionless just inside a doorway to his right. She had a bloody dent in her scalp and a spike of broken bone protruding from her twisted arm, and she wasn't breathing. Resisting the temptation to flee through the front door while he had the chance, he stepped over her and skulked on.

Hideous faces leered from the shadows. His heart jolting, he pivoted and pointed his gun before he realized that he'd merely glimpsed another macabre piece of art. In the course of the next two minutes he found two more Arcanists, one unconscious, his left eye gouged from its socket, and the other dead. Then he heard a contralto voice chanting in Latin.

Following the sound, he peeked through a doorway. On the other side was a spacious room furnished with desks and leather armchairs, evidently the heart of the library that had spilled out into the rest of the house. Row after row of books covered the walls from floor to ceiling, suffusing the air with the musty scents of old paper and crumbling leather.

Marilyn stood at the far end of the chamber, brandishing a crucifix with the coils of a snake rather than the body of Jesus draped around the cross. She was the one doing the chanting. A stocky, gray-haired man in the center of the room was doing his best to approach her. From the hunch of his shoulders and his laborious, lurching movements, Bellamy understood that he was having to force his way forward, as if the air around him had thickened to the consistency of mud. Presumably the artifact in Marilyn's grip was responsible.

Despite the uncanny aspects of the situation, Bellamy felt a pang of relief, because Marilyn's assailant was a human being. Obviously a formidable one, but not some horror that would freeze him in his tracks. He was going to be all right.

Suddenly the crucifix shattered, and Marilyn reeled backward. Released from his invisible bonds, her attacker scrambled after her. Bellamy lunged through the doorway, leveled his automatic, and shouted, "Stop or I'll shoot!"

The gray-haired man spun around, and Bellamy gasped. Because judging from the bloody holes, someone had *already* shot the intruder, once in the center of the chest and once in the forehead, and it didn't appear to have slowed him down at all. *There should have been exit wounds,* the agent thought uselessly. *That would have given me a little warning.*

The stranger charged. *Shoot!* Bellamy told himself. For a

moment, he didn't think he'd be able to, fearing that shock had severed the link between his will and his body; but finally his finger started squeezing the trigger.

The bullets staggered the gray-haired man, but he wouldn't fall down. Snarling, hands outstretched, he made a grab for Bellamy's throat.

Bellamy sidestepped and swept his arm in a block, but he wasn't quite fast or strong enough. His attacker missed his neck, but managed to grasp his shoulder and pull him backward.

Bellamy's spine slammed against the door frame. The gun nearly tumbled from his hand. Clutching frantically, he managed to keep his grip on it.

Using only his right hand, the gray-haired man grabbed him by the throat and jerked him into the air, a jolt that nearly snapped his spine. He began to strangle Bellamy.

Bellamy tried to swing the Browning into position for another shot. With his free hand, the gray-haired man struggled to immobilize the gun. Bellamy supposed that that was encouraging in its way, in that it implied the murderer *was* susceptible to gunfire. It was just that no one had shot him *enough* yet.

A roaring filled Bellamy's ears, and dark spots swam at the corners of his vision. He was only seconds from blacking out. Straining, he managed to force the pistol another inch toward the gray-haired man's torso. He couldn't tell if it was actually in line to hit the target, but he knew it was as close as it was going to get. He fired three shots, emptying the magazine.

The gray-headed man's mouth fell open. Then, to Bellamy's surprise, the slack-jawed expression of astonishment gave way not to a grimace of anguish or another snarl of rage, but to a smile. The agent had the feeling that he was looking into the face of a completely different person, someone who was *grateful* he'd been shot.

The gray-haired man collapsed, dragging Bellamy to the floor with him. Still choking, Bellamy scrabbled at the fingers constricting his throat. Finally, he managed to tear them away. He slumped on the floor, shivering and gasping.

Rapid footsteps pattered across the floor. Bellamy jerked his head up. Marilyn was running toward him with a knotted blue cord in her red-nailed hands.

It took Bellamy a moment to remember that she was a potential threat as well. And he was still too winded to wrestle with her. Hoping she didn't know it was empty, he raised the Browning. His hand trembled as if he were ninety years old.

Marilyn skidded to a halt. "It's all right. I want to bind *him*. This particular rope should hold him."

"He's dead," Bellamy croaked. He realized that he'd never killed anyone before, not unless you counted the statue. He wondered if he'd feel terrible once he'd had a chance to think about it. "Where were you when I needed you?"

"When the Cross of Hermes broke, there was a sort of backlash," Marilyn said defensively. "It stunned me. I came running as soon as I recovered my senses. Now please, let me tie him. You can't be certain he's dead, or that death will stop him if he is."

Bellamy supposed she had a point. He shifted himself away from what at least seemed to be a lifeless corpse. Marilyn knelt, rolled it on its stomach, and hog-tied it.

The agent wished that his heart would stop hammering, and that he could catch his breath. "At least one of the people who got attacked is hurt but still alive. He needs help right away."

"We have a doctor on retainer," said Marilyn. She reached inside her jacket and brought out a cellular phone.

"I think you should get an ambulance."

Marilyn shook her head. "The Arcanum is a secret fellowship. We can't afford to let the authorities know about this mess. Besides which, at the moment you're more or less operating outside the law yourself. Do *you* want to talk to the police?"

Not without a pang of guilt, Bellamy silently conceded she had a point.

"Our man is very good," Marilyn continued. She dialed, spoke tersely to the physician, and hung up. "He'll be right over. I just hope the neighbors didn't hear the shooting. You wouldn't think it to look at the old place, but we had a contractor install state-of-the-art soundproofing."

Bellamy dragged himself to his feet. "I know first aid," he

said, his voice still a rasp and his throat still aching. "I'll try to help your friend until the doctor gets here. *If* I can trust you not to jump me while I work."

"You can," Marilyn said. They began to retrace their steps through the enormous house. Lightheaded, Bellamy could have sworn that a sphinx in a painting winked at him.

"What happened here?" the agent asked.

Marilyn shrugged. "I didn't see the start of it, either. I was upstairs with you. But apparently the intruder somehow broke into the house and attacked everyone he encountered."

"How could he get hurt as badly as he was and still keep coming for us? What was he?"

A dead body appeared in the gloom ahead. Marilyn flinched. Perhaps she cared more deeply about her fellow Arcanists than Bellamy would have suspected. "He was supernatural," she said, her cool tone betraying nothing of her dismay. "Otherwise, the Cross of Hermes wouldn't have affected him. I can't be sure of any more than that, but I do have a theory. When statues and similar objects come to life, it's because a spirit has decided to inhabit them. It's also possible for a discarnate entity to possess a living human or animal body, and such beings can remain active in the face of damage that would incapacitate a wholly natural creature. That's because they don't feel the pain to the same degree that you or I would."

"I wonder if he was the Atheist." Bellamy scowled. "No. No, I don't. Maybe he committed some of the murders, but even if he did, my instincts tell me that he was only one small part of whatever it is that's going on."

"So do mine," Marilyn said.

They stepped into the next room and the body of the Arcanist with the missing eye came into view. Bellamy crouched and pressed his fingertips lightly against the side of the occultist's neck. The injured man's skin was clammy and his pulse was fluttery, but at least he still had one. "Get something to cover him up, and something we can use to prop his feet up."

Marilyn pulled an afghan off a sofa and draped it over her unconscious colleague. "This is my fault," she said. "I should never have brought you here. Paranormal creatures have arcane means of locating people they want to find. I should have anticipated that your enemies might track you."

"Maybe they did," Bellamy said. The wounded man had a blue handkerchief in his breast pocket. Bellamy removed it and packed one end in the Arcanist's ravaged eye socket in an effort to stop the bleeding. Despite his training and experience, the operation made him feel queasy. "On the other hand, they might not even have realized I was here. Maybe they decided to hit you for the same reason they apparently decided to kill Waxman, just to make absolutely sure the Arcanum wouldn't interfere in their plans."

Marilyn hoisted the injured man's feet onto an ottoman. "But except for R.]., none of us intended to meddle in their business."

"They may not have understood that," Bellamy said. "Or they may have figured that you guys were some of the very few people who might eventually catch on to what they're up to, and that if you did, you would feel obliged to get involved. Anyway, considering what's happened, you have to assume you're targets, which means you'd better clear out of this place for the duration."

Marilyn grimaced. "Yes. I thought we had the house sealed with magical wards, but evidently they don't work. But dear Lord! All the artifacts and books, unprotected! They could set the building on fire!"

"If they do, it'll be better if it burns without you inside it."

The transsexual sighed. "I can't argue with that. I suppose everyone should leave his home as well. Given that the Atheist located our headquarters, it's conceivable that he knows the identity of every member of the Chapter. Damn it!"

"Are you going to help me now?" Bellamy asked.

"What choice do we have?" Marilyn replied bitterly. "But we could still erase Astarte's memory and send her on her way."

Bellamy hesitated. The brainwashing would probably remove the girl from danger. But as he knew all too well, it was horrible to have something punch a hole in your mind. Much as she sometimes annoyed him, he could never subject her to such a violation.

"No," he said. "Now that she's come this far, maybe she's earned the right to go the distance."

24

Kevin Bolan awoke hot and sweaty, his nerves jangling with tension—the residue, he assumed, of some forgotten nightmare—and the bedclothes tangled. Beside him, his plump, curly-headed wife Dora slept on, a soft snore buzzing from her open mouth.

Bolan looked at the glowing face of the digital clock radio on the nightstand. It was almost seven. Time to rise and shine, and even though he felt as if he'd barely slept at all, he did his best to feel cheerful about it. A minister ought to be happy to get up Sunday morning.

Trying not to wake Dora, he stood up and shuffled into the bathroom. After urinating, he stepped in front of the sink. He was reaching to open the medicine cabinet when the image in the mirror caught his eye.

At first it was just a peculiar shape, as if his brain refused to interpret it. Then it snapped into focus. A misshapen head with two reptilian faces leering side by side, each with a fanged, scaly set of jaws, a pale forked tongue, and a pair of luminous amber eyes.

He squealed and stumbled backward into the doorway. His heel caught on the edge of the bedroom carpet and he tumbled onto his butt.

Dora bolted upright in bed. "What's wrong?" she cried.

"The mirror—" Bolan began, and then rapid footsteps pounded up the stairs. The minister yelped again before he realized that he must be hearing his bodyguard, rushing to his aid.

Clad in camouflage fatigues and combat boots, his CAR 15

assault rifle leveled, the red-faced, barrel-chested form of Glen McGinty burst through the door. "What is it?" he said.

Bolan belatedly realized that he couldn't really have seen what he thought he'd seen. Though his heart was still racing, his fear began to give way to embarrassment. "I'm sorry," he said. "I looked in the mirror, and I thought the face looking back wasn't mine. I guess I was still half asleep. Still dreaming."

"Good grief," Dora said, grimacing. She grabbed a handful of covers and pulled them up to her chin, shielding her heavy breasts with their prominent nipples, inadequately concealed by her thin cotton nightgown, from McGinty's gaze.

Even though Bolan approved of her modesty, he thought that in this instance, she almost needn't have bothered. McGinty was too caught up in his role of protector to cast a lustful eye in her direction. Stepping over the minister's legs, he stalked into the lavatory as if the Atheist actually might be lurking in the mirror. He peered suspiciously this way and that, whisked the shower curtain open, and finally, almost grudgingly announced, "All clear."

"Thank you," said Bolan, clambering to his feet. "I really *am* sorry to have made you race up here."

"All part of the job," said McGinty in his manliest tone of voice. "I'll be downstairs if you need me." He ambled out the door and closed it behind him.

"How much longer are you going to keep those people around?" Dora asked.

"Until the Atheist is arrested," Bolan said. "I'm sure the police will get him soon." He felt a twinge of guilt, because the second statement was a lie. Since he'd begun to fret about the murders, he'd read up on the subject of serial killers. Some of them operated for years without getting caught. Some were never apprehended.

"What do you think the odds are of the Atheist actually coming after you?" Dora asked.

"Probably slim," Bolan said, pulling off his striped pajama shirt. As always, he felt a pang of disgust at the ring of flab around his middle. "But for some reason, I can't stop thinking about the possibility. Call me timid, but that's the way it is. If

Glen and the other members of the militia want to guard me, and that makes me feel safer, what's the harm?"

"The harm is that we don't have any privacy," Dora said. "I hope you understand that I am not going to have relations with you as long as there's a chance someone might overhear. Besides, you've said yourself that the Tennessee Patriots' League are a bunch of gun-crazy yahoos. Have you talked to any of them about the Atheist? They think he's a secret agent working for the Trilateral Commission and the International Masonic Conspiracy."

"They may be eccentric," Bolan said, "but they're still my parishioners, and they're giving up their free time to help me. Please, can't you put up with them for at least a few more days?"

"Can't you try putting your trust in the Lord?" she replied, but then her expression softened. "Oh, all right. If it makes you feel better. Do you feel all right now? Did you hurt yourself when you fell?"

"I'm fine," he said. "Thanks for being so understanding."

She got out of bed and pulled on her quilted housecoat and fuzzy Chip 'N Dale slippers, souvenirs of a Disney World vacation two years ago. Then, to his surprise, she came to him, put her arms around him, and gave him a long kiss. "You really don't need bodyguards," she murmured. "I love you too much to let anything happen to you."

He felt a surge of desire and slid his hand onto her bottom, but she squirmed out of his embrace.

"I told you, no," she said, a hint of mischief in her dark brown eyes. "Not until we're completely alone. Besides, we don't have time. Get ready for work and I'll go start breakfast." She turned and exited the room.

Bolan sighed and reentered the bathroom, flinching reflexively as he glimpsed the mirror. But nothing peered back at him, nothing but his own round face, pale blue eyes slightly bloodshot and chin gray with stubble.

He brushed his teeth, shaved, and showered. The drumming water refreshed him and gave him hope that he might actually enjoy the rest of the day. As he dressed, the sizzle and aroma of frying bacon wafted up the stairs. His stomach growled.

He looked at his rickety tie rack, a gift from a parishioner with a distinctly limited aptitude for woodwork, and decided on the teal silk one. But as he reached for it, he faltered.

Or rather, his arm did. Nothing had distracted Bolan himself from his intent, but the limb simply froze in mid-extension, as if it had a will of its own. Numbness flowed from his fingertips down to his elbow.

Bewildered, he tried again to lift the tie off its peg. Instead of obeying, his hand closed, opened, made a tight fist, and opened once more. It snapped its fingers. Then, when the minister had forgotten all about the tie, it finally picked it up.

Bolan imagined his right hand flipping the neckwear around with uncanny dexterity, tying it into a noose, then tossing it over his head and choking him. He grabbed its wrist with his left hand, the still obedient one, and at that instant the numbness tingled away. His right arm shuddered, and the blue tie fell to the floor.

The minister gingerly flexed the fingers of his rebellious hand. It felt like *his* flesh once again, as much a part of his body as ever.

I'm too tired, Bolan thought. Dora's right, I've got to get over this morbid fear of the Atheist before I have a breakdown. I don't know why I'm so paranoid. I've never had these problems before.

He started to pick up the fallen tie, then, with a quiver of aversion, left it on the floor. He selected a red one instead, then headed downstairs.

He found McGinty and Dora in the kitchen. The self-styled militiaman was seated at the table spreading orange marmalade on a piece of toast, and she was scrambling eggs at the stove. "Perfect timing," she said. "Everything will be ready in a second."

"Great," he said, trying to shake off the rest of his anxiety. He sat down, reached for some toast, and his arm went numb and locked up on him again.

This isn't happening, he told himself. *It's all in your head.* Exerting every iota of his willpower, he strained to grasp the bread. His hand wouldn't budge. He made a tiny whimpering sound.

McGinty gave him a questioning look.

Dora turned around. "What is it?" she asked.

Bolan wanted to say, I *think I'm sick. I need to go to the hospital.* But as he opened his mouth to speak, the numbness shot all the way up his arm and into his head. To his horror, he heard himself say, "I'm all right. I just grunted because my elbow gave me a twinge. I guess I bumped it when I fell."

He tried to shout, *No, no, that's not what I meant to say!* But the words wouldn't come out. He felt as if he were a puppet and the numbness, the hand of the puppeteer, was controlling his mouth.

The dead feeling tingled through his entire body, and as his sense of touch faded, another mode of perception seemed to sharpen in compensation. Suddenly he felt the presence of another consciousness clinging to his own like a lamprey feeding on a fish.

This is demonic possession, Bolan thought, awestruck. He realized that even though its existence was an article of faith in his fundamentalist sect, he'd never truly believed in it until now.

The spirit squirmed Bolan's shoulders as if his hijacked body were a garment in which it was trying to get comfortable. Then it began to peer about the kitchen.

Bolan discovered that he could catch an echo of its thoughts. The forks and butter knives were too puny to bother with, and McGinty's rifle was leaning in the opposite corner, out of reach. But there must be some suitable weapon at hand.

No! Bolan thought. I won't *let you hurt them!*

To his surprise, the demon answered him. Though it was speaking silently, in thought alone, as he was, somehow its words still seemed cold and sibilant. *You can't stop me, mortal. I'm the presence you've been sensing. I have spent weeks Skinriding you, preparing for this moment. Now it's your turn to go where I lead.*

Bolan strained to close his hands into fists. To regain control. His fingers didn't even twitch. *Jesus, please help me!* he prayed.

Nothing can help you, the devil replied. *Stop fighting me and enjoy the bloodshed. You can if you try.*

Bolan felt the demon's attention fix on the silvery coffee pot. Two reptilian faces sneered from the curved reflective surface. The spirit took hold of the handle, hefted the pot experimentally, and then stood up.

McGinty looked up at his pastor, or the creature he still believed to be his pastor, with an expression of mild curiosity on his square, weather-beaten face. The demon smiled, swung the pot over Bolan's head, flinging coffee behind him, and then smashed the container down on the bodyguard's skull.

Bone crunched. The shock of impact jolted Bolan's arm, and hot coffee sloshed from the pot to burn his hand. He could feel the pain even through the numbness, but the devil didn't seem to mind it.

McGinty made a choking sound and fell out of his chair. The demon stamped thrice on his skull, mashing it out of shape, and then turned toward Dora.

She was still standing beside the stove. Her face was gray, her eyes so wide that Bolan could see white all the way around the irises, and her mouth hung open. *Don't just stare!* the minister begged her. *Run!* But of course she couldn't hear him, and she didn't move.

"All right, now we're alone," the spirit said. "Are you happy?"

Dora's mouth worked, but no sound came out.

"There's no pleasing some people," the demon said. The coffee pot upraised, he started toward her. Once again, Bolan struggled desperately to reassert mastery of his body, without hindering the spirit in the slightest.

For a moment it looked as if Dora still wouldn't move. Then she snatched up the cast-iron frying pan in both hands and swung it at her attacker's head, spattering eggs and hot grease.

Perhaps her sudden move caught the devil by surprise, because it didn't quite manage to block. The black skillet bonged against Bolan's temple, bringing another jab of pain. Everything went dark. Vaguely he felt his knees buckling, and the coffee pot slipping from his fingers. *Yes!* he rejoiced. Pass *out, you horrible thing!*

But then the world swam back into visibility. The demon lurched upright, wrenched the pan out of Dora's hand, and grabbed her by the throat. It shoved her down on top of the stove and began to choke her.

She thrashed madly, clawing at its hands and forearms, but couldn't break its grip. Flames licked along her torso as the burner set her housecoat ablaze. Before long the fire reached her throat and head, but the searing heat didn't make the spirit let go of her, either. A stink of burning hair and meat filled the air.

Finally, Dora stopped struggling. The devil slapped out the flames on Bolan's sleeves and then flexed his black and red hands, evidently making sure they were still functional. Tears flowed down the minister's face, and the demon wiped them away. Don't *whine, it* said. *You know very well that there were times when you wanted to kill her. I've fulfilled one of your fantasies.*

Why! Bolan wailed. Why *are you doing this?* He had the mad feeling that if he could convince the devil it had made a mistake, then Dora would be alive again.

To *settle an old score,* the spirit answered. *This morning's sacrifice is just one tiny part of a scheme that encompasses the Atheist murders and much more. We should both feel proud to be part of something so grand.* The creature retrieved the CAR 15 and then opened the back door. Outside, the dewy grass, the slender white steeple of the Third Baptist Church of Memphis, and the red roof of the Youth Fellowship building shone in the early morning sunlight.

Please, *God,* Bolan prayed, let *this end. Destroy this monster, even if it means killing me with it.*

Do you think we should begin with the church or the Sunday school? the spirit asked, examining the gun. I think, the children.

25

His rapier in one hand and a pistol in the other, Montrose prowled the muddy alley at the head of a ten-man patrol, looking for any Heretics who'd escaped the battlefield. Elsewhere in the Friar's Point Haunt, other irregulars and Legionnaires crowed whenever they ferreted a fugitive out of hiding, momentarily drowning out the hiss of the Nihils riddling the row of crumbling shanties on the Stygian's left.

Abruptly Montrose heard something shift in the shadows under the eaves of a nearby hovel. He peered, but saw nothing that might have made the noise. Perhaps one of the religionists was a Harbinger, with a Harbinger's ability to veil himself in shadow. Invoking his powers of flight, the Scot hurtled toward the shack. As he landed, he aimed his blade at the spot where he judged the Heretic to be.

The form of a small man with a gaping white cut in his forehead shimmered into view. He cringed against the wall. Montrose waited until he saw hope dawn in the other wraith's face, hope that the Stygian didn't mean to destroy him on the spot. Then, lunging, he thrust his blade into the Heretic's breast.

Pulsations of darkness swept through the religionist's body. He toppled, but vanished before his body hit the ground.

Grinning, Montrose pivoted back toward his men. Murderous ruffians though they were, they seemed to be eyeing him askance, and their wariness took the edge off his glee.

"What's wrong?" he asked.

The men looked at one another as if silently agreeing upon a spokesman. Eventually a Masquer, her translucent body shining with a golden inner glow, said, "I thought the idea was to take them alive when we can. Otherwise, there's nothing to sell."

Montrose blinked. "Yes. You're right, of course. I guess that in the heat of battle, we can all become overexcited."

"Do you want to go back to the command post? We can handle the mopping up."

Montrose scowled. "No, of course not. I'm fine. Come on." He stalked on down the alley and the guerrillas fell in behind him.

For a few paces, he wondered if something might actually be wrong with him. The Soulshaper was correct, they were supposed to be taking captives, and it was unsettling that he'd forgotten it. And though he'd worked hard to become as ruthless as the intrigues of the Stygian court required, he didn't ordinarily revel in needless slaughter.

But gradually his exhilaration seeped back and washed his misgivings away. The fugitive had been a Heretic, hadn't he? An enemy to all creation. As foul a thing as his own treacherous Louise. How could anyone feel remorse over slaying an such abomination? It was remarkable that Montrose and his army managed to contain their loathing sufficiently to drag *any* of the bastards to the barracoons.

A hulking cutthroat in a bottle-green top hat and cutaway coat stuck his head through the side of a shanty, checking the interior. When he pulled it out again, he said, "I don't see anything. But I *feel* them. Somebody's in there somewhere."

"Then I suppose we'd better search it," Montrose said. He glided through the wall, and the rest of the patrol followed. It only took a moment to find the trapdoor set in the rotting floorboards.

Montrose knelt and thrust his face through the hatch. The earthen cellar below it was dimly lit by the greenish glow shining up a set of plank stairs. The cool air smelled of vegetables gone rotten.

It would be tricky to slip one's body through the substance of the trapdoor, yet avoid plummeting through the steps as well. Grunting, Montrose shifted himself across the Shroud, gripped the edges of the door with his fingertips, and pulled. For a moment the warped, swollen wood resisted him, but then it jerked upward. The Scot surrendered to the pull of the Shadowlands, and his soldiers reappeared around him.

"Let's go," Montrose said. He charged down the steps with the guerrillas behind him.

The root cellar was lined with crudely built shelves. The sickly light of a single barrow-flame candle gleamed on row after row of dusty mason jars. In the corner stood four children, three boys and a girl, with a small, darkhaired woman behind them.

Startled, Montrose froze. Because even though he knew better, for an instant, in the dim light, the young wraiths resembled John, James, Robert, and Jean, his long-lost children, and the ghost behind them, their mother Magdalen, whom he'd loved deeply until his penchant for dangerous politics had driven them apart.

The tallest boy pointed a pepperbox pistol at Montrose's chest. His mother, if that was who she was, grabbed his arm and jerked the gun out of line. "No, Davy!" she cried. "There are too many of them. We can't fight them."

"Bind them," said Montrose to his troops. They hurried forward to obey.

The ruffians seemed to delight in handling both the woman and the children as roughly as possible. They slapped them, fondled them, and snarled threats and obscene endearments in their ears. The boys struggled frantically, while the little girl began to sob.

Montrose watched the proceedings with growing distaste. He searched for the delicious cruelty he'd enjoyed only moments before, but for the time being, it seemed to have abandoned him.

He reminded himself that the prisoners weren't *his* children. Indeed, judging from their homespun clothing, they were probably more than a hundred years old, not youngsters at all in any rational sense.

Yet with their piping voices and coltish frames, with the girl's terrified weeping and the boys' desperate defiance, they *seemed* like children. And in point of fact, Montrose had noticed that many wraiths who died before reaching adulthood retained childlike personalities forever after, no matter how many decades or even centuries of existence they experienced.

He wished he could turn away, but he knew he shouldn't. He mustn't look weak in front of the men.

The black-haired woman stared at him beseechingly. "We haven't hurt anyone," she said. "Why are you doing this?"

Because my *master ordered me to,* Montrose thought. *For sport. For revenge.* All three answers made him uncomfortable. "Because you're Heretics," he said aloud. "The agents of Oblivion."

"No!" the woman said. "Perhaps some Heretics do worship the devil, but we hate him as much as you Stygians do! Our beliefs are in the Bible, and that book over there!" With her hands already bound, she couldn't point, but she jerked her head at a dilapidated workbench in the corner, and the slim volume, bound in white leather, lying atop it.

"Thank you for calling it to my attention," said Montrose. "I wouldn't want to leave subversive literature lying around to corrupt the innocent. Perhaps the artificers can melt it down and make something useful." He shifted his gaze to two of the irregulars. "Take them to the stockade and then rejoin the search."

"You got it," said the taller of the pair. He shoved the woman and the younger boy toward the steps.

The little girl wailed. The woman cried, "I beg you! Do anything you want to me, but let the children go!" She kept pleading all the way up the stairs.

Montrose supposed that he really should confiscate the book. He walked to the workbench. When he saw the gold letters embossed on the cover, he faltered, and then, his hands trembling ever so slightly, picked up the volume and started leafing through it.

It was the old Prayer Book of the Scottish Kirk, in defense of which he and his fellow Calvinists had formed the Covenant and defied the Crown. The text had set him on the twisting path which eventually led him to fight for the murdered King and his faithless son, and finally put Montrose himself on the gallows.

He didn't know what to feel. Or rather, he felt too many things at the same time, contradictory emotions which ground together inside him. He hated the Prayer Book. How could he not, when it had prompted him to waste his life? Yet simultaneously, he remembered the reverence with which he'd once regarded it, and the knowledge that he was persecuting women and children for embracing its teachings sickened him.

The Masquer with the luminous flesh cleared her throat. "Are you okay?" she asked diffidently.

"Yes," Montrose said, "but you know, you were right. You don't need me for this, and there are matters I ought to take up with Fink. I'm going back to camp. You report to me when you finish."

"Will do," the Masquer said. Montrose got the distinct impression that she and her companions would be glad to be rid of him.

The Stygian headed back toward the edge of the Haunt. Soon he heard the sounds of his temporary headquarters, the drone of dozens of conversations, the clink of manacles, and the cracking of whips. Fink stood loitering at the edge of the weedy vacant lot into which the men were herding the captured Heretics.

"Hello, again," boomed the former pirate. "Considering the haul we made tonight, you don't look very chipper."

Uncertain that he actually wanted to confide in Fink, Montrose hesitated, but then the words started slipping out. "I suppose I'm in an odd mood. I'm wondering if there's a point to what we're doing."

Fink grinned. "If you don't see the point of getting rich, then Stygians are even odder than people say."

"I do see it," Montrose said. "I must, mustn't I, since I fought so hard to win a place at the Smiling Lord's right hand. But a philosopher once told me that the wealthiest, most powerful wraith is poorer than the neediest mortal pauper, and sometimes I think he was right. No matter how many trinkets we amass, there's a cold, barren quality to our existences that can never be dispelled. That's obvious here in the Shadowlands, where the Shroud makes the whole world ugly, but one can feel the bleakness even amid the splendors of the Onyx Tower."

Fink snorted. "You're right, you *are.* in a sour mood. If you've lost interest in money and power, can't you still be happy that you're making yourself useful? How many times have I heard you say that by persecuting the Heretics, we're protecting all creation from Oblivion?"

"And I suppose I still believe that. But what if I'm mistaken? What if that notion is just an excuse to justify our brutality?"

"Who cares?" Fink replied, casually loosening his pistol in its holster. "Your problem is that you think you *need* an excuse."

Montrose cocked his head. "I beg your pardon?"

"The way I see it," said Fink, "nothing means anything. Love, morals, patriotism, religion, the crusade to hold back the Spectres—it's all a crock, or at least nobody can prove it isn't. We only know one thing for certain. Ghosts who hang on to their emotions survive, and the ones who lose them fade away. So, you do whatever it takes to make you feel like you're still alive."

"Even if it means hurting people who don't deserve it."

"Isn't that how you got to be an Anacreon?"

Montrose smiled wryly. "One could certainly make a case that most of the rivals I stabbed in the back *did* deserve their comeuppance. One could also argue that they didn't deserve it any more than I did. Don't worry, Mike, I'm not turning milksop on you. But if we stop caring about right and wrong, aren't we virtually surrendering to our Shadows?"

"I don't believe in Shadows," Fink replied, "or anyway, I don't believe in mine. As far as I'm concerned, Shadow is just a word people use for the part of themselves they're afraid of. I'm not afraid of anything. But if you are, maybe you should do something about it."

"What do you mean?" Montrose asked.

"It seems like the more Heretics we hunt down, the more you enjoy making them suffer." Fink leered. "You're turning mean, like me. Which would be fine if you *were* me, or one of the other cutthroats in our happy crew, but it doesn't look natural on you. It could be that your Shadow's getting too much of a hold on you."

"You're suggesting I consult a Pardoner. I have to admit, it might not be a bad idea."

"The Three Stooges must have one or two confessors hanging around the Citadel."

"I'm not going to bare my soul to a man who might turn around and repeat what I said to Gayoso," Montrose said. "I'll go to someone in Under-the-Hill."

Fink nodded. "I suppose you can."

Montrose raised an eyebrow. "Is there any doubt?"

"There don't seem to be as many around as there used to be. I guess they moved on to other Necropoli."

Valentine had said the wraiths of Natchez were turning surly and violent. Perhaps the shortage of Pardoners was to blame. For a moment Montrose felt a pang of disquiet, as if he'd glimpsed one aspect of some grand and sinister design, perhaps even the menace Katrina the Ferryman had warned him of.

Then, grimacing, he thrust his misgivings aside. No doubt, as Fink had suggested, it was simply Natchez's bad luck that most of the local pardoners had decided to relocate at approximately the same time. And even if it wasn't, the spiritual health of the province wasn't Montrose's problem. He just wanted to finish crushing the Heretics and go home.

"I'm sure I can find someone suitable," he said.

26

Gayoso closed his office door, snapped his fingers to light the three stubby tapers in the candelabrum, and whispered the word which activated the invisible wards set about the walls. Supposedly the magical glyphs would keep out any intruder. Scowling, the Anacreon wished they could block the cheering and martial music which echoed through the Citadel as well. Evidently Montrose had won another victory, and was parading another coffle of captives through the streets, thus reaffirming his status as the hero of the hour. As far as Gayoso could tell, most of his subjects didn't even resent the fact that the Stygian had begun to withhold a portion of his loot, animate and otherwise, for shipment to the Isle of Sorrows.

Unmasking, Gayoso sat down behind his desk. Mustering his courage or setting aside his better judgment, he wasn't sure which, he reached through the front panel of the bottom drawer and brought out a tarnished silver hand mirror. He hesitated, and then looked into the glass.

At first, he saw only his own reflection. But gradually the image changed, though he would have been hard pressed to say exactly how, until finally it grinned when he did not. The mirror turned icy cold in his hand. "Hello," the reflection said. "It's been a while." The voice was Gayoso's own, but slightly tinny, as if passing through the glass distorted it.

Since he'd acquired the mirror nearly a decade ago, Gayoso had had ample opportunity to grow accustomed to the sight of his image coming to independent life, yet he still had to repress a shiver. Because he was fairly certain that the entity inside the glass was actually his Shadow.

Most of his fellow Hierarchs would have deemed him mad for trafficking with the creature commonly regarded as the most insidious, relentless enemy a wraith could ever have. But the being in the mirror had often helped Gayoso when he needed help the most. He was convinced that if he hadn't had the benefit of its advice, Shellabarger or Mrs. Duquesne would have murdered him long ago. He could only assume that the magic of the looking glass compelled his dark side to aid him, or else that the creature didn't aspire to destroy him but to turn him into a Spectre, a goal which necessitated keeping him alive.

"I need your assistance," Gayoso said.

"I'm yours to command," said the Shadow, smirking.

Gayoso wondered if his own features ever looked quite that unpleasant. "Do you know what's been going on?"

"How could I, when you haven't informed me?" the reflection said. "I don't even exist except when you choose to give me form and purpose."

Gayoso scowled. "Don't play games with me. I understand what you are, and I imagine you know everything that I do."

The Shadow smiled. "In point of fact, I know things you don't, or at least I have instincts and intuitions you lack. That's what makes me useful. All right, I won't play the ignoramus. You're worried about Montrose." Another skirl of brassy music penetrated the wall.

"Yes," said Gayoso. "Damn the man! I should have either helped him wholeheartedly or killed him when he first arrived."

"You certainly should have," the Shadow agreed. "If you'd asked me, I would have told you as much, but alas, you kept me locked away in my musty little drawer."

"I don't run to you every time I have to make a decision," Gayoso said. He suspected that if he didn't use the mirror sparingly, he might corrupt his soul beyond any hope of redemption. "But I need to know what's going to happen next. What are Montrose's intentions?"

The Shadow nodded thoughtfully. "That's an interesting question. In his place, would you hold a grudge? Would you want to deliver the impudent provincial who hampered your mission to the justice of the Smiling Lord?"

Gayoso scowled. "That's what I'm asking you. Does he mean to arrest me?"

"Perhaps he wants to usurp your office. At this point, your subjects might well support him. So, might Shellabarger and Mrs. Duquesne. And the Marquess would scarcely be the first Hierarch to decide that it's better to reign over a Shadowlands kingdom than to kiss Deathlord ass in Stygia."

"Don't give me *perhaps*. I don't dare move against him unless I'm certain."

"Even I don't know everything, dear brother. I can't foresee every twist and turn of the future, or spy into the depths of every soul we encounter. But I can tell you this. Montrose served a purpose, but he's on the brink of becoming a liability. I recommend we dispose of him before he does."

"How? An assassination?"

"No," the Shadow said. "Even if the attempt succeeded, everyone would suspect you. Your fellow governors could conceivably bring a charge of treason against you. It would be better if Heretics slew Montrose on the battlefield."

"Obviously," Gayoso said impatiently, "but he keeps winning. And every time he does, more outlaws slink out of their lairs to enlist in his army. No Heretic Circle in the region can stand against him, not anymore."

"No *one* Heretic Circle," the Shadow said. "But a missionary, a Sister of Athena, is putting together an *alliance of* Circles in Grand Gulf."

"How do you know that?" the Anacreon asked.

The creature in the glass ignored the question. "She just might be able to destroy Montrose, given the proper assistance."

"What kind of assistance?"

"Supply our Stygian friend with faulty intelligence. Tell him where the lady's followers are assembling, but grossly underestimate their numbers. With luck, when he goes to dispose of them, he'll leave some of his own force behind to tend to other business. Arrange matters in such a way that it's primarily *your* soldiers, not Shellabarger's or Mrs. Duquesne's, who are supposed to fight alongside his ruffians, and then make sure your men don't show up for the engagement."

Gayoso nodded thoughtfully. "Inaccurate reports. Troops arriving late for a rendezvous. It happens all the time. If I'm careful, no one will be able to accuse me of anything."

"You'll also want to warn the Sister that Montrose is coming," the Shadow said, "so she can set a trap. But your emissary mustn't refer to him by name."

"Whyever not?"

"I don't know," the Shadow said. Gayoso had the unsettling feeling that on this one point, it was lying. "But I sense it's important. And I see that if you follow the plan in every detail, Montrose will fall." The reflection smiled. "One way or another."

27

On his way from the Citadel to Under-the-Hill, Montrose noticed a newspaper box, the sides covered with spray-painted gang markings and the coin compartment levered open.

Although he'd long ago lost much of his interest in the affairs of the Quick, the size of the big black headline framed in the window caught his eye. Wondering if the United States had gone to war or experienced some spectacular disaster, he reined in Alexander and dismounted for a better look.

Stooping, he skimmed the first few lines of the story, and then, intrigued, shifted himself into the Skinlands to peruse the entire thing. His luminous white stallion and the webwork of Nihils in the sidewalk vanished. With the sizzling sound of the tiny cracks cut off, the dark, deserted street seemed almost unnaturally silent.

Wondering idly if someone might look down from one of the tenement windows, and what he would make of the masked, cloaked figure below him if he did, Montrose kicked the newspaper box. The window shattered. The Scot removed a paper and continued to read.

In the past three centuries, he'd seen more than his share of marvels and mysteries, but even by his standards, the newspaper story was odd. Ten ministers, four priests, two rabbis, and an imam had all gone homicidally berserk on the same Sunday morning. The police had had to kill the majority of them to halt their rampages. The remainder had committed suicide rather than be captured. The reporter who'd written the account seemed to be hinting that the phenomenon might have something to do with the serial killer called the Atheist, but apparently didn't have any real evidence to support such a speculation.

Montrose reflected that it was almost as if he had an opposite number on the other side of the Shroud, someone attacking the religious institutions of the living as ferociously as the Stygian was waging war on the Heretical sects of the dead. Once again, he had the uneasy feeling that some sinister design was unfolding around him. That he might even be a pawn in this scheme.

Scowling, he thrust the disquieting notion out of his mind. He knew very well why he was campaigning in the Shadowlands. To enhance his master's status among his peers. Moreover, he couldn't imagine what anyone could hope to gain by instigating both a crusade against the Heretics and a terrorist campaign against a few Quick preachers, or even how such an effort might have been accomplished.

Surely, Montrose reasoned, he suspected a connection only because his Shadow was trying to vex him with irrational anxieties, just as it had earlier filled him with self-doubt and delirious cruelty. All the more reason, then, to get himself to a Pardoner without further delay. He tossed the newspaper into a trash can and then allowed himself to slip back across the Shroud. His scarlet eyes glowing, Alexander whickered as if he'd been waiting impatiently.

"I know," Montrose said, patting the Phantasy's neck. "I have a morbid imagination, and I'm wasting your precious time. My humble apologies." He swung himself into the saddle and kicked the horse into a canter.

The ambiance of Under-the-Hill had changed since his arrival in Natchez. Many of the residents had seen fit to abandon their criminal activities and assist the campaign against the Heretics in one capacity or another. Consequently, the dark streets no longer felt quite so perilous. Yet paradoxically, with an abundance of newly enslaved Heretics available for gladiatorial combat, rape, and any number of other vicious amusements, the invigorating, nauseating miasma of sadism, terror, and pain had grown even thicker than before.

Montrose rode past a crowd of his irregulars who were

watching a Masquer forcibly sculpt a bound, shrieking male slave into the semblance of a beautiful woman. The troops hailed their commander jovially. Concealing a pang of disgust at their notion of entertainment, Montrose gave them a nod, but didn't stop to talk.

He turned Alexander into the mouth of a crooked alley. A large Nihil seethed in the pavement just before him, and the crumbling buildings pressing close on either side reeked of vermin and decay. Even allowing for the distortions of the Shroud, the scene was so ruinous that Montrose found it difficult to imagine anyone taking up residence here. And yet, as an informant had promised, a dimly glowing iron lantern, the emblem of a Pardoner, hung above a recessed doorway a few yards ahead.

Giving the Nihil a wide berth, Montrose rode to the lamp, which radiated the chill of barrow-flame. He dismounted, stepped to the door, and called, "Hello!"

"Come in," replied a reedy voice. "Anyone seeking absolution is welcome."

Montrose slipped through the substance of the door. The interior of the shack was as deteriorated as the exterior, with a sagging floor, a few sticks of marred and broken furniture, and great masses of filthy cobweb festooning the corners. To his surprise, the dusty strands shed a faint green light. Perhaps the Pardoner had used an Arcanos trick to make them glow.

The man in question sat at a rickety table in the exact center of the room. He was slight and stooped, and had chosen to conceal his features under a gray hood. Black stains, the stigmata of his craft, mottled his twisted, arthritic-looking hands. A miscellany of objects—brass finger cymbals, a fuming incense burner, long black needles with ebony heads, a jeweler's loupe—rested on the scarred wooden surface before him.

"Your custom honors me, my lord Anacreon," he said.

Montrose removed his glossy ceramic mask. "It would have honored you sooner, but you weren't easy to find."

"Salvation never is," replied the Pardoner, a hint of humor in his tone. "I refer to salvation in the most secular, non-Heretical sense, of course."

The Scot approached the table. The bitter scent of the incense stung his nose. "My Shadow has been restless lately. I'd like you to quell it. How much do you charge?"

"Whatever the client sees fit to give."

Montrose reached inside his mantle, brought out a bulging leather bag, and set it on the table. The oboli inside it clinked.

"My lord is most generous," the Pardoner said. "Please be seated."

The Stygian perched on a fragile-looking stool. Had he and it existed on the same side of the Shroud, he had little doubt it would have disintegrated under his weight. He set his mask on the tabletop. "I've been slipping into a sort of fever," he said. "A fever of anger. It makes me enjoy my task—the fighting and slave-taking—more than I should."

"Of course you enjoy it," said the man in the hood. "You aren't just shooting and stabbing rebels. You're getting even with the ogres of your past. People who betrayed you."

Montrose sighed. "I probably am. You have good eyes."

"It's all a matter of knowing how and where to look," the Pardoner said. "I also see that one betrayal in particular has left lasting scars. A woman you encountered in the last few months of your mortal existence, after you'd laid your wife to rest and imagined you were done with love forever. You thought the girl was an angel, but she sent you to your death."

Montrose's eyes ached as if they were still capable of shedding tears. "It's pathetic, isn't it? Louise sold me out three hundred years ago, and it isn't as if I haven't done anything since. I've won a place in the aristocracy of an empire that puts Scotland or any other mortal realm to shame. I've dallied with beauties who really *do* resemble angels, in a way coarse Earthly bodies never can. Why can't I forget her?"

"That isn't how we're made," the Pardoner said. "My master in the craft taught me that every ghost is inherently a creature of rage and regret. Were we not, we never would have entered the Underworld in the first place. The only way to rid yourself of your burden of passion is to confront and resolve it."

"And I missed my chance at that," Montrose said bitterly. "When I died, a Reaper seized me and sold me to the Black

Hawks to fight in the ranks. I wasn't a thrall, but I was the next thing to it. A few days later, our commander marched us off into the Tempest to patrol the roads. It was decades before I made it back to the Shadowlands. By that time, I was a Proctor. I could have attacked Louise, Argyll, Van Lengen, and all the rest of my enemies. But every one of them had already gone to his grave."

"Thus denying you your catharsis," the Pardoner said. "It must have felt like a final injury and an ultimate injustice. And it left an open wound in your psyche, a flaw for your Shadow to exploit."

"But I would assume, not anymore," said Montrose, "not anytime soon. Because you're going to put the genie back in its bottle."

"Let's hope so," said the Pardoner. "Take off your gauntlets and spread your hands on the table, palms down."

Montrose did as he'd been instructed. The man in the hood picked up one of the black needles, set the point against the middle finger of his client's right hand, just below the nail, and suddenly thrust it in. Somehow the thin shaft of metal pinned Montrose's digit to the surface beneath it as if it had actually plunged into the wood.

The pain was intense. Montrose felt waves of dissolution licking at the substance of his finger. Evidently the needle was made of darksteel. "Sweet Jesus," he gasped, fighting the impulse to pull the offending object out.

"It's necessary for your treatment," the hooded man said blandly, which actually sounded plausible enough. Many Pardoners employed scourging or other forms of physical chastisement to break a Shadow's power. "And it'll only be for a little while." He picked up a second needle.

When all ten of Montrose's fingers had been impaled, the Pardoner attached the small brazen cymbals to his own thumb and forefinger. He rose and began to circle the table in a slow-motion dance. Repeatedly pausing in mid-motion, he struck poses that reminded the Scot of the Deathlords and their totemic stances. The cymbals chimed. Each note seemed to echo for longer than it should.

Sick with pain, Montrose didn't realize the Pardoner had

stopped circling until the hooded man rested his gnarled hands on his shoulders. Startled, the Stygian jumped. The motion jerked his immobilized arms and produced a fresh burst of agony.

The Pardoner bent down and whispered in Montrose's ear. "Who do you hate?"

"Argyll. Hamilton. Van Lengen. King Charles and the Crown Prince." With each name, he felt a flare of overwhelming rage, as if the pain in his hands was intensifying his anger. And then something writhed in the depths of his mind. His Shadow was stirring. Alarmed, he tried to twist his head around to look the Pardoner in the face. He couldn't quite turn it far enough.

The hooded man massaged the clenched muscles in Montrose's shoulders. "It's all right," the confessor said. "This time, give in. Let the venom flow, so I can neutralize it. Who do you hate?"

"Heretics. Demetrius." The pain and fury sang on inside him.

"Who do you hate?" the Pardoner asked.

"John," Montrose said. He was appalled at himself, but with the rage wailing even louder, he couldn't deny that on some level, his declaration must be true.

"Your son?" the Pardoner asked. "Why?"

"I took him to war and he died. He broke my heart."

"Who do you hate?" the Pardoner asked.

"Magdalen. She refused to understand why I *had* to support the Crown, no matter what the cost. She stopped loving me. And finally, she died, too."

"Who do you hate?" asked the hooded man.

Montrose shuddered, stabbing fresh pain through his injured hands. The anger inside him was sickeningly intense. It felt as if it were shredding his spirit, and he wanted it to stop. "You know," he said. "We already talked about her."

"Say the name," the Pardoner insisted.

"Louise!" Montrose cried. "Louise!"

"What would you like to do to her?"

Images of torture and mutilation cascaded through the Stygian's mind. He felt his penis stiffen. "Tear her eyes out.

Rape her. Cut off her hands and feet. Hang her a thousand times, the way they hung me."

"Who do you hate?" the Pardoner asked.

"That's everyone," Montrose said.

"Who do you hate?"

"No one else, damn you! Finish this! I don't want to feel this way any longer!"

"Who do you hate?"

Montrose sensed his Shadow surging to the forefront of his mind, intermingling itself with his psyche so thoroughly that he lost any sense of a separate entity coexisting with him inside his head. In a strange, odious way, it reminded him of how it had felt to be mortal. At the same time, his anger seemed to change, from a white-hot blaze to something cold and heavy.

"Myself," he said. "I hate myself."

"Why?" the Pardoner asked.

Montrose sneered in self-loathing. "So many reasons. I led my men off to die in a lost cause. I killed my own boy that way. I ruined my life for the sake of principles scoundrels like Argyll and Hamilton disdained, and it turned out they were right, and I was wrong."

"Why else?" the Pardoner murmured.

"For trusting my betrayers. And for failing to win and hold their love. What was wrong with me? What ugliness did they perceive inside me, that made them feel it was permissible to forsake me?"

"Just a little more," the Pardoner urged. "Tell me the rest and the healing can begin."

"I hate the man I used to be," Montrose groaned. "But at the same time, I hate myself for casting his ideals aside. I don't know what to do or who to be!"

"You will," the Pardoner whispered, "because I'm about to tell you a secret, the greatest secret in all the universe. Once you leave this place, you may not remember it consciously, but even so, it will guide and inspire you for the rest of your days. Would you like to hear it?"

"Yes," Montrose said. He couldn't imagine what the hooded man was babbling about——it sounded like Heretical mumbo jumbo—but anything to end the pain in his fingers and the even more agonizing emotions festering in his mind.

"Here it is then. You deserve it."

"Deserve what?"

"Your own contempt. You're a monstrous, crippled thing who richly deserves every pain and humiliation existence has ever seen fit to give you."

"That's mad," Montrose said, and it certainly didn't resemble the pronouncement of any Pardoner he'd ever consulted before. Yet the truth was, it didn't seem insane at all. It simply seemed like a summary of his own confessions.

"Don't resist," the Pardoner said. "Once you know the whole truth, your personal piece of it needn't trouble you anymore."

"What is the whole truth?" Montrose asked desperately. He felt so vile, so full of despair, that it was a wonder Oblivion hadn't already claimed him. And if the Pardoner couldn't help him, he *wanted* it to.

"That no one else is any better than you," said the man in the hood. "Your own mournful history proves it. We all deserve to suffer. So, forget your qualms and scruples, my lord Anacreon. Pursue your ambitions with a vengeance. When you look down on the underlings and thralls, you'll know that no matter how foul and worthless a creature you may be, at least you're better than they are. And whenever you destroy someone, you'll know you've cleansed creation of a bit of filth, and perhaps even justified your own existence in the process."

Montrose struggled to evaluate what he was hearing. It sounded demented. Wrong. Yet it sounded *right*, also, as if it was the only possible remedy for his physical and spiritual pain.

As he began to succumb to the Pardoner's logic, he felt portions of his memory withering. He didn't forget his children or the friends who'd stayed faithful to the end, but a kind of significance drained out of his recollections. Soon he'd be able to think of them dispassionately, the way he might reflect on characters in a rather tedious play.

At the same time, the quality of his anger and self-contempt changed once again. At the core of the pain he discovered a kind of masochistic release. A promise that if he simply embraced his own inner putrescence, his shame would turn to joy.

Perhaps, he thought, the Pardoner still crooning blandishments in his ear, he *should* let go. Perhaps it was the only sensible course of action, and in any case, it certainly seemed the easiest. Then he noticed a flicker of movement from the corner of his eye. He turned his head to peer directly at it, only to find there was nothing there.

Confused and feverish as he felt, he still believed he knew what had just happened. As a Harbinger, he possessed the ability to peer into the Tempest, and occasionally he caught a momentary glimpse of the eternal storm even when he wasn't trying to. Invoking his Arcanos, he looked again—

—And beheld a trio of Spectres, gaunt, gray creatures seemingly made of tatters of darkness and lengths of twisted bone. In the bewildering hyperdimensional manner of the Tempest, the creatures were still standing at the fringe of their own chaotic realm yet simultaneously clustered around the table in this very room, watching Montrose and the Pardoner with avid interest.

The Scot suddenly realized that what the monsters really hoped to see was his Shadow, essentially a Spectre in embryo, taking control of him. And they very well might. Because the Pardoner was feeding the parasite!

"Get away from me," Montrose mumbled, the words so slurred that it seemed impossible the Pardoner would understand them.

But evidently, he did, because he said, "Don't struggle, my lord Anacreon. It's too late. And I promise, you'll be happier when it's over."

Montrose's memories continued to petrify, becoming gray and brittle. He felt the link between his mind and flesh attenuating. His sight began to dim.

Then from somewhere deep inside him came a surge of defiance, a thunderbolt of pure outrage altogether different from the cold, malicious self-loathing eroding his will. Bellowing, he leaped up off his stool, knocking the Pardoner backward, and ripped his hands upward with all his remaining strength.

His fingers tore free, but the resultant burst of pain was

indescribable. Blacking out, he collapsed to the floor. When he came to a moment later, his hands were dissolving into nothingness. The black pins fell tinkling to the grimy floor.

"I was too ambitious," said the Pardoner from behind him.

Montrose was in too much pain to move, but with an enemy present, he couldn't just lie helpless where he was. Somehow, he managed to clamber to his feet. The floor tilted and the glowing spider webs dimmed, as if he was in danger of losing consciousness again. He stumbled around to face the man who'd hurt him.

"I should have made your Shadow a little stronger and let it go at that," the Pardoner continued. "That's the usual practice, and you wouldn't have noticed a thing. But you're such a wonderful prize that I got greedy. Now I'll simply have to kill you." Edging forward, he reached inside his coat and brought out a knife. It looked as if it was made of chipped black stone.

Trembling, Montrose tried to veil himself in darkness. Nothing happened. He was too spent to use an Arcanos. He attempted to retreat. His Shadow contested his intent, and his feet wouldn't move. Straining, the Scot pitted every iota of his will against the parasite's, and finally broke its grip. The sudden release of tension made him stagger.

By the time he recovered what passed for his balance, the Pardoner was nearly within striking distance. Montrose snatched for his pistol before remembering that he no longer had any fingers to grasp it. The hooded man laughed.

"It is rather comical," Montrose rasped. "Although I might not see the humor if I hadn't been to France." With a silent prayer, though he couldn't have said to what or whom, he lashed out with a kick.

The *savate* attack caught the Pardoner under the chin and snapped his head back. Montrose kept kicking him, in the groin and then the knee. The knife tumbled from the hooded man's hand, and he fell to the floor.

The Stygian stamped on him, pulping flesh and snapping bones. By catching the Pardoner by surprise, he'd gained the advantage, but he was still half-crippled with pain. He didn't dare give his adversary a chance to counterattack. Besides, he *wanted* to keep hurting him. He wanted to mash his body into paste.

And eventually he did, more or less. Waves of darkness swept through the smaller wraith's flesh. His clothing slumped in on itself as the mass inside it dissolved. In another moment the garments were all that remained.

Gasping and shuddering, cradling the stumps of his hands against his chest, Montrose dropped to his knees. Then he remembered the three Spectres. Terrified that they'd slithered through the Nihil outside and were about to attack him, he looked frantically about, but didn't see any sign of them. Evidently, in the unpredictable manner of such horrors, they'd decided to leave him alone, even though he was currently easy prey.

His Shadow squirmed inside him, quiescent for the moment but swollen with newfound power. Since he would now be leery of asking *any* Shadowlands Pardoner for assistance, he guessed he'd simply have to control it through vigilance and willpower for the time being.

At any rate, he now had excellent reason to suspect that the honest Pardoners of the region weren't simply drifting off to other provinces. Someone was eliminating them to enable *false* Pardoners, practitioners of a corrupt version of the same Arcanos, to take their places, and *strengthen* the Shadow of every wraith who called on them for aid.

But *why?* What did it all mean?

Montrose decided he'd better find out. He couldn't neglect the campaign against the Heretics, but with luck, he could manage some inquiries on the side. He just wished he could shake the feeling that he'd waited too long to begin examining the overall picture. That whatever threat was advancing through the darkness, nothing could stop it now.

28

Looking feminine in her platinum wig and a lacy gray blouse, Marilyn nodded at the dark, recessed doorway across Ursulines Avenue. "That's it," she said. "At least, we think it is. But I still advise against this. Rumor has it that other people have gone into that house and never come out." Astarte grimaced impatiently.

Bellamy shrugged. "What are our options? I don't mean to knock the Arcanum. I never would have gotten this far without you and your friends. But the truth is, you don't seem to have any information that relates to the Atheist murders. Maybe the people inside that building do."

"If they *are* people," Marilyn said glumly, and indeed, the Arcanum's intelligence about the dilapidated Vieux Carre town house, like so much of its data, was maddeningly vague. The fraternity had circumstantial evidence that a group with occult connections had owned the structure since the early 1800s, but few real details except for the fact that the occupants generally convened at night. "God knows, I want to solve our problem as much as you do, but still, we should be patient. We might turn up the very facts we need tomorrow."

Bellamy shook his head. "There's no time for patience. People are getting hurt. The Atheist is still killing clergymen. It could be that he made all those ministers go berserk, too. And when I phoned my boss to get an extension of my leave, I found out Nolliver's dead."

"But you said his death was determined to be a suicide," Marilyn replied, "and that everyone knew he was a troubled individual."

"I'm not taking anything for granted," Bellamy said. "The point is that despite your help, the investigation's stalled. We haven't even been able to learn the identity of the possessed guy who attacked your house. I'm willing to run a risk to get things moving again."

"And I want to see whatever's inside there," said Astarte, her eyes shining in the moonlight. "You and R. J. gave me my first break, Marilyn. You showed me that the paranormal is real. Now I have to take the next step."

Marilyn frowned. "Suit yourselves, then. At least I warned you. If you don't come out by dawn, I'll phone the police anonymously, though I'm virtually certain they won't be able to help you."

"Thanks," said Bellamy. He and Astarte started across the deserted street.

"It's so sad," Astarte murmured.

"What's that?" Bellamy replied, studying the shuttered windows. It was impossible to tell if anyone was peeking out through the spaces between the slats.

"Marilyn wants to become a part of the supernatural so badly. Yet she's known for almost a year that this place is here, and she's never done what we're about to do. Deep down, she's chicken, and that will keep her from ever getting her wish."

"At least she'll be alive," said Bellamy. "You could use a dose of her caution herself."

Astarte stuck her tongue out at him.

They climbed up onto the stoop. No sound whispered through the door, and no light shone through the cracks around it. With its paint peeling away in long strips, the house seemed abandoned, as, perhaps, it actually was.

A pair of screw holes at eye level revealed where a knocker had hung, but it was gone now. Bellamy couldn't find a doorbell, either, so he rapped on the panel with his knuckles. In the quiet, the pounding seemed unpleasantly loud. He imagined *things* stirring in the shadows up and down the street, peering to see what all the racket was about.

No one came to the door. He knocked harder, until the heel of his fist began to ache. Still, no one replied. He turned the tarnished knob, but the door was locked.

"I guess we'll have to break in," Astarte said.

Bellamy scowled at the notion of doing so without a warrant or probable cause. He was used to upholding the law, not flouting it. But he was operating without the sanction of the Bureau anyway, in a situation where the old rules and procedures seemed absurd. "I guess we will," he replied, fishing in his pocket for his Swiss Army knife and lock pick.

Astarte looked disappointed when he brought them out. He guessed she'd been expecting some exotic gadget from a James Bond movie, or at least an impressive array of burglar's tools. But Bellamy wasn't called upon to pick locks nearly often enough to carry such a collection of hardware around, nor should he need it to get past what appeared to be a simple, old-fashioned mechanism.

He inserted the pick in the keyhole, then used the knife's screwdriver as a tension tool. As he exerted pressure, he felt the pins shiver, and then they clicked into the opening position.

He expected a momentary glow of satisfaction. That was what he usually felt when he finished such a task. Instead, a chill oozed up his spine, and he had to swallow away a dryness in his throat. Because he'd just made it possible to go inside, and as he suddenly realized, he didn't want to.

"Nice work," said Astarte. "Now open the damn thing."

"Okay," he said, closing the knife. "But, remember, let me go first, and do everything I tell you."

Astarte rolled her eyes. "Yes, sir, J. Edgar."

Bellamy eased the door open. The foyer beyond it surprised him. The chandelier was glowing, if only faintly, and dim illumination from other sources spilled through the arches in either wall. Evidently someone had taken pains to ensure that not even a hint of light would leak outdoors. Fresh white roses in a crystal vase, along with a general absence of dust and cobwebs, suggested that the interior of the house was being well maintained. Yet paradoxically, a faint but noxious odor, reminiscent of both rotting meat and the fetor of rats, hung in the cool air.

"Hello!" Bellamy called. His voice echoed through the building. "Is anybody here?"

No one replied.

"Let's look around," said Astarte. To his surprise, she took his hand and tugged him toward the doorway on the left. He considered extricating his fingers from her grip, but then thought better of it. Perhaps, for all her bravado, she needed the reassurance of the contact, and at least she wasn't restraining his shooting hand.

Beyond the arch was a parlor full of antique furniture dominated by a towering sculpture in the center of the floor. The construct was a twisted mass of junk, crushed fenders, bent, rusty nails, razor blades, flatware, and unidentifiable scraps of metal welded into a double helix. The component parts gleamed dully in the wan gray light.

Ordinarily, Bellamy didn't much care for abstract art. Surrounded by Victorian tallboys and ottomans, this piece was so out of place that it ought to seem particularly unappealing. Yet for some reason, it fascinated him. It seemed bigger, *deeper*, than it had any right to be, with faint fluctuations of shadow and phosphorescence rippling inexplicably at its core.

He stared at it for at least a minute, trying to puzzle out its true shape, before he realized that, even though the style was utterly different, for some reason it reminded him of the immense carvings in his dimly remembered nightmares. Obscurely alarmed, he wrenched his gaze away from it.

Astarte kept staring at it. He gripped her shoulder and gave her a gentle shake. "Are you okay?" he asked.

Blinking, she turned to face him. "I guess," she said hesitantly. "I wasn't asleep, but I feel like you just woke me up. Was it hypnotizing us, like Marilyn's runes?"

"It just *interested* you," said a silky baritone voice.

His heart jolting, Bellamy spun around. Astarte did the same. In the doorway to the foyer stood a small bald man. Despite the dim illumination, he wore heavy sunglasses, and despite the chill in the air, he smelled of sweat. Evidently, he'd crept up behind the intruders while the sculpture held them in its spell.

"Their art is *very* interesting," the bald man continued. "It speaks to the part of us that's the same as they are." He giggled.

There was nothing overtly monstrous or even threatening in the bald man's appearance, but something about him made Bellamy's skin crawl. Maybe it was simply because he was on edge. "I'm sorry we forced our way in here," he said. "But I'm an FBI agent, and we're on urgent business." He displayed for his credentials.

The bald man pressed his dark glasses back onto the bridge of his nose. "What can I do for you?" he asked.

"For starters, you can tell us who you are," Bellamy said.

The bald man smirked. "Charles Tamblyn. Which is to say, no one at all. I just work for Mr. Daimler and Miss Paris. They're the ones who can help you if anyone can." He sniggered, as if the idea of his employers assisting anyone was comical in the extreme. "Come with me." He limped toward the opening in the far wall. Bellamy noticed that one of Tamblyn's shoes was shorter than the other, with a built-up sole and heel.

Astarte shot the FBI agent a questioning glance. He gathered that she found Tamblyn unsettling also. Bellamy gave her a nod and then they followed the bald man on through the house.

The servant, if that was the proper term for him, led them through several more gloomy but elegant rooms and finally into a study, where golden flames crackled in the fireplace and an abstract oil, rendered predominantly in shades of blue and green, hung above the marble hearth. The painting had the same disturbing yet eye-catching quality as the huge metal sculpture, and as soon as Bellamy realized it, he hastily looked away.

The most handsome man he'd ever seen stood beside the fireplace in an exquisitely tailored three-piece suit, a goblet of red wine cradled in his hand. His hair was pale gold, his skin alabaster, and his eyes sapphire blue. Across the room, a slim woman in a long dress lounged on a leather couch. White gauze bandages concealed every inch of what would otherwise have been exposed flesh, from her scalp with its waves of chestnut hair down to her fingertips.

Astarte gasped. Bellamy wondered what she'd noticed, or thought she'd noticed.

"What have we here?" asked the handsome man.

"My name is Frank Bellamy," the agent said, displaying

his badge and ID. "I'm with the FBI. This is Emily Dodds, my assistant. I assume you're Miss Paris and Mr. Daimler?"

The bandaged woman inclined her head. The firelight flowed over her hair.

"We're sorry to disturb you," Bellamy continued.

Daimler chuckled. "You ought to be sorry to break into a private residence."

"We knocked," Bellamy said. "No one answered. And we're trying to stop a series of murderers. I assume you've heard of the Atheist."

"Yes," Daimler said, "but all I know about him is what I read in the papers. I can't imagine why you'd think otherwise."

"We believe the Atheist is involved in the occult," Bellamy replied. "We have reason to think that you are, too."

Daimler smiled. "I'm a suspect, then?"

Bellamy shook his head. "To tell you the truth, I'd never even heard of you until we broke in here. But a reliable informant told me that *everyone* who frequents this house has some connection to the occult. I came on a fishing expedition, hoping you have some pertinent information."

Miss Paris rose and sauntered toward the intruders, her long skirt swishing faintly. Head cocked, she circled them, looking them over. The faint, foul stink intensified. Evidently it was wafting from her bandaged flesh. Astarte quivered.

Daimler shook his head. A lock of golden hair slipped down his ivory forehead. "I must say, you seem to be grasping at straws."

"Tell me about it," Bellamy said. He could feel that Miss Paris had paused directly behind him. He tried to ignore her. "But sometimes an investigation is like that, and this one is worse than most."

"In fact," Daimler said, "I don't even live in New Orleans, or anywhere in what seems to be the Atheist's hunting range. An associate owns this house. He lends it to me when I visit."

"If you don't know anything about the Atheist," Bellamy said, "maybe he does. What's his name, and how can we get in touch with him?"

Daimler smiled. "I didn't say I didn't know *anything* that

might be helpful. Miss Paris and I collect information on all sorts of esoteric topics. But why should we share it with you?"

"How about human decency? You could help me save some lives."

Daimler grinned. "Aha. That clinches it. You don't have any idea what we are."

Astarte stepped toward him. "I do. I've been looking for you all my life."

"Do you think so," Daimler said.

"I know so," Astarte answered. She stuck her finger into the red liquid in his goblet, then touched it to her lips. "And here's the proof. This isn't wine."

Bellamy stared in amazement. Did she mean that the drink was blood, and Daimler was a vampire? The idea seemed crazy, but no more crazy than statues coming to life, or killers who were nearly bulletproof.

He almost reached for his Browning, but he didn't *know* that Daimler was a vampire, and in any case, so far, the blond man hadn't made any threatening moves. Possibly sensing Bellamy's confusion, Tamblyn giggled.

"If you think my choice of beverage proves me undead," said Daimler to Astarte, "then you underestimate your own species' propensity for cannibalism. But just for fun, let's say you're correct. What then?"

"Then maybe I'll give myself to you," Astarte said.

"What?" Bellamy cried.

Astarte glared at him. "Fuck off! It's my body and my choice!" She turned back to Daimler. "Here's the deal. You give Frank all the help you can, and I'll be your slave. I'll do anything you want."

Unpleasantly conscious of Tamblyn and Miss Paris, still standing behind him, Bellamy eased his hand toward his pistol. "Don't listen to her," he said to Daimler. "She doesn't know what she's saying."

"No," said Daimler, "she most certainly doesn't. Would you actually like to be one of my mortal servants, Miss Dobbs? Mr. Tamblyn is, and some people would say it's had a deleterious effect on both his social presence and his mental health."

Tamblyn snickered.

"I'll risk it," Astarte said.

Daimler stroked her lips with his fingertip, pausing for a moment to toy with the steel ring. Bellamy's muscles clenched with anger. "Because you think I'd become infatuated with you," the alleged vampire said, "and crave your blood. But what if I drank it all without giving you immortality in return? What if I simply killed you?"

Bellamy's fingers closed around the butt of his pistol.

"I'll take that chance," Astarte said. "I knew I was risking death when Frank and I broke in here."

Daimler nodded. "I admire your nerve if not your judgment. Perhaps I *should* grant your wish. Burn away all that beauty. Compel you to spend eternity in a body like mine."

Daimler seemed to crouch, but then Bellamy saw that he hadn't exactly *moved*. Instead, the blond man's body had changed form. Now it was bent and hunchbacked, with scablike moles mottling its twisted hands. His face had altered as well, the straight nose becoming a wrinkled pig's snout, the perfect white teeth rows of stained, jagged tusks, and the sapphire eyes a single bloodshot orb set off-center in his forehead. Astarte's mouth fell open, and her body quaked. She looked as if she were screaming, but she didn't make a sound. Seizing her, Daimler pressed his thin black lips against her throat.

Bellamy froze for a split second, then began to snatch out his pistol. Two pairs of hands grabbed him from behind.

The FBI agent snapped his arm backward in an elbow strike. The blow connected, and one set of hands slipped away. He glimpsed Tamblyn stumbling backward, clutching at his solar plexus. The servant's sunglasses fell off his face, revealing a ring of pustulant sores around each eye.

Miss Paris clutched at Bellamy with terrible strength, trying to immobilize his shooting arm with one bandaged hand and throttle him with the other. As they struggled, the putrid stench of her flesh became fouler and fouler. Tiny insects emerged from between her wrappings, jumped on the agent's body, and bit him.

He stamped on Miss Paris's foot. Bone snapped, and her

grip loosened. Wrenching himself free, he spun around and slammed the Browning against her temple. She staggered back against the wall, sending a still-life in a gilt frame crashing to the floor.

Bellamy shot her in the chest. He had no confidence that he'd actually incapacitated her, but with Astarte in Daimler's grasp, he couldn't waste any more time on her. Gripping the Browning in both hands, he whirled.

To his surprise, Daimler hadn't actually bitten Astarte. Rather, he was simply holding the thrashing girl in his arms, and now he pushed her away. "My compliments to your karate instructor," the cyclops said. "I didn't think you could actually get your gun out. Miss Paris will be sore for a while."

"Get away from him," rasped Bellamy to Astarte. She stumbled to his side. He glared at Daimler. "Get your hands up."

Instead of obeying, Daimler shook his head as if Bellamy had disappointed him. "I had plenty of time to bite her if I'd really wanted to, but she isn't Nosferatu material. Too innocent, though considering her punk regalia, I imagine she's annoyed to hear me say so." He gave Astarte a hideous leer. "I was only trying to teach her a little wisdom. Quixotic of me, considering the likelihood that neither of you will leave this house alive, but we all have our impulses."

"I'm the one pointing the gun at you," Bellamy said.

"Do you really think that matters?" Daimler asked. The FBI agent heard a floorboard creak behind him. He suspected Miss Paris was drawing herself to her feet. "I can guarantee you it doesn't. However, there is a chance that we can avoid any more unpleasantness."

Bellamy edged around the room until he had his back against a wall and could see Daimler, Tamblyn, and Miss Paris all at once. The stain on the bandaged woman's breast looked black in the firelight. From the location of the wound, the agent figured he'd hit the aorta. Were she human, her blood would be spurting. Instead, it was seeping out in a steady flow.

"What do you have in mind?" said Bellamy to Daimler.

"My people have a law," Daimler said. "It requires us to

kill any mortal who learns of our existence. But I've never been a stickler for rules, at least not when I can profit by ignoring them."

"Are you asking us to bribe you?" Bellamy asked.

Daimler chuckled. "Not with money. I have more than I'll ever need. Not with Miss Dodds's sweet blood and ripe young body, either. I'm not thirsty, and I'm no longer capable of sexual arousal. With information. I told you I collect it, as do most of my breed. Tell me everything you know about your friend the Atheist. If I find your tale significant, or at least intriguing, I'll let you off the hook. I might even help you, with the understanding that you'll share the rest of the story when you can."

"What if I bore you?" Bellamy asked.

"Then we finish our altercation," the cyclops said.

Suddenly Bellamy's eyes were drawn to Miss Paris. He had the peculiar feeling she was talking, even though she was standing silent and still.

And Daimler responded to her as if she had spoken. "You're right," he said. "But I like them. And it won't be the first time we've played fast and loose with the Traditions." He turned back to Bellamy and Astarte. "Miss Paris says that if we're even to consider setting you free, you'll have to promise never to try to learn any more about us or this house, or reveal to anyone that our race exists."

Bellamy hesitated. He didn't like the idea of holding out on the Arcanum. But on the other hand, Marilyn *had* kidnapped him, and anyway, stopping the Atheist, to say nothing of escaping this place alive, was a more important consideration. "It's a deal," the agent said.

"Excellent," Daimler said. He waved his blemished hand at a sofa and two armchairs clustered to form a conversation pit. "Then let's make ourselves comfortable. Charles, bring our guests some coffee." Tamblyn recovered his sunglasses, then hobbled from the room.

Bellamy hesitated. These creatures were hideous monsters. If Daimler was willing to show *his* true features, God only knew what sort of deformities Miss Paris was hiding inside her bandages. Bellamy had just shot the woman, and might well wind up fighting the two of them again. It would seem surreal to sit down and chat with them as if they were all old friends.

Yet events had taken much the same course with Marilyn. She'd seemed to go from enemy to ally in the blink of an eye, and given the proper circumstances, he could easily imagine her turning against him again. It was as if violence was so much a part of the world of the paranormal that all the inhabitants took it in stride.

Scratching at one of the tiny bugs still stinging his wrist, hoping they didn't carry some ghastly disease, he sat down on the sofa with the Browning in his lap. Daimler and Miss Paris settled across from him, and Astarte plopped down beside him.

Bellamy noticed her staring at the monsters. Though she was trying to hide it, there was loathing in her eyes, but now that the first shock of Daimler's transformation had passed, fascination as well. "You talked about your *race*," she said, a little hesitantly. "What *is* it?"

"Oh, we're vampires," Daimler said. "You were right about that much. It's just that we belong to what's generally considered one of the less desirable bloodlines. Now please, Agent Bellamy, tell us about your adventures."

Bellamy did his best, striving to be not merely clear, but entertaining. As he began to describe his encounter with Keene, Tamblyn brought the coffee service on a silver tray. It smelled good, but Bellamy was far too tense to drink any. It annoyed him when Astarte poured herself a cup, dumped liberal quantities of cream and sugar into it, and began to sip.

When he finally finished his account, Daimler said, "I'll have to let my host know that your Arcanum busybodies have discovered the existence of this residence. He may want to stop using it for a few decades, or even dispose of it altogether."

"Whatever," Bellamy said. "What I want to know is, how do things stand between you and us?"

Daimler turned to Miss Paris. Once again, Bellamy felt that she was speaking, even though she didn't make a sound.

The cyclops pivoted back toward his guests. "You can put the pistol away," he said. Some of the tension quivered out of Bellamy's body. "We are intrigued, and on an abstract level, we'll even agree that this Atheist person—or cabal—should probably be stopped. We'll help you to the extent that we can without inconveniencing ourselves."

"Good," Bellamy said. "What do you know?"

"Nothing relevant," Daimler said, "not yet. But I may be able to find something out. If I do, I'll contact you."

"You may not realize the significance of information you already have," Bellamy said. "Let me ask you some questions—"

"No," Daimler said. "I'm sorry, but I won't give you a single fact until I'm convinced you absolutely have to have it. Powerful as we are, my people only survive through secrecy."

Bellamy grimaced. "All right. We sleep in a different place every night, to keep the Atheist from catching up with us again. When you have something, mail it to me at New Orleans General Delivery."

"Very well," Daimler said, and then he hesitated.

"What is it?" Astarte asked.

"I'm reluctant to mention this," said the vampire, "because I don't really know what it means, and I don't want to alarm you unnecessarily. But from some of my reading, I suspect that the vision of the island city you both beheld was a glimpse of the Kingdom of the Dead. It seems an ill omen that you, Agent Bellamy, have been dreaming of the same place ever since. Let's hope it isn't summoning you."

29

Potter crept through the artificial jungle with his halberd leveled, mostly to keep from catching it on the low-hanging branches and lianas. As always, he was impressed by how well the artificers who'd built this environment had done their work. The yielding mass beneath his boots felt and smelled like decaying vegetable matter. The plant and tree sculptures were indistinguishable from living Earthly verdure. The sounds of nocturnal birds and insects whispered through the humid air. Only an occasional glimpse of one of the structures outside the park, the spindly white minarets of the Skeletal Lord's palace or the colossal black cylinder of the Onyx Tower proper, marred the illusion of a genuine tropical forest.

Despite Demetrius' ministrations, Potter had found himself growing edgier and more apprehensive by the day, and his Shadow increasingly restive. Evidently even the most skillful Pardoner couldn't entirely quell a person's masochistic side, not when the petitioner sensed terrible danger looming over his head.

And so, the Deathlord had ordered his animal handlers to release a Phantasy into the forest. With luck, a hunt would wake the magic of his mask almost as effectively as violence against a fellow human being. It would submerge his own flawed essence in the indomitable persona of the Smiling Lord, and in so doing, finally soothe his jangled nerves.

Up ahead, something made a coughing sound.

Potter crept forward, pulled a leafy branch aside, and saw his quarry for the first time. The menagerie keeper had chosen a truly magnificent animal, a cat striped like a Bengal tiger, twelve feet long from the tip of its nose to the root of its twitching tail. A pair of huge ivory fangs curved like scimitars from its upper jaw.

Perhaps because he was downwind of it, the sabertooth hadn't yet detected Potter. But he didn't want to take it by surprise, nor did he wish to kill it with a long, heavy weapon like the halberd. Either tactic might end the confrontation too quickly, denying him the catharsis he craved. He laid the lance on the ground and drew his dagger from its scabbard, then stepped into the open.

Instantly the sabertooth pivoted to face him. Its green eyes blazed.

"Come to me," said Potter, advancing. Already he felt more like an archangel, less like a man. He unfastened his voluminous mantle and it slipped from his shoulders.

The tiger snarled.

"No," said Potter, smiling. "You can't frighten me off and you can't avoid me, either, not for long. I'm going to kill you unless you kill me first."

As if it had understood him, the Phantasy charged.

Potter hadn't expected anything so big to move quite so fast. Even though he'd been awaiting its attack, he only barely managed to dodge out of the way. As it was, the cat's shoulder brushed him and knocked him reeling into a tree. His armor clanged.

As he recovered his balance, the sabertooth whirled and pounced at him. Sidestepping, he thrust at its neck with his darksteel blade.

The dagger punched into the tiger's flesh just above the shoulder. It was a serious wound, the ripples of darkness proved that, but it didn't finish the creature. Spinning, the sabertooth swiped at Potter with its paw, catching him on the hip. The blow hurled him to the ground, and the animal leaped on top of him.

He clutched at its throat, struggling to keep it from plunging its elongated fangs into his chest. Simultaneously he stabbed the beast, over and over again, while it raked his lower body with its hind legs. Its claws shredded his armor and the flesh beneath.

Yet he scarcely felt the pain, and for the first time in days, he wasn't even a little bit afraid. A pure and joyful savagery possessed him.

He dragged the dagger down the sabertooth's chest, cutting a gaping gray incision. For a moment the cat fought even more frantically than before. Thrusting its head down, it finally rammed one of its immense teeth all the way through Potter's shoulder. But then the beast began to shudder. It collapsed on top of him, nearly crushing him, and then its carcass melted away.

As he inspected his wounds, watching them begin to close, Potter reflected that it was a shame he couldn't hold on to the tiger's head and hide for trophies. Of course, the artificers could duplicate them, but that wouldn't be the same.

And then, abruptly, even though he'd ordered the jungle cleared, he sensed someone watching him.

Since he still felt godlike, the realization didn't trouble him. Heedless of the pain it caused him, he surged to his feet. Bits of his broken mail fell clinking to the ground. He summoned his halberd and cloak. The former streaked into his hand and the latter floated upward, spread itself like a pair of wings, swooped through the air, and draped itself around his shoulders. Holding the polearm across his body, he assumed one of the Smiling Lord's ritual stances.

"Come forward," he commanded.

No one answered.

"I know you're there," said Potter in his most magisterial tones, "just as I'm sure you know it's treason to spy on a Deathlord. Nevertheless, if you show yourself now, I'll be lenient."

Still, no one replied.

With the joy of slaughter still singing through his soul, Potter wasn't inclined to be patient. He'd hunt down the intruder, wring an explanation from the wretch, and then punish him as his temerity deserved. He opened his senses, looking, listening, feeling for vibrations in the earth, and sifting the myriad tastes and odors floating on the breeze.

He couldn't locate the spy. And that was peculiar. Even

before his ascension to his present office, he'd rarely met a ghost with perceptions as acute as his own, and Charon's grace had heightened them still further. Ordinarily, even Harbingers veiled in shadow couldn't hide from him. And yet he didn't doubt the veracity of the sensations, the small hairs standing up on the back of his neck and the chill oozing up his spine, that warned him something was amiss.

A pang of human disquiet disturbed the Smiling Lord's divine equanimity. Potter did his best to quash it. So what if he hadn't pinpointed the intruder yet? He'd simply have to move around until he did, in the same way he'd located the sabertooth. It wasn't as if he'd be in any real danger in the meantime. No lurking assassin could pose a threat to the Lord of War and Murder.

Scarlet lighting flickered and thunder rumbled in the eternal storm clouds overhead. His torn legs throbbing, Potter advanced on a stand of brush thick enough to conceal a human form. No longer meshing properly, two pieces of his battered armor scraped together.

A light prickling jittered across patches of Potter's skin. Over the course of several seconds the sensation intensified to a hot, stabbing pain. Certain he was under attack, he pivoted back and forth, trying to find his assailant. He still couldn't.

Another flare of agony wrung a grunt out of him. He decided he needed to see what was happening to his body, even though a part of him cringed at the prospect. He fumbled off one of his steel gauntlets.

His hand was changing, the fingers twisting, the knuckles enlarging, brown spots appearing on the coarsening skin. It looked as if it was withering into an old man's hand.

A wraith couldn't perish of senescence. That was an affliction of matter, not spirit. But Potter could feel his entire body altering, shrinking, becoming stooped and frail, and then a numbing trickle of Oblivion oozing through the core of his chest.

If this wasn't old age, it was a counterfeit, a weapon, just as lethal, and he suspected he had only a few seconds to find the enemy who was casting the curse against him. Any longer than that would be too late.

Dropping his gauntlet, he turned this way and that, peering about, the weight of his armor, unnoticed only a minute before, now pressing cruelly on his shoulders. He wheezed, unable to shake the panicky feeling that he couldn't catch his breath even though he knew he didn't need to. He seemed to feel a heart twinging and stuttering in his breast.

And worst of all, his vision blurred, and the sounds around him—the recorded jungle noises and the clinking of his damaged mail—grew muffled. If he hadn't been able to find his enemy before, the very notion seemed risible now.

Potter's knees buckled. He toppled forward.

No! he thought. With what little remained of his strength, he jammed the butt of his halberd against the ground and clung to the shaft as tightly as he could. The polearm held him precariously upright as if he were a drunkard leaning on a crutch. *I am the Smiling Lord. Charon's anointed lieutenant. I will not end like this.*

As if it had been waiting for this declaration of defiance, his mask invigorated him with a surge of strength. The arcane energy didn't halt his ongoing deterioration, but it might allow him to function for a little longer despite it. The world swam back into partial focus. Squinting, he peered about.

And at last he seemed to glimpse a shadow shifting between two tree trunks, though his sight was still so murky he couldn't be sure. He lifted the halberd and threw it like a spear.

The darksteel head of the weapon slammed into the center of the shadow's chest. Clutching at the shaft, the assassin dropped to his knees. But despite the deadly enchantments which Charon and Nhudri, the emperor's chief artificer, had laid on the halberd, the fellow's body didn't dissolve, nor did his wounding halt the progress of Potter's destruction.

The writhing thread of Oblivion in the Deathlord's torso grew like a fungus, extending tendrils into his head and limbs. He realized he only had time for one more attack.

Concentrating with all of his fading might, he struggled to conjure one of the greatest magics of the ancient Harbingers' guild, a trick so difficult that most modem students of their Arcanos never mastered it. For a moment nothing happened, but then he felt the power rise within him.

Suddenly the darkness around the assassin grew blacker, and then clutched at him with inky tentacles. He only had time for a startled yelp before the thrashing mass of shadow imploded around him, vanishing and taking him with it. Only the halberd remained, softly thumping to the ground.

Potter hadn't actually destroyed his attacker. He'd thrust him into the Tempest. But at least he was gone, and with his departure, his magic lost its bite. The Deathlord felt the seething mass of Oblivion inside him contracting. The gnarled fingers of his naked hand began to straighten.

Unfortunately, the fierce serenity he'd derived from the hunt was gone, too. Pain and terror had wiped it away. Feeling entirely human again—human, in horrible jeopardy, and utterly out of his depth—he slumped down on the ground.

30

The Pentium's monitor displayed a black step pyramid. The tiny figure at the top made a stabbing motion and then held up a crimson lump of flesh. Cheering blared from the speakers, and streams of blood ran down the sides of the monument. That image dissolved into a picture of a huge stone city, a bewildering complex of towers, castles, and bridges, on an island. The water around it turned inky black and began to spin, shaking the buildings apart, grinding the bedrock to shards, sucking everything down.

Chester was making his presence known.

Dunn grimaced. The cartoonish display was a waste of his time. And he always felt silly speaking out loud to a computer, even though when Chester was inhabiting the machine, he could hear him and even use the built-in sound system to answer back. The SAD agent wished that somebody else with a little authority, someone made of flesh and blood and consequently able to carry on a normal telephone conversation, had been available for a conference.

"Hi," said Dunn. "When you get done jerking off, you can let me know what's going on down there. Have you found Bellamy and the girl?"

The face of a middle-aged black man, a long, narrow countenance with wire-rimmed glasses and graying hair, appeared on the screen. Dunn assumed that Chester had looked like that when he was alive. He'd never been interested enough to actually inquire.

"No," said the ghost, his artificial voice a little tinny. "Or rather, our agent did find Bellamy at the headquarters of the

Arcanum. But she didn't manage to kill him or all the Arcanists either. She only nailed a couple, and then Bellamy stunned her by neutralizing her host body. By the time she came to, everybody had cleared out of the house, and we haven't found any trace of them since."

"Nice work," said Dunn, sarcastically. He reached into his jacket for his tobacco pouch.

"We'll get them," Chester said. The monitor showed Bellamy lying bloody and mangled in an alley.

"I don't know about that," said Dunn, sprinkling a line of tobacco onto a rolling paper. "Bellamy knows how to find people, which means he knows how to keep from being found. And no offense, but your crowd has certain disadvantages when it comes to a manhunt. I'm sure it's helpful to be invisible and walk through walls, but on the other hand, you can't question live people. Most of you can't even flip the pages of a motel register or rummage through a wastebasket, especially if the what-do-you-call it, the Shroud, is thick in that particular location."

"You're forgetting the Puppeteers," Chester said. The screen showed leering shadows riding piggyback on a line of stooped, naked, blank-faced human beings.

Dunn lit his cigarette and took a long drag, savoring the heat and flavor of the smoke. "I'm not forgetting anything," he said. "Most of the Skinriders are slated for other jobs. If you send them after Bellamy, you risk derailing the whole terrorism thing. I'll tell you what we'll do. I'll come down there and catch him for you. It's what I should have done in the first place."

Chester's face reappeared on the screen. "Can you get permission to come?" he asked.

Dunn shrugged. "Probably. If not, I'll go AWOL. I wasn't planning to stay on at the Bureau much longer anyway. After the big day, we won't need a mole in SAD."

"But until now, it's best if we have one," Chester said. "Don't do anything reckless. Let's stick to the plan."

"You have your priorities ass-backward," said Dunn. "SAD doesn't have a clue. With the damage I've done to their database, it'll be years before they get a clue. The Arcanists have never been players, not really, and Weiss and Waxman were a joke. But you worry about them and not a guy like Bellamy."

"Because they know something about our world, and he doesn't."

"You mean, he *didn't*. By now, the Arcanists have filled him in. And that means he could pose a problem. I admit it isn't likely, but given his skills and personality, it's possible."

Chester frowned. "And you're certain *you* could find him and take him down."

"Hell, yes. Because I'm an even better manhunter than he is. And as we already know, all I have to do is show him my other face to drive him out of his mind."

"You have a point, but I don't want to say yes or no, not right now. Let me talk to the others—"

"Hey," Dunn growled, "time for a reality check. My people and I don't take orders from you guys or even the honchos on the pyramid. We're your partners, not your flunkies. I wasn't asking your permission, I was telling you. I'm coming."

"Now you listen—" Chester shrilled.

Dunn laid his hand on the computer and discharged a crackling burst of electricity into the works. The device went dead, as did the light fixture overhead. The SAD agent heard the other FBI staffers in the surrounding offices exclaiming in surprise and irritation.

Since Dunn didn't know much about ghosts, he had no idea whether the zap had actually hurt or even inconvenienced Chester in the slightest. But it had seemed worth a shot.

31

Montrose reached the bluff south of Grand Gulf shortly after sunset. He couldn't see or hear anyone moving around the derelict church, and by the time he and his irregulars secured their flotilla and started up the trail, he was reasonably certain that they'd arrived in advance of Gayoso's Legionnaires, who were coming overland to check out reports of Spectre activity in Union Church.

As he clambered upward—it hadn't seemed especially practical to bring Alexander on a lengthy river journey—he felt his Shadow stir, a sensation like a heavy weight shifting in the depths of his mind. He'd been aware of the bloated mass of the parasite every minute since his visit to the false Pardoner. The nerve-wracking feeling made the stink of the local paper mill even harder to bear.

Yet swollen with strength as his dark side was, as far as he could tell, it hadn't actually tried to do anything to him. He wondered what it was waiting on, and hoped it wouldn't attempt to paralyze him in the midst of the battle soon to come.

"You're solemn this evening," said Fink, marching along beside him. Once again, Montrose was impressed by the other wraith's ability to gauge his mood despite his mask. "Aren't you worried about undermining my morale?" He leered at the notion that anyone or anything could dampen his fighting spirit.

"I was just thinking," Montrose replied.

"Still craving a Pardoner is more like it," the big man replied with flawless insight. Montrose had told him about his near-disastrous experience in Under-the-Hill. "You know, if you're worried about your Shadow getting even stronger, you can keep yourself out of the actual fighting."

"And wouldn't that do wonders for everyone's morale," the Stygian answered. "For all their virtues, our fellows are jumped-up bandits, not regular soldiers. They follow me because they imagine I'm braver and tougher than they are. If I tried to lead from the rear, they'd forsake me at the first setback."

"You have a point," the river man conceded. "It doesn't help their confidence when you look like you're going crazy, either, but on the other hand, maybe it doesn't hurt it an awful lot. They'll follow a lunatic if he's a cunning, vicious lunatic." He grinned. "Otherwise, I'd never be able to find a crew."

Montrose smiled. "Over the past few weeks, I've learned a secret about you, Mike. You aren't quite as mad as you let on."

"You repeat that, and you'll have to fight me all over again. How are you doing with the *big* secrets? Do you have any idea what these phony Pardoners are all about?"

The Stygian sighed. "Not yet. I still haven't found time to conduct anything but the most cursory investigation. But when we get back to Natchez, I'm going to *make* time." And hope he wasn't starting too late in the game for it to matter.

They reached the top of the bluff, which was as vacant as Montrose had anticipated. The dilapidated church, former sanctuary of the Valhalla Circle, creaked faintly in the breeze, its crumbling spire a notched black blade in the gloom. Down in the mortal settlement, electric lights were winking on.

"What now?" asked Fink.

"Wait, I suppose," Montrose replied. "You choose some pickets and scouts while I take a first look around." He soared into the air and lit atop the steeple.

Clinging there, he removed a small but powerful pair of binoculars, a treasure he'd recently discovered in the markets of Natchez, from a pocket, raised them to his eyes, and began to peer about. The gathering darkness made observation difficult, even for wraith eyes, but he glimpsed a flicker of movement at the edge of town, in a dark, decaying block of buildings that looked like a prime location for a Haunt.

Adjusting the focus, he looked a second time. What he saw made his muscles clench in rage.

Descending so fast he was nearly in free fall, his mantle billowing around him, he flew back down to the ground, where Fink stood giving orders to half a dozen irregulars. "Never mind what I told you before," Montrose said. "I spotted the Heretics, and it looks as if they're getting ready to make a run for it. If we don't go catch them immediately, they'll slip away."

Fink frowned. "Then they know we're here. I wonder how."

"Probably a sentry watching the river," Montrose said impatiently. "Or an Oracle sensed our presence. Either way, it doesn't matter. I want the rest of the men on top of the bluff in two minutes, and then we'll move out."

A lanky wraith in a faded denim jacket, one of the guerrillas to whom Fink had been giving orders, said, "We aren't going to wait for the Legionnaires?"

Montrose had to suppress an impulse to knock the fellow down. For a second, he had the uneasy feeling that his irritation was excessive, symptomatic of some problem, but on further reflection, he couldn't see why. No commander liked having his orders questioned. "Absolutely not," he said. "According to our intelligence, there are only a few Heretics down there, and that's the way it looked to me. We already cleaned out Grand Gulf once; how many *could* there be? Besides, when have we ever needed Gayoso's clowns to help us fight?"

The other wraith smiled. "Never. So why give them a cut of the loot?"

"No reason I can think of," said Montrose. "You men get ready. Rejoin your squads."

It took several minutes for the remainder of Montrose's troops to finish scrambling up the trail. He paced restlessly until the last of them reached the top. He forced himself to give the officers a few more seconds to assemble their units, then brandished his sword and shouted, "Let's go!" He set off running toward the town, and the irregulars pounded after him.

As he'd told Fink, the unruly guerrillas weren't cut from the same cloth as conventional soldiers. The force never maneuvered with any great precision. But they nearly always managed more order than this. At the moment they seemed less an army than a mob or a wolf pack coursing through the dark.

In other circumstances, that might have troubled Montrose, but in a raid like this, it shouldn't pose a problem. Speed was what mattered, striking quickly enough to keep the miserable Heretics from slipping through his fingers.

The derelict buildings he'd seen from atop the spire loomed out of the darkness ahead. About twenty-five wraiths, many carrying suitcases, backpacks, or bundles, were milling around in the open area between two crumbling tenements.

The Heretical grand alliance, thought Montrose with a sneer. The Sister of Athena who was supposedly putting the conspiracy together had clearly been less than successful in convincing the various sects to join forces. He studied the scene before him, looking for a woman who appeared to be organizing the evacuation, but he couldn't see one.

Someone shouted. Evidently a lookout had spotted Montrose's raiders surging out of the night. The irregulars on the flanks of the advance began to fan out, the better to envelop their prey.

Then a blinding glare and a deafening screech blasted the night apart.

32

Montrose staggered, squinting against the dazzling glare, fighting the impulse to throw his AK-47 away and use his hands to seal his ears.

Around him, his men stumbled. Some screamed and others fired their guns, apparently at random, the cries and the shooting barely audible above the endless shriek. After a moment other firearms barked in response, and the guerrillas began to drop.

Shielding his eyes, pivoting back and forth, Montrose tried to make out the source of the enemy fire. To his dismay, when he did manage to catch a glimpse of the terrain beyond the light, he discovered that it seemed to change from one second to the next. Formations of riflemen and hordes of hideous Spectres flickered in and out of existence. The contours of the ground flowed as if made of jelly. At one point the whole world inverted itself, and he felt as if he were about to plummet into the endless abyss of the sky.

At the same time, terror yammered through his mind. The screaming, the glare, and the disorienting transformations of the environment were simply too much. He wanted to rip the eyes from his head, ram a stiletto into his own ears, put his rifle in his mouth and pull the trigger, just to make the torment stop.

What prevented him was that he knew what was going on, or at least he hoped he did. A group of Sandmen were creating the glare and spinning disorienting illusions, while a choir of Chanteurs were singing to fill the Hierarchs with terror. Montrose had never realized that the practitioners of either Arcanos could work together to such devastating effect, but evidently, with practice, preparation, and, no doubt, a team leader possessing extraordinary knowledge of his mystic art, it was possible.

Bolstered by his comprehension, the Scot fought his incipient panic, insisting to himself that it wasn't *his* fear, not really. The Heretic bastards were putting it inside his head. And finally, it loosened its grip.

He peered about. Guns rattled, and arrows arced through the air. Many of his men were already wounded or gone entirely, devoured by the Void. Others, though uninjured, wept and shuddered on the ground. Some were still trying to shoot blindly back at their assailants. A few men tried to flee in what appeared to be the direction of the old church and the river. An instant later, they staggered and fell. Apparently, they hadn't been running *away* from the Heretics but directly *at* them.

A big man knelt on the ground a few feet away, pumping off rounds from a shotgun. It looked like Fink, though Montrose couldn't be sure in the glare. He scrambled toward him.

The world spun like a carousel, nearly throwing him off his feet. Something in the air, a tactile and olfactory illusion woven by the enemy Sandmen, burned his nose and eyes. An arrow, its force nearly spent, glanced off his mask. At last, he reached the man with the shotgun.

It was Fink. Grinning ferociously, he shouted, "Here's that setback you mentioned." Montrose could barely hear him over the wailing.

"Sandmen and Chanteurs," the Scot bellowed back, "working together. Sandmen hid most of the enemy behind illusions until we got to the piece of ground where they wanted us."

"Figured that out," answered Fink. "Don't know what to do about it, though, not when I can't tell where any damn thing is."

"I can." Montrose hoped that his memory and instincts weren't playing him false. "We're in a depression in the ground. The enemy has us surrounded on three sides. The town is that way." He pointed. "The Chanteurs and Sandmen are on one of the rooftops directly in front of us."

Fink eyed his dubiously. "Are you sure?"

"Yes," Montrose lied. "I'm a Harbinger and a general. Nothing can ruin my sense of direction, and I know where to position troops for optimum effect. If I were commanding the other side, I'd put the Sandmen and Chanteurs someplace they could stand together to coordinate their magic, overlook the entire battlefield, and enjoy a measure of protection. And if we're going to turn this fight around, we have to get up there *now* and stop the bombardment."

"How?" Fink asked. "It's one thing to know where they are. But to charge it blind, with the ground spinning under your feet and rows of gunmen in the way—"

"We can do it," Montrose said. "Grab a man or two, anybody who looks as if he can still fight."

Fink rose, pulled a mewling wraith with stubby jeweled horns off the ground, and shook him. Montrose grasped the shoulder of a youthful-looking wraith with a smoking revolver in either hand. "This way!" the Stygian shouted.

In the next few seconds, Montrose collected two frightened men, and Fink three. Not enough, but the Stygian doubted there was time to gather any more. Doing his best to block out the excruciating distractions of the glare and the shrieking, the fear still gnawing at his nerves, he focused his will and invoked his Harbinger powers.

A glittering circular hole opened in the ground before him. "In!" he bellowed. "Jump in!"

Grinning, Fink did so instantly, and the other men scrambled after him. Ordinarily any wraith would hesitate to leap into a Nihil. But conditions on the killing ground were so painful, so terrifying, that even the Tempest seemed preferable. Hoping that he hadn't sent his companions tumbling into the jaws of a Spectre, Montrose jumped after them.

He landed on a barren plain littered with huge gray boulders. A freezing wind, its ferocious howl faint in comparison with the screeching of the Chanteur choir, ripped at his hair and cloak, and blue lightning flickered in the churning clouds overhead. The Nihil he'd opened, a disk of shadow floating unsupported in the air, made a sizzling sound and vanished.

Fink looked this way and that. "What next?" he asked.

Montrose extended his arcane perceptions, studying the patterns of twisted and fractured space around him, and then said, "We go this way. Quickly, but warily. The Tempest is every bit as dangerous as you've heard."

Weapons ready, scanning the darkness for flickers of motion, the seven men skulked forward. "I think I get the idea," Fink murmured to Montrose. "We're going to pop back into the Shadowlands behind the guys who were shooting at us. It's a good trick. Why don't we use it all the time?"

"Because it can all too easily go awry," the Scot replied. Sensing a kink in the dimensional fabric off to the left, he led his troops in that direction. "The metaphysical structure of the Tempest is so complicated, so contrary, that often even the greatest Harbinger can't bend it to its will. I may not be able to create another doorway that will take us anywhere close to where we want to go. We may not get back for hours, even if it only feels like a few minutes to us. A gang of Spectres may jump us—"

Behind them, one of the men screamed.

Montrose and Fink whirled. "You and your big mouth," the latter said.

A few yards back, a patch of the hard, cracked ground had turned to mush and was sucking down the last two wraiths in the procession. Already the shrieking, thrashing irregulars had vanished up to their knees. At first Montrose thought the men were sinking of their own weight, but then he noticed the long, thin tentacles twining around them and dragging them down.

The comrades of the unfortunate soldiers hovered helplessly about the newly formed quicksand pit. They couldn't shoot the tentacles, not without hitting the prey in their clutches as well, and the pool was too wide for them to grab their friends and drag them to safety. If they tried, they'd only topple in themselves.

Montrose levitated and hurtled to the center of the pit. He tore at the tentacles gripping the man who'd sunk the deepest, but he couldn't rip them away. Grasping the wraith by the arms, he struggled to fly straight upward, only to find he didn't have enough lift to overcome the strength of the hidden monster. Its victim continued to slide from view. The Scot had to let him go to avoid being pulled down himself. Gibbering curses and pleas for help until the muck slopped into his mouth, the guerrilla went under with a ghastly slurping sound.

Turning, Montrose saw that the second irregular was almost gone. Only his hairless head and naked shoulders with their reflective brass-like skin remained above the surface. Snarling, the Stygian whipped out his rapier and began thrusting it into the slime.

The blade didn't contact anything solid. After a moment, additional tentacles shot out of the quicksand and tried to whip around him.

"Get away!" shouted one of the irregulars.

Doing his best to fend off the tentacles with his empty hand, Montrose kept stabbing. The unseen monster's arms lashed around his legs and yanked him downward, plunging his boots into the gelid quicksand. Then the point of the rapier finally punched into something solid.

The tentacles thrashed, loosening their hold. Montrose frantically flew upward, freeing himself from the tangle, and then looked down. The wraith with the brazen skin was nearly gone. Only his yellow hands remained above the surface.

Swooping downward, Montrose gripped them and then, straining, rising again, heaved the man out of the quicksand and set him on solid ground. Deep, steaming gashes spiraled around the soldier's body where the tentacles had burned into his flesh.

The Scot flew back over the pit. Hovering just above the surface, he plunged his arm repeatedly into the icy slime, groping for the other irregular. He couldn't find him.

After a few seconds, Montrose grimaced in frustration. For all he knew, the soldier was still alive, and mired within reach. But with scores of men in jeopardy back in the Shadowlands, there was no more time to fish for him.

The Stygian flew to the fellow he had rescued. "Can you walk?" he asked.

The brazen-skinned wraith gave him a shaky nod. "I think so."

Montrose turned to another of the irregulars. "You keep an eye on him, and help him if he needs it. Let's move."

Montrose resumed his place at the head of the column, and they hurried on. "That was pretty smart work," said Fink.

Montrose scowled, disgusted with himself. "Nonsense. I should have sensed the creature's presence before it attacked. Failing that, I should have saved both of our lads." As the two wraiths neared another towering boulder, the Scot perceived a crumple in the fabric of space. "This is the place."

Fink pivoted toward the four wraiths behind them. "Look alive, boys. We're going back to the fight."

Montrose invoked his Harbinger Arcanos. For a moment the dimensional fabric resisted him, but then a round black hole opened in the side of the rock. He checked his AK-47, making sure it was ready to fire, and then sprang through the portal.

To his relief, he emerged into the Shadowlands precisely where—and when—he'd intended, behind a line of Heretic gunmen in dark glasses, all facing in the opposite direction, and just in front of a crumbling brick tenement, on the roof of which the choir of Chanteurs was keening. Fortunately, now that he was out of the target area, their song failed to rattle him. Presumably the Sandmen were atop the building also, though from his vantage point, he couldn't see them.

Fink and the other irregulars scrambled out of the rift. Montrose pressed his finger to his lips, commanding stealth, and pointed at the rooftop.

Fink nodded, pivoted, and led the other raiders toward the tenement's front door. Montrose levitated. Though his blood was up, he didn't relish the idea of assaulting the rooftop alone. But his helpless men in the field of glare were dying by the second. He couldn't put off attacking until his allies appeared for fear they'd arrive too late.

He started shooting the instant he rose above the parapet, sweeping the assault rifle in an arc, cutting down Sandmen in gaudy clothing and Chanteurs clutching a miscellany of musical instruments. The deafening chorus of wailing ended abruptly.

As Montrose had hoped, he'd caught the Heretics by surprise. Alighting on the rooftop, he shot another pair of Sandmen, and then the rebels who were still on their feet struck back.

Some snatched pistols from holsters and started to shoot. Others used their Arcanos. Ghastly shrieks jolted Montrose, or even seared away patches of his skin. Bursts of glare dazzled him, and intangible fingers fumbled at his mind, trying to make him fall asleep.

Snarling, nearly berserk with hatred, he spun this way and that, striving to keep any of his opponents from getting a fix on him, hoping their own numbers would hinder them. The assault rifle blazed and vibrated in his grip.

Three more Heretics went down, their bodies dissolving in ripples of shadow. Grinning crazily, Montrose decided this kamikaze strike was going to work. He didn't even need the reinforcements still charging madly up the stairs. He was going to clear the rooftop all by himself.

Then a Chanteur wailed and blasted Montrose's legs out from under him. But as the Stygian fell, he glimpsed Fink and the other irregulars bursting through the walls of the enclosure that presumably capped the stairwell.

Fink bellowed and brandished his shotgun over his head. Crackling strands of electricity blazed across the rooftop, filling the air with the smell of ozone. Heretics, caught in the discharge, shuddered, and burned. The other intruders opened fire with their rifles.

The diversion gave Montrose the moment he needed to scramble back to his feet. He tried to shoot a Chanteur, a little man with a guitar strung across his back, discovered the AK-47 was empty, and clubbed the Heretic with the stock instead. Even as the musician dropped, the Scot reached inside his mantle for another clip.

From the corner of his eye, he glimpsed something flashing at him. As he pivoted, a tattered canvas lawn chair, hurled with considerable force, slammed against his shoulder. The Skinlands object sailed on straight through his body to vanish over the parapet. The impact didn't alter the course of its flight an iota. But it staggered Montrose.

He tried to regain his balance, and a second folding chair whizzed through his legs. He fell back down. A slender blond woman, no doubt the Spook who'd thrown the furniture, charged him, a *katana* in her upraised hands and a silver owl pendant, the emblem of the Sisterhood of Athena, bouncing on her breast.

And Montrose froze. Because the rebel leader was Louise.

For a moment he felt empty, as if his astonishment had smothered every other emotion, even the desire to survive. Then a wave of rage and hate crashed through him. Lurching to one knee, he jerked his rifle over his head. The Japanese sword clanged against the barrel.

He slammed the AK-47 into Louise's knee. Bone cracked, and she reeled backward. Dropping the rifle, he scrambled up, drew his rapier, and went after her.

Hobbling now, she started to cut at his head, then faltered, her blue eyes widening. He realized that, thanks to his mask, she hadn't recognized him until now. The enemy commander with the auburn lovelocks might have *reminded* her of the man she'd once betrayed, but if so, she'd dismissed it as a chance resemblance.

That she hadn't even known him infuriated Montrose still further. Screaming, he thrust the rapier through her forearm. Black light rippled from the wound. The *katana* tumbled from her grasp. Dropping his own weapon, he pounced on her, intent on ripping her apart with his hands.

They grappled, and he bore her backward. A dagger with a silver owl's head pommel and a curved darksteel blade popped into existence in her hand.

Once again, it was Montrose's turn to be startled. Because even delirious with fury, he saw that Louise's weapon was the knife Katrina had showed him.

Louise started to thrust it at his breast. Then something smashed down on top of her head, bone crunched, and she slumped in his arms.

Montrose raised his eyes, to discover that Fink had come up behind her and clubbed her with the butt of his shotgun. Though he was leering as savagely as ever, the hulking, black-haired wraith looked somehow less real, almost translucent, as if he'd been drawing on his Haunter's Arcanos so heavily that even his prodigious strength was nearly spent.

For a second Montrose wanted to strike his lieutenant for daring to intrude on what should have been an intimate moment. But ultimately, that resentment was puny, an ephemeral emotion. It couldn't divert him from the utter loathing he felt for Louise. And even though she wasn't conscious at the moment, it would still be delightful to mutilate her. After all, as long as he was careful not to do too much damage, she'd heal, and he could hurt her all over again when she woke up. He threw her down, straddled her, and began to tear open her garments.

"What are you doing?" Fink demanded.

"It's all right," said Montrose. "Leave me alone."

Fink grabbed his shoulder, yanked him to his feet, and slapped him. "Snap out of it," the river man growled.

Montrose thrashed, struggling to break the other wraith's grip. "You don't understand! It's *her!*"

"I don't give a watery shit who it is," Fink replied. "There's still a fight going on. By wiping out the sons of bitches up here, we've given our boys an outside chance of winning it, but only if their leader rallies them."

Montrose's frenzy lost its edge. Of course, the battle. He'd forgotten all about it. He gave his head a shake, trying to clear it. "I'm sorry. It's just that this woman—"

"Whoever she is, she'll keep!" Fink picked up the rapier and stuck the hilt in Montrose's hand. "Are you ready?"

The Stygian nodded. "Let's do it."

33

Montrose strolled from one group of irregulars to the next, inquiring about their welfare, joking with them, and listening to them boast about their valor in the battle. Most of the ruffians seemed to feel they'd won the victory over the Heretics more or less singlehandedly, and never mind the jibes of their comrades, who heckled the storytellers with accusations of poltroonery, martial ineptitude, or both.

Ordinarily the Stygian could have performed this duty gladly, taking satisfaction in the sight of every survivor, grateful that a visit from their commander could distract the men from the loss of fallen friends and the pain of their wounds. But tonight, with his hatred, frustration, and indecision grinding together, it took a Herculean effort just to smile, pay attention to what the guerrillas were saying, and offer an appreciative response.

But at last, the chore drew to a close. The final casualty was an amputee in a blue leather mask who was using a long spear for a crutch. The wispy shape of a new lower leg and foot, not solid enough to support his weight as yet, depended from his stump. Montrose kidded the fellow, a former highwayman, about his predilection for chubby women, clapped him on the shoulder, and bade him good night. Then he trudged over to one of the dilapidated tenements and slumped down with his back against the cracked brick wall.

After a minute he wished he'd gone farther away from what remained of his army. From where he was resting, he could hear the whimpering and weeping of the captured Heretics, whom his men, enraged by their near defeat, had brutalized even more thoroughly than usual. The moans reminded him of the one prisoner he was holding separately, on the roof where they'd tried to murder one another.

A hulking form lumbered out of the gloom. "I made the count," said Fink. "We lost half our men."

Montrose nodded. "That was about what I estimated." "Percentagewise, the losses are even heavier than on our first raid." Fink shrugged and sat down. "But it's war, right? People are going to die. What matters is that we won."

The Stygian sighed. "I suppose."

Fink cocked his head. "What's troubling you now, Anacreon? The Sister of Athena? What's the story on her, anyway?"

After a moment's hesitation, Montrose said, "I knew her when I was alive. Her name is Louise, and she was my lover. She also betrayed me to my death."

Fink grinned. "Ouch. No wonder you were so eager to torture her. So, what are you moping around down here for? Go pay her a call."

"I want to," Montrose said. "You can't imagine how badly I want it. But I'm afraid that if I do, my Shadow will grow even stronger."

"Mask and Scythe, man, are you going to let a little thing like that stand in the way of sweet revenge? Judging from past experience, if your Shadow *does* slip its reins, all it's likely to do is make you hurt Heretics, and that's what you want to do anyway."

"You have a point," Montrose said. "This is one of those occasions when my dark side and the rest of me are in accord. But there's another problem." He described his encounter with Katrina.

"*Forbear*," said Fink at the end of the story. "In other words, show mercy."

"Yes."

"Are you sure it was the same knife?"

"Absolutely," Montrose said. "Before Katrina picked me up, I met a Spectre wearing Louise's form. Evidently the creature was telepathic, and plucked her image from my mind. Katrina as much as told me the encounter was a portent—the Tempest is like that—meaning, no doubt, that I was destined to find the real Louise later on, but I was too thick to understand her."

Fink grimaced. "Your Ferryman was too cryptic by half. If she knew you were going to run into our friend on the rooftop, she should have told you flat out."

"She may not have known," Montrose said. "I'm no Oracle, but I'm told their insights are often jumbled and incomplete."

"Well, I think she scammed you, because she realized you hated Louise too much to pledge to spare her. And I say the trickery releases you from your promise, particularly since it was given under duress."

Montrose smiled ruefully. "I've been telling myself the same thing, but I'm not convinced."

"Well, who gives a piss anyway," said Fink. "Just break the damn promise. It wouldn't be the first time, would it?"

"No," Montrose said. "But you know, I've always tried to keep my word. Even when I was backstabbing my way up the ranks of the Hierarchy, if I actually made someone a pledge, I did my best to keep it. Considering the sins I *did* commit, it was probably absurd to cleave to that one scruple, but nonetheless, I did."

Somewhere in the gloom, an irregular began to sing a love song about a lady named "Michelle." The fellow was no Chanteur, but he had a pleasant baritone voice. The gentle strains of the ballad made a stark contrast to the anger seething in Montrose's breast.

"I wonder," said Fink, "why the Ferryman even cared. What's so special about this one Heretic?"

"I have no idea. Katrina implied, in the vaguest manner possible, that the business with the knife was linked to some mysterious challenge I have to face. It sounded like gibberish at the time, but now that we've stumbled onto the business with the false Pardoners, I wonder."

"Has it occurred to you," said Fink, "that you *have* to punish the bitch? She's a dangerous rebel. She killed half your soldiers. Even if our boys would sit still for it, it would be treason to let her off the hook."

"I know," said Montrose. "As a matter of fact, I even told

Katrina I wouldn't keep the promise if it meant neglecting my duty. But I *can* exercise some restraint. I don't have to tear Louise apart with my own hands."

Fink leered. "But you'll regret it if you don't."

Montrose nodded. "I will indeed." He stood up. "I need to make up my mind, and I'm not getting it done down here. Perhaps if I see her again, I'll be able to decide."

"Sounds sensible," said Fink. "Give her a welt or two for me."

Montrose entered the tenement and climbed the stairs. As he neared the roof, he faltered. *I don't have to do this*, he thought, surprising himself. *I never have to look at her again if I don't want to.*

But even as he framed the thought, he realized it was a lie. He *did* need to see her, even if a part of him cringed at the prospect. He stepped through the substance of a door with flaking paint and out into the moonlight.

Louise lay near one edge of the tar paper roof, her slender body wrapped in an extraordinary quantity of chains. Either Montrose's men had wanted to make certain she wouldn't slip her restraints with her Spook Arcanos, or else they'd simply decided to make her as uncomfortable as possible. A red rubber ball gag with a black leather strap filled her mouth, distending her cheeks, and a blindfold covered her eyes. A bored-looking guard with a crossbow sat on the parapet beside her.

Montrose hesitated again, then urged himself forward. "I want to be alone with her for a bit," he said to the sentry. "Wait on the stairs." Louise's head jerked around at the sound of his voice. The guard rose and sauntered to the stairs.

As Montrose knelt beside the captive, sorrow and a kind of bitter nostalgia rose inside him, not replacing his hatred but coexisting with it. *Dear God*, he thought, *what we shared together made me so happy, even in the midst of a desperate time. How did we ever come to this?* Discovering that he wanted to see her eyes, he slipped the blindfold off. They were the same clear blue that he remembered.

"Yes," he said, "it's truly me. Who would have thought we'd

meet again, on another continent, after all these centuries? It's a strange world, isn't it?"

She gazed up at him beseechingly. It made him grateful for his mask. He suspected his face was contorted with hatred or anguish, but he was in control of his voice. His tone was light, conveying the message that she was a miserable creature scarcely worthy of his notice. That he valued her as little as she had him.

"I find myself in a ludicrous situation," Montrose continued. "I'd like to spend the next few months torturing you, and send you to the Void when that grew tiresome. I'm sure you aren't expecting anything less. But before I knew who you were, I promised a benefactor I'd show you mercy. What would you do in my place?"

The strap securing the gag snapped, and the rubber ball popped out of Louise's mouth. Montrose reflexively lifted his hands to defend himself, but she didn't try to strike him with the object. It simply dropped to the rooftop.

"I'm sorry, James," she gasped. "I'm so sorry. I didn't know you were leading the purge. If I had, I never would have tried to destroy you. I would have arranged to meet with you. I would have found another way."

"As you did three hundred and fifty years ago?"

She gaped at him in horror. "You... you know about that?"

"Oh, yes," Montrose said. "Your fellow Judas Van Lengen was kind enough to enlighten me."

"I swear, I never *wanted* to betray you," said Louise. "I *loved* you—"

For some reason, that blatantly false claim disturbed the precarious balance of passions in Montrose's mind. "Liar!" he exploded, battering her with his fists. "Liar! Liar!"

She made a choking sound and went limp. Her head rolled sideways. Perhaps she hadn't yet fully recovered from the clubbing Fink had given her, and Montrose's blows had aggravated the injury anew. At any rate, he'd beaten her back into unconsciousness.

He hit her six more times before he was able to stop. Shuddering, he curled his fingers into hooks and reached for her eyes.

And then, somehow, he seemed to see himself from the outside, as an observer might. He beheld a gloating sadist about to inflict atrocities on a helpless woman, and though the prospect thrilled him, it now sickened him as well. He had a vague intuition that if he allowed himself to become such a vile, perverted creature, even for one brief interlude, he might never recover his true self again. He leaped to his feet and scrambled back several paces, like a mortal recoiling from a poisonous snake.

Still his body quivered with the lust to maim her. He turned his back on her, and the compulsion eased slightly.

"I won't hurt you any more myself," he said to the unconscious woman. "I won't even have you destroyed, not completely. But you *will* pay. I'm shipping you to Stygia, tonight, with instructions that you go to the Masquers, or the soul forges." He pictured her twisted into the shape of a hideous barghest, the magic in her iron muzzle warping her mind into that of a beast. Or sculpted into a torch, silently screaming as her crown of freezing barrow-flame devoured her. Or shattered into a handful of oboli, each coin retaining a splinter of sentience, just enough to suffer for eternity.

He smirked at the thought of her agony, then winced at another surge of shame and self-disgust.

"I'm sorry," he muttered, just as if Katrina were present to hear him. "I believe you were trying to help me when you extorted my pledge, and I wish I could keep it. But this is as close as I come."

He hurried to the stairwell before he could change his mind. As he descended, he sensed his restive Shadow stirring, swelling, invading his conscious mind. He frantically struggled to muster the will to repress it, until, suddenly, the world seemed dim and far away. He felt as if he were drifting off to sleep.

34

Chiarmonte, an Anacreon of the Order of the Avenging Flame and the Smiling Lord's spy master, was a small, gray man who generally carried himself with the diffidence of a mild-mannered clerk. He'd once told Potter he attributed his success as an agent of the commune of eleventh-century Venice to his unassuming demeanor. Now, however, he stood at parade rest with his iron mask cradled in his right hand. Potter, ensconced on a golden throne with red velvet cushions and eagle-claw feet, had the unpleasant feeling that he knew the reason for the other wraith's martial posture.

"You've come up empty, haven't you?" the Deathlord said.

Chiarmonte flicked his eyes at Demetrius, who was standing in the corner of the small audience chamber, the bluish light of the nearest barrow-flame lamp glinting on the sardonyx helmet tucked casually under his arm. It was a subtle gesture, but Potter had no difficulty interpreting it.

"You can speak freely in front of Demetrius," he said impatiently, exasperated that, even with his life in jeopardy, his lieutenants still insisted on playing their courtiers' games, angling for his favor by subtly casting aspersions on their fellows. "Your report, please."

Chiarmonte inclined his head. "Of course, my liege. I regret that I have *come up empty*, thus far. The Legionnaires assigned to guard the park on the night of the attack appear to be loyal. None of them deviated significantly from his story—"

"*Significantly?*" Demetrius interjected.

Chiarmonte's thin-lipped mouth tightened. "When you torture a man and his loved ones," he explained, "and refuse to accept his story, he's likely to offer a second one eventually, even if the original version was true. But none of those alternate stories checked out. Which is to say, in my opinion, the men kept faithful watch over the perimeter of the park, but failed to see the assassin slip inside. As far as our agents have been able to discover, so did everyone else who happened to be in the general vicinity."

"Perhaps it isn't all that important to identify the man," Demetrius said. "He used a distinctive weapon, the ravages of old age. Which suggests he was working for the Ashen Lady."

"I wouldn't leap to any conclusions," Chiarmonte said. "It's conceivable that some other enemy devised that means of attack precisely because it would divert suspicion to the Seat of Shadows." He gazed into Potter's eyes. "Frankly, Dread Lord, I think it would be rash to assume that *any* of your peers instigated the attack. Our informants in their households don't know anything about such a scheme. And you have a plethora of *known* enemies. Heretics, Renegades, Spectres, the Dark Kingdom of Jade—"

Potter shook his head. "None of them have access to the highest levels of the city."

"They certainly aren't supposed to," Chiarmonte conceded. "However, any defensive system can be breached."

"Perhaps," Potter said, "but I have other information indicating that someone on the Council is plotting against me."

Chiarmonte lifted an eyebrow. "Since I'm your chief of intelligence," he said a bit ironically, "perhaps it would be appropriate for you to share it with me."

Potter supposed he deserved the rebuke. The Venetian probably did have a right to know. But the Deathlord was reluctant to confide his troubling visions to anyone but Demetrius. They were too personal. It would make him look too human, and too vulnerable. "Its intimations derived from a mystical source. You don't need to know the specifics. There aren't any, really."

Chiarmonte sketched a shallow bow. "As you wish, Dread Lord," he said, his tone now entirely neutral. "Undoubtedly, you know best."

Wonderful, Potter thought sourly, *people are trying to* murder *me, and he has injured feelings.* "You're entirely right about one thing," he said, hoping to mollify the man, "it doesn't have to be the Ashen Lady who sent the assassin. Even if it was, we don't know how many other Deathlords were in on the plot. And until we do, we can't retaliate."

"I'll continue to investigate," Chiarmonte said. "I'll also confer with the captain of the household guard about tightening up security."

"Good," said Potter. "Carry on." Chiarmonte bowed and exited the chamber. "Idiot."

Demetrius cocked his head. "I've always thought him competent, if unimaginative."

"If he were competent, I wouldn't be in this predicament." Potter sighed. "Or perhaps that isn't fair. I don't know what to believe. I feel as if I'm not thinking straight. And that I might even be losing my bond with my mask. Its power it seems sluggish and remote. If I could tap it as easily as I used to, I would have crushed the assassin the instant I sensed his presence. I keep wondering if someone has laid a curse on me."

"If so," Demetrius replied, moving closer to the throne, "it's such a subtle malediction that none of your servants, with all our various Arcanos, can detect it. I think you're simply feeling the effects of stress."

"Then see if you can ease my apprehension," Potter said. "Scry for me."

The Greek frowned, but to Potter's relief, for once he didn't need to be coaxed. "Very well, my lord. As it happens, I stumbled on a new technique in a volume I found in one of your libraries. I suspect someone salvaged the tome from the ruins of the old-time Oracles' guild hall."

"Do you think it will serve us better than the cards, or studying the patterns in the clouds and lightning?"

Demetrius smiled. "We'll find out."

The Greek set his mask on the dais supporting the throne, then opened the leather satchel hanging at his side. A wavering glow shone forth, staining his swarthy hand and the folds of his toga. He reached into the bag and brought out a ball of luminous, opalescent jelly. Soul stuff, smelted but not yet transformed into wood, metal, or some other less disquieting material.

Demetrius said, "Please remove your gauntlets." Potter complied, and the Oracle handed him the glowing mass. It was cool to the touch, and oozed and squirmed feebly in his grasp.

"Knead it," Demetrius said. "Roll it around. Handle it until it feels right to you." Feeling a bit like a child playing in mud, or making snowballs, Potter manipulated the material for about fifteen seconds, then handed it back.

Demetrius backed two paces away from the throne, down the scarlet runner that ran from the dais to the door. Frowning with concentration, murmuring incantations, he began to draw long curling tendrils from the central mass. Occasional ripples of darkness, symptomatic of the Oblivion gnawing at the heart of all things, pulsed through the strands of light. Crude faces formed and dissolved, some blank and mindless, a few contorted in anguish, and one grinning and mugging with demented glee.

Before long the mass became a structure rather like a shrub, with multiple stems rising from a common base. The Oracle slowly, carefully released his creation, and it floated unsupported in the air. Then, murmuring once more, he moved to one of the lamps, removed the fluted chimney, and put the fingers of his left hand in the flame.

The residue of soul plasm clinging to his skin kindled instantly. Potter winced, but Demetrius didn't appear to be in any pain. He touched his hands together, setting the right one ablaze, and then returned to his creation. He began to caress the various tendrils, reminding Potter of a harpist plucking the strings of his instrument.

For several seconds his ministrations had no obvious effect. Then, suddenly, one section of the ectoplasmic sculpture caught fire. The embryonic faces screamed, a faint piping barely audible above the crackle of the blaze, and a stench like burning flesh suffused the air.

Three strands quickly burned away to nothing, leaving the rest of the structure unscathed. And as the cold flames finished consuming them, a circular window opened in the air.

Beyond it was a street of derelict bungalows, their crumbling facades and verandahs fissured with Nihils. A crescent moon shone among the tatters of clouds overhead. A pair of grievously wounded Legionnaires lay amid a litter of arrows, notched and broken swords, spent cartridges, and a fallen standard emblazoned with a fountain of liquid fire, one of the thirty-odd emblems of the Smiling Lord.

Potter leaned forward, trying to see more, but the window vanished.

"Is it working?" Demetrius asked. His normally mellifluous voice was a little rough, betraying a discomfort or strain his calm expression and easy movements denied.

"Yes," Potter said. "I saw a Haunt somewhere in the Shadowlands. There'd been a battle, and my troops lost it. Show me more."

"I'll try," Demetrius stroked the phosphorescent tendrils. Another piece of the construct exploded into flame, and a second window opened.

This time Potter beheld the Isle of Sorrows as if he were soaring high above it. From such an altitude, with only ochre lightning to illuminate the scene, it was hard to make anything out. The City of Dark Echoes was an intricate, bewildering mass of vague protrusions and myriad points of light. But after a moment he realized that one light looked peculiar. It was too large.

When he focused his attention on it, the window zoomed in on it like a camera, until he seemed to be hovering fifty feet above it. He saw that it was a great mass of barrow-fire, consuming his section of the palace.

He cried out, and the window closed.

"What did you see this time?" Demetrius panted.

Potter gestured impatiently, brushing the question aside. They could talk later. "Show me more."

"As my lord commands." Demetrius ran his burning fingers along the remaining strands of glow. More of them flared and vanished.

This time Potter saw himself, stumbling through the corridors of his fortress, his halberd clutched in his hands. Or rather, what was left of his halberd. The enchanted weapon's shaft had snapped midway down. What was even more horrifying was that some force had cleft the Smiling Lord's *mask* as well. One half of the steel visor still clung to the left side of his face, but his right profile was *exposed.*

The figure in the vision stopped, sucked in a deep breath, and bellowed. Potter couldn't hear him, but he could read his lips. "Guards! Guards!"

After a moment, the beleaguered Deathlord's mouth twisted in despair. *Because he doesn't hear anyone rushing to his aid,* Potter thought. *Impossible as it seems, there* isn't *anyone to come. He's been betrayed.*

The Potter in the vision hobbled on, until a ring of shadowy figures abruptly materialized around him. Snarling, their quarry whirled his broken weapon over his head, but never got a chance to use it. His enemies swarmed over him like wolves pulling down a fawn. Darksteel daggers flashed in their black-gloved hands.

The window snapped shut. "No!" Potter yelped. He glared at Demetrius. "More!"

"I'm sorry," Demetrius croaked, trembling. "There isn't any more." He motioned toward the luminous construct, and Potter saw that the last burst of barrow-fire had devoured all but a few wisps of it, and these were shriveling by the moment.

"There's a bit of plasm left," the Deathlord said. "Enough for one more effort." Demetrius hesitated. "Do it!"

"Very well." Looking as if he were struggling not to flinch, the Greek told hold of the last crumbling vestiges of his creation.

The final explosion was far more intense than those which had preceded it. The burst of terrible cold slammed Potter backward as if someone had clubbed him in the face. This time, no window opened. Instead, Demetrius fell down thrashing, his arms aflame from fingertips to elbows.

Potter leaped up and scrambled toward him. At the same time, clearly making a supreme effort, Demetrius rasped out another invocation. Despite the agony grating in his voice, the words of power seemed to resonate like the beats of a gong. The fires consuming his flesh winked out abruptly. So did the ones in the lamps along the walls, plunging the chamber into darkness. The Greek lay motionless.

Potter flung himself down beside his lieutenant, peering frantically, terrified that the man was about to melt away. At that moment, he felt that if Demetrius perished, his demise would leave him utterly friendless and alone.

But to his relief, there were no ripples of shadow eroding Demetrius's substance, not even within his charred and withered arms. After a moment, the Greek looked up at his master. "I think I see why that technique was abandoned," he whispered.

"I'm sorry," Potter said. "I shouldn't have goaded you onward when you knew it was time to stop."

"Please," said Demetrius, his voice a shade stronger, "don't say such things. I'm your servant. My only purpose is to obey you. It's for me to apologize, for bungling my task." A long, pale worm of ectoplasm wriggled down his forearm as his shriveled limbs began to heal. "If you could please move back, I'd like to try to get up. Marble floors are decorative, but they're also cold and hard."

"Of course." Potter helped Demetrius to his feet, put his arm around him, more or less carried him to the dais, and sat him down. "Is this better?"

"Yes," gasped Demetrius. Clearly, motion had aggravated the pain of his burns. "Thank you, my liege. May I ask what the divination showed you?"

"Nothing too alarming," Potter said sardonically. "Merely defeat, betrayal, and my own murder. But it was just like all the other visions. Incomplete. I still don't know which of the other Deathlords are plotting against me."

"Perhaps none of them are," Demetrius said. "Sometimes the shape of the future expresses itself *symbolically*—"

Potter gave him a withering stare.

"Forgive me," said the Greek. "I'm talking nonsense. The pain is making me lightheaded. Of course, when you see variations on the same horrible theme, time after time, when someone has already tried to slay you..."

"It was the same problem this time, wasn't it? You couldn't

show me everything I need to know because you haven't seen my deathmarks. Because you don't really know who I am."

"Yes," said Demetrius. A shiny white burn on the back of his wrist rippled and turned into dark, unblemished skin. "It's a technical problem. I'll keep searching for the solution."

"But what if you don't find it before the crisis comes?"

"I hope matters won't fall out that way. But even if they do, you still have Chiarmonte to gather intelligence by other methods."

"To the devil with Chiarmonte. He just admitted his spies can't discover anything." Potter took a deep breath, steadying himself. "I'm going to do it. I'm going to reveal myself to you."

Demetrius's dark eyes widened. "I'm honored, Dread Lord, but are you certain? I'm merely one of countless functionaries. Why should I be entrusted with your greatest secret?"

"You just risked your life and got burned trying to help me," Potter said. "If I can't trust you, who can I trust?" He lifted his hands to his visor, and then faltered.

Charon forbade this, he thought. He called it treason. And it will leave me vulnerable in a way that no Deathlord should ever be.

But the emperor was gone. Why should his laws outlast him if they were no longer useful? And Potter was already vulnerable in the way that mattered most. Every hour of every day, he sensed his unknown enemies closing in for the kill.

Quickly, before he could change his mind, he yanked the mask away from the rest of his helmet. A bolt of panic ripped through his mind, and he shuddered. His naked skin tingled in the cool air.

After a moment, his terror loosened its grip. Ridiculously enough, he now felt shy, flustered, as he had the first time he'd taken off his clothes in front of a woman. He looked at Demetrius. The Greek was trembling also, and had lowered his eyes.

For some reason, the other wraith's manifest anxiety made Potter feel calmer. "You have to look at me," he said wryly. "That's the whole point. I promise that no one is going to burst in and execute you for it. You probably won't even turn to stone."

Demetrius nodded and slowly lifted his head.

Potter envisioned the features his lieutenant was beholding. Straw-colored hair and pale blue eyes. Apple cheeks, a snub nose, and a rather weak chin. He smiled ruefully. "It's not nearly as impressive as it ought to be, is it?"

"You died younger than I would have expected," Demetrius said, a hint of compassion in his tone.

"I was fresh out of Eton, just beginning what was supposed to be a long and glorious career in Her Majesty's army," Potter said. "But I don't much regret dying young, not anymore. My true misfortune is that I died so *recently*. I was killed in the Sepoy Mutiny of 1857. Charon made me the Smiling Lord ten years later, even though I was only a centurion in his service at the time. I don't know what happened to the old Smiling Lord, or why the emperor chose me as a replacement. He wouldn't say. At first, it was terribly strange. I conducted myself as my mask prompted me, held myself aloof and mysterious, and even clever fellows like Montrose and Chiarmonte didn't notice the change. They treated me as if I were my predecessor, a demigod from the dawn of time, when they had inhabited the Underworld for centuries longer than I had."

"Even so, you were the emperor's choice," Demetrius said, "and you've managed to carry out the duties of your office. Does the date of your ascension truly matter?"

"What matters is that I'm virtually certain that most if not all of the other Deathlords *have* been around since the beginning. They helped Charon build the city and expel the Fishers. They've had millennia to amass knowledge and arcane power. I've always thought that if they ever realized how recently I joined their company, they'd regard me as a contemptible upstart."

Potter grimaced. "Such reflections didn't trouble me too much as long as Charon was running the show, and I was merely his deputy. But now I feel completely out of my depth!"

Demetrius climbed unsteadily to his feet and laid his burn-spotted hand on Potter's shoulder. "Don't despair, my lord. You've started down a new road tonight, and I promise that from now on, your existence is going to change."

35

Quivering with anger, Gayoso thrust his hand through the front of the desk drawer, grabbed the silver hand mirror, and snatched it out. Raising it to his face, he glared into it.

His own middle-aged countenance with its baggy eyes and curved, fleshy nose scowled back at him. His own features, and nothing more.

After a while, his angry expression wilted into one of puzzlement and dismay. Had the looking glass lost its magic?

Then, without warning, the handle of the mirror turned ice cold. His arm jerked at the chill. The reflection crossed its eyes and wiggled its ears. "Peak-a-boo," it said.

"Where have you been?" Gayoso demanded.

"You don't exactly look like a satisfied customer," the Shadow said. "I thought things might be pleasanter if I avoided you until your temper cooled down. Alas, it seems that I don't have the option. The djinn has to appear when you rub the lamp."

"If you were a djinn," Gayoso said bitterly, "you would have managed to grant your master's wish."

The Shadow lifted an eyebrow. "Do you mean that Montrose survived the surprise party we arranged for him?"

"You know damn well he did."

The Shadow sighed. "My dear twin. You don't comprehend my nature nearly as well as you suppose, so please don't make assumptions about what I know or don't know. Just answer my questions. It will make everything easier."

"Fine," Gayoso growled, "we'll do it your way. Yes, Montrose escaped along with half his men. He even won the battle, and he returned to the Citadel."

"Did the Sister of Athena inform the gallant Marquess that you tried to help her destroy him?"

"Apparently not," Gayoso said grudgingly. "And it seems that for some reason he shipped the woman to Stygia immediately after the battle, so she's no longer available for questioning. Thank heaven for small favors."

"That particular benefaction isn't small at all," the reflection said. "It leaves you in the clear."

"Temporarily, yes. But Montrose will want to know why the intelligence I supplied him was faulty, why my troops failed to keep their rendezvous with his, and why the Heretics were so well prepared for his arrival."

"As you observed when we were hatching this scheme, the answer to the first two questions is simple bad luck and human error. And as for the third, well, how should you know?" The Shadow grinned. "Ah, those diabolical Heretics! Who can fathom their cunning ways?"

"I did cover my trail," Gayoso conceded. "I don't think Montrose can prove anything against me. But I'm certain he'll suspect. And if he was tempted to dispose of me before, he'll be an implacable enemy henceforth, while Shellabarger and Mrs. Duquesne will be only too happy to help him bring me down."

The Shadow nodded somberly. "I can't find any fault with your analysis. I suppose we should have let sleeping dogs lie."

Gayoso stared at the mirror in disbelief. "*Let sleeping dogs lie?* Is that all you have to say?"

"We rolled the dice and lost. Such is the nature of existence." The Shadow smirked. "Let me know when I hit on a cliche you find comforting, and I'll expand on it."

"I don't want to hear you philosophize. I want you to help me dispose of the Stygian as you were supposed to do in the first place."

"Remember, it isn't wise to ask for my help too often," said the Shadow with a mockery of concern. "You wouldn't want to stain that pristine nature of yours."

"Damn your impudence!" Gayoso barked. "I *order* you to help me!"

"My goodness," said the creature in the mirror, "you're truly frightened of Montrose, aren't you? I can't say I blame you. Any man who could forge the scum of Under-the-Hill into an army, destroy many of the local Heretic Circles in a matter of weeks, and escape the trap we set for him is a force to be reckoned with it. Which makes this the ideal time for me to renegotiate my contract."

Gayoso felt a chill, one that had nothing to do with the length of frigid metal in his fingers. "What are you talking about?"

"Up until now, I've helped you out of the goodness of my heart. It's time I received a token of your appreciation."

"I don't have to pay you," Gayoso said. "The magic of the mirror compels you to aid me."

"Did you ever really believe that?" asked the Shadow. "How quaint of you. Actually, it's simply a means of communication. A glorified telephone."

Gayoso tried to tell himself the creature was bluffing. He couldn't make himself believe it. "What do you want?" he asked.

"Hm." The Shadow narrowed its eyes as if it were just now considering the point. "Good question. How about this? Jehovah asked Abraham to sacrifice his son, and what was good enough for the Creator should be good enough for us. Of course, you haven't seen your biological offspring in hundreds of years, but you do have some youthful wraiths among your subjects. Your children in a symbolic cum political sense. One of them will do."

"That's insane," Gayoso said. "I can't offer up one of my own people to the powers of darkness. The province would rise against me."

The Shadow rolled its eyes. "I'm not asking you to do it in front of the whole Necropolis. A private ceremony will suffice. I'll teach you where to cut and what to chant, the prayers to the Void and all that."

I won't do it, Gayoso thought. It would be a monstrous crime.

But would it really? In his years as a governor, he'd condemned any number of wraiths to suffering and death, sometimes simply because it was expedient. That was the nature of politics. Would this occasion truly be any different, merely because the victim had a childlike appearance, and

Gayoso recited the praises of the Malfeans?

No! the Anacreon thought. What's wrong with me, that I can even consider such an act? I don't have to resort to this. I can solve my problems by myself.

Yet could he? When he looked inside himself, he doubted it. For years he'd turned to the mirror whenever he felt himself to be in dire jeopardy, and now he realized that in one sense, the Shadow had already exacted a fee for its services. It had deprived him of his confidence in his own judgment and ingenuity.

Averting his gaze from the mirror, loathing the creature inside the glass and himself as well, he whispered, "One child. My selection." If he looked, he ought to be able to find one with an adult personality, perhaps even a rebel or a criminal.

"Agreed," said the reflection. "A single sacrifice will do nicely, this time."

Gayoso glared at it. "There won't be a next time. Once I'm rid of Montrose, I'm going to smash this mirror."

The Shadow sighed. "That would be wasteful to say the least, but it's your decision. Shall we discuss how you're going to bring about Montrose's downfall?"

Gayoso blinked. "Don't you want me to perform the sacrifice first?"

"Oh, I trust you. I think you understand that when someone makes a pact with an entity like me, the universe takes note, and exacts a heavy penalty if the fellow tries to welch on his end of the bargain."

The Hierarch swallowed. "Yes," he said, "I do understand that." He struggled to thrust his guilt and self-contempt out of his mind, and focus on the benefits of the covenant. "All right, how *do* I get rid of the Stygian?"

"For a long while now, Montrose's Shadow has been waxing stronger."

"How do you know that?" Gayoso asked.

"Creatures like me have means of communication and other sources of intelligence which a steadfast Hierarch like you"— the Shadow leered—"couldn't understand. It's one of the many reasons we're going to win. But let's concentrate on the issue at hand. When Montrose came face to face with Louise, the

Sister of Athena, he learned that she was the long-lost love who betrayed him to his mortal death. The person he hates more than anyone else in the world."

"And you knew that all along," said Gayoso, scowling. "That's why you didn't want the emissary to allude to Montrose by name. You thought that if the woman knew who was coming to fight her, she'd lose her nerve and run away. Why didn't you share this with me before?"

"If she'd destroyed Montrose on the battlefield, it wouldn't have mattered," the Shadow answered glibly. "To continue: When Montrose saw Louise, he fell prey to a terrible rage. He wanted to torture and ultimately destroy the lady with his own hands. Had he done so, his Shadow might have annihilated his psyche. He could have become a Spectre on the spot. But for some reason, he held back. Contenting himself with a less intimate revenge, he condemned her to torment at the hands of others. But even that expression of his hatred was enough to permit his Shadow to possess him temporarily. It knew from past experience that it couldn't compel him to commit suicide, or attack his own soldiers. Had it tried, he would have snapped out of his altered state of consciousness. But it was able to prompt him to a subtler means of self-destruction."

"And what was that?" Gayoso asked eagerly.

"Somewhere in his belongings," the reflection said, "you'll find a journal written in his hand, with his characteristic phrasing, although actually, of course, his Shadow penned it. You have to retrieve it quickly, before he stumbles across it himself."

"That could be difficult," said Gayoso, frowning. "He has his cutthroats guarding his section of the Citadel." Then he smiled. "But he likes Valentine, and his people know it. They'll let the little toad wander anywhere he pleases."

"Can you trust Valentine?" the Shadow asked.

"Yes. I know he helped Montrose at one point, but only because I hadn't ordered him not to. He's capable of small impudences like that, but ultimately, he doesn't have the nerve to sell me out. His position here is the only remotely pleasant existence he's ever known, and he's terrified of losing it."

"Good. Then he can steal the papers. When he passes them to you, have a first-rate Harbinger and a detachment of Legionnaires carry them to the Smiling Lord as quickly as possible. Your problem will sort itself out in nothing flat."

36

When he'd first seen it by the light of day, Bellamy had thought the motel lobby—a rectangular room paneled in oak, with a host of glassy-eyed bluefish, channel bass, cobia, and pompano mounted on the walls—looked rather comical. But at one o'clock in the morning, with no one else in view and most of the lights extinguished, some of the trophies floating in the shadows appeared less like fish with dopey expressions than hideous reptiles escaped from an ocean in hell, glaring balefully at any warm-blooded life that wandered into view.

No, they don't, Bellamy told himself firmly. *Turn off your imagination, or you never will get any sleep.* He took a drink from his can of Coca Cola, savoring the sweetness and the pleasant burn as it went down. Then he strolled across the room and flopped down on a sofa in front of one of the bay windows.

Beyond the glass, the branches of the pines stirred restlessly. The sailboats and cruisers tied up at the docks bobbed and lurched back and forth as if trying to break their moorings. Gray clouds like fists clenched above the black expanse of Lake Pontchartrain, occluding most of the stars. The causeway was a vague streak in the distance, fading away into the night as if some disaster had obliterated the middle section.

Bellamy grimaced. The thunderheads, the boats, and the bridge reminded him of the island city in his nightmares. He wondered if *every* sight he encountered from now on, no matter how mundane, was going to convey intimations of mystery and terror.

Something touched him lightly on the shoulder. He jumped, squawked, and grabbed convulsively for his gun.

"Chill!" said Astarte. "Don't shoot, Officer, I surrender."

Bellamy took a deep breath, trying to slow his pounding heart. "I didn't hear you walk up."

"Apparently not," Astarte said. Her mocking grin gave way to a gentler smile. "I guess you couldn't sleep, either. Bad dreams?"

Bellamy shrugged. "That and anticipation, I guess."

She sat down beside him. The rings in her eyebrow, nostril, and lip gleamed dully in the faint illumination. Still, without her black lipstick and eye shadow, she didn't look as self-consciously pugnacious as usual. "Try not to let the dreams bother you," she said. "You don't know that you're seeing the City of Death, and even if you are, it doesn't have to mean anything. Marilyn says that different people see different things when they stare at the magic writing, and she's never been able to find any kind of pattern to it."

Bellamy smiled crookedly. "You mean there's something about the paranormal, about her own dirty little magic tricks, that Marilyn doesn't understand? Hey, there's a shocker."

Astarte grinned. "What a snotty comment. Just because she pumped you full of drugs, kidnapped you, and was going to brainwash you, that doesn't mean you shouldn't try to be friends with her."

"That's what's sad," Bellamy said. "I *don't* hold it against her. Life has gotten so crazy that what she did doesn't seem all that outrageous or even particularly important. If I'd had any idea what I was getting myself into, I don't think I'd be here."

"Yeah, you would."

"Don't count on it. Every time something spooky happens, I freeze up for a second or two."

"Like the rest of us don't?"

"I guess you do, but I also feel my mind *squirm*. *I* think it's trying to crawl inside itself, the way it did on the night Waxman died."

Astarte made a fist and punched him on the forearm.

"Ow!" he exclaimed.

"You aren't going to choke again, no matter what we run into," she said. "I know you're not, so just get over it and give me a sip of your soda."

"Okay," Bellamy said, handing her the red and white can. She threw back her head and glugged down considerably more than a sip. He was surprised and discomfited to catch himself staring at the rhythmic pulsing of the muscles in her long, white neck.

She dragged the back of her black-nailed hand across her mouth and handed the Coke back. He could feel from the lightness of the can that there was hardly any soda left. "I'm the one who ought to feel like a chicken," she murmured.

Puzzled, Bellamy cocked his head. "Why do you say that?"

"Daimler and Miss Paris were the answer to my prayers. But when he changed, I choked. And even afterward, when the shock wore off, I couldn't offer myself again."

"I had you pegged the first time I ever read your posts on Grailnet," Bellamy said. "You really are out of your mind."

"Daimler showed us two faces," Astarte said. "How do we know which one was real, and which an illusion? Maybe he was testing my courage, the strength of my commitment, and I flunked."

"I think your mom read *Beauty and the Beast* to you one too many times when you were a kid. Miss Paris had her bandages on when you first walked in, before you ever announced that you'd figured out that she and Daimler were undead." He marveled in passing at how easily he now used the corny, ridiculous term, a word he couldn't recall ever speaking before. "And there was nothing illusory about the stink of her flesh, or those nits crawling around in it. She really was deformed, and I'm sure Daimler was, too."

"I suppose," Astarte said. "Still, beauty is in the eye of the beholder, right? Maybe they didn't seem ugly to each other, or to themselves. Maybe if they'd changed me, I would have felt like a goddess, not a cripple or a freak."

Bellamy shook his head. "What is it with you? Why are you so hot to become a part of the paranormal anyway, especially after the gruesome things we've seen? You've never really told me."

She shrugged. "I don't know if I can explain it. Except that lots of the time, life sucks. I don't mean the parts that make you mad, or break your heart. I mean when it's plastic and ordinary. You look at somebody you're supposed to love, or hate, and you don't feel *anything*, any more than you would if you were looking at a machine. Or you find yourself slumped in front of the TV, staring at some rerun that was shitty the first time, but you can't find the energy to get up and go do something else."

Bellamy smiled. "I don't think that happens to you very often."

"It happens to everybody," Astarte said somberly. "Everywhere you look, you see people just switching off, wasting time, like they were going to be around forever. On the other hand, sometimes you take a bite out of a peach, or hear a great song on the radio, or look at a robin outside your window, and your whole mind and body just lights up. And you think, this is it. This feeling of delight. This is the whole point of being alive. I've got to hold on to it. But you never can. It always slips away."

"And you think that for paranormal creatures, it doesn't. Life is an endless series of highs without any lows."

Astarte shrugged. "I figure that's why we call them supernatural. I'm not saying they don't ever feel grief or pain or fear. But at least they always feel *something*. "

"And that seems so wonderful to you that you'd want to be one, even if it meant becoming evil?"

"What's evil? Who are we to judge them when we don't know what they know, or understand what they understand?"

"In a weird kind of way, you have a point," Bellamy began.

Astarte grinned. "Hey, that's the first time you've ever admitted I might be right about anything. I feel all warm and squishy."

Bellamy chuckled. "I didn't mean you were right, just that I understand how you feel. Since I got involved in this mess, I haven't known what to believe about *anything*. For instance, maybe I should forget about the Atheist and try to destroy Daimler and Miss Paris. They might represent a bigger threat to human life than he does. There's no way to know. I'm flying blind.

"But I think we have to try to do the right thing, even when we're ignorant and confused. If we don't, we really won't be any better than robots." He smiled at her. "Whether you realize it or not, you care about right and wrong, too. If you didn't, you wouldn't have jeopardized your dream to help me. You would have offered yourself to Daimler with no strings attached."

She shrugged. "I never said I was consistent. You know what else is strange to think about? By this time tomorrow, we may have our answers."

He nodded. When he'd checked with the New Orleans Post Office yesterday afternoon, he'd received a letter from Daimler. The message, written in an elegant Spencerian hand, had provided an address where the mysterious men from Lafayette supposedly stayed when they visited the city. "It's possible. You know, I still think it would be better if you didn't come with me."

"Don't even try. I'm in, and that's that. Even if I didn't want to go, you need somebody to watch your back, and I'll be more useful than any of the Arcanists, not that you could convince one of them to tag along anyway."

He had to admit, she had a point. In the final analysis, all the surviving occultists, even Marilyn, had the temperament of scientists or scholars, not daredevils or cops. On occasion, they did willingly place themselves in harm's way, but only when they believed they understood the nature of the danger, and had taken appropriate precautions to protect themselves. They were more than reluctant to break into a strange building knowing only that it was occupied by people—or quasi-people—with ties to the paranormal, who were apparently to blame for scores of disappearances.

Bellamy didn't blame the Arcanists for their caution. He suspected that if he had had as much experience with the supernatural as they had, he wouldn't be so reckless, either.

"Okay," he said. "I just had to try to talk you out of it one more time."

"I know you did," she said. "It's nice, in a condescending, MCP kind of way. And it was nice when you tried to save me from Daimler." She put her arms around him and kissed him. The contrast between her warm, soft flesh and the cold, hard metal transfixing it was as arresting as he'd imagined it.

At first he kissed her in return, his tongue dancing with hers, his hands slipping inside her leather jacket to caress her body. He couldn't help himself. But gradually his sense of propriety reasserted itself. Extricating himself from her embrace, he shifted sideways on the sofa cushion, putting distance between them.

"You want to go to one of our rooms?" she panted. "Mine's closer."

Breathing heavily himself, he swallowed and said, "I'm sorry. I can't do this."

She frowned. "Why not? You told me you were divorced. And I *know* you like me."

"Yes," he said, wondering how she'd known it when he hadn't ever quite admitted it to himself.

"It can't be the difference in our ages," she said. "I'm legal, and you're only a few years older than me. Is it my look? The piercings, and all that?"

"No," he said. "The problem is that it wouldn't be professional."

"You're kidding."

"No," Bellamy said. "An FBI agent shouldn't get romantically involved with a fellow investigator, or anybody he meets in the context of a case."

"Are you crazy?" she asked. "You aren't here as an official FBI guy, remember? You're poking around on your own. You're already breaking the rules, and anyway, I'm not going to rat you out to your bosses."

"You have to understand," he said, "there's a *point* to this particular rule. It helps you stay sharp and objective."

She sighed. "And you can't see your way clear to just relax and let go, even for a few minutes."

"It wouldn't be for just a few minutes. If we went to bed, things would be different afterward. The feelings I have for you would be stronger than they are already."

"God, let's hope so."

"Look, I've always tried to be the very best cop I could be. I've always given one hundred percent, without letting anything distract me. And that discipline has worked for me. It's helped me catch a lot of criminals. And because it has, I'm not willing to put it aside, especially in a situation where *your* life is on the line. I care about you way too much for that."

She smiled crookedly. "I guess I have some options here. I could rip off my clothes or grab your crotch, and see if I could convince you not to be such a jerk. I could deck you. Or I could ask if there's a rule against you dating me after the case is over."

"No," Bellamy said. "I don't remember reading that one anywhere in the G-man handbook."

"Well, don't let it get your hopes up. I was just wondering. You had your chance." She leaned over and kissed him on the cheek. "Don't sit up all night," she said in a softer tone. "Try to get some rest."

She stood up and headed out of the lobby. Her hips seemed to sway more than usual, as if she was exaggerating the motion to tease him. As he watched her blend with the shadows, he did indeed feel like the biggest jerk on earth.

37

A rhythmic vibration shook the floor, so softly no mortal would have noticed. But Montrose perceived it without difficulty and even divined the source. A sizable company of wraiths was marching in step through the Necropolis.

Puzzled, the Scot frowned. He made a point of keeping track of the agendas of his fellow Anacreons' Legionnaires. To the best of his knowledge, no large detachment of soldiers should have been heading out of or into the Citadel this evening. He decided to find out what was going on.

Rising, he picked up his mask and pressed it to his face, strapped on his pistol and rapier, and wrapped himself in his voluminous mantle. As he fastened the silver collar clasp, he heard familiar footsteps pattering down the corridor outside.

"Come in," he called. Valentine stuck his head, crowned with a green and yellow floppy-horned cap, through the office door. "Hello."

"Good evening, Anacreon," said the dwarf. "Gayoso told me to tell you that a column of soldiers, from Stygia, by the look of them, is coming toward the Citadel. He suggested that all four of you Anacreons gather at the front entrance to greet the commanding officer."

"That sounds reasonable," Montrose replied. "Which Legion is arriving?"

Valentine hesitated, and then said, "If Gayoso knows, he didn't tell me."

"Well, I suppose everyone will know soon enough," Montrose said. "But I think I'll indulge my curiosity and find out now. If I fly up above the Citadel, I should be able to read their standards and banners. It's a pleasant night. Would you care to ascend with me? I promise not to drop you."

"No," said the dwarf, almost too quickly. "I have to get back to Gayoso. But..."

Montrose cocked his head. "What's troubling you?"

"Nothing! I'm just...nervous this evening. You be careful." He scuttled backward, pulling his head and shoulders back through the door. His running feet clattered back down the corridor.

I *always am careful*, Montrose thought. *But tonight, I shouldn't really have to be. Gayoso isn't likely to attempt to assassinate me in front of a group of newly arrived Stygian witnesses.* Shaking his head over Valentine's jitters, wondering if Gayoso had been abusing the small man, the Scot blew out the barrow-flame lamp, invoked his Harbinger Arcanos, and then strode through the cobwebs and grimy glass in one of the window frames.

He allowed himself to drop for an instant, enjoying the thrill of free fall, and then soared upward into the cool air. The ugliness of the decaying city, blemished and distorted by the Shroud, gave way to the unstained beauty of the moon and stars. He felt a pang of joy, and a mad desire to soar up and up forever.

Quashing the impulse, he peered across the Necropolis. Despite a lack of music or any particular attempt at ostentation, the Stygians were easy to spot. The column was climbing toward the Citadel from the south. The Hierarchs were wearing the same insignia and carrying the same black and scarlet flags as Montrose's original force, indicating that they were affiliated with both the Smiling Lord and the Order of the Unlidded Eye.

In different circumstances, Montrose might have worried that his master had dispatched a new force under a new general because he was dissatisfied with his original agent's progress. But the Scot had scored such an impressive series of victories that he couldn't credit such a notion. Perhaps the Smiling Lord was so pleased that he'd sent additional troops to enable Montrose to extend the scope of the campaign. Or maybe he'd provided fresh men and a new commander so that his valiant deputy could return home and be rewarded for his efforts.

To his surprise, Montrose realized that he couldn't quite anticipate how he'd react if it turned out that the Smiling Lord had recalled him. He still yearned for the splendors and luxuries of the Onyx Tower, and chafed at the thought of rival courtiers scheming to usurp his place in his absence. But he also had the obscure feeling that his recent adventures had stimulated dormant aspects of his personality, a valuable dimension of himself that had been in danger of withering away. If he left, he'd miss some of the people he'd met, Fink, Valentine, and others. And to some degree it would irk him to abandon the mystery of the false Pardoners—and the Atheist murders, if they were part of the same puzzle—for a successor to unravel.

Ultimately, of course, it didn't matter how he felt. He'd go if the Smiling Lord had ordered him to go, or stay if he wanted him to stay. He was just glad that he'd emerged from his fugue state before his fellow Stygians arrived.

Montrose's blackout had lasted nearly forty-eight hours. He'd awakened feeling more nearly himself than he had in weeks, his Shadow apparently having exhausted its strength maintaining the possession. At first, realizing what had happened to him, the Scot had been terrified, certain that the parasite must have run amok, reveling in perversions and atrocities.

But if it had, it had covered its tracks flawlessly, which seemed unlikely. It would want Montrose to discover its handiwork, to shame and sicken him. In point of fact, as far as he'd been able to determine, none of his associates had noticed anything even a little strange about his behavior. He could only assume that his psyche had managed to hold his malignant side in check, in a contest of wills inaccessible to memory.

He swooped toward the ground and alit in front of the Citadel's primary entrance. His fellow Anacreons, Valentine, and Fink had arrived before him. A smattering of Shellabarger and Mrs. Duquesne's soldiers were also present, as were a few of Montrose's irregulars, but only Gayoso, no doubt in an effort to make himself seem a better commander than his colleagues, had managed to turn out a full company of his men in all their somewhat tawdry martial finery. The wavering bluish light from the ring of torches gleamed on their weapons and on the black hourglass in Mrs. Duquesne's shriveled hands.

"Good evening," said Montrose.

"Yes," said Gayoso, a smug note in his voice, "isn't it."

Leather creaked, metal clinked, and cloth rustled. The newcomers had nearly reached the crest of the hill. A moment later their commander strode from the gloom, a lanky man with long brown hair whose outer garments were much like Montrose's, except that his mask was made of riveted crimson metal. The soldiers at his back were marching four abreast.

Montrose smiled, because he recognized the commander despite his visor. The inquisitor was Karl Reinhardt, a valued agent of the Smiling Lord these past two hundred years. Reinhardt had never seemed to aspire to a permanent position in his master's household, and thus had never posed a threat to Montrose's ambitions. As a result, though they weren't friends—the Scot made it a policy to avoid true friendship with men of equivalent rank—they shared a bond of respect, forged in a hard fought campaign against a horde of Spectres in 1832. It would be pleasant to talk to him.

A centurion bellowed a command, and the column halted. Reinhardt continued forward. "Good evening," he said in his German accent. "I bring the governors of Natchez greetings and instructions from the Seat of Burning Waters." He reached inside his cloak, produced a scroll bearing the Smiling Lord's seal, and handed it to Gayoso, who unrolled it without haste. Compromising their dignity a bit, Shellabarger and Mrs. Duquesne pressed in close to read the message also.

"Hello, Karl," said Montrose. "It's good to see you."

"I'm afraid you won't think so in a moment," the Grim Rider replied. "James Graham, Earl and Marquess of Montrose, Anacreon of my own Order, I have a warrant for your arrest."

"What?" Montrose exclaimed. "On what charge?"

"According to this," said Gayoso, brandishing the scroll, "treason." The gloating note in his voice was now unmistakable.

"That's absurd!" said Montrose. He'd worried that in his absence, his rivals would try to undermine his master's trust in him, but in light of his successes in the field, how could anyone have convinced the Smiling Lord he was a traitor? It didn't make sense.

"It's no use protesting," Reinhardt said. "I've seen the evidence against you, and even if I hadn't, I have my orders."

"What evidence?" Montrose asked.

"A journal in your handwriting. In its pages, you reveal your intention to conquer your own kingdom here along the Mississippi."

"I never wrote any such thing." Montrose pivoted toward the three governors. "Gayoso sent the papers to Stygia, didn't he? Well, he forged them, too!"

"As I mentioned," Reinhardt said, "the document is in your own hand. Chiarmonte did the comparisons himself, and said there isn't any doubt. Even so, the Smiling Lord was reluctant to accept your guilt. He had Demetrius examine the journal through some esoteric application of his Arcanos, and he too is certain that you wrote it."

Montrose felt as if he were trapped in a nightmare. The more Reinhardt explained, the stranger the situation seemed. Chiarmonte was a rival, but he couldn't quite imagine the Venetian falsifying the results of a graphological analysis, if only because of the pride he took in his professional expertise. Nor could he imagine the man conspiring with Demetrius to frame him. Chiarmonte wasn't unduly fond of Montrose, but, like most of the courtiers who'd attended the Smiling Lord for a century or longer, he loathed the upstart Oracle.

Then, suddenly, Montrose's intuition told him what had happened. In effect, his *Shadow* had framed him, writing the journal during the period when it was dominant. Now that he realized the truth, he sensed the parasite laughing in the depths of his unconscious.

And why shouldn't it? Montrose couldn't prove he'd been possessed, and he suspected the Deathlords, whose justice was often leavened with a generous measure of expediency, wouldn't regard it as an adequate defense anyway. If his Shadow had mastered him once, perhaps it would do so again, and put its treasonous schemes into effect. It would be safer to execute him and avoid the possibility. He struggled to suppress a surge of panic.

"Surrender your weapons," Reinhardt said.

"I give you my word," said Montrose, "I'm innocent." "It doesn't matter," Reinhardt replied doggedly. "I have orders to take you into custody and that's what I'm going to do. Unless you compel me to destroy you instead."

Montrose looked at Shellabarger and Mrs. Duquesne. "I've helped you people. I've rid your territory of subversives. I've brought prosperity."

"You also disrupted a reasonably comfortable status quo," said Shellabarger. Montrose could just barely make out the form of the governor's bulging, faceted eyes, glinting behind the openings in his hood. "You forced us to obey your orders. To be honest, I think I can cope with the pain of your departure."

"I'm a loyal Hierarch," said Mrs. Duquesne. "I wouldn't think of disobeying a command from any of the Deathlords." She glanced at Gayoso's troops and the ranks of Stygians. "Even if it were practical."

"Listen to me," said Montrose, "there are things happening along the river I haven't told you about. A new danger, from an unknown source. You need me to help you get to the bottom of it. I understand you have no choice but to return me to Stygia, but you could intercede for me. Assure the Smiling Lord that no matter what the evidence seems to indicate, you've observed me closely over the past few weeks, and you're certain I'm loyal."

Inside the lugubrious frown of her white glazed mask, Mrs. Duquesne's lips quirked in an ironic smile. "Tie my own fate inextricably to your own. An intriguing concept. But unfortunately, I never take it for granted that *anyone's* loyal. That's what makes me a successful politician."

Gayoso sneered at Montrose. "Did you really expect anyone to believe such a blatantly self-serving lie?"

"It's not a lie," Montrose said.

"Well," said Gayoso, "in the unlikely event that there *is* some mysterious menace lurking about, I'll deal with it. These soldiers didn't all come just to drag you back to the Isle of Sorrows, my lord Anacreon. Your military reputation isn't *that* fearsome. Most of them will remain in Natchez under my command, to continue the suppression of the rebels." He smiled coldly at his fellow governors, indicating that the balance of power had shifted, and that henceforth, they'd better stay on his good side.

"Give me your sword and pistol," Reinhardt said.

Montrose looked at Fink. The river man grinned and shrugged. The Scot had the feeling that if the odds hadn't been quite so overwhelming, his lieutenant might have tried to rescue him from his would-be captors, if only for the savage, reckless fun of it. But whatever bond of friendship had sprung up between the two wraiths, it wasn't enough to prompt the former outlaw to throw his existence away. And if he didn't make a move, none of the other irregulars would, either.

The Scot was tempted to try to veil himself in darkness, open a Nihil and leap through, or project himself onto the other side of the Shroud. But his Arcanos didn't work instantaneously, and as soon as he began to generate an effect, the Legionnaires would shoot him. If he truly wanted to escape both immediate destruction and the terrible justice of the Smiling Lord, the only hope was to surrender now and try to get away later. A chance so slim it was barely worth contemplating, but still, the only one he had.

As he unclipped his scabbard from his belt, he saw Valentine's homely features twist in anguish, and suspected the dwarf had played some part in his downfall. Betrayed by yet another friend. He supposed he should have been expecting it.

38

As Bellamy surveyed the rows of crumbling, whitewashed mausoleums, floating like islands in a sea of tangled brush and pearly ground mist, he felt his pulse ticking in his throat. Speaking lightly in an effort to alleviate his anxiety, he whispered, "Well, this figures, doesn't it?"

"What?" Astarte replied.

"That we'd wind up in a cemetery before this mess was over."

She smiled wryly, the moonlight gleaming on the steel rings in her piercings. "I don't mind as long as it isn't a permanent stay." She pointed. "That way?"

He nodded. "Stay alert." They slunk forward, down one of the lanes defined by parallel rows of dilapidated tombs. There didn't seem to be any copings, a fact which didn't surprise him. In New Orleans, with its high-water table, it was easier to lay the dead to rest above ground than to bury them.

Try as he might, he couldn't move altogether silently, any more than Astarte could. The weeds and long grass swished and rustled around their feet. He hoped it wouldn't matter.

Astarte took hold of his forearm, halting his forward progress.

"What is it?" he asked.

"No one's keeping this place up."

He repressed a sarcastic observation about her keen grasp of the obvious. "I noticed."

"So where are the signs that other trespassers have jumped the wall? Where are the condoms and beer cans?"

He frowned. "I don't know. I did see some graffiti on some of the tombs."

"All of it funny symbols. Hieroglyphics. Nothing in English."

"In other words, the cemetery has such a nasty reputation that people are afraid to trespass. Or when they do, the men from Lafayette kill them."

Astarte nodded. "That's what I'm thinking."

After a moment's hesitation, Bellamy said, "We already knew we were headed into danger. I'm not going to turn back. But if you want to—"

Astarte grimaced. "Will you get over that sexist crap? I just thought you ought to know we were already in the danger zone. Now come on." She crept forward, and he followed her.

Five minutes later they reached the eight-foot wall, itself a tomb riddled with vaults, on the far side of the cemetery. Bellamy hoisted himself up until he could peek over the top.

The house on the other side was a massive brick edifice that reminded him of a prison. Indeed, with its few narrow windows sealed behind burglar bars, it was an eyesore ugly and ominous enough to stand out even in one of the city's most miserable slums. As far as he could see, no lights were burning. With luck, it meant no one was inside, though he was by no means certain of that. The mysterious people from west Louisiana might be thoroughly at home in the dark.

Bellamy hauled himself to the top of the wall, and Astarte scrambled up beside him. They dropped to the other side and sneaked on, through a yard as overgrown as the cemetery. Bearded with long gray streamers of Spanish moss, the branches of a huge cypress blocked out the stars, making the night even blacker than before.

The intruders reached the back door without anything leaping out at them, or anyone shouting to announce their presence. Bellamy switched on his pencil flashlight, examined the entry, and found no evidence of an alarm system. Holding the light in his teeth, he took out his knife and pick.

After a moment's work, the lock clicked open. He cracked the door open and a faint but foul stench like the smell of rotting meat wafted out. He peered through the opening.

He was looking into a spacious kitchen. Flicking the flashlight beam this way and that, he sensed there was something odd about the room, and after a moment, he realized what. There were no pots and pans hanging from the hooks on the walls. He stepped inside and opened some drawers and cabinets. There was no cutlery, plates, or canned goods, either, and when he checked the faintly humming refrigerator, he only found wine, soda, and beer. Evidently the rotting smell was coming from another part of the house. No one prepared any food in here.

He listened intently, but didn't hear anyone moving around in the darkness ahead, just a nearly inaudible buzzing. Drawing his Browning from its holster, he led Astarte through the next doorway. The foul smell grew stronger.

The next chamber was a dining room, though it appeared as if it had been a while since anyone had used it as such. Many of the chairs lay shattered on the floor, and someone had carved sets of parallel grooves in the table. It looked as if a gigantic cat had sharpened its claws on the wood. Crudely painted on one wall was a black spiral like the design on a hypnotist's spinning wheel. Pointing to it, Bellamy gave Astarte an inquiring look. She shrugged.

Bellamy listened once again, and still didn't hear anyone. He and Astarte crept through the next arch. The stink burned in his nose and throat, half choking him. He swung the light around, and flinched at what he saw. Nausea squirmed in his stomach.

The large room was littered with human corpses and body parts. Most were little more than gnawed bone, pocked with tooth marks, but a few scraps of decaying meat remained. Enough to account for the stench and nourish swarms of flies, their wings the source of the ambient drone.

Bellamy told himself that he'd seen the handiwork of serial killers and even cannibals before, though it hadn't been on this scale. He had to get past his horror and function like a professional.

Astarte made a gagging sound. He took her in his arms, and she hugged him tightly.

"I'm sorry," he whispered. "I know it's bad. But we have to cope with it."

"I know," she said. "It's just that it's worse than seeing

Vulture die. Worse than feeling Mr. Daimler's teeth pressing into my neck. Worse than anything so far. But I'll be all right." She clung to him for a moment longer, then released him.

Bellamy played his light back and forth, trying to ignore the ghastly remains of the murderers' victims and see what else was in the room. The beam slid across a few pieces of dilapidated furniture and a collection of trophies and curios, many nearly as ghastly as the corpses and nearly all of them strange in one way or another.

Mobiles made of wire, sticks, and human bones hung from the ceiling, and someone had thumbtacked pairs of snapshots to the faded, floral-print wallpaper. The first picture in each set was a candid shot of a man, woman, or child. The second was a view of the body of the same individual, torn to shreds.

On the marble mantel reposed a long ivory tusk, so flamboyantly curved that Bellamy was certain it couldn't have come from any breed of elephant alive today. It reminded him of artists' conceptions of the hairy pachyderms that had walked the earth during the last ice age. And when he approached it, he discovered that it was carved with crude representations of gigantic sloths, cave bears, and other prehistoric beasts.

The skulls of two huge canines rested on a table. Each had been painted with the black spiral and a selection of other symbols. At first glance, Bellamy assumed that they were fossils, too. But on closer inspection, they looked too fresh, almost as fresh as some of the human bones littering the bloodstained floor.

An assortment of jewelry—bracelets, rings, pendants, and earrings—most of it rather large and primitive-looking, lay on the tiers of a bookshelf, along with a straightedged dagger the size of a Bowie knife. The color of the blade seemed a little off. Bellamy wondered if it might be made of silver rather than steel.

Once again, he looked at Astarte, asking her to interpret the significance of the various relics. Once again, she shrugged. So much for her claim to be an occult expert, he thought sardonically.

Denied any esoteric insights, he decided that for the time being, he'd better ignore what he couldn't comprehend—the meaning of the tusk, the canine skulls, and similar enigmas—and focus on what he could. Which was that he was virtually wading through evidence of multiple murder. For a moment, he felt a swell of satisfaction, and then it withered. He scowled.

Brushing a fly away from her face, Astarte asked, "What is it?"

"We've got all the evidence any cop could ask for to prove that certain people have been killed. But—"

"We still don't know who the men from Lafayette *are*," she said. "We don't know how they figure into the Atheist conspiracy, or even *that* they do."

"Right," Bellamy said. "When you think about it, it's even worse than that. We don't even know who owns this place. I mean, we got a name and a post-office box address out of the city records, but I've got a hunch they're just a blind. I'm sure you want to get out of here. So do I. But to get to the bottom of this craziness, I need to look around some more."

Her face pale, Astarte gave him a jerky nod. "It's okay. I can handle it. Hell, here's where they kill and eat, right? The other rooms *can't* be as bad as this one."

"I hope not." He listened once again. Except for the thrum of the flies, the house remained silent. "Let's go this way. Keep an eye out for any kind of papers. File folders. An address book. A wallet with ID in it. Whatever."

They crept on through the twisting passages of the house. As they got farther away from the room containing the corpses, the stink of decay gave way to another unpleasant smell like that of rats, but Bellamy didn't see any droppings, or any holes gnawed in the baseboards. He wondered if it could be the body odor of the men from Lafayette themselves.

Occasionally he and Astarte came upon a shredded, severed human limb, or the black spiral or some other cryptic symbol daubed on a door or wall. Once he somehow missed seeing one of the grisly mobiles, and walked right into the dangling lattice of cold, clinking bones. Squawking, he recoiled, and lifted his gun to shoot. But Astarte clutched his arm and said, "It's okay, it's okay!" Her intervention brought him back to his senses.

But despite a sprinkling of such artifacts, most of the

ground floor was sparsely furnished and seemed little used. When they'd searched it all, the two intruders climbed a broad, curving staircase. A soft hum whispered down to meet them.

Astarte gave Bellamy an interrogatory look. Now it was his turn to shrug. His mouth dry, he crept on up until, suddenly, he glimpsed a point of green light. Startled, he almost fired at it before he realized it was electric illumination, not the chatoyant eye of some lurking monster.

To be precise, it was an indicator light on the base of a computer monitor, shining through a doorway. And the faint whine was the sound of the PC's cooling fan. His shoulders slumping with relief, he motioned for Astarte to join him.

Compared to the filth, carnage, desolation, and bizarre decorations elsewhere in the house, the computer room, with its desk, file cabinet, and bookshelves seemed relatively normal, like an office that any ordinary person might set up in his home. Only a handful of clay and carved stone statues—a naked woman with two faces, a squat, warlike figure in a feather headdress—suggested a connection with the occult.

"This stuff is different from what we saw downstairs," Bellamy whispered. "The jewelry looked like something the Vikings might have made, but these—"

"Look Aztec or Mayan or Incan," Astarte said. "Do you think it means something?"

"I have no idea. I was hoping you would."

"All I know is that it makes me nervous that that"—she nodded at the computer—"is turned on."

"Some people leave their PCs on all the time. But even so, I'm not too thrilled about it either. We need to search this place, but keep listening for voices and footsteps. If somebody is around, it would be better to know about it *before* he steps into the room."

Something popped. Startled, Bellamy whirled, to see that the blank monitor had lit up. The PC's hard drive clattered softly.

A little hesitantly, he and Astarte edged closer, to see what the screen would display. Arcs of red and purple swirled inward like water vanishing down a drain, reminding him unpleasantly of the black spirals downstairs. Then the vortex gave way to a step pyramid.

"That looks Aztec, too," Astarte said, her pale face shining in the monitor's sickly glow.

"Yeah," Bellamy said, "except the ones in Mexico aren't jet black."

A shadowy figure atop the pyramid made an exaggerated, unmistakable hacking motion, and then held up a bulb of crimson flesh. Unseen multitudes cheered. Cascades of blood poured down the sides of the edifice.

The monitor zoomed in on the top of the monument for a close-up view. The priest conducting the sacrifice wasn't human. He was a creature with two scaly ophidian faces mounted on a single head.

"What does this mean?" Astarte asked. "Why is it showing this now? Does somebody know we're here?"

"I don't know," Bellamy replied.

The picture on the screen changed. Astarte gasped, and the FBI agent stiffened, because they were now looking at the island city from their shared vision. The water around it began to revolve, accelerating rapidly. With a grinding, crashing sound, the dark towers and even the bedrock beneath them began to break apart, until the whirlpool devoured it all.

After which, the swirling red and violet pattern reappeared.

Surmising that the entire animated sequence was about to repeat itself, Bellamy sat down at the computer. "You start checking the books and papers," he told Astarte. "Fast. I'll see what I can pull off the hard disk."

Typing rapidly, the keyboard clicking, he tried to enter commands. But no matter what he did, the PC wouldn't respond. It just kept showing the same scenes of bloodshed and annihilation. Finally, he gave up and checked the desk drawers. He didn't find anything interesting. To his surprise, there weren't even any floppy disks.

With a growing sense of desperation, he stood up and began to help Astarte ransack the bookshelves. A small spiral notebook, almost invisible between a massive dictionary and a textbook on the principles of accounting, caught his eye. He pulled it out and flipped it open. The pages were full of row after row of tiny symbols, neatly inscribed in ink.

He showed it to Astarte. "More Witches' Alphabet?" he asked.

She shook her head. "I don't recognize it."

"Well, it looks promising," Bellamy said. He stuffed it in his jacket pocket, and then a long howl reverberated through the house.

39

Astarte yelped. Bellamy involuntarily backpedaled across the office until his shoulders were pressed against the wall. His heart pounded, and his bowels felt as if they'd turned to water.

Beside him, someone laughed. He lurched around, and saw that the face of a thin, intelligent-looking black man had appeared on the computer screen. Its eyes bright with malice, it was doing the laughing. The image dissolved into the close-up view of the apex of the pyramid. Now Bellamy was the naked corpse on the altar, his gory chest hacked open, a raw cavity gaping where his heart should have been.

Bellamy felt his mind breaking up, his consciousness turning inside out. He put his knuckle between his teeth and bit down hard. The pain cleared his head to a degree.

Astarte stood wide-eyed and trembling.in the center of the room. When Bellamy touched her, she jumped. "It's just a yell," he said, "just noise. It's creepy, maybe there's even something magic about it, but we can't let it get to us."

She swallowed. "All right."

"I'd just as soon not meet what's doing the yelling," he said, "so we're leaving. Get out the gun Marilyn gave you." She fumbled the little automatic out of her jacket. "Do you remember what I taught you about how to use it?" She nodded. "Good. We'll move fast, but quietly, and we'll go down those back stairs we saw. I think it's less likely that anything will be waiting at the bottom. Got it?"

"Yes," she said, grimacing, a flicker of the old Astarte breaking through her dread. "I'm not stupid."

"Says who?" he said, forcing a smile. "You're here, aren't you? Come on, let's move."

Bellamy switched off his flashlight. The monitor went black at the same instant, plunging the room into almost total darkness. Astarte gasped, and his heart jolted in his chest. Peering warily this way and that, the intruders slipped into the hall.

They turned left, away from the main staircase, and a second howl split the silence. Astarte whimpered. Shuddering violently, Bellamy struggled to keep panic from overwhelming him. The unearthly wailing was invested with some supernatural power, without a doubt. What sort of creature possessed such a cry? He had a ghastly feeling that a part of him already knew. That he'd encountered such a beast on the night Waxman died.

Though the unseen creature howled again and again, it was impossible to tell from which direction the sound was coming. Each shriek slammed into Bellamy's mind like a hammer. He peered desperately into the shadows ahead, searching for the narrow flight of stairs he'd noticed before. He didn't see them. He wondered if, addled with terror, he'd led Astarte in the wrong direction.

Astarte gasped and spun around, nearly clubbing him with her gun. He pivoted. But whatever she'd thought she'd heard, there was nothing behind them.

They crept on around another corner, and finally spied the steps. Bellamy paused, listening, and heard nothing. He started down, placing his feet near the wall, wincing when, despite his care, one of the risers creaked.

He and Astarte reached the ground floor unmolested.

Just a few more steps, he told himself, just a few more steps and we'll be out of this place.

Their path led them back into the room with the corpses. Bellamy hesitated for a heartbeat, deciding between the front and rear doors, then turned toward the foyer.

"Bad choice," said a pleasant bass voice behind him.

Bellamy spun around. A shadow stood in the darkness a few feet away. It struck a match with its thumbnail, and when it lifted the flame to light its hand-rolled cigarette, he saw that it was Bill Dunn.

"This is a rough neighborhood," the SAD agent continued. "You go out on the street, you might get mugged. Whereas the cemetery is usually peaceful this time of night."

Settling into a marksman's stance, Bellamy aimed his Browning at Dunn's face. The other man didn't look as if he were wearing a Kevlar vest, but in the gloom, it was impossible to be sure. "You're in on it, aren't you? Part of the Atheist conspiracy."

Dunn grinned. "Well, duh, Sherlock. Of course I am. I pressured Nolliver to discredit you. I whacked him when he got squeamish. I even took time off from the Bureau to hunt you down. So much for that Windjammer cruise vacation I was planning."

"You're under arrest," Bellamy said.

"How did I know you were going to say that?" Dunn replied, exhaling a plume of smoke. Bellamy caught a whiff of the acrid vapor even through the stench of the rotting bodies. "The sad thing is that catching you was so easy that so far, it hasn't been any fun. I'm impressed that you found our little home away from home here. I'd be interested to know how you did it. But when Chester phoned me to say you'd broken in, there went my chance to shine as a detective. By the way, did you meet Chester? Black guy, dead, runs around inside computers, thinks he's Steven Spielberg?"

"Put your hands up," Bellamy said.

Dunn ignored the command. "And then when I was following you around the house, I could have killed you any time. Even with fear sharpening your senses, you didn't see me. So I decided to reveal myself in this guise to give you a sporting chance. To make our final meeting at least a little bit interesting. Don't disappoint me."

"Is he crazy?" Astarte whispered. "Or on drugs?"

"I hope so," Bellamy murmured. Better that than the alternative, which was that Dunn was like Daimler, possessed of powers so formidable that he had no reason to be afraid of a gun. He raised his voice. "Listen to me, Bill. You can't hurt us. It's the other way around. We're leaving, and we're taking you with us. If anyone or anything tries to stop us, I'll shoot you. Do you understand?"

"Sure," said Dunn, staring at them. Even in the darkness, his eyes seemed to glow. Bellamy felt the beginnings of a tremor in his arms, and struggled to hold the Browning steady. "Fact is, you shot me before, though I know you don't remember it. An amazingly lucky shot, too, right in the eye and round and round my brain until it just about cut my spinal cord in two. Anything less wouldn't have bothered me much, and I would have left your body beside Waxman's."

"What are you?" Astarte breathed.

"Something pretty cool," said Dunn, his gaze still boring into Bellamy's skull. Bellamy felt frightened and lightheaded at the same time, as if he were about to faint. A part of him was screaming for him to shoot, shoot now, but some force kept him from translating the impulse into action. "Something you monkeys are afraid of all the way down into your DNA. I gather you're a big fan of the occult, sweetheart, so why don't I give you a demonstration."

Dunn's body swelled, shoulders broadening, limbs lengthening, the front of his face extending into a foaming muzzle, stretching his smile into a fanged grin like the leer of the Big Bad Wolf. He lifted his enlarging hands, now gloved in black fur and sporting long, curved claws, and ripped his clothing apart to accommodate his growth.

Bellamy recoiled and fired at the same time. As near as he could tell, the shots flew wild. He felt his awareness contracting, caving in on itself, and for a second, he was grateful. Then he glimpsed Astarte from the corner of his eye.

Tears streaming down her face, her pistol hanging forgotten at her side, she stood paralyzed, like a rabbit hypnotized by the stare of a snake. Bellamy wasn't the only one whose mind was shutting down.

Except that he mustn't let it happen, not if it meant abandoning her to die. He bellowed wordlessly, a primal roar that expelled the panic from his mind. He was still terribly afraid, but the dread had lost its ability to cripple him. In fact, he sensed that no matter what terrible thing happened, he'd never freeze or lose himself again, and for one instant, in the reeking darkness, surrounded by the dead with a demon looming over him, he experienced a crazy flash of joy.

He grabbed Astarte and screamed in her ear. "Run!" He shoved her toward the front door and she began to stumble along under her own power, gaining speed with every step. He pivoted and, his hands now steady, resumed firing, emptying the clip.

By now Dunn was so tall that his head nearly brushed the ceiling, a stooped, gaunt, but horribly powerful-looking apparition with pointed, batlike ears and lambent eyes, his flesh exuding the bestial fetor that Bellamy had smelled elsewhere in the house. The hail of bullets slammed into his face and the cigarette fell from his jaws, showering orange sparks on its long descent to the floor. Clutching at his wounds, Dunn staggered and dropped to one knee. And then laboriously started to get up again.

Bellamy suspected that, gun or no, it would be tantamount to suicide to keep fighting Dunn at close range. Whereas outside, sniping from a distance, he might conceivably have a chance, might at least prolong the encounter long enough for Astarte to get away. As he wheeled to run, he caught a glimpse of the dagger.

If Dunn was the werewolf he more or less appeared to be, a silver blade might hurt him in a way lead bullets couldn't. Unfortunately, Bellamy figured that the odds of him getting past the monster's talons and inhumanly long reach to deliver a mortal blow were pretty close to zero. Still, he detoured and grabbed the knife on his way out, then sprinted on through the dining room and kitchen. Behind him, Dunn roared.

When Bellamy opened the door, his eyes widened in surprise. The world was veiled in sheets and tatters of white. He could barely see the trunk of the cypress just a few feet away. While he and Astarte had been inside, the fog had risen and thickened.

So much for shooting Dunn at long range. On the other hand, maybe the mist would allow him to evade the creature altogether. He ran on across the overgrown yard. As he reached the wall, he heard the monster chasing him, its claws clicking on the kitchen floor.

Bellamy scrambled over the wall, dashed a few feet to the left, and then hunkered down behind a tomb to reload the Browning. An instant later, he heard a soft thud. It sounded as if Dunn hadn't had to climb over the barrier. He'd simply hurdled it.

Bellamy listened intently, but except for the muted rumble and clatter of a freight train rolling down the rails a block away, he didn't hear another sound. Finally, he peeked around the side of the mausoleum. All he saw were the vague forms of the other vaults and coils of gray-white mist.

Apparently, Dunn had moved off in another direction. Bellamy wished he could be certain it was because he'd shaken the monster off his trail, but he couldn't shake the nasty suspicion that the creature was merely toying with him.

Still, Bellamy was alone for the moment, and he meant to make good use of the time. The dilapidated tomb in front of him had a long crack running down the front. On impulse, he removed the notebook from his pocket and stuffed it into the fissure. If he survived, he could retrieve it later. If not, there might be one chance in a million—well, maybe a billion— that someone would find and decipher it, and in any case, its disappearance might cause the Atheists some worry. Then he reloaded the Browning, wincing at the small clicks and snapping sounds the operation entailed.

He wondered if he should double back. Clamber back over the wall, go around the house, and into the shabby, nearly deserted streets beyond. Dunn might not be expecting that. But after a moment's consideration, he decided against the idea. Chester the unfriendly ghost was probably still keeping watch in the house as he had before. It would be better to exit the cemetery in another direction.

Bellamy thought that the east wall was a little closer than the west. Crouching, gun in one hand and dagger in the other, he headed for it. Tendrils of cool, wet mist caressed his face. Broken statues—a headless Madonna, her hands folded in prayer, an angel with chipped wings and a crumbling, leprous face—loomed out of the murk.

Then he heard a sniffing sound, and intuited instantly

what it was. Dunn was near and searching for his scent like a bloodhound.

Bellamy threw himself down behind the cover of another tomb, then looked frantically about. He didn't see Dunn.

The snuffling grew louder. Bellamy still didn't see the werewolf. His heart pounded, and his mouth was dry as sand. *Damn it!* he thought. *Dunn's ten feet tall. Even in the fog and the dark, I should be able to see him when he's obviously right on top of me.*

A vague shadow, almost invisible in the murk, fell on the ground before him. He smelled a faint, foul odor, monster mingled with tobacco smoke. He reflexively hurled himself forward, not consciously comprehending until a split second later what had spurred him into motion. Dunn had silently climbed up on the tomb Bellamy had counted on to protect his back and was reaching down to maul him.

Claws snagged the right side of Bellamy's face, ripping gashes in his flesh as his momentum carried him free. Blood gushed. He sensed that Dunn had more or less torn his ear off, but there was no real pain, not yet, not with the adrenaline flooding his system, only pure sensation. He was just glad the talons had missed his eye.

He whirled, pointing the Browning. At the same instant, Dunn bounded over the tomb and struck a backhand blow at his quarry's shooting arm. The impact snapped bone and flung Bellamy's hand to the side. The pistol flew from his grasp.

Dunn snarled and lunged, jagged, yellow fangs bared and huge hands clawing. Spinning to the side, Bellamy narrowly blocked the monster's first slashing blow, and just as Dunn's striding foot was about to contact the ground, he hooked it with his own and jerked it.

Thrown off balance, the werewolf stumbled. Bellamy rammed the silver knife into the creature's solar plexus.

Dunn went down, but even as he did, his hands shot out, sunk their nails into Bellamy's flesh, and wrenched him down on top of his adversary. Locked in a clinch, the human couldn't pull the knife out of Dunn's body for another thrust. So, he jerked it back and forth, trying to enlarge the wound. Meanwhile the werewolf bit him, clawed at him, tearing and flaying the flesh from his bones.

Until, to Bellamy's amazement, Dunn's attacks began to slow and weaken, to diminish into a spastic scrabbling, and he wondered if he'd gotten lucky yet again—if by some miracle he was actually going to win.

Then Dunn gripped him by the shoulders. Even through the werewolf's musky stink, Bellamy smelled ozone, and his hair stood on end. An instant later, something crackled, and every muscle in his body convulsed.

He thought he could feel, even smell, his flesh burning, although it could have been his imagination. At any rate, he understood what was happening. Dunn was frying him like an electric eel. Another paranormal danger he hadn't had any way to anticipate. Had he still been capable of vocalization, he might have screamed at the unfairness of it.

His awareness began to collapse, not into the protective embrace of madness, not this time, but into the deeper oblivion of death. He thought of Astarte, wished that he'd made love to her, and then the world went black.

The End of The Ebon Mask

Dark Kingdoms will continue in The Onyx Tower

About the Author

Richard Lee Byers is the author of forty fantasy and horror novels including Called to Darkness, his first Pathfinder novel, Blind God's Bluff, the start of a new urban fantasy series, and Prophet of the Dead, the latest in a series of books set in the Forgotten Realms universe. His novel The Spectral Blaze won Diehard GameFAN's award for the Best Game-Based Novel of 2011.

Richard is also the creator of The Impostor, a post-apocalyptic superhero series. He has published dozens of short stories and writes a monthly feature for the SF news site Airlock Alpha.

Richard lives in the Tampa Bay area, where he spends much of his free time fencing and playing poker. He is a frequent guest at Gen Con and Florida SF conventions.

He invites everyone to Follow him on Twitter (@rleebyers), Friend him on Facebook, and add him to your Circles on Google+.

Curious about other Crossroad Press books?
Stop by our site:
http://www.crossroadpress.com
We offer quality writing
in digital, audio, and print formats.

www.ingramcontent.com/pod-product-compliance
Lightning Source LLC
Chambersburg PA
CBHW031548240626
47153CB00002B/420